UNDISCLOSED

By

NY Times best-selling author

Steve Alten

A&M Publishing, L.L.C.
West Palm Beach, FL

Other titles by Steve Alten

MEG SERIES
MEG (Viper Press, a division of A & M Publishing)
The TRENCH (Kensington/Pinnacle)
MEG: Primal Waters (Tor/Forge)
MEG: Hell's Aquarium (Tor/Forge)
MEG: Night Stalkers (Tor/Forge)

MAYAN DOOMSDAY SERIES
DOMAIN (Tor/Forge)
RESURRECTION (Tor/Forge)
PHOBOS: Mayan Fear (Tor/Forge)

The LOCH NESS Series
The LOCH (Tor/Forge)
VOSTOK (Tor/Forge)

GOLIATH (Tor/Forge)

THE SHELL GAME (Tor/Forge)

GRIM REAPER: End of Days (Tor/Forge).

THE OMEGA PROJECT (Tor/Forge)

SHARKMAN (VIPER Press, a division of A & M Publishing)

DOG TRAINING THE AMERICAN MALE
(WJM Books, a division of A & M Publishing)
A comedic novel, written under the pen name L.A. KNIGHT

UNDISCLOSED

By

NY Times best-selling author

Steve Alten

UNDISCLOSED

Published by A&M Publishing, LLC
West Palm Beach, FL 33411
www.AMPublishers.com

ISBN: 978-1-943957-05-7

Library of Congress Control Number: 2017937983

Printed in the United States of America

Special thanks to NASA for the incredible pictures that are throughout this book.

ACKNOWLEDGMENTS

It is with great pride and appreciation that I acknowledge those who contributed to the completion of UNDISCLOSED.

First and foremost, many thanks to Dr. Steven M. Greer, and his wife Emily, for giving me access and permission to incorporate the information Dr. Greer painstakingly acquired from hundreds of hours of incredible testimonials by military, intelligence personnel, and scientists who were eyewitnesses to UFOs, extraterrestrials, Unacknowledged Special Access Projects, zero-point-energy, subterranean bases, and other secrets woven into the storyline of this book.

My thanks to the dedicated team at A&M Publishing: Tim Schulte, Barbara Becker, Belle Avery, Michelle Colon-Johnson, Doug and Lisa McEntyre at Millennium Technology Resources, as well as my dear friend, Mark Maller, and our cover artist, Erik Hollander of Erik Hollander Design (ErikHollanderDesign.com). My gratitude to my long-time agent Danny Baror and Heather Baror-Shapiro at Baror International.

To my wife and soul mate, Kim, our children (Kelsey, Branden, Amanda & Chad) and grandchildren (Savannah, Leanna, & Alexandra). Finally, to my readers: Thank you for your correspondence and contributions. Your comments are always a welcome treat, your input means so much, and you remain this author's greatest asset.

Steve Alten, Ed.D.

To personally contact the author or learn more about his novels,
go to www.SteveAlten.com

UNDISCLOSED is part of ADOPT-AN-AUTHOR,
a free nationwide teen reading program for
secondary school students and teachers.
For more information, click on www.AdoptAnAuthor.com

Author's Note

On Saturday, December 14, 2013, at approximately 11:10 p.m., my wife, Kim, and I were returning home from dinner and a movie. As we drove through our neighborhood, I noticed something bizarre moving toward us in the night sky—pale amber lights like nothing I had ever seen. There were eight to twelve of them flying in staggered pairs, approaching from the south, less than a thousand feet (estimated) above Route 441/State Road 7 in Palm Beach County. They were far too silent and smooth to be helicopters and they were definitely not planes. As they came closer and passed almost directly overhead, we could see the outline of a … well, their saucer-shaped vessels.

By this time, I had parked the car. Kim and I stood and watched them, the two of us incredulous as they moved north through a cloudless night sky … until, pair by pair, they simply faded into the ether. Let me be clear here, they didn't move out of range or shut off their lights or disappear into a cloud bank—they slipped out of existence.

My wife and I were both fifty-three at the time, and neither one of us in our combined one-hundred-plus years on this planet had ever seen a UFO. Far from being scared, we felt exhilarated, like we had just been treated to something very special.

Three days later, we drove to Miami Beach and had dinner with Dr. Steven M. Greer and his wife, Emily—the first time the four of us had ever met.

I discovered Dr. Greer's work in 2010 while writing my eleventh novel, *Phobos: Mayan Fear*. I write "faction"—fictional thrillers woven in fact, and I sweat the details. Extraterrestrials played a small part in the storyline I had been working on, and during my research, I had come across a YouTube video of *The Disclosure Project*. I was blown away by both the encounters and integrity of these eyewitnesses, many of whom held top security clearances in the military. I emailed Dr. Greer seeking permission to use excerpts of these testimonials between chapters as a means of entwining fact with fiction. The Greers generously agreed. I thanked them in the acknowledgment and sent a signed book when the novel was published a year later.

In August of 2013, I received an email from Emily. She loved the book and said Steven would like to meet me—perhaps we could have dinner together when they came down to Miami Beach in mid-December.

Of course, the first thing we spoke about was our UFO experience three nights earlier. Dr. Greer explained that these close encounters happen to many of the people he is going to meet for the first time, the ETs "checking us out." I've since learned that advanced species communicate through consciousness; it was during meditation that Steven Greer discovered how to initiate his own close encounters.

Having spent several hundred hours with Dr. Greer, a thousand more researching his work, and a few startling moments in the presence of far more intelligent (and peaceful) life forms not from our planet, I can tell you without a shadow of doubt that the public is being lied to. UFOs and extraterrestrials exist—that is fact, not fiction. It took an emergency room medical physician to figure out how to communicate with them, and the path led him down a dark rabbit's hole. This is his story and it is ours, told in the hopes that, by awakening the masses, we can veer humanity off our current path—a path purposely intended to lead us to Armageddon—and instead usher in an era of universal peace.

—Steve Alten, Ed. D.
　February 10, 2017

While many of the characters in this book are real, and the evidence and history of UFOs and ETs woven into the storyline is based on actual testimonials from eyewitnesses in the Armed Forces and Intelligence Services ... this novel remains a work of fiction.

For Kim ...

PART 1

"We already have the means to travel around the stars, but these technologies are locked up in black projects and it would take an act of God to ever get them out to benefit humanity."

—Ben Rich, Former Head of Lockheed Skunkworks 1975–1991

UCLA School of Engineering Alumni Speech
March 23, 1993

PROLOGUE

North Philadelphia, Pennsylvania
September 5, 2032

MICHAEL ANDREW SUTTERFIELD crept down the staircase, the soft whirring sound of the blender helping to cover the report of the wooden steps creaking beneath his weight. Bypassing the kitchen and his mother, the twelve-year-old made his way through the dining room to reach the basement door.

Another flight of stairs led him down into the cellar. Squeezed among the washer and dryer and a handyman's work station was the pod. Sphere-shaped and twelve-feet-in-diameter, the device was anchored in a seven-foot-high aluminum frame which enabled the object to rotate 360-degrees. The exterior shell was white, composed of fiberglass and tinted plastic. Emblazoned across its midsection in navy-blue was: *GVP-5000*.

A control panel featured a retinal scan and emergency shutdown switch. A digital clock displayed the time as 07:39 a.m. EST. Three names appeared in the USER menu.

Sutterfield, Edward M.
Sutterfield, Tina K.
Sutterfield, Michael A.

Retrieving his personal headpiece and visor from its charger, the adolescent pressed his name on the touch-screen and submitted to the retinal scan.

The pod immediately cracked open, revealing a padded black bucket seat which rotated into position for its occupant, its four female receptors moving to accommodate four male sensory devices built into Michael's neoprene body suit.

The boy was about to climb in when he heard, "Freeze, mister."

His mother descended the wooden stairs, carrying an 8-ounce glass filled with a pink smoothie.

"C'mon, Mom, it's the first day of school. Do you want me to be late?"

"It's only 7:39. Class doesn't activate until eight, and you're still grounded."

"Twenty minutes of zero-gravity … what's the big deal?"

"No."

"Ten?"

"No! Here, drink this."

"I'm not hungry."

"Drink it anyway. The machine will shut down if it senses your blood sugar is low." She handed him the strawberry-banana protein shake. "So, your first day of junior high school, huh? A chance to meet new friends."

"Whatever."

"Michael, can you at least try?"

"Five minutes of zero gravity?"

"Dad told me you selected a science and space curriculum. That sounds exciting."

"They do CE-5."

"He told me. He also said the training sessions won't begin until after you pass all your prerequisites."

"A nutless monkey could pass them." He checked the time display on the side of the pod … 07:41. "Come on, Ma! It calms me down."

Tina Sutterfield could see her son was getting hyper … then again, he knew all the right buttons to push to get her to acquiesce. "Fine. You can stay in zero gravity until school starts, but first drink your smoothie."

Michael drained his breakfast in one steady gulp, handing her the empty glass while expelling a loud burp.

"That's disgusting."

"Can I go now?"

"Did you feed Myrtle?"

"She died."

"What? When?"

"I don't know? Last night, I guess. I went to feed her this morning and she was on her back."

"Honey ... I'm so sorry."

"I chucked her in the trash, she was starting to smell. Can I go now?"

Squeezing her eyes in defeat, she managed, "Go."

He climbed inside the pod, sealing the hatch before his mother could lean in to steal a first-day kiss.

Tina watched the machine activate. Then she headed up two flights of stairs to her son's room.

The terrarium was empty.

She and her husband had found the box turtle on a walk around the park. The reptile's left rear leg had been crushed by either a bicycle tire or a jogger. Against her better wishes, Edward had brought it home for Michael to nurse back to health; father and son accessing the turtle's internal anatomy on a zoological app inside the GVP.

Locating the wastepaper basket, she found Myrtle's remains. While she had wanted to believe the creature had flipped over and suffocated on its own, the evidence suggested otherwise.

Tina examined the incisions that had extricated the turtle from its shell. *Clean cuts ... he's getting better.*

She wiped back tears. *Maybe he'll be a veterinary surgeon ...*

Arguably the most popular technological development since the iPhone, the prototypes of what would eventually become the *Global Village Pod* had originally been designed by the entertainment industry to enhance the video game experience by encapsulating the user in a holographic world that transcended reality.

By merging the system with cell phone technology, the GVP evolved into something far greater.

Almost overnight it seemed, new virtual apps hit the market, allowing executives to "virtually attend" a business meeting, saving travel time and money. Families could get together in any location, real or imagined. Sporting events and concerts, both live and pre-recorded, could be experienced from the best seats in the house.

A new line of sensory body suits raised the bar, allowing one to experience everything from being weightless aboard the International Space Station to the appendage-numbing temperatures and effects of extreme altitude training during a simulated assault on Mount Everest. A medical app replaced doctor visits while a line of interactive adult entertainment apps "virtually" put strip bars and prostitutes out of business, begetting a line of marital counseling apps.

But the Global Village Pod's most important contribution to society was its ability to provide a high quality, individualized and affordable education for everyone, regardless of their household income level or location.

By law, attending kindergarten through sixth grade remained mandatory for a child's social development; however grades seven through twelve, college, post-grad, and all vocational training were now offered in the interactive realm of the Global Village, saving state and local governments billions of dollars while placing public and private schools on a level playing field, allowing each student to learn at their own pace.

While the GVP changed the way the world learned, played, worked, and socialized, its primary function served a new division inside the Department of Homeland Security. Its neural sensors were able to analyze the brain waves of its users, allowing it to identify and track the five percent of the population exhibiting the traits of a sociopath.

The blind caterpillar crawled in excruciatingly slow endless circles along the bottom of the empty glass jar. Every two or three laps it would stop and raise its furry head, as if searching the void for landmarks.

The hologram of the attractive Chinese-American woman sat across the table from the boy, the teacher's looks and age strategically selected to hold the adolescent's interest while still establishing her as an authority figure.

"Mr. Sutterfield, I am still awaiting your answer. Please describe what you see."

Michael rested his chin on the table, rolling his eyes. "For the twentieth time, I see a hairy worm crawling along the bottom of an empty jar. When's lunch, Amy? I'm starving!"

"You are in junior high school now, Mr. Sutterfield. Temper your hunger and think *deeper* please. And you will address me as Ms. Shau."

"Think deeper? I don't know what that means."

"Perhaps a different perspective might help."

The tiny holographic jar suddenly expanded so that it engulfed the boy, who found himself trapped inside the glass container with the caterpillar, which circled him like a three-foot-high wiggling mass of fur.

Michael knew the caterpillar was blind; his tutor had told him that when the exercise had commenced almost an hour before. He rapped his knuckles against the inside of the thick glass jar, a sense of claustrophobia building.

Sensing the disturbance, the caterpillar's head rose to investigate. For several seconds it blindly searched along the inside of the lid before dropping again to circle.

What do blind caterpillars want?

How does a blind caterpillar even know it's blind?

And then it came to him, sparked by his reading assignment.

"It's a metaphor."

The hologram of Amy Shau joined him inside the jar. "Elaborate please."

"It's a metaphor for humanity, prior to the D.E."

The attractive Asian woman smiled. "And how is a blind caterpillar sealed in a jar a metaphor for humanity prior to the Disclosure Event of 2017?"

"The caterpillar's blind, so it doesn't know it's sealed inside its jar, therefore it must keep searching."

"And what is it searching for?"

"A branch to spin its cocoon from; without it, it can never fulfill its destiny."

"And what is its destiny, Mr. Sutterfield?"

"Its destiny is to become a butterfly. See, that's the metaphor. Humanity's destiny was to sprout our wings as a species—you know—live in peace … explore the galaxy. Only we didn't, we just blindly walked around in circles for over a century until the D.E. finally occurred … at least that's what I read in my history book."

"Very good. And who placed humanity in the jar?"

"Uh … I don't know."

"The answer, Mr. Sutterfield, are the ones who *profited* from keeping humanity sealed in the jar. There was an old expression used before the Monetary Reforms of 2022: Always follow the money."

"I don't get it."

The jar disappeared, Michael once more finding himself seated across from his tutor.

"The seventh grade curriculum is quite different from Grammar school. In addition to an introduction to the new sciences, there is a great deal of focus on consciousness and spirituality. You will be taught the most effective ways to meditate. Assuming you pass all of your prerequisites, you will join twenty-four other classmates on three week-long CE-5 training retreats."

Michael smiled. "I am so ready for that."

"Not yet. Before any student can begin CE-5 training, they must understand the circumstances that led to humanity being trapped in a jar during the 20th and 21st centuries."

"Why is that so important, Ms. Shau?"

"Because Michael, if the Disclosure Event had *not* happened when it did, the entire human race would have become extinct."

2017

Before the Disclosure Event …

1

Washington, D.C.
January 20, 2017

THE PLATFORM MEASURED over ten thousand square feet and had been built from scratch, its construction "officially" initiated when a single nail was ceremoniously hammered into a plank back on September 11, 2016.

Two thousand VIPs were seated on the riser, huddling beneath scarves and umbrellas … anything to stay dry in the cold rain. Another hundred thousand visitors encircled the Capitol Building beneath a smoke-gray winter sky as the forty-fifth American ever to be elected to the highest office of the land took the oath:

"I, Donald John Trump, do solemnly swear that I will faithfully execute the Office of President of the United States, and will to the best of my ability preserve, protect and defend the Constitution of the United States."

The new President of the United States accepted the congratulations of the Chief Justice of the Supreme Court before kissing his wife, Melania, to a loud cheer from the partisan crowd—

—while millions of demonstrators protested the event across the country and around the globe.

Adam Shariak located the TV controller beneath a stack of folders and muted the flat screen television mounted on his office wall. Politics had never interested the former Apache helicopter pilot and decorated Iraqi war vet until he had become managing director of Kemp Aerospace Industries. With billions in defense contracts at stake, Adam's CEO, Dr. Michael Kemp, had made it clear which politicians he expected his staff to support. Of course, that gesture paled in comparison to the seven-figure donation Kemp Aerospace made to the Super PAC which forwarded the defense contractor's agenda.

A history buff, Adam could only imagine how America's founding fathers would have reacted had they known about the Supreme Court's 2010 Citizens United ruling which allowed corporate interests to dwarf the rights of the individual. Given a rewrite today, he imagined the authors of the Constitution would have imposed some serious limitations on D.C.'s "professional politicians," no doubt beginning with term limits.

Adam reached for the Levitron Anti-Gravity Top—a gift from his girlfriend, Jessica, on his thirty-ninth birthday. With an expertise born from a thousand twists, he pinched the tip of the device between his thumb and index finger and gave it a sharp spin, the torque causing the top to lift away from its magnetic pad like a flying saucer.

Watching the anti-gravitic device caused his thoughts to wander.

What had ever happened to the promise of flying cars … or the exploration of our galaxy? Forty-five years had passed since man had last set foot on the moon—a full eight years before he was born. By now mankind should have had thriving lunar communities with space travel having become as common to humans as commercial air travel. We certainly had the ingenuity; Kemp's teams were providing technology to the Defense Department that far exceeded anything NASA had contributed in the last twenty years. Even the new laptops and PCs possessed more computational power than anything on board the space shuttle.

Had we simply lost interest in our own evolution?

Adam glanced up at the TV set, the split screen showing the new president's supporters on one side, the demonstrators on the other. Fifty years ago America had found itself in a similar tug-of-war over its own morality. Five decades after Vietnam, a different kind of war dominated the news.

Fifty years. No space travel, no cures for cancer, same old gasoline-fueled combustion engines … same old hatreds—only now the venom could be shared more efficiently and impersonally by email and Twitter, the country hopelessly split down the middle by two political parties that refused to compromise.

He had found himself in a similar conversation two nights earlier at a Defense Department dinner.

"Don't fret it, Shariak. What's important to us is that the new president knows war is good for the economy."

Adam Shariak was born into the life of a nomad. The only child successfully conceived by Air Force Colonel William Shariak and First Lieutenant Sara Jernigan-Shariak (there were two prior miscarriages), the boy had "redeployed" seven times in three different countries before he had entered kindergarten. By the time he was given the standard military ID card issued to children with parents in the Armed Forces, Adam had forgotten half the places he had lived.

Being raised on a military base can be especially challenging for a child. Friendships are short-term with moves frequent, forcing one to become resilient to change. Conversely, the military life encompasses rigid routines, with family members often treated as soldiers, forced to accept a code of honor and self-discipline foreign to their peers. While these traits are valued in the work force, a "military brat" often feels like an outsider in the non-military world.

Sara Jernigan-Shariak had been the glue that held the family together. Whether it was Kansas, Texas, or the military base in Turkey, the moment Adam's mother unpacked the apartment or duplex or hotel room, it not only functioned as a family unit, but as the boy's home-school and his personal training center.

If Colonel Shariak had to rise at 4:30 a.m., then so did his family. After feeding her "men" breakfast, Sara would pack a lunch and she and Adam would hike to a park. Thirty minutes of calisthenics would get the blood circulating to the brain for history, science, and math. Lunch was followed by an hour of reading, the rest of the afternoon reserved for team sports. Basketball was the easiest for Adam to practice by himself—the outdoor courts were usually empty until the local schools let out—but Sara soon realized that her young protégé preferred football. There were organized leagues to join during the fall and spring and drills that Sara incorporated into their off season routine to further her son's skills as a running back—his favorite position.

When he was thirteen, Adam attended class at the local middle school. If the coach was lucky, they'd have the gifted athlete for an uninterrupted season of football and track. Unfortunately, Colonel Shariak was kept on the move as the United States Armed Forces prepared for the first Iraq war, and his son's social and athletic life suffered as a result.

Things changed when Adam turned fifteen and made the Ayer Shirley Regional High School varsity football team as a sophomore. When his father was ordered to report to Frankfurt, Germany a month into the season, the starting fullback made it clear to his parents that he was not leaving Fort Evens. And so the Shariaks split up—the colonel and his wife heading overseas; Adam moving in with Head Coach Adrian Reeves and his family.

It was in Germany that Sara noticed a small lump in her left breast. A biopsy revealed the tumor; blood tests that it was malignant. Surgery was performed, the colonel and his wife deciding not to tell their son about it. Weeks of chemo followed. Unfortunately, the cancer had metastasized to Sara's lymph nodes.

Sara's physician informed the colonel that it was just matter of time. Complicating matters was that his wife was too weak to handle the trip back to the states to see Adam, whose high school football team was competing for a division playoff spot.

And so Adam never knew that his mother was sick until after she passed away.

Adam was devastated. His mother had been his most trusted friend; now the colonel had not only kept the teen from her when she was sick, he had also robbed him of his only chance to say good-bye.

The anger the sixteen-year-old directed toward his father only escalated when the colonel returned to Massachusetts the following October with his new bride.

Marilyn Hall worked as a nurse at the base hospital in Frankfurt. Sara had been her patient; upon her death she had become the stabilizing force in Bill Shariak's life. A widow herself, Marilyn also had a son, Randy, who was in his first year at Harvard Law School.

Adam was furious; his mother's body was still warm in the grave, and now his father had married her nurse? The teen refused to talk to the couple, let alone move in with them. As far as he was concerned, Coach Reeves was his father now.

That became a problem when his surrogate parent accepted the offensive coordinator position at Indiana University in February of Adam's junior year. If the teen had any hope of earning a football scholarship, he had to compete his next two seasons at Ayer Shirley Regional High School—and that meant moving in with the colonel and his new wife.

The situation quickly became toxic.

Twice-a-week mandatory counseling sessions gradually eased Adam's anger toward his stepmother, but the wall he had erected between himself and the colonel would not come down. Despite focusing his rage on the football field, the season was a disappointment as the new head coach ran an offense without a fullback, forcing Adam to learn a new position—tight end.

Relegated to the bench, Adam lost his motivation. His grades suffered and he contemplated dropping out of school, his only enjoyment coming from playing video games.

When Marilyn noticed these games were military-oriented contests featuring combat helicopters, she convinced William to teach his son to fly.

A flight aboard one of the base's Sikorsky helicopters led to private lessons with the colonel and hundreds of hours of practice on a flight simulator, which quickly replaced the teen's video games as his favorite activity. Adam worked hard to impress his father, and it wasn't long before the colonel allowed his son to take the co-pilot's controls while in the air.

A relationship slowly matriculated, aided by Marilyn, whose loving personality was similar to that of Adam's mother. Stepbrother Randy drove in for Adam's football games his senior year, solidifying the family unit. By the time he graduated high school, Adam Shariak could pilot a chopper better than most adults could drive a car.

The teen received one offer to play Division-I football, and that was from his old high school coach who was now installed as the offensive coordinator at Indiana University. Adam rarely played, and when he did, his role was relegated to blocking. And then, on a nationally televised game on Thanksgiving weekend against perennial powerhouse Ohio State, Indiana's starting tailback suffered a concussion and Coach Reeves decided to give his adopted son a shot.

Adam started the second half as the team's halfback. He ran for 126 yards and scored two touchdowns before tearing the ACL in his left knee. The injury officially ended his playing career. It was a bittersweet tale—a taste of success … only to be yanked away, and the pattern would repeat itself throughout his adult life.

Adam spent the rest of his senior year rehabbing his knee. Upon graduating Indiana with a degree in engineering, he promptly enlisted. Upon completing officer's training, "Captain" Shariak was assigned to the Army's 1st Battalion, 4th Aviation Regiment where he would spend the next two years training to pilot the AH-64D Apache

Longbow helicopter.

It took incredible dexterity and coordination to fly the warship. It wasn't enough that his four limbs were responsible for four completely different tasks, his eyes also had to function independently as well. A monocle positioned over his right iris immersed him in a virtual world of fluctuating instrument readings while the eyepiece covering his left eye maintained a real world view.

For most of the first year he suffered terrible headaches as his two eyes competed for dominance.

It took Adam six months just to learn how to fly the air machine, six more to master its weapons system, and another half a year to put everything together until he finally felt combat-ready.

Two months later, his battalion deployed to the Middle East to join Operation Iraqi Freedom.

The city of Karbala had initially been bypassed by American forces in favor of a direct advance on Baghdad. Adam's team arrived in time to provide air cover for the U.S. 3rd Infantry Division which had engaged Saddam's Republican Guard just southeast of the city.

Captain Shariak and his co-pilot, Chief Warrant Officer Jared Betz, were flying their third combat mission over Karbala when a rocket-propelled grenade struck their Apache, sending their helicopter slicing sideways through the hot desert air. Somehow Captain Shariak was able to aim the plunging airship between two buildings, tearing off the rotors while funneling the crash into a semi-controlled landing, avoiding thousands of Iraqi civilians.

The impact collapsed the cockpit like a steel accordion, shattering Adam's left femur. Pinned beneath the wreckage, the captain ordered his co-pilot to abandon him in order to evade capture. By the time Betz returned with help, Captain Shariak was gone; eyewitnesses claiming the American pilot had been taken prisoner by Saddam's forces.

Gravity recaptured the spinning top, slowing its inertia. Adam allowed it to die on the magnetic pad, checking the time on his vintage *Three Stooges* desk clock, a graduation gift from his stepbrother, Randy.

Five-twenty. Dinner reservations are at seven-thirty. If we leave here by six we should get to the restaurant with about ten minutes to spare.

Timing was everything in D.C. On normal days the traffic was merely horrendous; with the inauguration it would be impossible. For someone who considered himself a shut-in, downtown was the last place you'd find Adam Shariak on a night like tonight ... but tonight was "special."

Considering all he had been through, he was amazed to find himself blessed to even have the opportunity to plan such a momentous occasion.

The Iraqis that had captured Captain Adam Shariak were members of Saddam's elite Republican Guard, led by a sadistic commander named Abu Anas al-Baghdadi. Adam's injuries were serious—his broken femur became infected and swelled to twice its size, gangrene quickly setting in. Al-Baghdadi needed his injured American prisoner kept alive, so he assigned the pilot's health to one of the young girls who he had kidnapped and turned into a sex slave.

Nadia Kalaf was fourteen. Her mother had been a nurse before the Fedayeen had gunned her down; therefore Al-Baghdadi assumed her daughter had to know something about first aid. The commander made it clear—if the American died before the Fedayeen could acquire Intel from the pilot then the girl would join him, only her death would be far more gruesome.

What the Iraqi sociopath didn't know was that the girl wanted to die. And so she allowed gangrene to set into Adam's wounds ... only to reverse course days later once she got to know the American pilot.

By week's end, she had decided to help him escape.

Captain Shariak awoke in a hospital bed at Ramstein Air Base in Germany. The infection that had nearly killed him was gone; so too was his left leg, amputated above the knee.

Losing a limb had a devastating impact on Adam's psyche. Flying helicopters was far more than his occupation; it had become everything to him.

Without a left leg, he was permanently grounded.

17

Two months later he found himself back in the states at Walter Reed Hospital in Bethesda, Maryland suffering from extreme depression.

Eight months of physical therapy enabled him to get along with a prosthetic leg; but it would take several years of counseling before Adam finally accepted his fate and could move on.

By now the two wars had produced more than six hundred amputees. Adam had been fitted with a prosthetic, but the change in his gait caused horrible back and sciatic nerve pain which ran down his buttocks.

As an engineer, Adam believed he could improve the design of these artificial limbs. Pulling some strings, the colonel managed to get his son a civilian appointment at DARPA (the Defense Advanced Research Projects Agency) in their RE-NET lab. Reliable Neuro-Interface Technology was a new science which focused on thought to control an artificial limb using the signals sent from the body's existing muscles and nerves.

One of the problems amputees experienced with RE-NET prototypes was pain caused by the tight-fitting socket joints needed to initiate osseointegration—the direct connection between living bone and the electrodes within the artificial limb. Adam's solution was to incorporate metal foam in the design; a porous bone-like material used in smart satellites which he believed would allow signals to pass from the brain into the prosthetic device.

Believing the prototype would find a better home in the private sector, Adam's supervisor arranged a meeting with Dr. Michael Kemp, a former NASA rocket scientist and the founding partner of Kemp Aerospace Industries. Kemp Aerospace was a private D.C. firm whose expertise in satellites enabled them to feed off the scraps of defense contracts awarded to "Beltway Bandits" like Lockheed Martin, Northrop, SAIC, E-Systems, EG&G and MITRE Corporation.

Adam Shariak's "K Street" connections (Randy was now a Senator and sat on the Senate Appropriations Committee) enticed Dr. Kemp, who had been looking to hire a new managing director.

Adam passed on the offer, until the CEO agreed to fund a new subdivision that would specialize in the design and manufacture of smart prosthetic limbs.

During his first six months on the job, Kemp Aerospace's new general manager cut costs and increased the company's profit margin by thirteen percent. Unfortunately, the security clearances on the large defense contracting projects were often above top-secret, meaning Adam had to exclude himself from participating in project meetings, reducing his role in the eyes of some of his employees to that of a glorified secretary.

Thankfully, he had Jessica to get him over the hurdles.

Dr. Jessica "Juice" Marulli was a five-foot, four-inch blonde dynamo with an athletic figure and sharp tongue. Her father, Captain Al Marulli, was an F-16 test pilot; her mother, Dr. Barbara Jean Singleton was an engineer at Lockheed-Martin. Like Adam, Jessica had grown up a military brat, her tutors and private coaches serving as surrogate parents. Short, but packing a lot of power, Juice Marulli was an all-state gymnast, but it was her grades and lineage that earned her a full scholarship at Cal Tech.

Eight years and three degrees later, the aerospace engineer and magna cum laude was being recruited by Lockheed-Martin. Unfortunately, there were too many security issues to overcome with mother and daughter working at the same facility in such varying capacities, so Jessica was sent to work at one of Lockheed's subcontractors ... Kemp Aerospace.

A workaholic with no time for a social life, Jessica found herself very attracted to the company's new managing director. Staking out her claim before any of the other single (or married) women at the company made their move, Dr. Marulli invited the former Apache pilot over for dinner.

Adam rarely lost his cool, but the blonde bombshell intimidated the hell out of him. It wasn't just her looks, her high I.Q., or her security clearance—it was the way in which she had looked at him after she had texted him her address, as if her brown eyes were undressing him right there in her lab.

With the exception of one particularly horrible blind date set up by his sister-in-law, Melinda, Adam's social life had been non-existent since he had lost his leg. When asked, he offered the usual excuses about focusing on his work or not meeting the right person, and yes, he'd definitely try out those Internet dating sites. But the reality was that it was the awkwardness of having to deal with his prosthetic leg during sex that kept him from asking women out.

The blind date with his sister-in-law's girlfriend had actually gone well until things became hot and heavy in the bedroom. When the woman asked him to remove the prosthetic because its sharp edges were scratching her Adam obliged, only the site of his mangled stump made her so squeamish that she quickly excused herself to use the bathroom.

She then claimed to have a hangover and left, never to be heard from again.

Embarrassment being the mother of invention, Adam set out to design a prosthetic limb that not only functioned well but was covered in an artificial flesh that looked and felt real to the touch. The new leg was coated in a soft and porous heat-conducive foam embedded with wires. An electrical charge warmed the leg; a small dial controlled the temperature.

He finished the prototype just in time to wear it on his dinner date with Jessica Marulli.

Adam showed up at her townhome dressed in a sports jacket, tee-shirt, and jeans, carrying a dozen red roses and a stuffed animal. He rang the doorbell, his heart fluttering like a virgin on prom night, his artificial leg pumping out heat.

Jessica answered the door, wearing only a gray tee-shirt which barely covered her groin. "You bought me a Koala bear... how sweet."

The sight of the scantily-clad blonde caused Adam to break out in sweat. "Am I early? I mean ... you're not dressed."

"No ... I thought we'd have sex before we went out to eat. That okay with you?"

He barely managed to nod when he was suddenly overcome by the stench of burning plastic.

"Adam, are you just happy to see me or are your pants on fire?"

They would laugh about it later—Adam rolling on the front lawn, Jessica drenching him with the garden hose. Yes, she had known he was an amputee and as she quickly demonstrated she had no problem dealing with his stump. What endeared him to her was the lengths Adam had gone to please her, and she promised to help him work out the technical challenges of the prosthetic flesh.

Jessica only had one rule—that they keep their personal life private and out of the workplace because of "security issues."

Jessica, will you marry me.

Adam inspected the two slips of paper before carefully replacing them for the ones he had removed from the fortune cookies that had come with his lunch. His plan was to swap out the fortune cookies at dinner when the check came. While Jessica was reading his marriage proposal he'd remove the engagement ring from his other pocket and place it on the table in front of her. It wasn't much—an oval-shaped three-quarter carat diamond set in a twisted gold braid. The jeweler had given him an extensive education on cut, clarity, carats, and color and he had opted for the largest white diamond he could afford.

A petite package of perfection … just like Jess.

He glanced at the desk clock again—his heart skipping a beat as his laptop screensaver obliterated the Kemp Aerospace Industry logo to alert him that he was receiving a call on a secured line.

Adam clicked on the ACCEPT MESSAGE icon and then typed in his password.

A moment later he found himself being stared down by a former three-star general.

Thomas J. Cubit was a military advisor with hundreds of contacts in the Defense Department who now made millions of dollars working in the private sector. A bit of a ball-buster with a wry sense of humor, the fifty-six-year-old Philadelphia native never hesitated to let Adam know that the military industrial complex had eyes everywhere.

"General? I thought our call was scheduled for next Wednesday?"

"This is courtesy call, Captain. Lockheed's engineers need Dr. Marulli on site in early August."

Adam split the screen, accessing his monthly planner. "How long will you need her for?"

"At least a month."

"A month? Sir, Dr. Marulli's overseeing two of our biggest projects; I can't spare her for that long. How about Nick Mastramico?"

"Dr. Mastramico doesn't have the necessary clearances."

"He has his Q clearance, General. That's sufficient to program the satellites."

"Not in a command post. If Strategic Command goes into a full alert, anyone not wearing a Zebra badge or higher will have exactly sixty seconds to vacate the facility before our marines shoot them."

"What could possibly cause a full alert?"

"I'd tell you, Captain, only you don't have the clearance to discuss it! Now pay attention: Lockheed will have a private jet waiting for Dr. Marulli at the Martin State Airport in Baltimore on the third of August at thirteen hundred hours; make sure your girlfriend is on it. Or should I say your fiancée."

Adam felt his face flush.

"Going with a smaller stone. . . it's a good move. At least you'll know if she really loves you." The general winked. "We'll talk more on Wednesday. Cubit out."

The connection severed, the screensaver returned.

Bastard ... probably has my office bugged.

Adam leaned back in his chair and peered through the horizontal slats of the silver Venetian blinds. The window looked down onto an extensive work area that was roughly the size of a high school gym.

The satellite, part of a black ops project code-named *Zeus*, occupied most of the Plexiglas-enclosed suite of Lab-3. The rectangular-shaped device was twelve feet high and eight feet wide, with a depth just under six feet. It stood upright like an onyx wall, its two solar panels, attached to either side of its frame, folded inward. As large as it was, the object was merely a three-hundred-pound replica used by Kemp's design team to test the configuration of its internal circuits under space conditions. The actual satellite was a four-ton monstrosity—one of twenty that were housed at an unknown location—most likely a secret military base.

Jessica was not inside the work station, which meant she was probably inside the CHIL.

Adam stood up from behind his desk, pausing to allow the internal pistons of his new prosthetic device to align with the working muscles of his right leg. A remarkable piece of machinery, the artificial limb's titanium skeleton extended from his stump all the way to its five working toes, all of which were capable of flexion and extension. The weight, length, and musculatures of the limb matched that of his right leg, down to the temperature of the spongy flesh-like skin.

To complete the visual, he had waxed the hair off of his real leg.

Adam had nearly trashed the device on its first day as he struggled to coordinate the complex movements of the fake appendage with his right leg. It had taken him hours just to learn how to sit without falling over sideways, his frustrations quelled only by Jessica's patience.

"I'm sure this is a lot like flying the Apache, Adam. Your brain is being asked to control two completely different limbs and coordinate these independent movements so that you can walk. The problem is that your right leg's brain is thirty years ahead of your prosthetic device, which was literally born this morning. As your brain learns to compensate, the smart chips embedded within the joints of your left limb will segregate the successful movements from the failures and over time you'll learn to walk without consciously thinking about it."

"Assuming I survive the thousand falls that await me. How do I use the bathroom without ending up in the urinal?"

"I could strap a board to your ass."

Focusing his thoughts, he walked with a slow, steady cadence to the elevator.

The Collaborative Human Immersive Laboratory, known as CHIL, was an enclosed motion-capture suite located next to Lab-3. Created by Lockheed-Martin, CHIL utilized virtual reality to allow production designers and engineers to test the components of a satellite in a computer-generated world where they could duplicate the frigid conditions of space.

Adam found Dr. Jessica Marulli inside the "cave," dressed from head to toe in a black and orange trim nylon body suit adorned with silver sensors. With her eyes concealed behind a head-mounted display, the aerospace engineer had morphed into her own personal avatar, moving through a virtual world only she could see.

She paused, sensing his presence on an internal display. "Adam?"

"Sorry to bother you. General Cubit just informed me that you'll be working at Lockheed the entire month of August and through the fall. When were you going to tell me?"

"It's not my place to tell you. This is a highly-classified project. Things don't filter down in the usual manner; you're either in the loop or you're not. When Central Command wants me I have to go. You know the deal."

"It doesn't mean I have to like it. With you gone that long, I'll need to bring in another chief engineer. It's not like I'm hiring a substitute math teacher."

Jessica removed her helmet, shaking out an entanglement of blonde curls. "And here I thought you were upset because I'll be gone for so long."

Adam looked around, wondering if there was anyone in the control room.

"It's just us," she said, reading his thoughts. "I told Khrys King she could leave early; it's her kid's birthday."

"And it's our anniversary. Are we still on for dinner, or do I need to okay it with the general?"

"Actually, I've got another /three hours in here. Is there any way we can move the reservation back to nine?"

"On the night of the inauguration? They're booked solid."

"So we'll skip Chen's. Let's go to Tosca's, my treat. Call Maria, she'll squeeze us in."

"Italian? I was really in the mood for Chinese."

"I thought you had Chinese for lunch? And the traffic's going to be crazy. Why don't we just order takeout?"

"Takeout ... yeah, whatever." He reached into his left jacket pocket. "I saved the fortune cookies from lunch. Will that work?"

"Adam, you shouldn't bring food into the lab."

"Pick one."

"Is this really necessary?"

"Just humor me."

She rolled her eyes and then pointed to one of the cookies. "You'll have to open it for me; I'm not taking off these gloves. And don't get any crumbs on the floor or Dr. Mastramico will blame me."

He pulled off the partially opened wrapper and cracked open the stale cookie, passing her the fortune.

She gripped the message in her cyber-gloved fingers, turning it right-side up. "What is this?"

"What does it say?"

She looked at him, unsure. "Is this real?"

"I don't know. Are you having an affair with the chef at Chen's?"

24

"Adam—"

He handed her the felt-covered box.

Jessica took it, her gloved hands shaking. "You were going to do this tonight at dinner and I ruined it, didn't I?"

"It's okay."

Using her teeth, she pulled the gloves from her hands and opened the box, her eyes tearing up. "Oh my God—"

"I know it's small. Maybe you can use your visor to create a larger virtual diamond."

"Shut-up." She placed the ring on her finger. "It's perfect. And yes, I will absolutely marry you. Yes, yes, yes."

She leaned in awkwardly and kissed him, careful not to make contact with the silver sensor balls adhered to her body suit.

Instead of pulling away, she continued to rest her forehead against his. "I love you, Adam Shariak."

"I love you, too Jessica … Shariak." Adam smiled.

"Jessica Marulli-Shariak. My father would disown me if I gave up our family name."

"I accept the terms of your surrender. I'll call Tosca's and see if they can get us in around nine."

"Forget Tosca's." She placed her headpiece on the floor, then unzipped the nylon bodysuit and carefully slipped out of it, revealing a crimson bra and matching silk panties.

"Take off your clothes; we'll screw first and eat dinner later."

2

Avenue of the Americas
New York City
April 18, 2017

THERE ARE MANY PERKS associated with being a former U.S. president, among which is having American taxpayers pick up the tab on your office space after you leave the White House. The most expensive lease was George W. Bush's 15,678-square-foot Dallas headquarters, tallying $701,636 a year in rent. Bill Clinton's Harlem office ran a more modest $399,931 annually, though he had moved out in 2011 in favor of a midtown Manhattan address.

The Clinton Global Initiative, one of a dozen foundations set up by the former president and his team, occupied 30,000 square feet on the 42nd floor of the Time-Life Building. Two more floors were subsequently leased by Hillary Rodham-Clinton leading up to her presidential run in 2015.

Established in 2001, the Clinton Global Initiative targeted a variety of causes, including AIDS, obesity, poverty, and global warming. Despite raising hundreds of millions of dollars in donations, the organization often struggled to balance the conflicts between the philanthropic goals of the former president, his money-making interests, the political ambitions of his wife, and the ever-increasing involvement of their daughter, Chelsea.

In the wake of Hillary's failed presidential campaign, Bill's agenda involved seemingly endless meetings with the foundation's attorneys and accountants in an attempt to resolve a myriad of post-election matters.

When the morning session with the Board of Trustees threatened to drift past noon, Clinton excused himself for a scheduled conference call.

Lisa Ann Hughes looked up from her desk as he entered the waiting area of his private office suite. "He's waiting for you inside. I know—hold all calls." She handed him a large plastic Styrofoam cup with a straw. "I ordered you a protein smoothie."

"Thank you, darlin'." He drained half the cup, then entered his office to find an old friend waiting for him.

Joseph G. Rangel was a former White House counsel whose friendship with William Jefferson Clinton stretched back decades. Well-connected with corporate executives and A-list celebrities, as well as government and military officials, Rangel preferred to operate in the shadows rather than the glare that seemed to follow the ex-president everywhere.

Built like a wrestler, the squat, muscular man rose from the cream-colored leather sofa to greet his friend, a dossier held in his thick left hand.

Bill Clinton gave Rangel a warm embrace. "We don't have much time; I've got a call with the Cuban ambassador at one. Is that him?"

"That's our guy."

Clinton took the file and settled himself in his favorite easy chair. Retrieving his reading glasses from a breast pocket, he opened the dossier, quickly scanning the information.

"Captain Adam Shariak, United States Army, retired. Apache helicopter pilot and trainer. Wounded during combat operations in Iraq ... purple heart ... the requisite security clearance for being a captain in the Armed Forces. Defense Sciences ... managing director at Kemp Aerospace—why him? What's so special about Adam Shariak?"

"When his Apache went down he was captured by members of Saddam's Fedayeen. He had a broken femur, life-threatening gangrene, and God-only-knows what other injuries. Ended up losing his left leg. They tortured him for a week but never got a thing out of him."

"Geez. How'd he get out of that?"

"He charmed the girl nursing his infection into helping him escape."

"So he's tough and empathetic; good. What's your insertion point?"

"The Under Secretary of Defense–Comptroller. The Deputy Secretary of Defense has been vetting him for several months. His confirmation hearings should happen in late spring."

"Does he even know he's a candidate?"

"He will by tonight."

"And Trump knows nothing about this?"

"It's a minor appointment to him, justified as political payback. My guy on the inside was afraid to call Shariak a war hero after all the abuse Trump gave McCain."

"You do realize that Shariak will serve as one of the chief advisors to the Secretary of Defense?"

"With oversight responsibilities for all military installations, operational energy plans and programs, major weapon systems, missile defense programs, and drum roll please … all space and intelligence programs."

"You are good, my friend. Is he married? Any kids?"

"He recently got engaged to the chief aerospace engineer at Kemp."

The former president looked at her photo. "Brains and beauty."

"And a Zebra security clearance, which I've been informed will soon be bumped to Cosmic Clearance."

Clinton looked up. "She'll be on the inside. Jesus, Mary, and Joseph, you're a cold sonuva bitch."

"You asked me to do a job. You think you're going to accomplish anything by being half-pregnant? We both know a job title means didleysquat or we wouldn't even be having this conversation. Dr. Marulli is a potential means of getting Shariak on the inside, something that was denied to you for eight years as president. If you know of a better way to pierce the gauntlet, tell me."

"No, no. You're right." Clinton closed his eyes, pinching the bridge of his nose. "What's the potential blowback to Shariak?"

"For now, he's flying way below the radar. Once he enters the rabbit's hole and starts asking questions he'll attract some low-level interest. His stepbrother is Senator Randy Hall."

"As in Head of the Senate Appropriations Committee Hall? Good Lord, Joe. What happens when they perceive Shariak as a threat?"

"They'll offer him a bribe. If he takes it we'll lose him. He won't take it."

"The cabal will set him up or issue a TWEP order. I don't know, Joe.

I don't want another Bill Colby on my hands."

"Shariak's a civilian; Colby was in the cabal's inner circle. It wasn't until he decided to sneak out plans for a free energy device that the radical element of MAJI murdered him. Damn sociopaths; it's that fear factor that has kept the silent majority in line."

"I've met some of these guys at a few CFR (Council on Foreign Relations) meetings; you look into their eyes and it's like Dick Cheney—there's no soul."

"Are you going to tell Hillary?"

"Absolutely not. The less people who know, the better."

"Which brings up a major hurdle. Shariak will need to be directed down the rabbit's hole sometime after the Senate hearing and it can't come from my guy on the inside."

"Why not?"

"He and Shariak have a history. Besides, this has to look non-partisan and come from a higher authority."

Clinton pinched the stress knotting in his brow. "Where and when?"

"It has to be at an event you'll both be attending. Maybe a golf outing?"

"As long as he's not in our foursome." The former president handed him back the folder. "I've got to go. You did real well, Joe."

"Bill, you never told me why you decided to put this in play."

"It would have happened if Hillary had won the election; she had already started planting seeds on the Kimmel Show. Papa Bush had actually set out to do this years ago with Gorbachev and Pérez de Cuéllar. The bastards kidnapped Secretary General de Cuéllar and put the fear of God into him and Gorby's wife. Something similar had been staged years earlier with Hans-Adams's brother."

"The Liechtenstein prince?"

"The abduction changed his mind, just like it did with the Secretary General. As for me, traveling around the world … my recent trips to India and Africa…you see the poverty, the effects of malaria and Ebola—it tears you up inside. We've accomplished more with our Global Initiative than anything we did during my eight years in the White House. But this, Joe—this is a game-changer. This is a tide of good that raises every boat on the planet."

"Just be careful, my friend. These are some seriously fucked up people we're dealing with, and they don't like sharing their toys."

3

Kemp Aerospace Industries
Washington, D.C.

THE CORPORATE WORKOUT ROOM had been Adam Shariak's idea. When he had first accepted the job at Kemp Aerospace, he had committed to a two-year lease on a one bedroom apartment in Greenbelt Station, along with a gym membership at a local club. Once he and Jessica began dating, he had practically moved in to her townhome.

Unable to afford a second gym membership, he made an "executive decision" to convert a barely used employee lounge into a weight room.

As it turned out, he and Jessica were the only ones who ever used it.

The blonde's legs were pumping out miles on a stationary bike, her lower body no match for her thumbs, which flitted across the keyboard pad on her iPhone as she texted and listened to music on her headphones.

Adam watched her for a moment before laying back on the incline press beneath a forty-five pound barbell, each side holding and additional hundred-and-twenty pounds of iron plates.

Two-fifty-five … Two good reps, three if you want to impress your woman.

Positioning himself beneath the bar, he inhaled a deep breath and exhaled as he lifted the weight off of the stand, then drew in another breath as he lowered the barbell to his chest.

Exhaling, he pressed the first rep with relative ease.

Glancing to his right, he saw she had missed his Herculean effort and went for another rep—

—big mistake.

Touching the middle of the bar to his chest, he managed six inches before the barbell resettled on his sternum.

Sucking in several quick breaths, Adam attempted to raise the weight again, managing to get it three-quarters of the way up before his strength waned and gravity turned the barbell into a hood ornament.

No problem, he had left the collars off for just such an emergency.

Tilting the right side of the bar down, he wriggled the loose plates, attempting to slide a hundred-and-twenty pounds off one side while preventing the other side from smashing onto the rubber flooring—only the plates weren't sliding off the rusted surface of the barbell like he had expected.

With his sternum beginning to bruise, he was about to try the left side when two hands reached down and gripped the middle of the barbell, helping him guide it back onto the incline press.

He sat up, turning to face his rescuer—surprised to see it was a woman.

She was Jessica's height, with short brown hair and gray eyes which matched her business suit and skirt.

"That's a lot of weight to be flipping sideways, Captain. You should have a spotter."

"He has a spotter," Jessica stated, positioning herself between her fiancé and the woman. "I'm his spotter. Who the hell are you?"

She held up her identification card. "Anna Curtis, special assistant to General James Mattis. I'm here to discuss your nomination as Under Secretary of Defense–Comptroller."

Jessica served Adam a bowl of pasta, then waited while he poured them each a glass of wine. "Shall we toast to your new career?

"I haven't said yes."

"You will. This isn't something you turn down, Adam. I didn't even know you knew 'Mad Dog' Mattis."

"I served under him briefly, but he was the colonel's friend. The last time I saw the general was six years ago at my father's funeral."

"With a nickname like 'Mad Dog,' I imagine he's the shoot-first and ask questions later type."

"The exact opposite. Yes, he'll drop a quote here or there about Iran that may cause a few pulses to race, but when you've spent as much time in the sandbox as Mattis has, there's a greater desire to maintain stability over engaging in another war."

"Sounds like someone you could work under … what's wrong?"

"I dunno. This whole thing feels out of left field. Hell, Jess, I'm not even qualified to attend half the meetings at Kemp; how can I even consider taking on a position like Under Secretary of Defense?"

"Trump's president. Is he any more qualified than you?"

"To be Under Secretary or president?"

"Under Secretary. You're already more qualified than him to be Commander-in-Chief."

"I'm just not sure a majority of senators will agree with you. My own stepbrother laughed himself into a wheezing fit when I told him."

"Randy will be there for you when it counts. Accept the nomination and see what happens. Worst case scenario—you're back at Kemp managing defense projects in the blind."

"Thanks."

She laughed, forcing her sauce-covered kiss past his defenses.

4

Senate Confirmation Hearings
Capitol Hill
Washington, D.C.

SENATOR ROBERT HARDY GIBBONS, JR. banged his gavel. "Good morning. The committee meets today to consider the nomination of Captain Adam Ulysses Shariak to be Under Secretary of Defense–Comptroller. Before we begin, I want to welcome the eight senators who are new both to the Senate and to our committee. Joining us in 2017 are Senators Brian Ziarnik, Marcus Eberlein, Stephen Wood, and Vincent Renzulli on the Republican side and Senators Melanie Hurt, Jimmy Cain, Kevin Banks, and Joe Horning on the Democrat side. In the past this committee has worked across party lines to support our troops and their families and America's national defense mission; it is in this spirit that I'll begin.

"Having served two tours in Iraq as a member of the U.S. Army Signal Corps, it is my honor to introduce our nominee. Captain Adam Shariak comes from a military heritage; his paternal grandfather served in Korea, his father Colonel William Shariak served in Operation Desert Storm. Like his grandfather and father, Adam Shariak has served our country honorably and with distinction. In 2003 he deployed to Iraq with the Army's 1st Battalion, 4th Aviation Regiment. While flying a combat mission, his Apache was hit by a rocket-propelled grenade. Somehow Captain Shariak managed to guide the airship away from a crowded marketplace where it crash-landed. The impact collapsed the Apache's cockpit and snapped the femur in the captain's left leg. Trapped and in terrible pain, Adam Shariak ordered his co-pilot to hide before the enemy arrived.

"Captain Shariak was captured, held in a bunker, and tortured. Despite a gangrenous left leg which he'd end up losing, he managed to escape. Although Captain Shariak has never worked in the Defense Department as a paper-pusher, I believe his credentials in the field make him uniquely qualified for this position, which is why I support his nomination to replace the outgoing Under Secretary of Defense–Comptroller. I know many of you have questions; we'll begin with Senator Renzulli."

The Republican from Connecticut leaned forward to speak into his microphone. "Captain Shariak, everyone in this chamber appreciates the sacrifices you have made for our country. My concern is the role you would play as one of the chief advisors to the Secretary of Defense. This committee has received so little background on you, yet the administration has pushed us to render a quick decision. I think many of us would like to know more about your beliefs as it pertains to the war on terror—particularly the escalating conflict against Islamic State. For instance, what is your opinion in regard to how President Obama handled ISIS?"

Translated: My brother, Senator Hall, is a Dem … what are my politics?

Adam Shariak took a deep breath. "Senator, we're dealing with a complex, multi-pronged situation. I appreciate President Obama understood that dropping bombs on Syrian villages like the Russians were doing is not how you win the battle that could potentially decide whether Islam will be ruled by radicals or moderates."

"Then you support President's Obama's failed policies?"

"As the DoD's Comptroller, I will support whoever occupies the Oval Office."

"That's not what I asked. I asked if you support Obama's failed policies when it comes to dealing with an enemy that wants to kill innocent Americans."

"With all due respect, Senator, reducing the issue down to a yes or no question indicates a desire to make my nomination a political issue. You can certainly do that if you wish, but if you really want to know what I think about ISIS, then give me enough latitude to answer the question properly."

Randy Hall leaned over to Jessica Marulli and whispered in her ear. "They have no idea who they're dealing with."

She smiled. "They're about to find out."

Senator Renzulli held out his hands. "Okay, Captain … enlighten us."

"My Apache team escorted the first boots on the ground back in 2003. Whether or not you agreed with the invasion of Iraq, the Iraqi people, at that time, clearly supported our presence. The Iraqi army had agreed to cooperate with General Jay Gardner in order to control looting while working with us to bring the power and water utilities back on line. And then Rumsfeld did a one-eighty, replacing General Gardner with Paul Bremer, a civilian who had no concept of the lay-of-the-land or the historic conflict between the Sunnis and Shia.

"Bremer's first decree was to ban all members of the Ba'ath Party from holding office; his second was to dismantle the Iraqi army. With two strokes of the pen, Bremer essentially took 400,000 well-trained Iraqi soldiers who had access to caches of hidden weapons and rendered them jobless, while excluding them from ever having a stake in their own country's future. This is what is known in the military as a major cluster-fuck. The commandos quickly organized, turning Iraq into a Guerilla war zone. Instead of peace, Iraqi civilians suddenly had to deal with suicide bombers and cities without electricity, food, and water. It wasn't long before al Qaeda, which was run by Sunnis and had never been in Iraq under Saddam, took root under the guidance of Abu Musab al-Zarqawi.

"Under Saddam's rule, Iraq's minority Sunni party controlled the middle-class. In 2006, Nouri al-Maliki—a Shiite—took over as Prime Minister. Instead of building a coalition government, he outwardly favored the Shiites while purposely neglecting to provide electricity and other essential services to Iraq's Sunni Arab cities. Worse, he looked the other way while Shiite militias ran rampant, killing Sunnis wherever they went in what amounted to an ethnic cleansing.

"In an attempt to combat al Qaeda and involve the Sunnis, General Petraeus created Awakening Councils—forces of armed Sunnis willing to fight the extremists. Instead of integrating these 100,000 moderates into the Iraqi army and police force, Al-Maliki opposed the program. Fearing a coup, he purposely kept his army weak. He later accused his Sunni vice president of being a terrorist, all of which only further served to alienate the Sunni population."

Senator Renzulli signaled to Chairman Gibbons. "I wanted a yes or no answer about the last administration's handling of ISIS; instead I'm getting a history lesson on the Iraq war."

Adam Shariak interjected. "I'm about to answer you, senator. After U.S. forces killed Zarqawi, he was replaced by Abu Bakr al-Baghdadi who merged his al Qaeda forces in Iraq and Syria and announced the creation of ISIL, the Islamic State in Iraq and the Levant. His first target was Mosul, a Sunni Arab city located in Northern Iraq, home to two million people. Having been abused by al-Maliki's government for five years, Mosul's Sunni population practically welcomed the Islamist radicals into their city. Al-Baghdadi then declared ISIL's territory a caliphate—a state governed in accordance with Sharia law. The Islamic State is very well organized, with four separate security services that keep both the jihadist and civilian populations in line. Each of these services reports to an emir, who in turn follows the orders of the men whose faces are always cloaked in black.

"Senator, these cloaked men who are the true leaders of Islamic State are, in fact, members of Saddam's former Ba'athist army, the ones Paul Bremer dismissed back in 2003. Just as they are doing now, these same officers in the Fedayeen carried out similar campaigns of terror under Sadaam. With Syria's President Assad waging war on his own people, and President Obama pulling our troops out of Iraq, the Ba'athist commandos saw ISIL as the perfect vehicle from which to retake Iraq and rule the region. They essentially overran Syria's military bases, took all of Assad's Russian-made tanks and weapons, and used them to take control of Syrian oil wells and refineries. Using their knowledge of the smuggling networks developed under Saddam back in the 1990s to avoid U.N. sanctions, these former Ba'athists have been selling the crude at discounted prices while raking in hundreds of millions of dollars in profits. And who is buying the oil and the stolen Syrian artifacts, Senator Renzulli? We are.

"You asked me about President Obama's initiatives. Before you evaluate his administration's policies you need to understand the Islamic State's endgame. The Fedeyeen wearing the black cloaks want control over the region. To get that, they are unleashing the jihadists—the religious radicals in the Muslim faith. Their goal is to convince the rest of the Islamic world that an apocalyptic process is underway which will lead to a confrontation between an army of Muslims and the Western crusaders… equating us with the Romans. Everything they do, from these public beheadings to the terror plots in Paris, is designed to elicit violent responses from the West that keeps moving us down the road leading to Armageddon. President Obama understood that."

"If that's true, Captain Shariak, then why did his policies fail?"

"They failed because Saddam's former Ba'athist officers are running Islamic State's territories like a business, generating several billion dollars which the jihadists want to use to purchase weapons of mass destruction. To prevent that from happening, we need to cut off the flow of funds coming from Turkey. Iraq may be salvageable if we can convince Baghdad that they need to have new elections to establish a coalition government with a place at the table for Sunnis and Kurds. As for Syria, that's more complicated. Assad has to go, but it's a mistake to support the Syrian rebels, most of whom are affiliates of al Qaeda. While President Trump scored points with Putin by calling out Turkey for buying oil from ISIL; the real supporters of Islamic State are the Saudis. Unless you force our biggest supplier of oil to stop funding terrorism and its messages of hatred which target Israel and the United States, we'll never defeat radical Islam."

The half-empty chamber broke out in a smattering of applause.

Joe Rangel was seated in one of the upper rows, out of range of the C-SPAN cameras. He glanced down at his iPhone screen as a new text message appeared:

GOTTA LOVE THIS GUY. I'M WAITING IN THE BULL PEN.

5

The White House
Washington, D.C.
July 2017

ADAM SHARIAK FOLLOWED the press secretary past a security checkpoint and through the West Colonnade, his left sciatic nerve slightly inflamed from the long walk from the parking lot. Entering the West Wing, they were intercepted by Kelli-Lynn McDonald, Donald Trump's Chief of Staff.

"Mr. Under Secretary, President Trump apologizes. He's been in a photo shoot and breakfast get-together with the Clemson Tigers … I guess you know they won the 2016 College Championship."

"I may have heard a rumor."

"Well, there's a game tonight between the Cubs and Nationals and the president wants you to join him in his luxury suite. Be sure to arrive thirty minutes early so you two can talk."

Nationals Park
Washington, D.C.

Located in the Naval Yard section of Washington, D.C., Nationals Park seated a cozy 41,500 fans, while offering a view of the Washington Monument and Capitol Building from the first baseline bleachers.

Adam had attended more than fifty games since the new park had opened back in 2008; many with his brother, Randy who had season tickets along the

39

third baseline. Jessica preferred the back and forth pace of hockey—after the first two innings she had spent the rest of the game texting on her iPhone.

He arrived at 5:40 p.m. for the 7:05 start. Access to the luxury suites was from a private entrance beneath the stadium. After swiping his ticket, the attendant called for a personal concierge—an older Caucasian man in his eighties who went by the name of "Pops."

"Pops, Suite 18."

"Eighteen it is. Sir, if you'll come with me—"

He followed the spry man onto an awaiting elevator and up to the suite level which featured a private mezzanine that looked like a Las Vegas-style sports bar, every wall covered in giant TV screens.

Pops led him to the first suite by the elevators where two stadium security officers were posted outside the metal door, the outside of which was receiving a new numbered plate and corporate sponsor's logo from a maintenance man.

"Here you go sir, allow me to show you inside." Using his pass key, the old man unlocked the door and held it open for Adam, who entered.

"Nice …"

The suite was divided into a kitchen and dining area, card tables, sofas and recliners, a pool table, and two levels of luxury seating in front of an unencumbered view ten degrees down the third base side of home plate.

Pops pointed to the two rows of buffet tables lined with empty metal trays. "You're a bit early. Food arrives in about forty minutes, along with the bartender and waitresses. Bathrooms are to the right. If you need anything, just pick up the service phone. Secret Service should be by anytime, I'm guessing."

"Thanks." He reached into his wallet for a tip, but the concierge waved him off and left.

Adam glanced at the wall clock … 5:56 p.m.

For the next few minutes he watched the players stretching and jogging in their warm-up jerseys while the first group of Nationals prepared to take batting practice. Bored, he moved to the pool table and selected a cue stick from one of two wall-mounted racks.

He turned as the door opened and a muscular black man dressed in a dark suit entered the suite, the ear piece identifying him as Secret Service.

"Name?"

"Excuse me?"

"Who are you?"

"Adam Shariak, Under Secretary of Defense."

"Shariak, huh?" The big man checked his iPhone. "Name's familiar, but you're not on my list which means ya'll don't belong here."

Adam reached for his ticket as the secret service man reached for his gun.

"Whoa, big fella, I'm just showing you my ticket. See … Suite 18."

"This is Suite 8."

President Bill Clinton walked in, placing a reassuring hand on the big man's shoulder. "Easy, Samson. They're changing out the door plates. Pops probably got confused."

"Mr. President … I'm so sorry."

"Nonsense. Nothing to be sorry about. Samson, this is Adam Shariak, our new Under Secretary of Defense. I caught your confirmation hearing on C-SPAN. Best explanation of ISIS I've heard. You were direct but succinct; forcing that senator to accept the fact that every military action creates a ripple effect throughout the Middle East… that dropping bombs and deploying more American troops is exactly what these radicals want us to do."

"Thank you, sir."

"Too bad Trump wasn't watching."

"I'm actually supposed to—"

"Say, Shariak, you any good with that pool cue?"

"Not very."

"Good, rack 'em up. Samson, maybe you can close that drape before you leave so I can see. The sun's blinding me."

"Yes, sir." The secret service man pulled the curtains closed and left.

"Sorry about Samson. He gets overprotective."

"Do you know if he played nose tackle at Ohio State?"

"I believe he did."

"I think he recognized me. Way back when, I played fullback at Indiana. OSU always beat the tar out of us, but in my senior year, I had a pretty good second half against the big fella."

Bill Clinton's face lit up. "I'll be damned. I remember that game. You ran for about a hundred and thirty yards in the second half and almost led your team to a huge upset."

"You have an excellent memory, sir."

"For some things." Clinton gestured to Adam to have a seat at one of the card tables. "Mind if I ask you a personal question? Your head coach at Indiana hadn't played you all season. What made him change his mind at halftime?"

"Our starting tailback was hurt. We were losing twenty-seven to nothing in our only nationally-televised game of the year and coach was pissed. So he asked a bunch of seniors for their advice. When he came to me I said, 'just give me the damn ball coach, and we'll score."

"Give me the damn ball and we'll score … I love it. And you did score—three touchdowns if memory serves."

"Two. I tore up my knee before we scored on that last drive."

As Adam watched, President Clinton removed a small stack of three-by-five cards from the back pocket of his slacks. Making eye contact with Shariak, he pressed an index finger to his lips for silence, causing Adam's pulse rate to jump.

"I love football," Clinton said, "it really is America's game."

Reaching into the pocket of his windbreaker, he removed a small keychain with a flashlight. Turning it on, he aimed the purple light at the first card in his hand, causing a message to appear in yellow ultraviolet ink:

READ CARDS SILENTLY—DO NOT REACT. CONTINUE MAKING SMALL TALK.

Seeing the urgency in the former president's eyes, Adam nodded.

"My game was rugby; I played on the rugby club when I attended Oxford. Ever play rugby, Shariak?"

He flipped to the next card:

YOU'VE BEEN WONDERING WHY YOU WERE SELECTED TO BE UNDER SECRETARY …

"Yes!"

"Really? Where'd you play?"

"Play what? Football?"

Clinton shot him a "stay focused" look. "Rugby."

"Rugby? Sorry … no. Just football."

The former president turned over the next card:

WE RECRUITED YOU TO COMPLETE A MISSION VITAL TO HUMANITY'S FUTURE.

You recruited me? How the hell did you recruit me? And who's we?

"I loved rugby. Of course, they don't wear helmets like they do in American football."

AS UNDER SECRETARY, YOU'LL HAVE ACCESS TO ILLEGALLY-FUNDED SPECIAL ACCESS PROGRAMS.

"What is … I mean … no helmets … that's crazy."

"It is crazy."

FREE CLEAN ZERO-POINT-ENERGY TECHNOLOGIES EXIST.

Adam felt light-headed, the scene surreal. *Free energy? What the hell is he talking about? Why is he doing this? Is the suite bugged?*

"So Shariak … how are you getting along with President Trump?"

"We've never met. Tonight … it's our first meeting."

Clinton turned to the next card, responding, "I read where the Doomsday Clock has advanced thirty seconds since he's been in office."

IT IS CONTROLLED BY A ROGUE SECRET CABAL IN PRIVATE/ MILITARY INDUSTRIAL SECTOR … VERY DANGEROUS!

"I read that … the Doomsday Clock. It's symbolic, of course."

"And yet it's representative of our times … the threat of nuclear war … the effects of climate change. Trump has no regard for the environment … to him it's simply a speed bump for the economy.

PATENTS HAVE BEEN DENIED, TECHNOLOGY CONFISCATED AND BLACK-SHELVED. SCIENTISTS HAVE BEEN KILLED … ALL TO SAFEGUARD FOSSIL FUEL PROFITS.

"So … what am I supposed to do … as Under Secretary?"

WE NEED YOU TO BRING ZERO-POINT-ENERGY TO THE WORLD.

Adam felt the blood drain from his face.

Bill Clinton removed a cigar from his windbreaker and lit up. "Do you have any children, Mr. Under Secretary?"

"Children? No, sir."

"I'm a father and a grandfather. I fear for them; I fear for their generation. We're doing the same things we've done over the last century—burning fossil fuels to create energy. We're killing ourselves and the planet, and this new administration is taking off the brakes. I've traveled a dozen times around the world since I left the Oval Office and the things I've seen would break your heart. Africa's dying. India's a cesspool; its population is drowning in sewage. Pakistan's ripe for a coup, and the EU can't hold back the tide of immigrants escaping from the Middle East. Did you know the hottest-selling products in China these days are respirators? In Bulgaria, it's radioactive nuclear material. It's only a matter of time before ISIS or al-Qaeda or another one of these radicalized Islamic groups gets hold of enough plutonium to set off a dirty bomb ... or your new president decides the best way to deal with Kim Jung Un is to strike first."

Clinton turned to the last message.

FIND DR. NEALE MANLEY...

"You wanted the ball, Mr. Under Secretary ... run with it."

TRUST NO ONE.

As Adam watched, the forty-second President of the United States pressed the lit end of his cigar to the stack of three by five cards, the ash immediately igniting the chemically treated paper, instantaneously burning everything into a solitary cinder.

A moment later two Secret Service agents escorted Pops into the suite.

"Hell son, we got to get you out of here, you're in the wrong place."

8:12 p.m.

JESSICA KEYED INTO HER TOWNHOME to find Adam seated on her den sofa by the lit fireplace, a bottle of wine and two glasses on her coffee table.

"You're home early. How was the game?"

"Trump never showed, his Chief of Staff said he decided to take the First Lady to a concert." Adam handed her a glass of wine. "Jess, I need to pick your brain."

"But first, you felt the need to ply me with alcohol?"

"It's a strange subject. One of my assistants was going on today about something called zero-point-energy. I spent most of the afternoon reading about it. Is there any basis for it, or is it just theoretical nonsense?"

She slipped off her shoes and took a sip of wine from her glass. "Just because it's theoretical doesn't make it nonsense. By definition, vacuum fluctuation or zero-point-energy is an ambient field that harbors the energy state of life. According to quantum physics, every cubic centimeter of space that surrounds us has enough energy in the ambient field to power the entire country for a day. Again, it's all theoretical."

"If it's all theoretical, why were Nikola Tesla, T. Townsend Brown, John Keely, Viktor Schauberger, and Otis Carr harassed and their work confiscated under the Warfare Act? Why was Professor John Searl and Adam Trombly poisoned?"

"Baby, that's Conspiracy Theory 101. Believe me; if zero-point-energy really existed we'd have it."

"Enough energy in a cubic centimeter of space to power the country for a day? I can think of a few groups that might prefer the status quo."

"Where's all this coming from?"

"I'd tell ya, only your security clearance is too high."

Leaving her glass on a coaster, Jessica straddled Adam's lap, nuzzling his neck. "Maybe we can raise your clearance to meet mine."

Science Applications International Corporation HQ
Tyson's Corner, Virginia

The 2011 silver Jeep Grand Cherokee inched its way south on Interstate 495, its driver more focused on the thoughts swirling through his head than the morning rush hour traffic.

Adam Shariak had never met Dr. Neale Manley, but he knew who the physicist was. Jessica had worked with him before she had joined Kemp Aerospace, the two of them succeeding in developing a simple oscillating electronic circuit that put out more energy as resistant heat than was required to drive the device. Manley's employer, Science Applications International Corporation (SAIC), had bought the design, along with the services of Dr. Manley—much to Jessica's chagrin.

"Might" always seemed to overcome "right" when it came to dealing with corporate giants, and SAIC was one of a dozen major defense contractors feeding at the massive trough of the United States Defense Department's annual $600 billion military budget. So entwined was the Pentagon with its suppliers that there was a perpetual revolving door among government personnel serving in the private sector, and both political parties abused the system. In December of 2012, Deborah Lee James had been president of SAIC's technology and engineering sector. A year later, Chuck Hagel swore her in as Secretary of the Air Force.

Meeting Dr. Manley—let alone picking his brain about zero-point-energy—seemed a daunting task. From what Jessica had told him, the physicist was involved in what she termed, "Weird Science and Freakin' Magic." Though she refused to elaborate, Adam got the gist—Manley and his work were off-limits, even to the new Under Secretary of Defense.

He decided on an innocuous "front door" approach, instructing his secretary to schedule as many "meet and greets" with military contractors during the next three days as possible. To save drive time, he had her book him into the local Hyatt Regency.

Science Applications International Corporation was his first stop on his list.

The flow of morning traffic opened up as the silver Jeep Cherokee entered northern Virginia. Adam Shariak exited the Capital Beltway in Tyson's Corner, a commercial center that was home to the corporate headquarters of some of the biggest tech companies in the world.

Turning off Leesburg Pike, he followed signs to the gated entrance of the SAIC campus, its fourteen-story-high concrete and glass structure looming ahead.

Sam Mannino, former Air Force Chief of Staff and current CEO at SAIC, led him into his office suite. "It's good to finally meet you, Captain Shariak. You did a nice job running Kemp Aerospace; though it's still a bit unusual for a high-ranking government post to be filled by a nominee hailing from such a small supplier."

"I would think the CEO of an $8 billion employee-owned tech company would appreciate an occasional victory for the little guy."

"Touché. So what's on your mind?"

Adam removed his iPad from its small carrying case. "I'm a bit concerned about SAIC's backlog of signed business orders. At the end of the last quarter it tallied approximately $7.4 billion, of which $2.1 billion was funded. The biggest red flag is your progress on the Marine Corps' new Amphibious Combat Vehicle."

Sam Mannino typed a command into his desktop computer. "SAIC was awarded a $121.5 million firm fixed-price contract to produce thirteen prototype amphibious vehicles, with options for 60 low-rate initial production vehicles and 148 full-rate production vehicles. The full value of the contract is just over $1 billion."

"Correct. However, the base period of performance for the new program was expected to be completed in September. Before he left office, you petitioned my predecessor for another eight months. Why the delay?"

"Son, when I took over as CEO of SAIC, the U.S. Attorney for the southern district of New York had just won a $500 million judgment against us for over-billing on a project to modernize the city's payroll and timekeeping system. Half a billion dollars is a lot of money, even for a corporate giant like SAIC. We had to make cutbacks, and cutbacks lead to extensions."

"And delays on contracts lead to fines. Like when Kemp Aerospace was ten days late on one of our contracts to provide circuit boards to SAIC because one of our suppliers in the Midwest was held up due to a snowstorm—an act of God which cost us $40,000. To a small supplier like Kemp, that's a lot of money. But, as they say, what's good for the goose is good for the gander. Translated: Paybacks are a bitch."

Sam Mannino's face paled.

"Hey now, no worries; September's still two months away."

"Mr. Under Secretary, surely we can work something out? Perhaps we can subcontract Kemp to help us on the Amphibious CVs?"

"That smells too much like a bribe to me. Strong-arming suppliers isn't what I'm about; nor is creating an adversarial relationship. My goal is to work with you, Mr. Mannino. You've got your eight months, not a day longer."

The CEO smiled in relief. "Thank you. And yes, I want to work with you, too."

"Just make sure every one of those ACVs performs as advertised. I don't want our marines getting their socks wet because something leaked; if that happens you're gonna need more than a plumber to save your ass from me."

"Understood." Sam Mannino shook Captain Shariak's hand. "How about lunch? There's a terrific Italian place a few miles from here."

"I'd love to, but I have to be at MITRE Corp. in forty minutes. However, there is someone I'd like to say hello to while I'm here."

Adam followed the armed security guard out of the elevator onto the seventh floor. They passed through a gated checkpoint and proceeded down a white-tiled corridor, security cameras sealed in tinted purple globes were mounted along the ceiling.

The guard led him to a bank of three elevators. "These three shafts run to our sub-basement levels." The guard swiped his passkey and entered his security code. The middle door opened and they stepped inside.

There was no control panel; no buttons to push. The guard looked up at a camera lens. "SB-5."

Before Adam could grab hold of the interior rail, the floor beneath his feet plummeted and stopped, the entire descent taking less than two breathless seconds.

The guard smiled as the door hissed opened. "Pretty cool, huh? For a moment you were actually suspended in mid-air. It's like a rush of butter-flies in your gut."

"Felt more like I swallowed my gut."

Adam followed him off the elevator and down another corridor, this one interspaced with metal doors. They stopped at a sealed room labeled LAB SB-5.

The guard swiped his card, causing the door to unlock. "Dr. Manley is expecting you. I'll wait for you out here."

"Thank you." Adam entered, the door requiring extra effort to push in against a cushion of air. The moment the door clicked shut a green light flashed on above an identical door six feet away. Pushing the handle down, he again fought a cushion of air and entered.

"Wow."

It was as if he had been transported to a tropical island—twenty feet of pink sand and a cluster of coconut palm trees were all that separated the lab's covered, open patio from an azure sea. Small waves lapped gently along the shoreline with a soothing crash and sizzle; cool gusts of briny air ruffled his hair. So realistic was the effect that for a confusing moment Adam was actually convinced he was in the Caribbean.

"It's the latest in holographic design."

He turned to find a white male in his early sixties, dressed in a floral *Tommy Bahama* shirt, shorts, and sandals. His chestnut-brown hair was long and graying around the temples, his tan complexion contrasting nicely with his gray goatee.

Adam extended his hand. "Shariak. I'm the new DoD Comptroller."

"I suppose that makes you the most powerful man in Washington—after the Vice President and dog catcher."

"Are you Dr. Neale Manley?"

"Who else would I be?"

"I don't know. Maybe you're his cabana boy."

The older man walked to the porch's bamboo rail. As he touched it, that section of the holographic projection materialized into a door. Opening it revealed a bathroom.

The physicist removed a white lab coat from a hook and slipped it on. "Do I pass inspection, Mr. Under Secretary?"

"Actually, this is more of a social call. About five years ago you worked on a project with Dr. Jessica Marulli. She asked me to say hello."

"Ah, Juice Marulli … what a sweetheart. How do you know her?"

"We're engaged."

"Then that makes you a lucky man, though still no more important than dog-catcher."

"I'm in town over the next three days; thought maybe I could treat you to dinner."

"Is Jessica with you?"

"No."

"Then what's the point?" Dr. Manley removed a tube of antibiotic gel from his coat pocket, squeezed a drop of the clear liquid onto his palm, and rubbed his hands together. "Nothing personal, Mr. Deputy, but it's not like we can talk shop, and I have no time for meaningless acquaintances."

Adam withdrew a business card from his pants pocket and handed it to the physicist. "In case you change your mind."

Dr. Manley waved it off. "If I need you I know where to find you. Your fiancée's a good egg. Tell her I said hello."

The scientist surprised Adam by extending his hand.

He dutifully shook it, the physicist's palm still slightly moist with gel.

Ten minutes later, Adam climbed back into his jeep. *Well, that was a waste of time.*

As he started the car he noticed his right palm was tingling. He rubbed it against his pant leg, only it grew worse, becoming sharp pins and needles.

Adam stared at the flesh, which had turned bright pink where he had shaken hands with Manley.

The gel? What was in it? Did he poison me?

As he watched, a message appeared in his normal skin tone, the scrawled words standing out against his flushed, irritated flesh:

8:15 p.m. Miyagi's Sushi Bar. McLean, VA.

McLean, Virginia
8:04 p.m.

FOLLOWING HIS IPHONE'S DIRECTIONS, Adam turned on Chain Bridge Road and then made a left onto Curran Street. He saw the restaurant and parked; the lot half empty.

Miyagi's was a small private establishment, the tables packed close together on a bamboo wood floor, its two sushi chefs working in tandem behind the glass-enclosed bar.

Adam stood at the counter behind a party of four waiting for a table and a man paying for takeout. He searched the dining area, only Dr. Manley wasn't there.

An Asian girl in her mid-teens gave him a warm smile. "For here or to go?"

"Table for two. I'm meeting a friend, only he's not here yet."

She glanced at one of the chefs, who signaled her very subtlety with two fingers. "Okay. We seat you first."

Overhearing their conversation, one of the women in the party of four protested. "Excuse me, but we were next."

"*Hai*. You are next party of four." Grabbing two menus, she motioned for Adam to follow her. She led him around a maze of tables and past the sushi bar, then beyond a red and white checkered curtain separating the kitchen and restrooms from the dining area. Turning left, they followed a small corridor past cases of bottled water, empty syrup canisters, and kegs of beer to a door labeled PRIVATE.

She knocked twice, paused and knocked twice again.

A dead bolt slid back and the door opened, revealing a Japanese man in his fifties, dressed in a white collared shirt, red bow tie, and black slacks. He nodded to Adam and then stepped back, allowing him to enter the small office.

Neale Manley was seated behind a desk, feasting on sushi rolls stacked on a decorative miniature wood boat. He waved Adam inside.

"This is Komura, the owner of this fine establishment."

The Asian bowed his head. "Mr. Ambassador, it is an honor."

Squeezing past Adam, he closed the door behind him.

"Mr. Ambassador?"

"I told him you were the Deputy Ambassador to Japan. Bolt the door and sit down, we don't have much time."

Adam slid the dead bolt in place and sat in the folding chair across the desk from Dr. Manley, who was unscrewing a pen, refitting the ink cartridge backwards inside the barrel shell—the connection causing a faint high-decibel sound.

"White noise. In case anyone's listening."

"Is that why you were so short with me this morning?"

"SAIC's ceilings have eyes; its walls have ears. Now pay attention, we only have about twenty minutes before your to-go order is ready and you're out of here."

"My to-go order?"

"I can't be seen with you, Shariak. I agreed to brief you and point you in the right direction, but after tonight we don't cross paths again. Is that understood?"

Adam grabbed two spider rolls off the back of the serving boat, shoving them in his mouth. "I'm listening."

Dr. Manley pulled the food out of Adam's reach. "What I'm about to tell you represents the tiniest acorn in the forest of the biggest kept secret in the history of the planet. If the world's population knew how they've been lied to … how they've been purposely denied the good life that can be provided by free, clean energy systems because of a few selfish, greedy sociopaths, there'd be anarchy. There needs to be a revolt, the public needs to demand these technologies be made available. Not to bring them out is nothing short of a crime against humanity.

"Since you're not a quantum physicist like your fiancée, I'll try to explain this in terms as simple as possible. Whether you accept what I say or not is ultimately up to you, but like that prosthetic limb you're limping around on, reality is simply reality and the truth is the truth. To begin, our third-dimensional physical universe is literally swimming in an all-pervasive sea of quantum energy; only, like ignorant fish, we remain unaware of the water's existence. Maybe a more appropriate metaphor is that, from our perspective, we can't see the forest for the trees. For scientists, the clues have been around for over a century but one has to think outside the box in order to understand them.

"Dr. Harold Puthoff was one of the first to conduct a search for this quantum sea of energy. Minus 273 degrees Celsius or zero degrees Kelvin is the absolute lowest temperature in the universe. According to the laws of Newtonian physics, all molecular activity should cease at absolute zero and no energy should exist. Of course, scientists used to say the same thing about the bottom of the ocean—no light, no energy—no life. And then we actually bothered to send a submersible into the depths to check things out for ourselves and, lo and behold, we found energy spewing out of hydro-thermal vents and an entire food chain existing on chemosynthesis—the primordial soup that led to the origin of life on this planet.

"Dr. Puthoff made a similar discovery. When he measured absolute zero, instead of an empty vacuum he was shocked to find a 'seething cauldron' of energy—a plenum of space where every square centimeter was filled with matter. Appropriately, he named it zero-point-energy. I prefer to call it the domain of W.S.F.M.—Weird Science and Freakin' Magic.

"It is zero-point-energy that causes subatomic particles to jiggle and then literally jump in and out of existence. What is actually happening is that the photons collide and are absorbed by other subatomic particles. The process excites them into a higher energy state, creating an energy exchange between the zero-point field and our physical world. Although they appear for only thousandths or millionths of a second, their appearance is yet another indication that something truly magnificent lies just beyond the physical realm and the limitations of our five senses—an endless supply of energy.

"Two more experiments have proven the existence of the zero-point-energy field. The first is the Casimir Effect. By placing two plates made of conductive materials in a vacuum facing each other, Hendrick Casimir theorized that if zero-point-energy actually existed the total amount of energy between the surfaces of the plates would be less than the amount elsewhere, leading them to be drawn together—which is exactly what happened. A more dramatic experiment and an example of the W.S.F.M. deals with a ZPE-related phenomenon called sonoluminescense—the transformation of sound waves into light energy. If you fill a small spherical glass with water, resonate it with harmonious sound waves of 20 KHertz, and then blow a very tiny air bubble into the center of the flask the air bubble will rhythmically heat up to an incredible 30,000 degrees Celsius before imploding in an ultra short flash of light."

"Okay, Dr. Manley, I'm willing to accept the existence of this amazing ocean of energy we're all swimming in. How do we tap into it to power our homes and fuel our cars?"

"Good question. First, it's important to understand that all of our present sources of electrical energy, from batteries to nuclear power plants, have one intrinsic problem in common. When the electrical current is fed back to the source that initiated it, it kills the source of the virtual photon flux within the vacuum."

"You just lost me."

"Let's go back to basics. Constructed within the walls of this building is an electrical circuit made up of copper wire. Flowing through the copper wiring like a river, is an electrical current, its movement generated by the separation of positively-charged protons fixed in the copper atoms, the negatively-charged electrons moving through the wire. What initiates that separation of atoms is a dipole—an electromagnetic device.

"Place a canoe in a river and off you go. Plug a lamp into a socket and the electric current flows through the copper wires into the bulb's filament, and we have light. One problem: In a normal three-dimensional electrical circuit, any excess energy that is generated is lost when it kills the dipole. As a result, the energy in the magnetic field dissipates, leaving only about a 30% return for the load, making the systems we've been using for over a hundred years incredibly inefficient. Of course, the power company wants the circuit to be inefficient. After all, they're profiting from every amp we use; and the fossil fuel and nuclear industries also get a nice chunk of that change since it's their fuel that powers the dipole.

"To figure out where things went wrong when they could have gone so right, we go back to the turn of the 20th century and Nikola Tesla. Far more brilliant than Edison or Einstein, Tesla realized more than a hundred years ago that humans may exist and think in three dimensions, but nature actually prefers to work in four dimensions—the fourth being time-space. By applying a high-voltage system to an electromagnetic field in a counter-rotating vortex he allowed nature to reorganize the flow of charges within the vacuum of a generator at the speed of light, essentially incorporating the fourth dimensional aspects of zero-point-energy. What's more, instead of fading, Tesla discovered the flow of energy in the vacuum would continue forever without losing so much as a drop of its load. Think of it as tapping into an oil well; once you hit a geyser you no longer need a drill, the pressure simply takes over. Tesla also figured out that, by using a permanent magnet as the dipole, you can pass the flux back through the permanent magnet and it won't get destroyed, provided it is welded into the material.

"Tesla's other challenge—which you just asked about—was figuring out a way to catch the energy. His solution was fairly simple—he found a material that separated the magnetic field from the magnetic field vector which flows unceasingly from the magnet, yielding a current of energy that could last another 15 billion years and beyond—a true over-unity system.

"In 1901, Tesla was preparing to use the planet's own magnetic field as a giant dipole in order to broadcast electricity to ships at sea without wires—an experiment that would lead to free energy and change the world … only J.P. Morgan intervened. The wealthy industrialist had invested in copper wire to use in homes and businesses and he decided that giving energy to the people without charging them for it was simply un-American. Before Tesla could conduct his experiment, J. P. Morgan got his cronies in Washington to shut it down and confiscate all of the scientist's papers and inventions, leaving him destitute.

"It's a pattern that repeats itself throughout our history, every scientist who has ever figured out how to tap into the zero-point-energy field is shut down or silenced by the powers that be. Remember, it's not enough to invent a ZPE device, you also have to sell it to the right people who won't quash it, otherwise you must manufacture the design yourself and that requires money. Either way you'll need a patent, and therein lies the second problem. Section 181 of the U.S. Patent law allows the government to arbitrarily determine if a technology or device poses a danger to our national security. Rogue elements within the Department of Defense, CIA, NSA, the Federal Trade Commission, and the Department of Energy have abused this interpretation of the law in their attempt to safeguard the world's status quo. T. Henry Moray's breakthrough work was ignored by the patent office, his lab ransacked. You want flying cars running on free, clean energy? T. Townsend Brown, one of the founding fathers of electrogravitics, discovered that he could access zero-point-energy by utilizing high voltages of 20,000 to 200,000 volts, causing his charged capacitors to lose their vessel's mass and levitate off the ground. Big Oil wasn't too keen on the competition so the authorities denied Brown a patent and confiscated all of his work. Other inventors are lured into partnering with bogus companies that black-shelf their inventions.

"Back in the 1980s, Stan Meyer was working as an engineer at a plant that built microwave systems; the scientist had observed that at very low frequencies, water would go straight into hydrogen and oxygen. Based on this observation, his twin brother Steve helped him develop a circuitry where he could put an electrode in water and, at a certain voltage, create what is called Brown's Gas, a magnetically-charged hydrogen and oxygen mix that essentially replaced gasoline with water. The Meyer boys retrofitted a dune buggy to run on water and word spread. Next thing they know, the CIA contacted Stan to discuss retrofitting a Lear jet using their invention.

"Stan was nervous, he insisted on meeting in a public place—a local Cracker Barrel restaurant—for lunch. Stan took one drink of his beverage, grabbed his throat and rasped, 'I've been poisoned!' He ran out to the parking lot, collapsed and died. Bottom line: If it's a threat to the fossil fuel industry, it gets shut down."

"And this is all being perpetrated by whom?"

"A secret government within the government … an international cabal composed of some of the wealthiest most powerful people on the planet. The name has changed over the years, from MJ-12 to Majestic-12, to SECOR and PI-40. These days we refer to the entity as MAJI, which stands for the Majority Intelligence Committee."

"You said 'we.' You're a part of this?"

"So is your fiancée, only they haven't brought her into the inner circle yet."

"Jessica is part of MAJI?"

"She'll deny it, of course. But that satellite project you have her working on is strictly Unacknowledged Black Ops. It's so compartmentalized that she probably has no clue what its real purpose is, and no, I'm not going to discuss it—for her sake. Understand something, Shariak—there are thousands of people who have been exposed to bits and pieces of the technologies I've just described, along with other projects that would blow your mind. Most of these men and women are decent, hardworking people like Jessica who, given a choice, would love to see these new energy systems shared among the masses. In fact, I'd guess upwards of eighty percent of MAJI secretly wants these unacknowledged projects to see the light of day. Unfortunately, as you move up the food chain into the bank and oil cartels, the military industrialists and religious fanatics—that's where you find the sociopathic element that runs the cabal. Trust me, these guys you don't fuck with."

"Why did Clinton send me to you?"

"Clinton's just a figurehead. There are bigger fish in this sea with a lot sharper teeth. As for me … I'm just the first in a series of currents meant to keep you swimming in the right direction. My job was to brief you on zero-point technology so you recognize it if and when you come across it."

"Where do I go from here?"

"I'm going to give you the name of a civilian who has more information about ETs, UFOs, and the cabal than any man alive. Years ago when Clinton was still smoking cigars in the Oval Office, a meeting was arranged between this civilian and a member of MAJI who was fed up with the cabal black-shelving zero-point technologies just to keep the oil oligarchs happy. So the MAJI guy decided he was going to give this civilian a zero-point-energy device along with $50 million in seed money to mass produce them."

"What happened?"

"He went missing right before the meet. Nine days later they fished his body out of Potomac River."

"Geez. Who was he?"

"William Colby."

"Wait … Bill Colby? The former CIA Director?"

"As I said, these guys you don't fuck with. Colby's death was a warning to Clinton. Obama received his warning shortly after this same civilian prepared a briefing for his administration."

"What kind of warning?"

"It happened on December 9, 2009. The president was in Norway with his family to receive the Nobel Prize. While he was there, MAJI launched a scalar missile over Oslo. Scalar waves are very different from electro-magnetic waves; they can travel over immense distances at super-luminal, faster-than-light speed with no loss of energy. The scalar left an eerie blue spiral in the night sky. Look it up on YouTube; the effect was witnessed by thousands of people who had no idea what it was or how easily it could have taken out Air Force-One. Obama knew; he was put on notice that he may be president, but the cabal still calls the shots. After that, he decided to leave the UFO-ET subject alone."

"No wonder Clinton was scared. But if presidents and former CIA Directors can't bring this technology into the public domain, how am I supposed to do it?"

"Hell if I know. My guess is that someone within the inner circle thinks they can sneak you below the radar long enough to put you in position to succeed. Regardless, you're going to need the help of the civilian I told you about. He's quite brilliant and super-skeptical; you'll have to win him over to get him to trust you."

"How do I do that?"

"By opening your mind to the possibilities that there is far more to existence than what you were taught in school … that the truth has been

59

hidden and the knowledge stolen—concealed between conspiracy theory and conspiracy fact, and your ability to distinguish between the two just may save your life."

"I understand."

Dr. Manley shook his head. "You haven't a clue. Once you enter the rabbit's hole, you'll be considered a threat to the status quo. Zero-point-energy will not just replace fossil fuels, Shariak, it is the game-changer that will eliminate hunger and poverty, pollution and climate change, disease and war … it will skyrocket the global economy and place every nation on an even playing field. Free, clean energy unlocks the door to humanity's evolution as a species and we've possessed the key for 70 years, only the gatekeepers refused to allow us to use it in order to protect the oil oligarchs and the military industrial complex. It is the new physics that allows us to explore the galaxy and beyond."

"Wait … are you saying we have the means to travel faster than the speed of light?"

"Yes. Only we didn't invent it. We reverse-engineered it."

"Reverse-engineered it? From where?"

"Not from where … from who—"

"—extraterrestrials."

Hyatt Regency Hotel
Tyson's Corner, Virginia
9:37 p.m.

ADAM WAS SEATED at the small work desk in his hotel room, finishing the last piece of sushi from the to-go order that had been waiting for him at the cash register. His thoughts were focused on the recent events that had accompanied his appointment as Under Secretary.

A clandestine meeting with a former president ... notes written with invisible ink ... a secret rendezvous in the back of a Japanese restaurant ... and now they have me chasing extraterrestrials?

Has the world gone insane?

He belched, clearing enough room for a few palate-cleansing strips of ginger. There were only empty containers remaining on the coffee table. Somehow Dr. Manley had known exactly which rolls were his favorite.

The thought lingered as he retrieved his laptop, intent on learning everything he could about the "informed civilian" Dr. Manley insisted he meet next. Logging on the internet, he was about to search for the ET expert's name when he paused.

If they can access my history of sushi takeout, they can certainly access my web search.

Leaving his laptop, he pocketed his room card, grabbed a can of ginger ale from the small refrigerator's overpriced offerings, and headed downstairs to the hotel's business center.

The room was empty and dark, the motion sensors causing the overhead fluorescent lights to flicker on as he swiped his key and entered.

There were three computer terminals separated by privacy cubicles. Situating himself at the station on the left, he logged on using his room number, making a mental note to bury his search history when he was finished.

He typed in the name Dr. Manley had given him—finding no shortage of references.

Dr. Steven Macon Greer was a medical doctor. He had left a successful career as an E.R. physician and the chairman at the Department of Emergency Medicine at Caldwell Memorial Hospital in Lenoir, North Carolina to launch the *Center for the Study of Extraterrestrial Intelligence* (CSETI). According to his bio, this bizarre journey had been seeded back in 1965 when nine-year-old Steven and a few of his friends had witnessed an oval-shaped, gleaming silver ETV—an Extraterrestrial Vehicle. Over the following weeks, the boy began experiencing lucid dreams and night encounters with beings that were clearly "not from our planet."

In 1990, Greer founded CSETI in order to create a diplomatic, research-based initiative to contact extraterrestrial civilizations. Three years later he founded *Project Starlight* which sought out government whistle-blowers willing to violate their security oaths by sharing insider knowledge about UFOs, extraterrestrial intelligence, and advanced energy and propulsion systems. Hundreds of men and women had come forward, including former astronauts, commercial pilots and intelligence and military personnel.

In 1998 Greer gave up his career in medicine to work full-time on *The Disclosure Project*, preparing for what he hoped would be an event that would crack the dam of secrecy surrounding extraterrestrials and UFOs.

Adam found the YouTube link and clicked on it.

The DISCLOSURE PROJECT
National Press Club, Washington, D.C.
May 9, 2001

He forwarded through an introduction from a Hollywood actor, hitting

PLAY when a tall, muscular man with a receding hairline appeared. In his late forties and exuding a commanding presence, the headliner took center stage before dozens of news networks and reporters.

"Good afternoon. We are here today to disclose the truth about a subject that has been ridiculed, questioned and denied for at least fifty years. The men and women who are on this stage and some 350 additional military and intelligence witnesses to the so-called UFO matter and extraterrestrial intelligence can prove, and will prove, that we are not alone.

"In 1993, I met with a group of military advisors to this project out in the countryside in Virginia, and we decided that it was time for civilians, military, intelligence and other people to come together and disclose the truth about the subject which is called UFOs. Since that time, I have personally briefed a sitting director of Central Intelligence, James Woolsey, President Clinton's first CIA director. I have personally briefed the head of the Defense Intelligence Agency; the head of intelligence of the Joint Chiefs of Staff; members of the Senate Intelligence Committee; many members of Congress; members of the European leadership; the Japanese Cabinet and others. What I have found is that none of them are surprised that this is true, but they are uniformly horrified that they have not had access to these projects.

"Our witnesses, who now number over 400, have worked inside the CIA, NSA, NRO, Air Force, Navy, Marines, Army, all divisions of the intelligence and military communities, and include corporate witnesses as well as contractors to the government. Many of these individuals have been involved in black budget, covert unacknowledged special access projects—projects paid for unknowingly by the American taxpayer to the tune of $80 billion per year or more, many of which involve technologies that can change the world forever.

"The reason we are coming forward now is that we are asking for the U.S. Congress and for President Bush to move toward an official inquiry and disclosure on this subject. This issue has the most profound implications for our future as a species, for national security, and for world peace. If declassified and used for peaceful energy generation and propulsion, these technologies, many of which were reversed-engineered from downed extraterrestrial vehicles, would solve the looming energy crisis definitively, would end global warming, and would correct the environmental challenges that the Earth is facing. It is also critical that we begin to debate, as a society, the dangers of placing weapons in space. If indeed, as we can prove, it is true that we are not alone, and that space is a territory we are sharing with other civilizations, it could be a very imprudent, destabilizing thing to place weapons in space. This is not being debated because it is off the national and international radar screen. It needs to be placed on it and we are here today to do so.

"We can establish through eyewitness testimony that these objects of extraterrestrial origin have been tracked on radar going thousands of miles per hour, stopping and making right-hand turns. We know they use anti-gravity propulsion systems which scientists in the United States, Great Britain and elsewhere have reverse-engineered. These objects have landed on terra firma; some have been disabled and retrieved by teams within the United States. Extraterrestrial life forms have been retrieved and their vehicles have been taken and studied thoroughly for at least 50 years.

"We can prove, through the testimony and documents we will be presenting, that this subject has been hidden from members of Congress and at least two administrations that we are aware of, and that the Constitution of the United States has been subverted by the growing power of the secret groups overseeing these classified projects and that this is a danger to our national security.

"There is no evidence, I wish to emphasize, that these Interstellar life forms are hostile toward us, but there is a great deal of evidence that they are concerned with *our* hostility. There are times when they have neutralized or rendered inert the launch capabilities of intercontinental ballistic missiles. Witnesses here today will describe those events to you and establish that these intelligent beings have clearly shown that they do not want us to weaponize space. Despite these warnings, we are proceeding down this very dangerous path.

"While this is a matter of the most pressing import, I know many in the media would prefer to joke about 'little green men.' In reality, the subject is laughed at because it is so serious. I expect people to be skeptical, but not irrationally so, because these men and women have come forward and they have their credentials. They can establish who they are and they have been first-hand witnesses to some of the most important events in the history of the human race. Some of the men with us today were charged with handling the nuclear weapons of the United States; as such, their word was trusted on everything of great importance to our national security. We must trust their word now. As Monsignor Balducci said in a recent interview at the Vatican, 'It is irrational not to accept the testimony of these witnesses.' So be skeptical, but not close-minded."

Adam advanced the video, stopping at a witness—a Caucasian man in his early seventies, his long hair thick and white.

"Good morning. My name is Harland Bentley. Between 1957 and 1959 I was a PFC in the United States Army, stationed north of Washington, D.C., on a Nike-Ajax missile base, close to Olney, Maryland. In May of 1958 at about 6 a.m., I heard a noise outside that sounded like a pulsating transformer. I sat up in my bunk, looked out the window, and saw a craft heading for the ground. It crashed; pieces broke off and it immediately took off again.

"The next night I was on radar duty. I get a call from the Gaithersburg missile base. He says, 'Hey, I got twelve to fifteen UFOs outside, fifty to one hundred feet above me.' So I asked him, 'What does it sound like?' He took his head mike off, held it out the van window, and said, 'Here!' It was the same sound I heard the previous morning, except there were a lot more of them. My radar was on stand-by, so I immediately turned it on and got the blip just outside of the ground clutter. I marked it on my radar screen; all of a sudden they took off as the sweep came around, hitting the blip. When it came around and hit it again, that blip was two-thirds of the way off my radar scope. In order to get that far, at a constant velocity, that's 17,000 miles an hour. I will testify before Congress if necessary and explain exactly what happened. Thank you."

Adam fast-forwarded to a female eyewitness, her blonde hair and features somehow familiar. *I've seen her before …*

"Good morning everyone. My name is Donna Hare and I worked at Philco-Ford Aerospace from 1967 to 1981. During that time, I was a design illustrator draftsman. I did the launch slides and moon landing slides, and also projection plotting boards—lunar maps for NASA. We were a contractor, but most of the time I worked on site in Building 8. I had a secret clearance, which was not that high, but I was able to go into the restricted areas.

"One day during down time, which was between missions, I entered a NASA photo lab across the hallway. I was talking to one of the techs in there, and he drew my attention to a photograph—a NASA photograph. It had a dot on it and I said, 'Is that a dot on the emulsion?' He smiled and said, 'Round dots on the emulsion don't leave round shadows on the ground.' This was an aerial photograph of the Earth; it had pine trees on it, and the shadows of the craft or whatever it was were in the same angle as the trees.

"By its very nature it was a UFO—and I wanted to clarify that to the gentleman who was talking to me. At that point I realized it was being kept secret because I asked him, 'What are you going to do with this piece of information?' And he said, 'We always airbrush these out before we sell them to the public.'

"After that, I decided I would ask questions of other people that worked there. And I found that I had to ask them away from the site, never on site. A guard told me that he was asked to burn some photographs and not to look at them. There was another guard guarding him, watching him burn the photographs. He said he was too tempted; he looked at one and it was a picture of a UFO. And he was very descriptive—I can go into that later with anyone. He told me that he was immediately hit in the head and knocked out. He had a big gash on his forehead and was terrified.

"Another incident: I knew someone in quarantine with the Apollo astronauts. He told me that the Apollo astronauts saw craft on the moon when we landed. He too was afraid; he said that the astronauts were told to keep this quiet; they're not allowed to talk about it. My boss didn't know about it, some people who sat right next to me didn't know about it. It's very strange, because I don't know how they can do it, but they can let some people know about it but not others. I am willing to testify before Congress that what I'm saying is true. Thank you very much."

Adam looked up as another hotel guest attempted to enter the business center using his room key. Caucasian and in his early seventies, he wore a black suit and tie and a striped dress shirt. White eyebrows and sideburns stood out against pink flesh tones, his short-cropped greasy gray hair fashioned by a barber on a military base.

Unable to align the passkey's magnetic strip, he gave up. Tapping the glass door with his wedding ring, the guest motioned to the lock, his piggish ice-blue eyes stared unblinkingly at Adam, bearing the hardened gaze of a sociopath.

"Can you let me in? My key doesn't seem to be working."

Manipulating the mouse, Adam clicked off the YouTube link, the cubicle's partition shielding the computer's monitor from the stranger's glare. "Ask the front desk."

The man's face flushed red. A telltale jiggle of the handle revealed the spark of anger, then he forced a smile and left, heading for the front desk.

Adam quickly located the Chrome menu in the top right corner of his screen and opened a tab displaying the computer's *browsing history*. Opening the drop-down menu on the History tab, he selected the *Beginning of Time* tab as the time range, and deleted the computer's browser history as the guest returned with the night manager.

The man with the white eyebrows and soulless eyes entered, allowing the door to close on the manager's apology. "You could have let me in."

"Sorry, I was watching porn." He winked. "Didn't want to use the company laptop. You never know when Big Brother is watching."

Collecting his empty ginger ale can, Adam pushed past the older man and limped out of the business center, heading for the elevators.

Norfolk, Virginia
July 19, 2017; 2:47 a.m.

LOCATED ON SEWELL'S POINT PENINSULA, the U.S. Naval Station in Norfolk, Virginia is the largest military base of its kind, supporting ships and submarines operating in the Atlantic and Indian Oceans as well as the Mediterranean Sea.

Admiral Mark Hintzman, Commander-in-Chief of U.S. Fleet Forces, had been in a deep sleep when the call had come in. Groggy, he checked the text.

"Christ … is this really necessary?"

His wife, Jayne sat up in bed. "Is what necessary? Who is it?"

"I'm needed on the base."

"At three in the morning?"

"It's nothing. Go back to sleep."

"You'd better not have a mistress, Hintzman."

"I'm sixty-two years old with two bulging discs and a swollen prostate— what the hell am I going to do with a mistress?"

Limping to the walk-in closet, he located a pair of jeans, a wool sweater and sneakers, and carried them into the bathroom to dress. By the time he exited his wife was already snoring.

Entering the kitchen, he debated whether he had time to brew a cup of coffee when the military limo pulled up outside his home. Putting on his windbreaker jacket, he yanked open the laundry room door and stepped out into the brisk night air.

Admiral Hintzman acknowledged his driver and climbed in the back seat. He nodded off before they had pulled out of the residential complex.

Ten minutes later he was awakened. "Sir, we're at the gate."

Rolling down his window, the Admiral flashed his Zebra security badge, the cold penetrating the vehicle's cocoon of warmth. Satisfied, the armed marine raised the steel barrier, allowing the vehicle access inside the perimeter fencing.

A poorly-lit asphalt driveway led to an innocuous steel-framed, one-story prefabricated building that looked more like a supply shack than anything which would warrant the presence of a high-ranking officer.

The driver parked before a solitary entrance guarded by two marines armed with M-16s. Exiting the limo, the admiral offered his badge to one of the men's flashlight beams, the other guard holding open the reinforced steel door.

Admiral Hintzman entered the building, following a dimly lit access corridor to a third checkpoint—a steel gate safeguarding a pair of elevators. He entered his Zebra security code on a touch panel, waited until the magnetic bolt retracted, then pushed open the gate as one of the elevator doors opened to greet him.

He stepped inside and held tight to the rail as the car dropped twenty stories into the depths of a dome-shaped, hardened steel and concrete bunker constructed to withstand the direct impact of a hydrogen bomb.

The elevator opened to his assistant, a young woman with a smile that always seemed to charm him, no matter how dour his day.

Sophia Pregadio handed him a fresh cup of coffee. "Woke you again, didn't they?"

"Our visitors have no respect for the working man. I like the new hairstyle."

"Nice try. I added the gold highlights two months ago."

"Sorry. Where am I headed?"

"Conference Room-A. Director Solis is already inside with the night-shift nerds."

"Not the South African?"

"Sunny Pilay? Don't you remember? You had me transfer him to Pine Gap."

"I forgot. Nice enough fellow; I just couldn't understand a damn thing he was saying. Let the Aussies deal with him."

"The new lab coat is American. Erin Driscoll."

"Do I know him?"

"Her. She's the strawberry blonde who got sick at the New Year's Eve bash. Oh yeah … Dr. Death decided to make an appearance."

"Christ. Did he bring the vampire queen?"

"She's in the break room."

"Probably feeding on bloodworms. The two of them make my skin crawl. Is that it?"

"General Cubit is on his way."

"Good. I'll watch the show from the theater until he gets here."

"Are you hungry?"

"No. Wait, do we have any more of that chocolate cheesecake I had at lunch?"

"I'm sure I can find you a slice."

"Good girl. Tell the general where to find me … and get him a slice, too." Admiral Hintzman headed down a ramp leading to a pair of double steel doors which opened automatically as he approached.

The command center, often referred to as "the theater," resembled NORAD's war room, only its equipment was far more advanced. Technicians worked in open stations in a semi-darkness that was lit by colorful giant LED screens which occupied the entire six-story-high forward wall, the maps able to pinpoint the precise location of every air craft, warship, and submarine—friend or foe—in the world.

Everyone's attention was focused on the thirty-by-fifty-foot center screen, its map zooming in upon Maine's eastern seaboard where six to eight objects, color-coded in yellow, were flitting on and off the screen like fireflies. As the admiral watched, one of the lights raced east over the Atlantic as if shot out of a cannon, stopped on a dime, and then soared ninety degrees to the south and off the screen beyond the range of their radar.

A number flashed in the lower right corner. Velocity: 7,665 mph.

A pair of objects blinked into existence over Nova Scotia. Admiral

Hintzman followed them as they streaked west across the Atlantic, their color fading from gold to aqua-blue, indicating the bogeys had submerged.

They disappeared, only to reappear seconds later over the coastline of Portland, Maine.

Velocity: 13,812 mph.

"Putting on quite a show for us tonight, huh Marko?"

The Admiral turned to a man in his mid-fifties. Like Hintzman, he was wearing casual attire, his sandy-brown short-cropped hair poking out beneath a Central Florida baseball cap.

"How are you, Tommy?"

"Good as can be expected. Matthew's entering his second year in law school; Andrea's back in Boca with our daughter and …" Cubit glanced up at the main screen as four red dots, flying in a diamond formation, crawled slowly across central Maine, heading for the coast. "Here come the F-16s."

"If you ask me, this entire exercise is a waste of taxpayer money. It's not like we're ever going to catch them."

"*Attention. Admiral Hintzman and General Cubit, please report to Conference Room-A.*"

"Xavier sounds cranky."

Hintzman nodded. "Our director has uninvited guests."

"Johnston?"

"And the Goth queen. She's in the cafeteria eating bugs or whatever it is witches eat."

"I wish someone would put a silver bullet in both their devil-worshiping hearts."

"We should talk about that sometime."

Sophia Pregadio approached, handing each man a slice of chocolate cheesecake on a paper plate. "Hurry up and eat this; I stole the last two pieces from Director Solis's refrigerator."

Conference Room-A was a 2,000-square-foot chamber featuring a balcony that overlooked the theater. Tonight its sliding glass doors remained closed and tinted, the four large flat screen LED monitors inside all tuned to the map featured on the command center's main screen.

Xavier Solis, former Directorate of the CIA's Special Activities Division, sat at the head of the oval smart table. On Solis's left was Lillie Becker, co-chairman of the Council of Foreign Relations. On his right was Dr. Erin Driscoll; seated beside her was Dr. Michael Kemp, CEO of Kemp Aerospace. The two scientists were focused on the data scrolling across their iPad screens.

Seated at the opposite end of the table from Xavier Solis was the older Caucasian man, his piercing ice-blue eyes red-rimmed from having just driven three hours in the dark from Tyson's Corner, his white eyebrows furrowed in concentration as if his mind was seeking a way to mentally obliterate the dancing yellow dots from existence.

Rory Johnston was twenty-six the year Adolf Hitler invaded Poland. The amateur pilot had just accepted a job teaching history at a high school in upstate New York and was worried about being drafted when he met Sandra Donahue at an Arts Festival. A struggling artist, Sandra was sharing a trailer with six people. Rory bought three of her paintings and asked her out.

Two weeks later, he asked her to move in.

A month later she informed him she was pregnant.

A devout Catholic, Rory convinced Sandra that they were meant to be together and asked her to marry him. Uncertain whether the child was even his, she nevertheless accepted, and the couple exchanged vows at Johnston's church.

Alexander Rory Johnston was born on April 7, 1939. His father worked two jobs to make ends meet; his mother stayed home and painted, often leaving the infant alone in its crib while she worked ... and drank and cursed her life.

Two weeks after the Japanese attacked Pearl Harbor, Rory received his draft notice.

After completing basic training, Private Johnston was informed that his experience flying qualified him to be trained as a bombardier. He was sent to England and, over the next four years, participated in more than a hundred combat missions. He returned home to a five-year-old son who did not recognize him and a wife who was just as distant.

Sandra confessed that she was having an affair with the principal at the high school where Rory had worked and that she wanted a divorce.

Rory packed his belongings and left. He returned later that night—drunk and quite violent.

Alexander was playing in his room when he heard his mother yelling at the stranger. An object smashed against the other side of his wall, followed by a chorus of grunts and screams ... then silence.

The boy waited, his pulse a steady sixty beats per minute. After a long moment he entered the hall and peeked through the open master bedroom door. He saw his mother spread-eagled on the floor, blood pooling in her mouth, the telltale purple imprints around her collapsed esophagus.

Hearing a noise coming from the master bathroom, he ducked beneath the bed.

Alexander watched through the reflection of the medicine cabinet mirror as Rory Johnston freed a length of chain link from the sky light and fashioned it into a noose. The boy grew excited, waiting until the groan that told him the stranger had stepped off the edge of the tub.

Alexander approached the bathroom gallows, far more curious than fearful. Suspended above the floor was an animated bag of flesh fighting to contain Rory Johnston's soul. The boy studied everything—his father's bulging eyes, the pulsating cords of blood vessels popping along the swelling neck, the herky-jerky leg movements ...

The internal battle caused the body to sway and spin, and suddenly the former history teacher realized he had an audience. Purple lips mouthed silent objections, flailing arms commanding his son to leave.

The boy held his ground—the Grim Reaper's protégé intent on counting down the final twitches of life until the stranger's soul slipped free of its physical purgatory and escaped into the unknown.

His mind intoxicated by endorphins, Alexander spent another twenty minutes examining his parents' vacant corpses before the police arrived. The night was an education in forensics—the child reveling in what would become his life's passion: Thanatology: the study of death.

Alexander Johnston entered his teens, moving from one foster home to the next, his

hobby of killing stray cats and raccoons tarnishing his surrogate family's welcome. Seeking human subjects, he lied about his age and enlisted in the army when he was sixteen, the armed forces providing him with a "license to kill." He quickly worked his way up through the ranks, demonstrating a lethal creativity on the battlefield that impressed his superiors. After enrolling in and graduating from Officer Candidate School, Colonel Johnston was chosen to command a Green Beret unit participating in clandestine operations in Vietnam and Thailand. One of these Special Forces—Project Phoenix—was responsible for the torture and killing of civilians in My Lai and later in El Salvador.

As educational as killing had become, what the colonel really desired to learn were methods of separating the life force from the body, an act which he believed would induce instant death. Believing this hidden knowledge existed among the more primitive cultures, Alexander Johnston resigned his commission and set out to find it, traveling to Tibet to converse with monks and with shamans in the Amazon jungle. He studied voodoo with witch doctors in Togo and feasted on human flesh with the cannibals of New Guinea. From the Russians he learned the art of psycho-correction; from former CIA officers, remote viewing and other paranormal exercises—until he was convinced he could use telepathy to interfere with the brain's electrical activity and chase the life force from the body.

Three years later, Colonel Johnston presented his "soft option killing" theories to Major General Sebastian J. Appleton, Director of U.S. Army Intelligence and Security Command. Appleton was enthusiastic, and suddenly the man who had spent hundreds of hours staring at goats had a new position as Director of Non-Lethal Programs working out of the Los Alamos National Laboratories. Here, the colonel was able to focus on mind control and psychotronics while gaining access to black budget projects which used advanced technologies necessary for his project's success. He worked side-by-side with Dr. Igor Smirnov, a psychologist from the Moscow Institute of Psycho-Correlations who had designed a technique to electronically analyze the human mind—a necessary step in order to learn how to influence and control it.

In 1992, Colonel Johnston married Yvonne Dwyer, a practicing Satanist and self-published author on the occult. At twenty-six, Dwyer was half the colonel's age, but she saw in his eyes a youthful madness waiting to be exploited.

By day they lived the lives of semi-celebrities as the colonel became a popular TV and radio guest, debunking UFOs while presenting lectures on "non-violent warfare." They rubbed elbows with billionaires, religious leaders and political power brokers, with the colonel being invited to sit on the boards of several powerful military contractors—allowing him unprecedented access into top-secret facilities and their black-shelved technologies. Behind closed doors, "Dr. Death" and his bride drank tiger's blood and consumed the umbilical cords of newborns while participating in Satanic rituals—the biggest being the annual festivities at the Bohemian Grove.

    Every July, two thousand elitists from all over the world—including former presidents and government officials, CEOs of major corporations, bankers, Big Oil executives, and members of the Trilateral Commission, the Bilderberg Group, and the Council of Foreign Relations—were invited to the Bohemian Grove, a private compound located in a Redwood forest 65 miles north of San Francisco. On the first night of this pilgrimage, all the invited guests gathered at a clearing by the lake for the opening event, known as the Cremation of Care ceremony. There, guarded by the 45-foot-tall statue of an owl, Bohemians dressed in dark brown robes would pretend to struggle to ignite a bonfire required to burn a human effigy referred to as "Dull Care," a symbol representing the burdens and responsibilities of the world leaders in attendance. The assembled then prayed to the giant owl, a Canaanite idol known as Moloch, that was used long ago to sacrifice children. Wild applause would erupt from the inebriated crowd as an aura of light appeared around the statue's head when the pyre was successfully lit, the sound system blasting human cries into the night in a pagan ritual that bound the rich and powerful to darkness.

Admiral Hintzman followed General Cubit inside the conference room, the two men situating themselves in vacant chairs farthest from Colonel Johnston's end of the table.

Director Solis looked up from his iPad as the two senior commanders entered. "Admiral … General; my apologies for asking you to join us at this ungodly hour, but this is the third night in a row we've had activity off the coast of Maine and it's becoming very difficult to keep stories and photos out of the paper."

The Admiral pinched the bridge of his nose, too tired to hide his annoyance. "What would you like us to do, Xavier? Ask the ETs to go home?"

"I really don't see a problem," General Cubit said. "There's ten thousand reported sightings a year; almost none of which ever get any traction. With our birds in the area, the ETs will slip back into transdimensional space and that will be that."

Director Solis powered off his iPad. "That's part of the problem, General. The governor of Maine is demanding to know why our F-16s are buzzing his coastline. He's pushing the White House, the White House is pushing the Pentagon, and the Pentagon is pushing me."

"In a few months we may not have to worry about dispatching fighter jets anymore," Lillie Becker stated. "From what Dr. Kemp was telling me, the lead engineer working on *Project Zeus* has discovered a telltale zero-point-energy flux which appears just before these ET vessels pop out of transdimensional space ... a possibly telltale indicator we've been looking for."

"It has potential," Michael Kemp replied. "Of course, we won't know anything until we get Dr. Marulli to the Cube. My firm simply doesn't have the necessary technology or support staff to complete the project."

Director Solis seemed positively giddy. "Good God, man, let's fly her out tomorrow!"

General Cubit shook his head. "Let's not jump the gun. There's absolutely no consensus among the voting members of Council to greenlight *Zeus*."

"Agreed," the admiral said. "*Zeus* was insanity back when it was called *Star Wars*. We're dealing with civilizations that are tens of thousands ... maybe millions of years more advanced than us. Up until now they've been incredibly tolerant, considering we took out a dozen of their vehicles, killing their crews in the process. Start blasting them as they come out of transdimensional space, and things could get ugly quickly."

"Now just a damn minute," the director said, swiveling in his wheelchair to face the two dissenters. "They've interfered with our ICBMs, they've declared the moon off-limits—last time I checked, this was *our* planet."

"Which we're systematically destroying," Erin Driscoll interjected.

"Young lady, if we want to destroy it, then that's our prerogative."

General Cubit rolled his eyes. "That makes no sense at all, Xavier."

"Enough," Colonel Johnston said, his voice just above a whisper. "This

76

isn't about *Zeus* or F-16s or Jesus coming to fly the born-again Christians off to heaven. These ETs are buzzing Portland, Maine for the same reason they buzzed Joshua Tree and Lisbon … because Steven Greer is out there on the beach with his followers, conducting another one of his damn CE-5 camp-outs."

"They're on private property, Colonel," General Cubit said. "It's not a crime to sit in a circle and meditate."

"I heard there's a reporter with them from the local CBS affiliate," Michael Kemp added. "The last thing we want is another Phoenix Lights situation."

"Then it's agreed," Colonel Johnston said. "We need to take Greer out, once and for all."

Admiral Hintzman turned a menacing glare at the white-browed older man. "Get it through your head, *Dr. Death*, that is not going to happen. Greer's set up a Dead Man's Trigger; you incapacitate him or send a wet works team after him, and we'll be dealing with something far worse than a bunch of UFO sightings."

"He has a lot of supporters out there," Cubit added, "including members of MAJI."

The colonel shrugged, typing something on his iPad. "Shit happens, general. Maybe the metastatic cancer will return."

Admiral Hintzman stood, his face turning red. "Pull another stunt like you did back in '97 and I'll make sure you and that witch you married are burned at the stake."

Alexander Johnston smiled coldly. "You're not my commanding officer, Admiral. I've met with several members of Council who share my concerns. Nothing will happen to Greer for now, but it's interesting to see where your loyalties lie."

Gathering his iPad and coffee, Colonel Alexander Johnston exited the conference room.

10

Washington, D.C.
July 29, 2017

IT WAS 11:15 BY THE TIME ADAM finished his breakfast meeting with the board of directors at Northrop-Grumman. A valet delivered his silver Jeep Grand Cherokee and he drove off the corporate complex, taking the northbound ramp out of Fairfax onto Interstate 495.

Seventy-two hours had passed since his bizarre conversation with Dr. Manley in the sushi restaurant. The issues they had discussed had lost their sense of urgency in the wake of an itinerary with military contractors which kept him busy from seven in the morning through midnight, and now Adam just wanted to get back to Jessica's townhome and crawl into bed—preferably with his fiancée.

The highway was free of traffic, allowing his mind to wander. Adam's personal opinion about the existence of extraterrestrials had always come down to a combination of logic, simple mathematics, and time. In our galaxy alone, it was estimated there were 400 billion stars and a trillion planets. Even if the odds of intelligent life existing on other worlds were a million-to-one, there would still be over a million inhabited planets in the Milky Way. Scientists estimated there were 200 billion *more galaxies* in the observable universe. Then there was the age of the universe; surely 14 billion years was enough time for evolution to take hold within these unreachable alien worlds.

Adam corrected his thoughts. *Unreachable to us, not for a civilization tens of thousands or even millions of years more advanced than our own.*

Logic aside, it was the emotional component surrounding other beings visiting Earth that fueled his skepticism. While there were thousands of UFO sightings reported every year, most were ignored by the mainstream media, with the eyewitnesses shrugged off as either being drunk, mistaken, or a little crazy. That was what had made the testimonials in Steven Greer's 2001 *Disclosure Project* so compelling. These eyewitnesses were not just credible; many of them were former members of the military entrusted with top security clearances. And yet the one constant that prevented Adam from "drinking the Kool-aid" was the fact that he had never personally seen an extraterrestrial craft himself.

Nor was he interested in looking for one now. The issue at hand was not whether flying saucers and little green men existed, but whether zero-point-energy systems were being deliberately kept out of the public domain by a cabal operating both within and outside of the government.

If this was true then the question was: Just how far had the cancer spread?

Shariak had no doubt that secretly-funded projects existed; the CIA and NSA had been operating unchecked and off-the-books for decades. As Deputy Under Secretary of Defense, he had the authority to investigate any matter involving weapon systems; the problem was that the applications of any secret technologies would have been farmed out to private corporate entities like the military contractors he had just visited. Before he started "shaking the bushes," he needed some direction, and that meant a face-to-face with Dr. Steven Greer.

According to Greer's website, he was on some kind of retreat in Portland, Maine until the end of the week. The good news was that he was scheduled to give a talk in D.C. the following Thursday. Adam had reserved a seat. After the lecture he would arrange a private get-together and lay his cards out on the table. If Greer could help—great. If not, Adam's next meeting would be with Bill Clinton where he'd politely hand him back his baton.

It was just past noon when he arrived at Jessica's home, excited to find her white Infiniti parked out front. Leaving his bag in the car, he knocked on her door to surprise her.

"It's open."

Adam entered to find two packed suitcases by the front door. "Jess?"

"Adam? I'm in the kitchen!"

He found her packing her laptop. "What's going on?"

"Hey, baby. I thought you were the driver. General Cubit called; Lockheed-Martin moved up our timetable. I have to be at Martin State Airport in Baltimore in less than an hour. I tried calling you but—"

"My phone died on the way home and I packed the charger. Will you really be gone a month?"

"Maybe two. Aw, don't look so sad; Cubit said he'd fly me back for a few long weekends if all goes well."

"If I had known, I would have pushed my trip back."

Adam heard a car pull up. He glanced out the kitchen window at the limo. "First class."

"Nothing but the best." Jessica opened the front door for the driver. "You can take these two suitcases; I'll be out in fifteen minutes."

"Yes, ma'am."

She shut the door, turning to Adam. "Let's go."

"Where?"

"Upstairs for a quickie. It's a private jet … they can wait."

Adam opened his eyes, feeling refreshed from the afternoon nap. He was still naked in Jessica's bed, his fiancée's scent mixing with his own; her perfume lingering in the bedroom though she had kissed him good-bye over an hour before.

Reaching for his prosthetic leg, he pulled the harness over his stump, making sure the electrodes commanding the smart joint were all aligned. Twenty minutes later he emerged from the bedroom in jeans and a polo shirt, wondering what there was to eat.

Adam headed downstairs, his eyes glancing at the photos mounted along the wall on his right, the assorted colors and sizes of the frames laid out like a jigsaw puzzle.

He was halfway down the steps when he saw the worn black and white image.

The photo had been taken outdoors, the three women and a child posing in front of a Lockheed U-2 spy plane. The blonde on the right was a younger version of Donna Hare, one of the eyewitnesses who had testified in *The Disclosure Project* video. The dark haired, blue-eyed woman on the left appeared to be a test pilot, a jumpsuit tag identifying her as *L. Gagnon*.

As for the attractive woman in the middle holding her two-year-old daughter—it was Dr. Barbara Jean Marulli, Jessica's mother.

The 6,538-square-foot waterfront estate was located on a private two-acre lot in Annapolis, Maryland's prestigious *Wardour on the Severn*. A housekeeper led Adam past the grand entrance and through the gourmet kitchen to the foyer. "She's waiting for you out back by the pool."

"Thanks, I know the way."

Adam exited out the French doors. The late afternoon sun was at his back, the July heat at its worst. The emerald green waters of the Chesapeake were spread out before him, sparkling beneath a cobalt blue sky. Three small docks and deepwater slips were anchored along the private shoreline shaded by a cluster of towering pine trees.

The stone path led to an Amish-built carriage home set between the main house and the waterfront. He found Jessica's mother sunning herself in a padded lounge chair by the outdoor pool. She was dressed in a white and navy trim tennis outfit from an earlier match, her eyes concealed behind designer sunglasses.

Dr. Barbara Jean Singleton-Marulli was in her mid-sixties, though she could have easily passed for fifty. A competitive gymnast in high school, it was her athleticism that had blossomed in Jessica … along with a passion for science.

Adam scuffed his shoes on the cement, attempting to alert his future mother-in-law that he was there without startling her.

"Hello, Adam. I heard you when you rang the doorbell. There's a spread by the bar. Grab something to eat and join me."

He entered the cottage through the open sliding glass door. A deli platter and assorted rolls, breads, and desserts occupied the bar—leftovers from an earlier lunch. Tossing two slices of rye bread onto a paper plate, he made himself a turkey, mayo, and Muenster cheese sandwich, grabbed a bottled water from a cooler of melted ice, and headed back outside.

Barbara Jean was finishing a text message on her iPhone with one hand, the other dabbing sweat beads with a towel.

"Captain Marulli around?"

"He's at the club." She looked up, offering Adam a cold smile. "So? How is my daughter? I hardly ever hear from her. You'd think she'd want to be more involved in her own wedding plans."

"She's been busy."

"Frankly, my husband and I were surprised when she told us the two of you were engaged. Jessica is like me—a workaholic. I was twenty-three when Kelly Johnson recruited me straight out of Cal Tech. My first project was the F-117 Stealth Fighter, and I ended up marrying one of the pilots. Thirty-two years I worked at Skunkworks, spending fourteen-hour days in the lab right up until I went into labor with Jessica."

She powered off her cell phone. "Okay, Mr. Deputy Under Secretary, what was so important that you needed to drive all the way out here to talk to me about it?"

"Jess has an old black and white photo of the two of you taken at Lockheed; she can't be more than a few years old. There's a woman standing next to you; her name is Donna Hare. I saw her on a YouTube video done in May of 2001 at an event called *The Disclosure Project*. She testified about seeing undoctored NASA photos taken on the far side of the moon which revealed … structures."

"What kind of structures? Oh, good God, you drove all the way out here to ask me about aliens?"

"And other things."

"Adam, I didn't know Donna Hare. We had a mutual friend in Lydia

Gagnon, the test pilot in that photo. I don't know anything about moon bases or aliens … Jesus."

"What about the F-117's design?"

"What about it?"

"How much of it was reverse-engineered?"

"Reverse-engineered from what?"

"A downed UFO."

Barbara Jean covered her grin. "This is a joke, isn't it? Did Juice put you up to this?"

"You worked in Lockheed's Skunkworks Division. I thought maybe you might have had access to the stuff Colonel Corso wrote about in his Roswell book."

"Adam, Phillip Corso was bat-shit crazy. Do I need to worry about you now?"

"Someone I know wanted my opinion about the subject. I was curious if you knew anything."

"About UFOs?"

"More about the energy source that supposedly powers them."

Barbara Jean wiped the sweat from the back of her neck. "It's too hot out here, let's go inside."

He grabbed his bottled water and paper plate and followed her inside the cottage, feeling foolish.

Barbara slid the glass door shut behind them and locked it. "What do you know about wine?"

"About as much as I do about UFOs, I suppose. Why?"

"So your trip out here isn't a total waste of time I'll give you a quick lesson; that way you can impress my daughter the next time you two go out to dinner."

Barbara led him through a short alcove off the kitchen to an arching wooden door. Opening it, she felt for a light switch before descending a narrow spiral staircase that took them into the basement.

Artificial legs were not designed to maneuver down tight spiral stairwells, forcing Adam to hop a step at a time. Sound seemed to mute as he followed her deeper into the bowels of the foundation and into an expansive wine cellar. The floor, racks, and cabinetry were made of cherrywood. Bottles of wine lined both walls.

Barbara searched the racks for several minutes before selecting a dust-covered burgundy. "Clos de Vougeot, Grand Cru, Leroy 1961. It's the captain's favorite."

She placed the bottle on a granite-topped island situated beneath a white panel of light in the ceiling. Opening a side drawer, she located a cork screw and expertly popped open the bottle. Sliding two inverted wine glasses out from an overhead rack, she poured just enough for a taste test into each one.

"There are four basic steps in evaluating a wine. The first is color. It's best to hold the glass up to a white background." Barbara demonstrated, using the overhead panel. "With a red wine, we're looking for a darker color which occurs during fermentation when the juice is left in contact with the skins. A dark color is associated with a more intense flavor. Brown means the wine is old. All red wines eventually brown with age, but you don't want too much cloudiness. Blush wine grapes are fermented with only limited contact to the skin; white wines are fermented with no contact."

Adam nodded politely, wondering how they had gone from UFOs to judging wine.

"Next is the smell test. Once the wine is poured you want to swirl it around in the glass to release its natural aroma. Immature wines carry little or no bouquet, while a mature wine carries a robust fruity aroma."

She inhaled, Adam following her lead. "Smells good."

"Can you detect a hint of oak? That comes from the barrel where the wine was aged. Older bottles may only exude an aroma for a few moments after uncorking, so it's best not to let an older wine breathe too long before drinking it."

"Older wine, short breaths … got it."

"Finally we get to the taste test. Taste is totally subjective, but we're looking for two things—a rich flavor and an aftertaste. A good wine made from ripe grapes will linger in your mouth; an unpleasant bitter aftertaste means the wine is high in acidity. Go on, drink up."

Adam drained the glass, the burgundy carrying a fruity taste with a bit of a kick.

"Do you like it?"

He didn't, but he nodded anyway. "To be honest, I'm not much of a drinker."

She filled his glass. "Keep chasing after zero-point-energy, and trust me, that will change."

"Wait ... what?"

"Let's sit down." The retired engineer led him to a small sitting area composed of a loveseat, two wooden rocking chairs and a leather recliner. She settled in on the loveseat and filled her wine glass to the brim, Adam opting for one of the rockers.

"My husband and I bought this property twelve years ago. When we added the wine cellar, we had electromagnetic sound dampeners installed within the walls of the foundation ... too many eyes watching and ears listening." She paused to drain her glass. "I assume you have a Q-clearance?"

"Yes."

"Q-Clearance is nuclear, and nuclear is *bubkus*. I have a Cosmic Clearance. It's about forty clearances above Q-Clearance ... it's at the top, there's nothing higher. Ninety-nine percent of the politicians on Capitol Hill and ninety percent of the assholes in the Pentagon have no idea it even exists. Only about twenty-five people in the world at any given time carry a Cosmic Clearance, and none of them are presidents or heads of state. But some of them are quite nasty. I'm telling you this because if I get too buzzed and reveal certain things to you that I shouldn't, your ability to keep your mouth shut may very well determine if I'll be around to attend your wedding in September ... which would really be a nice thing considering we're footing the bill."

Adam felt his heart racing. "What's said down here stays down here."

"Good. Now ask your questions."

"How long has all this been going on?"

"You mean, how long have other intelligent species been visiting Earth? Who knows? Archaeologists have discovered cave paintings and Egyptian hieroglyphics which suggest extraterrestrial-human contact might trace back thousands of years. The more recent documented interactions with UFOs began in the 1940s during World War II. Allied pilots and crewmen reported seeing strange orb-like objects of light buzzing our bombers during combat sorties. The Nazis apparently saw them as well, and before too long, everyone started referring to them as 'foo fighters,' which translates as 'fire' in French and German. These orbs, which could be described as energy drones, often disrupted electronics aboard our warplanes while affecting gravity. Occasionally one would pass transdimensionally right through one of our bombers, freaking out the crew.

"FDR was very concerned and he dispatched General Jimmy Doolittle to the Allied theater of operations in Europe to find out if this was some kind of new high-tech Nazi secret weapon. Doolittle reported back that the objects were interplanetary in nature.

"Sightings increased after we dropped A-bombs on Hiroshima and Nagasaki. New Mexico became a UFO traffic magnet, and for good reason. The first nukes were created in Los Alamos and tested in Alamagordo and Whites Sands.

"Then two years later, everything changed. On June 24, 1947 there was a UFO sighting that made the international news. Eight nights later, three saucer-shaped ETVs, each fifty-feet-in-diameter, began buzzing Roswell Air Force Base, home of the 509th bomber squadron, the only wing in the world equipped with atomic weapons. Two of the UFOs crashed. One went down southwest of Corona, New Mexico. The second crash site was discovered in Horse Mesa, west of Magdalena, New Mexico. The 'official story' is that Roswell had been using a high-powered radar system that was set on a certain frequency which disrupted two of the ET crafts' propulsion and navigation systems, causing them to collide. Having spent time with Colonel Phillip Corso three decades later, I can tell you what really happened.

"Roswell had secretly developed a pulsed scalar longitudinal electromagnetic weapon, the beam of which struck two of the three ETVs at supra-light speed as the crafts were phasing out of transdimensional space-time. The pair collided and one was completely destroyed, the second was salvaged … along with its dead thirty-six-inch-tall hominids. They were classified as Greys, after their gray skin tone.

"Between June of 1947 and December of 1952, the military's EMS weapon brought down thirteen extraterrestrial spacecraft; eleven of them in New Mexico, one each in Nevada and Arizona. Two other crashes occurred in Mexico and one in Norway. Sixty-five bodies were recovered, including one ET that was kept alive for three years."

"A live alien?"

"From the Roswell crash. By the way, the whole 'alien' thing … they find that term a bit derogatory. They prefer extraterrestrial."

"What happened to it … the surviving ET?"

"It was a Grey. They called it EBEN, short for Extraterrestrial Biological Entity. It was hairless, with a bulb-shaped head and big black eyes that had no exterior lids. From the autopsy reports I've read, the ET's internal anatomy was chlorophyll-based, and it processed food into energy and waste material in the same manner as plants. The EBEN had a solitary organ that did the job of both a heart and lungs, but they had multiple stomachs which performed different digestive processes. They also had an organ that would take every single bit of moisture out of whatever they ate and fed the body; so they had no need to drink a lot of fluids.

"The EBEN brain has eleven different lobes, and where the spinal cord met the brain, there were two little bulbs on each side. The eyes were very sophisticated with optic nerves that went into different anatomical parts of the brain than human optic nerves …

"These beings are thin and wiry, but their muscles are fibrous and quite strong, especially the legs. The hands are thin and double-jointed, and each of its four long fingers possesses a suction-tip. Its sexual organs are internalized, but the scientists assigned to the EBEN were pretty sure it was a male. According to the ET, there were female EBEN, just none on any of these ships.

"They didn't have any ears, but they had a canal with an organ or gland—a little bulb that they could hear out of. They didn't have vocal cords like we have. I read a briefing that indicated a procedure was performed on the EBEN which allowed it to talk or make sounds. None of that was necessary since they communicated telepathically."

"Where did they keep it?"

"The live one? At first, Fort Dietrick, Maryland, then at Wright-Patterson Air Force Base, and later at the Huntsville Redstone Arsenal.

"Our scientists learned a lot from EBEN, all of which was compiled into what became known as the Yellow Book. Unfortunately, the ET became ill in late-1951. Several medical specialists were brought in to treat it, the team headed by a botanist. Realizing it was dying, the United States began broadcasting radio signals into deep space in an attempt to demonstrate peaceful intentions to what was obviously a superior entity. The group tasked with overseeing this project—code named SIGMA—was the National Security Agency, created by secret Executive Order on November 4, 1952. The NSA was assigned to monitor all communications, both human and extraterrestrial, while maintaining secrecy regarding the UFOs' presence."

"So, the CIA and NSA were both created in response to these UFO events?"

"Correct, though the first secret task force to investigate the ET phenomenon was organized under the name *Project Sign* and evolved into *Project Grudge* a year later. A low level disinformation project named *Blue Book* was created to fool the public. Meanwhile, 'Blue Teams' were trained to recover the downed ETVs, later evolving into Alpha Teams under *Project Pounce.*

"Both the CIA and NSA were given complete autonomy through a series of National Security Council Memos and Executive Orders which legalized their covert activities and kept Truman and his advisors out of the loop, allowing them to maintain plausible deniability in the event any information leaked to the public. This buffer effectively gave the intelligence community the legal right to keep future presidents in the dark regarding UFOs."

"What happened to the Grey?"

"The EBEN died in June of 1952. Spielberg's movie, *E.T.* was loosely based on these events."

Barbara Jean refilled her glass with burgundy. "Imagine you're President Truman. On your watch, the military's secret weapon has shot down thirteen UFOs, and the lone ET you've held captive for the last three years just croaked. Harry S. knows he's dealing with civilizations whose technology is light years ahead of ours, so you can imagine he'd be freaking out a bit, worried about an alien invasion.

"Truman contacted our allies to warn them about what happened. He also reached out to the Soviet Union. Turns out their top-secret weapon bases were also being buzzed by ETVs. They decided maintaining secrecy was more important than sharing the information with their respective governing bodies and risking a leak. A new world order was necessary, one that operated without oversight, allowing it to move quickly in the event of an ET invasion. This secret government became known as the Bilderberg Group, named after the hotel in Switzerland where they first met. They continue to meet there every year and it is this group, not the United Nations nor the G-8 that sets global policy.

"Dwight D. Eisenhower took office in 1953. During the president's first year as Commander-in-Chief, nine more UFOs were downed in the United States; four in Arizona, two in Texas, and one each in Louisiana, Montana, and New Mexico. There were also thousands of reported sightings. Knowing he had to be proactive without involving Congress, Eisenhower enlisted the help of his friend, Nelson Rockefeller, a fellow member of the Council on Foreign Relations. With the CIA busy placing the Shah of Iran in power and the NSA eavesdropping on Castro, Rockefeller decided a new agency was needed that would be solely dedicated to UFO encounters while overseeing the incredible technologies that were being acquired through reverse-engineering of all their downed space craft.

"Majestic-12 was launched a year later as an independent agency operating on a black budget. Its first members were said to have included Rockefeller; Secretary of Defense, Charles E. Wilson; CIA Director, Allen Dulles; Secretary of State, John Foster-Dulles; Chairman of the Joint Chiefs of Staff, Admiral Arthur Radford; and FBI Director, J. Edgar Hoover. There were also six men selected from the Council on Foreign Relations and six from the JASON Society, a scientific group formed during the Manhattan Project. Policies could only be mandated by a majority vote of twelve, thus the name."

"Barbara, our government is known for leaks. How has MJ-12 been able to maintain its hold on secrecy for so long?"

"Internal compartmentalization is the key. As a scientist, if you are working for a USAP—an Unacknowledged Special Access Project—your task is so job-specific that you can't see the rest of the puzzle, or even the piece you're working on. As a USAP director who has a need to know, I've found myself on several different occasions being escorted into a secret underground facility for a coming-to-Jesus talk. The good news, you're told, is that you are going to be paid very well for the rest of your life. The bad news is that if you speak outside the circle of trust, it won't be a very long life. Every member of Council has a bullet with their name on it just waiting to be popped into the chamber. Keep in mind that rank has no bearing when it comes to black ops. If you are involved in a USAP and your C.O. calls you into his office and asks you about it, your response is simple—as far as you know, no such project exists. Say anything else and you might end up like James Forrestal."

"What happened to him?"

"As I mentioned, Forrestal was appointed by Truman to be the country's first Secretary of Defense. As such, he was engaged in the UFO agenda from Day One. Being a very idealistic and religious man, he believed that the public should be told about the situation. When it looked like Dewey would win the presidential election, Forrestal began pushing to talk to leaders of the opposition party and Congress. After Truman pulled out the upset and was reelected, Forrestal was asked to resign.

"Leaving office didn't render Forrestal any less of a potential threat; it just placed him lower on the media radar. It wasn't long, however, before the former Defense Secretary began acting paranoid, telling friends and family that he was being watched. There were reports of a mental break-down and suicide attempts, which led to his forced admittance to the Bethesda Naval Hospital where he was kept under 24-hour watch in a private room on the 16th floor, his family denied visitation rights.

"Over the next several months there were indications he was improving and that his brother, Henry, was demanding his release. On May 22, 1949, around 2 a.m., James Forrestal's corpse was found on the third floor roof of Bethesda Hospital. Authorities claim the guard had left his post and the former Secretary of Defense had used the opportunity to escape to a kitchen across the hall where he tied one end of his bathrobe sash around his neck, the other end to a radiator by the window. Pushing out the screen, he attempted to climb out along the edge and hang himself, only the knot slipped and he fell thirteen stories to his death."

"What can you tell me about these zero-point-energy devices? Have you ever seen one?"

"Anything of importance is kept in one of these vast subterranean complexes built by Bechtel. Now it's time for you to go; I'm tipsy and I've said way too much."

It was dusk by the time Barbara Marulli awoke from her catnap. Adam was gone, her future son-in-law having left a few hours earlier.

Collecting the empty burgundy bottle and cork, she trudged up the spiral stairwell to the first floor. She tossed the bottle in the recycling bin and turned on her iPhone, dialing the memorized number.

The phone rang, a male voice picking up on the third ring. "Speak."

"It's me. It went as well as can be expected."

11

Martin State Airport
Baltimore, Maryland

WHEN JESSICA MARULLI had been told that a private jet would be waiting for her at Martin State Airport to fly her to her on-site assignment at Edwards Air Force Base, she had expected the usual G-500 Gulfstream. To her surprise, the chauffeur parked the limo beneath the starboard wing of a Boeing 767-33A/ER jumbo jet.

"All this is for me?"

"Yes, ma'am. Go on up, I'll bring your bags."

Jessica exited the vehicle and ascended the mobile staircase.

Her eyes widened as she stepped inside the commercial airliner. First-class was not a foreign concept to the physicist; her parents' careers having afforded them the good life. But what awaited her inside the cabin was an entirely different level of luxury. Everything in the wide-bodied cabin aft of first-class seating had been gutted, the interior converted into a mini-mansion. The forward section was dominated by a plush ivory sofa mounted along the starboard side, its treble-clef-shaped curvature matched by a marble coffee table. Behind it was a concave mirrored privacy wall, the effect of which seemed to double the size of the forward compartment. Violet cushions matched the thick-pile carpeting which stood out smartly against the padded ivory walls. Moving aft led her to a dining room that seated twenty, the rectangular table anchored beneath three small chandeliers. The middle compartment concluded with a fifteen-foot flat screen TV and an assortment of recliners, sofas, and love seats that were no doubt put to good use on long flights by the jet's owner and his entourage.

A closed set of mirrored double doors separated the middle section of the plane from the aft compartment.

Jessica knocked. Receiving no reply, she tried the handle and pushed her way inside.

"Oh my Gawd."

The heart-shaped, king-sized bed was covered in a mink quilt, the fur reflected in the mirrored ceiling. An entertainment center included another large flat screen television. A small workout area consisted of a stationary bike, a treadmill, and a six-station gym.

Guess the owner likes to watch himself in action ...

She ran her fingers across the smooth-as-silk fur blanket as she walked past the bed to inspect the bathroom. Gold faucets accentuated the black marble sink. Thick violet towels were stacked in racks by a completely enclosed glass shower as wide as six phone booths. A black porcelain toilet and bidet were harbored in a private water closet.

"Impressed?"

She turned to find General Thomas J. Cubit standing by the open double doors. He was dressed in what appeared to be a golf outfit.

"General Cubit? I didn't know you'd be accompanying me to California."

"Someone has to brief you on your new assignment."

She groaned. "Seriously? I haven't finished my work on *Zeus* and you're already adding more to my agenda?"

"The new assignment *is Zeus*. We considering having you take over as the project's director."

Adrenaline coursed through Jessica's bloodstream. "What happened to Scott Hopper?"

"Dr. Hopper had a few personal issues which forced him to vacate the position. Join me in the entertainment center; we're about to taxi to the runway and the crew wants us buckled in ... some ridiculous FAA regulation."

She followed him out of the bedroom suite, her mind racing. As a Team Leader, her work up to this point had been confined to overseeing the guidance system of *Zeus*—the military's new satellite array. As project director of an Unacknowledged Special Access Project, she would have to be brought inside the inner circle.

Mother said she was fifty-two when she took over her first USAP; I've got her beat by fifteen—

She shook her head as if to knock the toxic thought out of her brain. *Stupid! You can't even drop a hint about the promotion ... not to your family or to Adam ... not to anyone.*

"Dr. Marulli?"

"Sorry ... I'm coming."

Edwards Air Force Base Complex
Mojave Desert, California

The Mojave Desert covers 54,000 square miles, extending east from Southern California into Utah, Nevada, and Arizona. Edwards Air Force Base is located in the southwestern corner of the desert not far from Lancaster, California. In addition to its airfields, the complex includes the China Lake Naval Weapons Center and the Fort Irwin Military Center, as well as the restricted air space above all three facilities.

There is another section of the complex—only this one cannot be found on any map.

The 767 jumbo jet touched down on a sand-swept tarmac surrounded by flatland. To the west, snow-capped mountains rose in the distance; to the east an unpaved access road led to a security gate—the only entrance through a ten-foot-high steel perimeter fence, the barrier topped by coils of barbed wire and outfitted with security cameras.

The only structure in the area was a 2,000-square-foot prefabricated building concealed beneath an open-ended hangar, its camouflage-painted roof large enough to accommodate the jumbo jet which taxied to a stop beneath the flat-roofed structure. A dust-covered SUV was parked outside the building, its doors advertising *Mojave Environmental Services.*

A garage door rolled open, releasing a man in overalls driving a motorized set of steps. Aligning the top of the stairs with the aircraft's forward door, he honked twice.

The exit swung open, releasing one of the jumbo jet's two VIPs.

The desert heat blasted Jessica in the face as she stepped off the 767. High overhead, the hangar roof blocked the afternoon sun—along with the cameras aboard any orbiting recon satellite. As she descended the steps she saw a tech remove her luggage from the plane's cargo hold.

General Cubit remained on board. He would be flying on to San Francisco for a week-long holiday with his wife in Carmel. While Cubit played golf at Pebble Beach, Jessica would be occupied with an intense seven-day orientation—assuming she accepted the directorship of a USAP.

"It's a security issue, Jessica. This particular project requires the director to have something called a Cosmic Clearance. The process normally takes several years to complete—your review, by the way, began eight months ago. Unfortunately, our need to complete critical work on *Zeus*, combined with Dr. Hopper's unexpected departure, forces us to accelerate things quite a bit. As we speak, Council is voting on the issue. If you're approved they'll offer you the position, at which time you'll be fully briefed on *Zeus*."

"How do you expect me to blindly accept a position without knowing what the job entails?"

"Did I mention the salary?"

"It's never been about the money, General."

"You'll receive a million a month to start."

Jessica felt the blood drain from her face. "Twelve million a year?"

"Plus perks. Six weeks paid vacation, access to the best hotels in the world. You'll be able to buy yourself a decent engagement ring."

She flashed him a look to kill.

"Sorry, that was out of line. But make no mistake, this is a game-changer for you and Adam. The only caveat being that he can never know what you're working on."

"Who's paying my salary?"

"Does it matter?"

"It does to the IRS. Somehow I suspect my accountant may need to be briefed."

"That will all be handled for you. As for the funds, they'll be wired directly into your account on the twelfth of every month from a non-profit cancer research foundation."

"You mean the CIA?"

"This is black budget research, Dr. Marulli. If you want to work on the most advanced sciences known to man you have to tell a few white lies and you also need a Cosmic Clearance. Opportunities like this are rare, even for someone possessing your talents. My gut tells me you'll be approved by Council but they'll want your answer the moment you enter the Cube."

The two MPs were waiting for her at the bottom of the stairs, each Marine armed with an M-16.

"Good afternoon, Dr. Marulli. If you'll come with us please."

She followed them inside the prefabricated building's front door to a waiting room that looked like something straight out of the 1960s. The floor was black and white checkered linoleum, the walls done in fake walnut wood paneling. Framed posters, faded and yellowed with age, featured antiquated information about California's environmental laws. Six chairs faced an unplugged RCA television set, the foam stuffing visible on the split-open worn vinyl cushions.

An open door on the left revealed a supervisor's office. A familiar gray-haired man dressed in a plaid shirt and worn jeans sat with his hiking boots propped atop a wooden desk. Brown eyes, magnified behind reading glasses, looked up from an issue of *Sports Illustrated*.

"Dr. Marulli."

"Afternoon, Fred. How's the wife?"

"Meaner than a bobcat. I see you hitched a ride with one of the hotshots."

"Guess I'm moving up in the world." She joined the two MPs who were waiting for her in the break room.

As she stepped inside, one of the marines shut and locked the door behind her while the second guard moved to the soda vending machine, the only modern piece of apparatus in the visitor center. Inserting a credit card in the pay slot, he selected ROOT BEER.

Internal magnetic locks snapped open, allowing the marine to slide the false outer door aside—revealing an awaiting elevator.

Jessica stepped inside. She held on as the doors sealed.

The subterranean base, known as the Cube, was the only one Jessica Marulli had ever visited. She suspected Vandenberg Air Force Base had a similar underground complex, as did Groom Lake. Two years before she had worked with a loose-lipped army engineer from Riverside, California named Matthew DeVictor. In an obvious attempt to impress her, the former officer at Bechtel described operating a nuclear-powered boring machine that could drill a tunnel seven miles long in a single day.

"We called them subterrene machines and they were massive, as long as the Space Shuttle with a diameter three times larger. On board was a compact nuclear reactor that circulated liquid lithium from the reactor core to the tunnel face, generating exterior temperatures in excess of 2,000 degrees Fahrenheit. That's hot enough to melt rock so there's no excavated soil or stone left to remove ... no telltale evidence. As the lithium loses some of its heat, it's circulated back along the exterior of the subterrene which cools the vitrified rock, leaving behind a smooth, finished, obsidian-like inner core—perfect for their unidirectional Maglev trains. I hear those puppies can travel at speeds in excess of 1,500 miles an hour. They have an entire underground rail system that connects one subterranean complex with the next.

"The Bechtel Corporation has been building these underground cities for the secret government since the 1940s. At first it was a response to the Soviet's nuclear threat, but over the last thirty years, it's shifted into something else entirely.

"The biggest project I ever worked on was the one located beneath Denver's International Airport. The complex is over twenty miles in diameter and goes down eight levels. It houses the new CIA headquarters—Langley's just a front. One of my buddies, a structural engineer named Stuart Martin, worked on and off the project for six years on account of them constantly changing construction companies in order to prevent any one particular group from knowing too much. It never bothered Stu; being one of the few structural engineers around with experience working underground, he'd just bounce from one company to the next as a freelancer. If you check out the surface area adjacent to the Denver airport, you can see these small concrete ventilation stacks that resemble mini-cooling towers. They're spread out across the entire surface area, some of them partially hidden behind shrubs. Of course, you can't get too close—the perimeter's fenced in.

"My last day on the job, I saw workers hanging Masonic symbols and bizarre murals on the walls featuring burning cities. To be honest, it scared the piss out of me. Bad enough no one knows about these facilities; to think some whacked out religious cult is involved makes it even worse. Of course, they scare the bejeezus out of you when you're hired, letting you know in no uncertain terms that if you ever talk about anything, you'll get the Jimmy Hoffa treatment."

The elevator descended rapidly with no indication of how deep it was going. After thirty seconds it slowed to a smooth stop, its doors opening to reveal a short Caucasian woman in her mid-forties.

Sandy Lynn Bagwell greeted Jessica with the same southern charm she reserved for all her Zebra-level guests. "Good afternoon, Dr. Marulli. It's been quite a while since your last visit. We've missed you."

"Thank you; it's nice to be back." She glanced nervously to her left where two more armed MPs were waiting.

"Dr. Marulli, come with us."

Jessica followed the two men down a wide white-tiled corridor, its walls papered in navy blue. They stopped at the first door on the left—a knobless steel barrier with a built-in security device.

One of the guards slid his identification card in the slot, causing a magnetic bolt to activate. "In you go."

Jessica pushed the door open, her hands shaking.

She jumped as the guard slammed it shut behind her, extinguishing the corridor light, leaving her in complete darkness.

"Hello?"

She was afraid to move, unable to see her hand in front of her face.

"Is there a reason you have me standing in the dark?"

Her pulse raced, her breaths turning rapid and shallow as her anxiety rose.

Stay calm … they're testing you.

"Stay calm … they're testing you."

The voice was female but not her own, nor was it human—its cadence computer generated.

"You can read my thoughts?"

No response.

You can read my thoughts?

We can do many things. Telepathy is the most efficient method of communication, don't you agree, Dr. Marulli?

The voice was male, this time human.

Telepathy may be efficient, but how does one function without the ability to filter every inner thought from the rest of the world?

What thoughts would you filter? Another male telepath asked. Feelings of anger? Hatred? Lust? The desire to hurt another?

Or perhaps the need to deceive? A human female voice suggested.

Jessica felt off-balance and vulnerable, afraid to think. The effect of the darkness magnified her fear, penetrating every fiber of her being, reducing her to nothingness … to an unutterable thought.

A primal urge saved her from the madness.

I have to pee.

No response.

I said I have to pee. Since you can read my thoughts you know I'm not attempting to deceive you. You can either guide me to the nearest toilet or I'll pull down my pants and piss on your damn floor.

A light appeared, revealing a bathroom and giving the chamber depth.

She made her way slowly across the room, her eyes gathering as much information as she could, her fingers counting each stride.

Entering the bathroom she pulled the door shut, dropped her pants and sat down on the toilet.

Seven fingers ... about fifteen to twenty feet from the bathroom to the exit. Circular chamber, the walls composed of some kind of dark, porous material, which means they probably can't read my thoughts outside of this room.

Can you?

Hello?

She smiled to herself. *I wonder how long they'll allow me to sit here before they lose patience and have to send someone in to get me?*

She glanced up at the door, its interior knob equipped with a lock. Reaching for it, she pushed the center button in.

Jessica relieved her bladder. When she was finished, she pulled up her pants and flushed, then lowered the toilet's lid and sat, waiting for her hosts to make the next move.

After a minute the lights flickered on and off.

Come on, guys. You'll have to do better than that.

"If you are finished," the female voice spoke out loud, "please join us in the chamber."

"So you can play more head games with me? I don't think so. I came here of my own free will to do a job. I didn't ask to be promoted, but if this is the way you treat your Cosmic Clearance candidates you can count me out."

"Dr. Marulli, this is Paul Sova. We met several years ago at Lockheed Martin. Do you remember me?"

"You worked with my mother."

"And now I'd like to work with you. You have my word—no more head games."

Jessica exited the bathroom.

The chamber was lit, revealing an oval conference table situated at the center of the circular room. Twelve chairs were occupied by ten men and two women. A vacant thirteenth chair was positioned on Paul Sova's left.

The tall, dark-haired rocket scientist from North Dakota waved her over, his hazel eyes failing to reflect the ceiling lights.

He's a hologram … they all are. General Cubit's presence at the far side of the table confirmed her theory.

"You are quite right, Dr. Marulli," Dr. Sova said, still tuned into her thoughts. "We are joining you from all across the globe."

Jessica glanced around the table. With the exception of Paul Sova and the general, none of the facial features of the other ten virtual attendees were in focus.

"Who are you people?"

"We serve on Council's selection committee," one of the men replied, his voice distinctly Australian. "You have been approved for promotion in the science and technology sector."

"There are four sectors, Dr. Marulli," said a man in a white lab coat, his dialect revealing his nationality to be Chinese. "Besides science and technology, there are representatives of the military, business and commerce, and security."

Jessica rubbed her eyes, the blurred faces of the holograms giving her a headache. "I'm a little confused. Who is Council? What do you do?"

The image of Paul Sova smiled. "Essentially, we run the world."

PART 2

"... The stories I have heard from these people, who are more highly qualified than me to talk about UFOs, leave me in no doubt that aliens have already visited Earth. When I learned that aliens really do exist, I wasn't too surprised. But what did shock me when I started investigating extraterrestrial reports a decade ago is the extent to which the proof has been hushed up."

—Astronaut Edgar Mitchell, Ph.D.

Sixth person to walk on the moon.

"Yes, aliens really are out there, says the man on the moon."

—Anonymous

The People [a London Newspaper], October 25, 1998

EVALUATION REPORT—FALL SEMESTER

Michael Andrew Sutterfield
SS #711-19-0878
GVP Unit: PA-762-32443
AGE: 13 years, 1 week
GRADE: 7
SEX: Male

ACADEMICS:
Student has made acceptable progress in mathematics, language arts, history, and the sciences. Student demonstrates an aptitude in quantum physics and expresses a desire for space travel.

SOCIAL SKILLS:
No racial, anti-Semitic, or other human prejudices demonstrated toward GVP instructors during the student's first semester.

NEURO-BEHAVIOR PREDICTORS:
A flat line in neuro-synaptic activity was detected during Phase-III of the Risch-Avery protocol, indicating potential sociopathic tendencies. Series S-1 through S-6 will be added to the curriculum and student retested in twelve weeks.

North Philadelphia, Pennsylvania
October 17, 2032

"Today's lesson is on consciousness. Mr. Sutterfield, are you listening?"
Michael Andrew Sutterfield glanced at his new instructor. He estimated Joseph Williams to be in his early thirties. Half black, half Irish, bald and

heavy-set, Michael found the man and his habit of posing questions he already knew the answers to be quite annoying. He wondered if the system had generated the character just to agitate him.

"You know I'm listening. It's just you and me in this pod."

"What was I speaking about?"

"Consciousness, what else?"

"The topic annoys you?"

"When will I be ready for CE-5 training?"

"An understanding of consciousness is a prerequisite for CE-5 training. Consciousness goes hand-in-hand when communicating with our ET delegates."

Michael sat up. "Okay, teach me."

The interior of the *GVP-5000* transformed into a two-man vessel, Michael's instructor strapped in next to him. One moment they were looking up at a brilliant blue sky, the next they were hurtling into a black velvet tapestry sparkling with a billion stars.

"Sweet!"

"I'm guessing this is your first simulated flight into space?"

"If you know it's my first simulation, why ask?"

"Perhaps I am attempting to *simulate* conversation?"

They continued soaring out into space until the Earth was centered in the forward view screen.

"The universe is not only teeming with a multiplicity of intelligent life both in the physical and spiritual realm, Mr. Sutterfield, but the universe itself is a living, intelligent entity. One of the great fears the religious community had about disclosing the existence of other intelligent non-human species is that it would challenge the established religious dogmas. In fact we've learned that there is a unified singularity that runs through all existence—a pure cosmic consciousness that confirms God is absolutely part of the equation and we are all bound to it and to one another. And yet there is also separation, good and evil, the physical universe and the spiritual.

"To 21st century humans, the existence of non-human species that are far older and far more advanced than us was initially made frightening by the taboos the covert government had assigned to extraterrestrial vehicle sightings. While some of these civilizations may be tens of thousands or hundreds of thousands of years older than ours, there are also those that are millions of years more advanced. These species have evolved to exist outside of the physical realm, their appearances conjuring labels of angels and avatars."

"But why Earth? What made them come here?"

"They were concerned. Among intelligent biologics, there is a natural progression that determines whether a maturing Type-Zero civilization will survive. Energy is the key to equality, and equality is what ultimately transforms a Type-Zero civilization into a Type-1 civilization. It is at this point that the dangers of splitting the atom are replaced by zero-point-energy. Type-2 civilizations terraform other worlds within their solar system while Type-3 civilizations—the highest level attainable for third dimension physical beings—have mastered transdimensional, faster-than-light travel, uniting them with the community of intelligent beings within their galaxy."

Michael nodded. *Screw humans. I want to know what the aliens know ... I want to live how they live.*

"Man had discovered zero-point-energy as far back as the early 1900s, only the technology was purposely stymied. From the 1950s on, a cabal composed of oil oligarchs, bankers, and defense contractors secretly black-shelved all ZPE breakthroughs, as well as all clean energy and anti-gravitic technologies. Greed not only caused billions of people to suffer needlessly, but the forced extension of the fossil fuel age was poisoning our planet."

The view of Earth disappeared, becoming a river reflecting a clear blue sky. Brown-skinned children were playing along a grass-covered shoreline, elder men fishing from a modern pier.

"Do you recognize this city, Mr. Sutterfield?"

"I don't know ... somewhere in India maybe?"

"Correct. This is the Yamuna River in New Delhi ... the way it looks today thanks to a robust economy ushered in by zero-point-energy. Over a hundred state-of-the-art sewage and water treatment plants were opened in the last fifteen years. New clean energy industries have taken root, employing what was once a destitute and dying lower class. Now observe the same scene twenty years ago."

The image changed, the river darkening into brown sludge, its putrid surface specked by islands of garbage. Piles of refuse lined the shore. The pier was gone, replaced by a wrought-iron bridge, its belly bleeding rust into the waterway. Naked children bathed and drank in the shallows while adults unabashedly squatted into the cesspool, emptying their bowels.

"That's disgusting. Don't they have toilets?"

"The toilets are backed up with raw sewage, and there are no sources of clean water. And it wasn't just the Yamuna. Eighty percent of India's human waste ended up in its rivers, which could no longer support life. Dysentery and disease swept through the country, the death toll in the millions. But water pollution was not their only problem. Air pollution, caused by vehicles and coal-fired plants had created dark cloud banks of smog which covered much of India and China, blotting out the sunlight needed to grow crops while altering weather patterns in North America."

The scene changed again, this time to an African village where half-naked dark skinned natives were running in fear from dark-skinned soldiers firing assault rifles. Several women carrying young children were chased into a white stucco church.

The teen found the violence enticing. "Where is this place?"

"At the time, the nation was known as South Sudan. The country remained divided by a civil war between multiple tribes that raged for decades. The men assaulting those women were members of the White Army, a heavily armed Nuer civilian youth brigade. Invading a Dinka village, they would steal their livestock and then rape and mutilate the women, butchering the men and enslaving their children. Unable to farm, the people were systematically starving to death. Things got so bad that two million Africans actually abandoned their homes to live in refugee camps. One of the poorest countries in the world, South Sudan and its people had no future … until a new energy technology was introduced in Africa.

"This is New South Sudan today."

As Michael watched, the image of the burning straw thatched huts faded into a modern rural community of brick and mortar. An agriculture center sat adjacent to miles of corn fields, the crops supplied with water from feeder pipes linked to high-tech industrial wells powered by small hockey-puck-sized devices—the zero-point-energy unit humming with power.

The view changed. Rising silently in the sky, Michael looked down upon a new network of tarmac roads connecting African village to African village. Soaring higher, he passed over a gleaming metropolis before heading west over the Sahara.

What was once tens of thousands of square miles of empty desert had been transformed into farmland communities, the crops, orchards, and grasslands drawing water from man-made reservoirs. Above-ground pipes connected these enormous caches to city-size filtration plants situated along the Atlantic Ocean.

Michael knew about these giant desalination factories; each was powered by a zero-point-energy device no larger than the pod he was now sitting in. The Sahara Project was not only feeding the African and Asian continents with pesticide-free food, but the artificial lakes and reservoirs—each built with retractable roofs—had been strategically placed to disrupt the intense dry summer heat rising over North Africa's desert—the cause of Atlantic Ocean-bound hurricanes. As a result, man could now diffuse one of the deadliest and most costly weather systems on the planet.

With free, clean and abundant energy, anything was possible.

His instructor continued the tour, contrasting the problems of the past with the solutions of the present. They traversed the Persian Gulf where oil refineries and rigs had been replaced by modern neighborhoods; then flew over the California coast where desalination plants similar to the ones used in the Sahara. They ensured the harsh droughts, which had threatened to extend the desert all the way to the Pacific coastline, would never return.

After a few more stops, Michael found himself back in space, staring once more at the Earth.

"We are now observing our planet as it appeared twenty years ago."

"It looks about the same to me."

"The extinction threat cannot be seen by the naked eye."

As Michael watched, a lime-green haze appeared to bloom over North America. "What is that?"

"Methane. It is a greenhouse gas thirty-five times stronger than carbon dioxide. For decades methane had been escaping from underground coal seams and at natural gas rigs. The oceans absorbed much of this methane, along with CO_2 from coal plants and carbon monoxide from cars. Then a new technique known as fracking was introduced.

"Fracking released intolerable levels of methane gas, but because the gas was invisible and the fracking generated vast amounts of wealth, humanity was slow to act. Then, in 2017, the Trump Administration removed virtually every environmental safeguard, and within two years, our planet experienced a runaway greenhouse effect.

"Over three hundred million people died of cancer and respiratory illnesses related to methane poisoning from 2019 through 2021; their deaths kept hidden from the public. Another two billion starved when the planet's ecosystem shut down because of banks of smog clouds which blanketed parts of Earth's atmosphere, cutting off the amount of sunlight needed to grow food.

Only the planet-wide shut down of fossil fuels, coupled with the advent of zero-point-energy and new technologies which eventually reversed greenhouse gases, prevented Earth from ending up like Mars—

—a dead world."

12

Dallas, Texas

THE LATE NIGHT TV HOST sat behind his studio desk, allowing his wife, Claire, to powder the shine on his forehead.

Richard Gatenby was born and raised in Portsmouth, a city in the south of England. He had dropped out of school at sixteen, was married by nineteen, and spent most of his free time playing football (rugby) where his "win or die" persona could be properly directed. When a brutal tackle by two rivals sidelined him with a broken leg and a ruptured thigh muscle, the weekend brawler channeled his gregarious personality into a satirical talk show called "Let's Get Randy with Dickie." Uploaded onto YouTube, the videos quickly went viral where he was discovered by a program director for a local FOX affiliate in Dallas, Texas … and another talk show phenomenon was born.

Gatenby chased his wife back behind the curtain as his producer signaled that they were coming out of commercial. Locating the teleprompter, he waited for his D.J. and co-host, Kyle Knori, to finish playing *Abracadabra* by the Steve Miller Band.

"Thank you, K.K. My next guest is a retired United States Army Colonel who has written a book about aliens … and not the ones we're building a wall to keep out … let's give a big Dickie welcome to Colonel Alexander Johnston!"

The white-haired man in his seventies waved at the studio audience as he strode across the stage to occupy the vacant couch next to the tattooed Brit.

Dickie held up the hard cover book that was lying on his desk. "The

111

book is called, *UFOs and Extraterrestrials: All You Need to Know*. Personally, I need to know a lot. But before we talk about the book, let's get a bit randy, shall we? You've had an interesting career, Colonel. Back in 'Nam, you commanded Special Forces 'A' Teams."

"That's correct."

"Ever kill anyone?"

"Suffice it to say, I've seen my share of death."

"You've not only seen your share of it … I understand you earned a degree in it?"

"Thanatology. It's the study of death and dying and the psychological mechanisms of dealing with them."

"Seems like a strange major. For the final, did you have to go out and kill someone?"

The colonel grimaced through the sustained applause and laughter.

"The subject of thanatology deals with the thoughts and reactions of the dying, something that varies from culture to culture. How an oncologist or priest prepares a terminal patient for death in America is far different than what a shaman in the jungles of Thailand will do. I was most interested in the multitude of reactions of the dying."

"Is that how you earned the nickname, 'Dr. Death?'"

The colonel forced a smile. "That was more of an academic nickname."

"After 'Nam, you returned to the states where you went to work at the Los Alamos National Laboratory. This is a place normally associated with a whole lot of death and destruction, yes?"

"True. Los Alamos is where the U.S. government conducted its top-secret nuclear weapons programs."

"But that's not what you did?"

"No. My focus was on developing non-lethal warfare programs."

"Is that because of all the death you witnessed in Vietnam?"

"I just felt that there were more efficient methods of subduing an enemy than scorching the earth with napalm."

"For instance?"

"Well, let's say your village was being threatened by a hostile air force. Instead of shooting them down, you could direct an electromagnetic pulse that would scramble their controls and have them dropping out of the sky."

The colonel smiled at the applause.

"Speaking of things dropping out of the sky … UFOs. Are they real, or is this all nonsense?"

"Before I answer that, Dickie, let's be clear here—I am not your average Joe. I've spent most of my adult life in the military and as a government liaison. Having spoken to hundreds of pilots and radar personnel, my view on UFOs is that, of the tens of thousands of sightings on record, approximately 5% remain unexplained. Having investigated both the military's and the government's responses to these unexplained sightings, I am convinced there is definitely something to these encounters. However, I can also state unequivocally that there is no government or military cover-up, no conspiracy."

"What about Roswell?"

"As I've detailed in my book, the Roswell crash was nothing more than a top secret military program called *Project Mogul*. It was essentially a weather balloon experiment that a bunch of yokels turned into an episode of *War of the Worlds*. Unfortunately, the American public, God bless 'em, can get a little riled up."

Boos rose from the studio audience.

The colonel responded with a smirk. "Settle down. I didn't say I don't believe in UFOs. I was simply telling you the truth about Roswell."

"Dr. Death, have you ever heard of Steven Greer? We had him on the show two weeks ago talking about his new book, *UNACKNOWLEDGED: An Exposé of the World's Greatest Secret*, and I think he might disagree with you about Roswell."

"Dr. Greer is a charlatan."

More boos.

"Now, hear me out. Greer makes a lot of money taking groups out to the desert and other remote areas to talk to the aliens. It's a bunch of nonsense, and it's one of the reasons I wrote my book—to protect the unsuspecting public from being ripped off."

The host held up his hands, attempting to calm his audience. "Easy now. The man has a right to his opinion, just as you have a right not to buy his book."

The boos changed to applause.

"I don't think they like you, Dr. Death."

The colonel's face flushed pink.

"Colonel, I understand you were part of a group of researchers and scientists who investigated reports of cattle mutilations and other strange alien occurrences. Was that our Mexican aliens sneaking over the border, or were these actual ETs?"

"It's hard to say, Dickie."

"Whoa … fella. This is public TV. You can't say 'Dickie' and 'it's hard' together."

Laughter.

"Hey Al, I just realized … we've got a Dickie and a Johnson sharing the same stage. This interview just turned into a sausage party!"

More laughter, followed by wild applause—prodded by the producer.

"Actually, it's Johnston … Colonel Alexander Johnston."

"Do aliens have penises? You never hear about that, only the anal probes. Wish we could talk more about aliens and alien sex but that's all the time we have for this segment. The book is called, *UFOs and Extraterrestrials: All You Need to Know.* The author, Colonel Death … I mean *Johnson.* We'll be right back with Theresa Ritter and her flock of sheep dogs."

Before the colonel could correct the annoying Brit again, he was cut off by the Steve Miller Band's *Abracadabra.*

"Thanks for being a good sport, Colonel."

The white-haired military man's eyes seemed to burn through the back of Richard Gatenby's skull.

"You will not sleep well tonight."

The vault was located underground, two miles beneath the Dugway Proving Grounds near Provo, Utah. The man who had personally trained the "Army grunts" operating the EMS unit stood just outside the tunnel entrance to the facility, awaiting instructions from his commanding officer.

Scott Muse swallowed the bile rising in his esophagus. He chased it back down with a sip of bottled water, then dug inside the pocket of his lab coat and fished out the roll of antacids. Peeling back the foil, he popped two of the chewable tablets into his mouth, hoping to settle the acid reflux. He had stronger stuff at home—prescription meds. But much like his job, they carried the threat of long-term side-effects.

Seven and a half more months and you can retire … assuming the colonel lets me walk.

What if I got my gastro guy to write up a report saying that I have cancer of the esophagus? He'd have to let me go then.

Or what if it really is cancer and the bastard gave it to me …

Four decades had passed since the engineer had been recruited straight out of the University of Cincinnati by NASA on the recommendation of Wernher von Braun, the German rocket scientist who had practically founded the U.S. space program. The year was 1975 and Muse—then a doctoral candidate—had published his second paper on anti-gravitics. Von Braun recognized a budding genius and set out to recruit him before health issues forced his own retirement. Interviews were conducted, an offer made—and then another recruiter came calling.

Major General Sebastian J. Appleton identified himself as the Director of U.S. Army Intelligence. A project under his command had run into technical challenges and he wanted Scott to join their team. An interview was arranged, the candidate flown first-class into Salt Lake City, where a limousine drove him south to the city of Provo.

A generic tour of the military base led to dinner at Scott's hotel where Appleton made the engineer a lucrative offer. It was far more money than what NASA had on the table, but there were also red flags. Scott and his wife would have to move to Utah, and the project was strictly top-secret—no doubt funded by the Pentagon. In the end, the choice came down to science versus the military, and Muse passed.

But Appleton had one more card to play.

At four in the morning, Scott was awakened in his hotel room by two MPs who loaded him into the backseat of an awaiting car. After being forced at gunpoint to sign a national security oath, he was blindfolded and driven to an unknown destination. Forty minutes later, he found himself standing besides the Major General on a barren plateau beneath a pre-dawn gray sky.

Towering before them, floating ten feet off the ground was a flying saucer.

"This is what we call an ARV, an Alien Reproduction Vehicle. We built it by reverse-engineering the extraterrestrial crafts that were downed over the last three decades by our scalar weapon system. Although the ARV is not nearly as advanced as the real thing, it's fully capable of accessing any star system in the Milky Way. As you can see, it uses anti-gravitics, similar to what you wrote about.

"Join us, and you'll find yourself working on cutting-edge technologies you never dreamed of."

"And if I don't?"

"Then you're free to go. Of course, if you ever discuss any of this we'll bring you back and let you pick out a burial plot."

Forty years …

Appleton was not exaggerating, the projects involving ET technologies were so far above the latest developments in physics they essentially reduced his degrees to toilet paper. But while the work was exhilarating, MJ-12's autocratic rules and the paranoia their military force instilled on a daily basis took its toll on his nerves.

And why couldn't they share these incredible technologies with the rest of the world? Zero-point-energy alone could eliminate hunger and poverty, not to mention the benefits to the environment that would come from replacing fossil fuels.

Dr. Muse knew he wasn't the only one who felt this way. As the years passed, he grew bolder, openly discussing the matter with colleagues as he attempted to push the envelope of tolerance.

Appleton responded by transferring him into another USAP—a covert intelligence program overseen by the man known and feared within the subterranean communities as "Dr. Death."

Colonel Alexander Johnston had developed a psychotronic device which used scalar waves to alter a subject's consciousness, behavior, and decisions. Add some stage craft, and suddenly the "evil aliens" were abducting good-hearted, blue-collared suburban folk whose stories held up to lie-detector tests.

Set high enough, a scalar wave could literally separate the spark of consciousness that was the soul from the physical body, killing the subject.

It was the ultimate mind-control device, free of any congressional oversight, and as Scott Muse soon learned, the subjects were not always random civilians.

The engineer's first VIP was the brother of a Crown Prince whose family ran a powerful banking empire in Europe. Coordinates to the man's sleep chamber inside his castle were provided by members of a covert paramilitary group operating in conjunction with the CIA.

Using a reverse-engineered Alien Reproduction Vehicle and man-made extraterrestrials cloned in a lab, the brother of Prince Hans-Adams of Liechtenstein awoke in bed, only to find his body paralyzed as it was atomized and whisked on board a flying saucer. For the next several hours, four-foot gray-skinned extraterrestrials probed and prodded the terrified human, all the while communicating through mental telepathy that aliens were responsible for every conflict on Earth since man first fell from the trees.

Their final message before he was released dealt with a plan to enslave humankind.

Scott Muse later learned why the man had been targeted. An ally of Dr. Steven Greer, the prince was contemplating funding his project for disclosure. Following his brother's abduction, the Prince changed his mind, donating a large amount of money instead to fund a black budget weapons program designed to thwart an alien invasion.

Scott Muse answered his iPhone on the first ring. "Yes, Colonel?"

"Has the subject's coordinates been obtained?"

"Yes, sir."

"Then let's put the fear of the Almighty in him."

Muse entered the vault where two of his crew were seated at their electronic surveillance stations. "Is he asleep?"

"Yes, sir."

"Take him."

Having locked onto the subject using his iPhone, the EMS operator powered up the scalar device.

Richard "Dickie" Gatenby awoke to discover his voice box was frozen, his body completely paralyzed. To his utter horror, he was no longer in his bedroom—instead, he was lying naked on a cold metal table, staring up at strange floating colored lights.

He choked on his breath—his airway constricting as the extraterrestrial leaned over him, revealing bulging lidless black eyes, its skin gray and hairless. Using a probe, the four-foot biped pried open his mouth and set to work on his upper gum line.

The throttle of noise coming out of Gatenby's throat was more of a high-pitched grunt than a scream—he had not felt the sharp stab, only a slight pressure and the momentary sensation of warm blood drizzling down his chin.

A second Grey appeared, its four-digit hand cold and clammy as it probed Gatenby's lifeless right arm. A pinch was followed by the sensation of more blood being drawn.

The talk show host passed out.

He awoke to feel himself floating. A wave of pins and needles passed through him and suddenly he was outside, staring at a cloudy night sky until his atomized body passed through his home's second story window, his astral mind returning to his physical body with an electrical *zap*!

"Ahh! Ahhh!"

"Dickie? Dickie, wake up!"

He felt Claire's hands on his shoulders, her grip shaking the paralysis from his body. Sitting up, he rolled out of bed and staggered to the window, his fingers separating the slats of the Venetian blinds so he could see outside.

Gone …

"Dickie, what is it?"

Staggering into the bathroom, he fumbled with the light switch as he examined his upper gums in the mirror.

Nothing there … wait!

Feeling a tender spot with his tongue, he pulled back his upper lip—

—revealing a white mouth sore.

"Dickie, are you all right? You look as pale as a ghost. And you're trembling."

"That bloody colonel … he did something."

"It was just a bad dream."

"No, Claire … this was real!"

"What was real?"

The English talk show host contemplated a response. He knew what he had experienced was real; he also realized how it would sound to his wife.

You'll lose her. She'll insist on having me see a psychiatrist and when I stick to my story and insist I'm right, she'll assume I took too many shots to the head playing rugby and she'll leave me … right after she has me committed.

"Sorry, Claire. What I meant was it seemed real. Just a bad dream …"

"Come back to bed."

Bed? Hell, no … I'll not be sleeping anytime soon.

"You go on, hon. I'm just going to fix a cup of tea."

Scott Muse gazed at the subject's vital signs coming across the EMS monitors in real time. Fear, anxiety, confusion, depression—he had seen it all before. And yet the engineer knew that the target had gotten off lucky.

Colonel Johnston was not a man you'd want to provoke. Wearing the calm mask of a sociopath, it was the thanatologist's presence among MAJI's Council that kept the more progressive members in check.

Yet even they had stood up to Dr. Death a decade ago when he had used the EMS weapon to remotely deliver malignant cancer cells via scalar waves to a congressman and two civilians who had become a thorn in MJ-12's side.

Two had died—the politician and a woman. The lone survivor was the man who had been responsible for briefing high-ranking members of the Pentagon about UFOs and the ET's technology—

—Dr. Steven M. Greer.

Washington Plaza Hotel
Washington, D.C.
August 3, 2017

ADAM SHARIAK HANDED his ticket to security. Placing his coffee on the desk, he held up his arms to allow a second guard to pass a hand-held metal detector over his body, the device squealing as it moved over his left pant leg.

"It's a prosthesis."

"I'll have to pat you down."

"Knock yourself out."

Adam waited while the man ran his palms up and down his pant leg and stump, a chore he was forced to endure whenever he entered a Federal building or made his way through airport security.

"Thank you, sir. Enjoy the presentation."

He limped inside Ballroom-C, surprised at the size of the crowd. Twelve hundred folding chairs faced the small stage and lectern and almost every spot was occupied. He managed to locate a vacant seat in the middle of the tenth row but had to squeeze his way past an obstacle course of unyielding feet and purses in order to reach it.

Settling in, he noticed a familiar face working security. *Tech Sergeant Hershel Eugene Evans, United States Air Force ... Been a while, amigo.*

Adam turned back to the stage as a tall, muscular Caucasian man in his late fifties strode toward the podium to enthusiastic applause.

"Good morning. My name is Dr. Steven M. Greer and I am the founder of the *Disclosure Project* and CSETI, the Center for the Study of Extra-terrestrial Intelligence, as well as the Orion Project. I would like to welcome all of you to this presentation on the secret government and the UFO cover-up. You're going to learn things that have been kept from every sitting U.S. president since John F. Kennedy, representatives in congress, heads of state, and members of the Joint Chiefs. I know this, because in many cases, I was the one who briefed them.

"What I speak of now will sound like *Conspiracy Theory 101*, and yet it is absolutely true, and we have thousands of classified documents and hundreds of eyewitnesses with top security clearances to prove it. Whether you accept anything I say this morning is up to you, but what I say now is absolutely true: There are two U.S. governments … the government of *We The People* represented by our elected officials, and a shadow government made up of mid-level functionaries whose roots trace back to a black budget organization launched in 1956 by President Dwight D. Eisenhower. This group, which was known back then as Majestic-12, was tasked with overseeing and keeping from the public the most astounding discovery in the history of the world—the existence of extraterrestrial life. It is this secret regime which covertly runs the USAPs—the Unacknowledged Special Access Projects—which are presently being funded to the tune of $80 billion a year in taxpayer money, without the knowledge of the American people, nor the oversight of congress or the president. When it comes to these two governments, the right hand does not know what the left hand is doing, and in many cases, they don't want to know. Innocent people have been murdered, including members of my team, close friends, military personnel, intelligence directors, and scientists. They were not murdered because they witnessed UFOs—millions of people share these close encounters. They were killed because they were perceived as a threat to bring out advanced energy technologies that would change the lives of the seven billion people living on this planet."

Adam felt the blood rush from his face.

"How did this all come about? Let's get that out of the way first since it is the easiest part to explain. UFOs are *real;* they are of extraterrestrial origin and they have been around for decades, if not centuries."

All eyes looked up as a large overhead screen came to life. The first video footage was taken using a night telescope, the heavens appearing emerald green. Moving rapidly within a visual sphere across a brilliant tapestry of stars was a triangular object, its underside appearing as three points of light.

The scene changed to a day shot. What began as an iPhone selfie on a crowded street in London, turned to the skies high above the city where several white saucer-shaped objects darted in and out of the clouds at incredible speeds, only to come to a complete stop before taking off again.

The next video was filmed by a passenger from their window seat inside a South Korean commercial jet. Several thousand feet below the aircraft, a white disk-shaped object suddenly darted above a cityscape, moving incredibly fast. This was followed by a dusk shot taken in Mexico City of two circular craft soaring majestically overhead.

The next scene was a night shot overlooking the city of Jerusalem. Hovering above the Dome of the Rock was a dazzling, spinning drone-like speck of light. It remained steady for a good thirty seconds before suddenly launching straight up and disappearing into the heavens in a split second.

The final footage was taken of the moon using a high-powered telescope. Leaping off the lunar surface, like sparks from a flame, were dozens of white specks—fast-moving craft scattering into space.

Greer continued, "Watching these videos, the mind still struggles to accept that any of this is real, and yet instinctively, we know that it is. The conflict is that, all our lives, we've been told by the government and the official 'gatekeepers of the truth' that UFOs aren't real, and that anyone who believes in ETs is crazy. In a sense, the UFO provides its own best cover; for to believe in it and discuss a sighting is to welcome ridicule.

"To be honest, my own first reaction to what you just saw and are about to hear was, 'Yeah, right.' Understand, I am not a NASA scientist nor a member of any covert organization. I am an emergency room physician and the former chairman of the Department of Emergency Medicine at Caldwell Memorial Hospital. But then confirmation after confirmation, and independent corroboration after independent corroboration, convinced me the information I was being made privy to was real, and by then I was saying, 'Oh God ...'

"The information I am about to reveal comes from private meetings and long discussions I have had with very senior and relevant military, intelligence, political, and private corporate sources. The search for truth regarding these secret projects has brought me to heads of state, royalty, CIA officials, NSA operatives, U.S. and foreign military leaders, politicians, and high-tech corporate contractors.

"The process began in earnest in July of 1993 when a small group of military and civilian personnel involved with the UFO matter met, at my request, to discuss how my group could best liaison with the government. In the previous year, CSETI had facilitated two near-landing events of ET spacecraft in England and Mexico and we wanted to be sure, given these incredible developments, that we could proceed with our mission with a measure of safety for both our team and for the extraterrestrial visitors, whom we regarded as our guests. We wanted a senior point of contact within the chain of command who knew what we were doing. We wanted to be clear that our actions should be regarded as a citizen's diplomacy effort—that a stand-down order was in place that protected us from any military intervention in the U.S. or abroad.

"Over the next several months that followed, members of our team participated in discussions and briefings with government, military, intelligence, political, international and private leaders from around the world. What we learned seemed surreal, unimaginable and bizarre. Beginning as early as World War II, officials in the U.S. government knew we were not alone, that there were advanced machines flying around in certain regions of the European conflict which neither belonged to the Allies nor to the Germans. Referred to as 'foo-fighters,' these vehicles, whether solid or harbored in an energy field which enabled them to pass through solid objects, were clearly extraterrestrial in nature.

"It quickly became apparent from the many sightings of UFOs at our nuclear installations, that our Interstellar visitors were quite concerned with the testing of atomic weapons used on Nagasaki and Hiroshima, as well as the development and testing of the far more lethal hydrogen bomb that followed World War II. The downing and retrieval of ET spacecraft in 1947 in the Roswell, New Mexico vicinity, and in 1948 in Kingman, Arizona forced the Oval Office and military into action.

"How did these interstellar propulsion systems work? Were there weapons on board? In the wake of World War II and the burgeoning Cold War, there was a real concern about falling behind the Soviets. What if these new technologies were leaked out? To say we were facing a quantum leap in technological capability is an understatement, and of course, we wanted it for ourselves. National security demanded that this entire matter be kept quiet at all costs. And no cost was spared in doing so.

"But there was one very large and busy fly in this ointment: The ETs were flying over the skies of America, sometimes in formation, and before thousands of witnesses. How do you hide that?

"The answer is—the mind hides it. In an Orwellian twist, it was found from past psychological warfare efforts that if you told a lie often enough, and the lie is repeated by 'respected' figures in authority, the public will accept it as fact. One of the masters of psychological warfare during World War II was put in charge of this diversionary tactic in the late 1940s. General Walter Bedell Smith helped coordinate the psychological warfare components of this ET problem and helped launch the big lie: UFOs, even though millions had reported seeing them, did not exist.

"For every sighting which made its way into the public eye, there would be an official denial, and worse, public ridicule of the observers themselves. Harvard Astronomer Donald Menzel was trotted out to tell the world that it was all hysteria; that UFOs were not real; that it was all embarrassing nonsense. The CIA upped the ante by staging alien abductions, relegating future ET or UFO encounters to shlock newspapers, leading any respectable journalist and scientist to avoid the subject like the plague.

"In the mid-1950s, a new model for covert projects evolved. By then, the entire UFO matter had been largely privatized and ran ten levels deep in the black ops community. It was also operating outside the constitutional chain of command of the United States or any other government. First hand witnesses have told us that President Eisenhower was furious. This was a former five-star general who had seen the ET spacecraft and bodies for himself, and yet suddenly, he was being kept out of the loop? Is it any wonder that this conservative Republican president made it a point to warn the American public about the 'military industrial complex' in his last address to the nation? Clearly, President Eisenhower realized he had lost control of his Frankenstein's monster.

"Fast forward to June of 1963: President Kennedy is flying to Berlin to deliver his famous speech proclaiming 'I am a Berliner.' On board Air Force One is a military man who relates the following: *On the long flight to Germany, Kennedy began discussing the UFO matter with me. He admitted that he knew the UFOs were real—he had seen the evidence—but stated the whole matter was out of his hands and he didn't know why. Kennedy said that he wanted the truth to come out, but that he couldn't do it. And this was the President of the United States, the Commander in Chief of the armed forces!'*

"But there was someone who JFK had been sharing this information with who did want to talk … and it got her killed."

Greer placed a document onto the overhead projector. Dated 3 August 1962, the wire-tap report was typed on CIA letterhead and stamped TOP-SECRET. Worn with age, certain sections were difficult to read, but the subject's identity was quite clear: Marilyn Monroe.

"This document, which has been authenticated by experts, describes how Marilyn Monroe—who had been recently jilted by the Kennedy brothers—was upset and hurt, and called Robert Kennedy and a socialite in New York—an art dealer friend of hers. According to this transcript, Ms. Monroe states her intention to set up a press conference and inform the public about what Jack Kennedy had told her regarding objects from outer space that had crashed and been retrieved in New Mexico in the 1940s. President Kennedy had apparently confided to her during pillow talk that he had seen the ET craft and debris from the UFO crash. This still top-secret document is dated the day before the night they found Marilyn Monroe dead. Since being presented with this document, I've located someone who was with the Los Angeles Police Department intelligence unit who helped facilitate the wiretapping and monitoring of Miss Monroe up to the time of her death, and actually knew how they killed her. There is no doubt that she was murdered by agents of the United States intelligence community, her death made to look like an overdose. As you can see, this document was signed by James Jesus Angleton III, the legendary fanatical mole hunter and leak stopper within the CIA. This document, in my opinion, was a death warrant for Marilyn Monroe because it summarized what she was intending to do rather imminently. I don't think she knew what she had stumbled onto, in terms of the kind of blowback her intentions were going to generate. When I showed this document to the actor, Burl Ives, a friend of the late actress, he said, 'Marilyn Monroe and I knew each other very well and I can tell you this: All of us who knew her were sure she had been murdered, but it wasn't until seeing this document that I knew why.'

"Some of the people that Burl knew were good friends with Ronald Reagan. He was able to confirm an exchange that I had heard from other sources that had been with the president during the screening of *Close Encounters of the Third Kind*. This movie was more of a docudrama than sci-fi. The storyline was inspired by secret Air Force files Steven Spielberg managed to gain access to while visiting Wright-Patterson Air Force Base. Ronald Reagan turned to the people who were at the White House screening and said, *'There are only a couple people in this room who know how true this movie really is.'*

"The Center for the Study of Extraterrestrial Intelligence has been engaging in what we call CE-5 or Close Encounters initiated by humans. In order to communicate with species that may be thousands to millions of years more advanced than ours required us to think outside the box. There is no question that extraterrestrial life forms have found their way to our planet, the question is ... how does a biological travel across vast interstellar distances within the specie's natural life time? Further, how does one communicate with their home world across such vast distances of space?

"Let's begin by examining the challenges of interstellar travel just within our own galaxy. The Milky Way is approximately 100,000 to 180,000 light years in diameter—a light year being the distance a beam of light will travel in one year at a speed of 186,000 miles per second. If an extraterrestrial life form comes from a star system say, a thousand light years away—a distance considered within our own galactic neighborhood—then it would take one thousand years for the life form just to get to Earth traveling at light speed and another thousand years to get home again. That's two thousand years.

While these travelers could technically be cryogenically put to sleep for the trip, everyone they knew on their home world would have long since died, rendering this method of travel unlikely. Further, using the methods of communication available to humans—radio, microwaves, TV or any other electromagnetic signal—it would again take a thousand years for a transmission traveling at the speed of light to communicate with an ET's home world once they arrived on Earth, and another thousand years for the ET's planet to answer back. In either case, it's safe to assume that any star-faring civilization must have developed technologies that allow them to skirt beyond the boundaries of linear space-time—a term we refer to as interdimensional or multidimensional shifting. That we have yet to discover the means to detect these other-worldly dimensions does not mean they do not exist. Gamma rays have always existed; yet it took a scientific breakthrough to discover them.

"What lies beyond the crossing point of light? What does one experience when you exceed the speed of light? What exists beyond this third dimensional barrier?

"It may surprise you to learn that humans are quite capable of accessing these higher plains of existence. As a teen, I studied Sanskrit and read the Vedas, the ancient sacred literature of India. I learned about meditation and the concept of transcendence, which fit quite comfortably into my psyche. When I could find free time, I'd take long bike trips out into the countryside. Seeking a connection with nature, I'd lie in a field and practice meditation. At times I'd find my consciousness leaving my body to observe other parts of Charlotte, or to visit other areas of the world. During several out-of-body experiences, I even ventured into space."

Adam choked on a laugh, following it up with a cough.

"When I was seventeen I injured my left thigh. A horrible infection developed in my leg and spread throughout my body. I became septic, which means my bloodstream was infected, and I broke out in a very high fever. I was spiraling toward death, not fully understanding the severity of my condition. It brought me to a near-death experience where I found myself suddenly released from my body. I was carried out into the depths of space—a place where I already felt at home. Then I experienced what I now understand to be God consciousness, where my individuality became faint as it merged with the unbounded pure infinite Mind ... there was no duality. This lasted for what seemed to be an eternity because a normal sense of time disappears in that state of being. I could see all of creation, the vastness of the cosmos, and it was beautiful beyond words. From our limited third-dimensional perspective I had died, and yet there was nothing frightening about it—only infinite awareness, joy, and the perception of an endless perfect creation.

"Eventually, two brilliant and scintillating lights approached out of the stars. I now understand them to have been Avatars—manifestations of God. They appeared as brilliant points of light ... pure, conscious energy. As the Avatars came near, I entered a state of oneness with them. It was incredibly beautiful. Communication existed, only non-verbally. Imagine instead of saying the word 'apple,' the actual image of the apple is received. And within *that* conscious image is the pure idea form of the apple itself—its essence. That is how information was being transmitted to me, and I am convinced it is how ET civilizations communicate instantaneously over great distances.

"I have no sense of how long this union lasted. I was affected by the beauty of it all, yet felt very overwhelmed at the same time. Eventually the episode moved into more of a linear style of communication. One of the Avatars said, *'You may come with us or return to Earth.'* I had the presence of mind to ask, *'Well, what is your will?'* And the being replied, *'It is our desire that you go back to Earth to do other things.'* I became depressed, having no interest at that point in coming back to the physical world. But I somehow knew the highest response of human will is acceptance of the Divine will, and I agreed to return. I lost consciousness and fell back into my body with a sort of *whoosh*.

"I was back in my body, but I must have been out long enough to lose conscious connection with all of my neural centers. My sensory input was working; I remember seeing the maple tree outside the little apartment, its branches moving in the wind against a street light. But I couldn't move. I thought I had been so damaged from this severe infection that I'd been paralyzed from a stroke. Fortunately, that turned out to be a temporary phenomenon; we now know that in the case of prolonged near-death experiences, it takes time for the person to be reconnected to their physical body.

"Then I felt a being in the room with me; it was sent there to test my will to live. It was a frightening but perhaps a necessary, experience which forced me to use my willpower to remain here. This force was trying to pull my soul back out of my body. I had to exercise volition to remain in the physical and keep my astral body of light and my consciousness integrated with it. And after about half a dozen tries, I nailed it and remained here. It was only then that I regained full use of my motor skills.

"This near-death experience not only altered my life, it prepared me for the challenges still to come. I now know from direct experience that God does exist, as do His messengers. I learned that death is not to be feared, that in fact, there is no death—only an inter-dimensional transformation from one state into another ... a state that is accessible to our extraterrestrial visitors.

"This was confirmed to me many years later by a gentleman who had worked in the Air Force and also with Kelly Johnson at Lockheed Skunkworks. His excuse for contacting me was to offer to be one of the CSETI military witnesses to UFO events, but what he really wanted was to get my feedback on an experience which he'd had in the mid-1960s. At that time he was studying a tradition which helped people to experience out-of-body or astral projections. One day his teacher told him that he was ready to have such an experience fairly soon, and in fact that evening, he indeed had his first OBE. But what happened shocked him. As soon as he left his physical body, he shot straight up through the ceiling and out of his house into space—only to slam into the side of an extraterrestrial spacecraft hovering over Earth in a higher dimension. His spirit literally rocked the spacecraft and he popped inside the vessel whereupon he saw some ETs at a console. He said, 'Steven, they looked over, saw me, and their expression seemed to say, *'My God, man, why don't you watch where you are going?'*"

Dr. Greer paused as members of the audience laughed and applauded.

"I have no doubt that this man was telling me the absolute truth about what he experienced—that the form of energy of his astral projection or lucid dream matched that of an extraterrestrial craft hovering in interdimensional space. This makes perfect sense, for it is within this state of consciousness that human to ET communication takes place.

"I have taught members of our team how to remote view our location to any passing ETs, and we use this technique to vector them to our location. We also use musical tones and high-powered lasers. With these tools and techniques, we have succeeded in initiating contact with extraterrestrials that are biological beings which rely on spacecraft, as well as advanced species that are non-physical yet sentient and perfectly capable of communicating with humans.

"These ET civilizations are all capable of interstellar travel and they operate on the other side of the light/matter barrier as easily as we use radio signals and fly on jets. They communicate instantaneously using thought energy. This is their reality; their cell phone and automobile. This is their existence technologically, theoretically and everyday practicality. But it looks like magic to us.

"I'm sure it looked like magic to those scientists who were assigned to reverse-engineer those downed spacecraft, but within ten years, they had learned enough to reverse gravitational fields and access zero-point-energy. And there's the rub … there's the crime against humanity. Because we've had the means to eliminate poverty, pollution, climate change and disease for six decades, and yet those few individuals running the secret government have chosen to deny the rest of the world. And that's why I'm here with you today—not to convince you that UFOs exist, but to mount a campaign among the uninformed masses that forces the secret government to turn over the technologies that can change our world."

Adam followed the exiting crowd out of Ballroom-C. He found the security guard he was seeking standing by an unmarked door.

"Tech Sergeant Evans?"

The North Carolina native's dour expression broke into a smile. "Captain Shariak?"

"In the flesh … and titanium. How are you, Gene?"

"Good … you know. Did my two tours, then spent five years at Andrews securing communications for VIP aircraft."

"How long have you been working private security?"

"About six months. Not much money, but it has its perks. I did a Taylor Swift concert a few weeks ago; that was cool. God, it's good to see you. The last time I saw you …"

"Was the day before my chopper went down."

"Yeah. So, what have you been up to?"

Shariak fished out a business card from his wallet and handed it to Evans. "My new job."

"Under Secretary of Defense? Damn … Hey, if you hear of any openings, I'm available."

"I'll keep that in mind. Dr. Greer is really something."

"He's definitely out there."

"Think you can score me some private face time? I had a few questions for him that I'd prefer to ask him alone."

"Wait here." Eugene Evans knocked twice on the door and entered.

He returned three minutes later. "Sorry, Captain. Dr. Greer's really busy. He said he'd try to reach out to you later in the week."

"Thanks. Listen, it was good seeing you … you look great. And good luck with the new job."

"Thanks, Captain. You take care."

Adam followed the exit signs down the carpeted corridor, unaware another pair of eyes were watching him as he passed by.

14

Edwards Air Force Base—Subterranean Complex
Mojave Desert, California
August 2017

THE GEOLOGY OF THE TUNNEL glistened like polished obsidian—an effect caused by the nuclear powered boring machine which had been used to scorch through the earth more than fifty years earlier, just as Matthew DeVictor had described to her two years before.

Jessica Marulli felt the MP's eyes on her as she ran her palm across the smooth surface. Her suitcases had been brought out to the underground station, the subterranean train set to arrive any minute to whisk her to another location where she would spend the next six to eight weeks—

—unless Council had voted against her bump in clearance and she was to be killed.

Too nervous to sit on the bench, she focused on the glass-like geology, her trembling fingers a result of overwrought nerves and extreme fatigue. She had not slept in two days—the last thirty-seven hours courtesy of Council's security measures.

Dr. Elizabeth Hull had introduced herself as a psychiatrist. Fit and in her early forties, the native of Mickleover, a suburb of Derby, England, talked endlessly during her four shifts with Jessica while the two of them were locked up together in an eight-by-ten-foot concrete cell, brightly lit by fluorescent lights.

"We find sleep deprivation to be a far more effective tool to determine a candidate's potential security risk than, say, water-boarding. I'm not saying we'd ever water-board a member of our team—we'd never harm anyone ... unless, of course, their actions warranted it."

There was only one chair in the room and it was always occupied by one of her two keepers, the other being a bearded Ivy Leaguer named Jack Stack, who gazed at her with predatory eyes but refused to say a word. The "Odd Couple" rotated places on random shifts, adding to Jessica's disorientation.

Jessica bounced her back against the cell wall, using the pain to keep herself awake and to block out the woman's grating voice.

"I've had many a candidate refer to me as Lizzie Borden. Have you ever heard of Lizzie Borden, Dr. Marulli?"

"She was an axe murderer who killed her parents."

"That she was. Let's see ... how did that poem go?"

Jessica chanted as she bounced. *"Lizzie Borden ... took an axe ... and gave her mother forty whacks. When she saw ... what she had done ... she gave her father forty-one."*

The Englishwoman nodded, making notes. *Subject's cognitive skills are still functioning after 28 hours without sleep ... a tough egg to crack.* *"Did you know the rhyme was all wrong? It was created by a reporter in order to sell newspapers. Lizzie actually gave her stepmom eighteen whacks and her father eleven."*

"Who gives a shit about Lizzie Borden?"

"I imagine her father and stepmom when she came at them swinging that axe. Did you know she was acquitted? There's a lesson here—no dear, don't shut your eyes. If you lean against the wall and shut your eyes, Jack Stack will return with an electrical collar and you don't want that. We have a rhyme about Mr. Stack ... would you like to hear it?"

"No."

"Jack Stack will take no flack when his subjects want to lean. Close your eyes and your neck will fry because he is so mean."

"How much longer?"

"We agreed any inquiries about the time would add an additional fifteen minutes. You now owe us forty-five more minutes. Now what was I saying?"

Jessica struck the wall harder.

"Cooperate and I can subtract time as well. Dr. Marulli? Hello?"

"Lizzie Borden ... some kind of lesson."

"Right. What I was going to say is that it doesn't really matter if it took Lizzie one whack with the axe or forty-one. What's important here is that something caused her to snap and kill her parents. You'd never kill your parents, would you Jessica?"

"No."

"And yet, that's exactly what you'd be doing if you disclosed the things you've seen and are about to see. That act would initiate a TWEP. Do you know what a TWEP order is?"

"I'm hungry."

"Terminate With Extreme Prejudice. You'd be killed, but since your mum has Cosmic Clearance, she'll know why you were killed and blame some of the members of Council. Which means they'd have to kill her too, as a preventive measure ... yer dad as well. It's not fair I know, but you can see Council's logic. The oath your parents took long ago would take a back seat to seeking revenge for their daughter's death, forcing—"

She had gone after the woman, exhaustion and rage pushing her over the edge—which she later realized had been the purpose of the exercise.

Before she could wrap her fingers around Elizabeth Hull's slender throat, the electrical circuits woven into her jumpsuit engaged, unleashing a ten second, 40,000 volt burst.

When Jessica opened her eyes, she was stretched out on the floor.

Elizabeth Hull leaned over her. *"Council needs your help, Dr. Marulli, but there remains a few members among those in the inner circle who are a bit paranoid about allowing you access. It's not just the threat of dealing with your mother; there's also your fiancé."*

"I've never said a word about my work to Adam."

"True. But now you're engaged to be married."

"You don't need to worry about me anymore ... I quit."

"That option no longer exists. Anyway, in a few days your new clearance will give you access to hidden knowledge reserved only for a privileged few, and I promise, you'll be over the moon. Not to mention a salary that more than compensates for respecting our code of silence."

"Money doesn't compensate me for this torture."

"Oh please, don't be so dramatic. So we kept you awake for awhile and hit you with the equivalent of a taser. Navy SEAL candidates endure far more for far less. Consider

this a valuable conditioning exercise ... an ounce of protection that ensures a pound of loyalty—and with it, your family's safety."

She heard no telltale rumble. One moment the tracks were clear, the next the Maglev train had simply appeared, the windowless seventy-foot steel bullet's chassis riding above the tracks on a magnetic cushion.

A side panel slid open. Jessica entered a plush cabin lined with rows of reclining bucket seats. The MP set her bags inside and left—she was the only person on board.

A message flashed on a wrap-around LED screen:

PLEASE TAKE A SEAT AND BUCKLE UP.

She sat down in the nearest seat and snapped the belt in place—

—the Maglev pulling two Gs as it accelerated effortlessly on a velvet cloud, its lone human passenger slipping into unconsciousness.

"Jess? Jessica, wake up dear."

She opened her eyes. The Maglev had stopped, its side panel open. Disoriented, she was not sure if she had slept ten minutes or ten hours.

The dark-haired, blue-eyed woman seated next to her was in her mid-fifties, her face very familiar.

"I know you."

"Actually, your mom knows me. Lydia Gagnon. I was one of Council's inner circle of twelve who interviewed you."

"Where am I?"

"Let's call it Oz."

"I suppose that makes me Dorothy. Are you Glynda, the good witch?"

"I like that ... Glynda."

"Are there any wicked witches down here I should know about?"

"Just one. And she's married to the Colonel. We'll discuss him later."

"Seriously, Lydia, where am I?"

"Jess, you've been granted Cosmic Clearance, but it's conditional."

"In other words, I'll be working in an underground complex for the next six weeks with no concept of where I am."

"It's not so bad. Up until now you've lived in a black and white world. I'm here to show you the colors of the universe."

ADAM FOLLOWED INTERSTATE 64 west through Virginia, the rolling hills of the Blue Ridge Mountains accompanying him as he made his way through Rockfish Gap. Rising along the steep elevation, he was greeted by a breathtaking view which enticed cars to pull over (illegally) along the shoulder of the road to snap photos with their iPhones.

A road sign at the highway's crest confirmed he was heading in the right direction: **Charlottesville–12 miles**.

He had received the message on his cell phone during his Friday morning staff meeting. The call was from Steven Greer.

"Mr. Under Secretary, my bodyguard tells me you'd like a private get together. I can meet you at three p.m. on Friday; after that I'm busy for the next few months."

Adam already had plans; Randy had seats behind home plate for the night's Nationals vs. Giants game. For nearly an hour, he debated the pros and cons of meeting with Greer before cancelling with his brother.

Adam exited the highway in Charlottesville. He got lost twice on country backroads before locating the entrance to the Greer's sixty-five acre farm. After being buzzed in at the gate, he followed a gravel road up to the two-story, five-bedroom house.

He was greeted at the front door by the warm smile of a gray-haired woman in her early sixties. "Hi, I'm Adam Shariak. I'm here to see Dr. Greer."

"I'm Emily, Steve's wife. Come in. I'm so glad you made it in before the fog; the driving can be treacherous. Steve's in his study, getting everything ready for our group. Fortunately, most of them arrived at the hotel earlier this afternoon. Do you think you'll be joining us?"

Before he could answer, Dr. Greer emerged from the study, extending his hand. "Mr. Under Secretary, thanks for driving all the way out here on short notice. Why don't we talk in my study. Em, can you get me at five? I need to meditate before our guests arrive."

Adam followed him into the twenty-by-thirty-foot room—part library, part office. Furnishings had been moved to the periphery to accommodate fifteen folding chairs which were set up in a circle around a Persian rug, the leather high-backed office chair reserved for Dr. Greer.

"Are you comfortable in that folding chair, Mr. Under Secretary?"

"Fine."

"So then, what can I do for you?"

"I'm not sure exactly. To be honest, I feel a little bit like one of King Arthur's knights, sent on an impossible quest to find the Holy Grail."

"The Holy Grail being …?"

"A zero-point-energy device."

"Interesting. And who put you on this quest?"

"Bill Clinton."

Dr. Greer threw his head back and laughed. "I'm sorry, but there's a delicious irony to all this."

Adam told Dr. Greer about the changing of the suite door numbers and the invisible ink and flashcards.

"Clinton really did that? With his access, you'd think he'd have used something from this century."

"The guy seemed pretty determined to deliver the message."

"The guy was president for eight years. If he really wanted to deliver the disclosure message to the masses, all he had to do was go off-script during a live State of the Union address, and the genie would have been out of its bottle. Like I said during my talk, presidents have become place holders. The real power is held by a secret cabal made up of high-ranking members of the Federal Reserve, four private banking cartels—who also happen to own four of the largest oil companies in the world—and defense contractors."

"Technically, that includes me … at least it did. I was managing director at Kemp Aerospace before they nominated me to be Under Secretary."

"No offense, but you're a peon. We're talking about guys like Dick Cheney—there's your poster boy for the secret government; lots of blood on his hands. These guys don't care, Shariak ... they don't care because they don't *feel*. Caring about other living creatures is not in their algorithm; they're immune to emotion. You think these ghouls want clean, free energy? They're all about war and population control; they don't give a damn about anyone but themselves."

"In your talk a few days ago ... you said you briefed Clinton."

"I said I prepared his briefing. Laurance Rockefeller delivered it. Laurance supported our efforts, but like Clinton, he felt it was too dangerous for him to personally pursue disclosure."

"Be honest; am I wasting my time?"

"Probably. Don't feel bad; it's a question I've asked myself a million times."

"How do you even know these zero-point-energy devices are real? What if it's all—"

"They're real. I have a close friend who is the third highest ranking official at the Naval Research Lab; he told me he's been inside the NRL's secret vault and saw papers dated October 1954 that confirmed and referenced mastering gravity control through a bubble in space time generated by zero-point-energy We also have government and military witnesses who have testified about the existence of Alien Reproduction Vehicles which incorporate both anti-gravity and zero-point-energy technologies. Hundreds, if not thousands, of witnesses have seen them accelerating at thousands of miles an hour, only to stop on a dime and reverse directions. Then you have the occasional scientist who doesn't need the reverse-engineering instruction manual; he's made a breakthrough on his own. He knows if he tries for a patent, the Federal Government will confiscate his work. So he attempts to sell the device in secret, only the contacts he's speaking with are all MAJI or CIA, or DIA, and he still ends up dead. Sadly, I've seen that happen several times."

"But you yourself have never personally seen one?"

"No, Mr. Shariak. The closest I came was when Bill Colby, the former

CIA Director, had made arrangements to deliver one to me, along with $50 million in seed money … they killed him before that happened."

"No disrespect, but how do you know—"

"According to investigators, Colby suddenly, and for no apparent reason, decided to go canoeing on the Potomac River at 8:30 at night. Nine days later the police found his body at a spot where they had already searched—nine days being enough time to hide the real cause of death from a coroner."

"If they killed Colby, why haven't they gone after you?"

"Oh, they have. The first time happened while I was staying at the St. Moritz Hotel in New York City. I was in town to meet with several VIPs about the *Disclosure Project*. At four in the morning, I suddenly started convulsing from a seizure brought on by a directional psychotronic weapons system."

"What exactly is a psychotronic weapon?"

"It's a high-end electronic beam which falls under the military's Orwellian 'mind fuck' term of 'Non-Lethal Weapons Systems.' The head of this secret program is another sociopath named Colonel Alexander Johnston, also known by his nickname: Dr. Death. Using this faster-than-light EM pulse, Johnston attempted to forcibly extricate my soul from my physicality—it literally felt as if I was being microwaved from the inside out. Had they succeeded with the astral extraction, it would have killed me. Fortunately I knew how to fight back, having experienced something similar during my near-death experience as a teen, but it was still quite terrifying.

"These EMP attacks continued every night for a week. One of the worst experiences actually took place during a congressional briefing … this was in April of 1997. The colonel decided that he needed to be at this meeting. When I refused he said, 'Oh, I'll be there anyway, Dr. Greer.' He wasn't there physically, but during the briefing I was struck by a pulsed electromagnetic energy wave which hit me so hard it nearly knocked me out.

"Six months after these attacks, Congressman Steve Schiff of New Mexico and I both contracted skin cancer, and my assistant, Shari was diagnosed with breast cancer. Congressman Schiff had been trying to get the Roswell information out. All three of our cancers metastasized.

Metastatic means that the cancer originated from a primary tumor somewhere else. And yet in all three cases, our oncologists could find no primary tumors anywhere."

"What do you suspect happened?"

"I can't prove it, but I'm convinced our cancers were induced electronically. At a subtle level of electromagnetism, you can transmute elements and transfer something from one place to another, infecting someone electronically. Dr. Death has apparently mastered this technique."

Dr. Greer cleared the emotion in his throat. "Shari and the congressman both died. My survival was a fluke. Our family had a golden retriever named Yami; the dog always stayed close to me when I was home. We must have both been hit at the same time; our veterinarian found a malignant sarcoma on the dog's left triceps muscle and had to remove his leg. To this day, I'm convinced Yami absorbed enough of the intensity from the EM weapon to save my life."

"And they haven't gone after you since?"

"I've become a very public figure, plus I've created a 'Dead-Man's Trigger.' If something happens to me, there will be hell to pay."

"This cabal sounds like something straight out of a James Bond movie."

"MAJI's not all bad; in fact a silent majority among the cabal's younger generation now believes zero-point-energy should be released. Unfortunately, it's the hardliners—like the colonel and a certain former Vice President—who maintain order in the ranks by terminating people like Bill Colby. Fear goes a long way, Mr. Shariak."

"I know; I have my share. What I'd like to know is why Bill Clinton chose me."

"Clinton was just the messenger … a figurehead whose 'personal aura' forced you to take this quest seriously. I really don't know why you were chosen. You're not exactly someone who carries an impressive resume, plus you only have a Q clearance. Hell, my mailman has a Q clearance. You need Zebra or higher just to access the subterranean bases where these reverse-engineered technologies are being kept."

"The guy I met with before you—he said these energy devices are game-changers. No more poverty … no more pollution—"

"Correct. Zero-point-energy essentially replaces jet engines, steam ships, internal combustion engines, gasoline, oil, public utilities, rockets, and paved roads. In the aggregate, you're talking about several hundred *trillion* dollars of world activity; by comparison the entire U.S. budget is a mere three to four trillion dollars. But this isn't just about money, Mr. Shariak, it's about control. Free energy is a tide that raises every country's boat. No more haves and have-nots; every nation on equal footing. Do you think the United States or Britain want that? How about Trump's pal, Putin? Do you think he wants to lose control over his neighbors to the south? Whether you believe it or not, we've mastered the technologies that will eradicate poverty, hunger, climate change, and disease, and we did it back in the mid-1950s. Only a bunch of rich oil oligarchs, bankers, military suppliers, and the top dogs at Goldman-Sachs don't want the world to change; they like things just the way they are."

Dr. Greer looked up as his wife entered the study. "Is it five o'clock already?"

"No, but I've been listening to the weather report. A cold front is moving in. The highway patrol has closed the Interstate because of fog. I called the hotel but they're booked solid, mostly with our group. The B and B's too."

"What does that mean," Adam asked.

Dr. Greer forced a smile. "It means, Mr. Under Secretary, that you're our houseguest for the night.

16

Subterranean Complex—Midwest USA

JESSICA FOLLOWED LYDIA GAGNON out of the Maglev train. She was barely able to keep her eyes open, the nine-minute catnap doing more harm than good. "I can't do this, I need sleep!"

"That's first on the list." The older woman wrapped an arm around her waist, leading her across a deserted platform to seven pairs of elevator doors. "We're going to check you in, order you a nice hot meal, then let you get a good night's rest before we begin your orientation."

Lydia inserted her identification card in the security slot servicing the last elevator on the right, and then stood before a twelve-inch-square section of dark glass, submitting to a retinal scan.

After twenty seconds the set of elevator doors labeled #7 opened, revealing an interior entirely different from the ones servicing the underground complex beneath Edwards Air Force Base.

Larger than a freight elevator, the compartment looked like something out of a futuristic subway train. Fifteen one-inch-in-diameter vertical poles were anchored from the floor to the ceiling. Set in three rows of five across, each held a small plastic seat which swiveled 360-degrees around its pole.

Jessica watched as Lydia mounted one of the seats so that she was facing the pole. Swiveling around to face the 'smart-glass' mounted on the wall to her right, she said, "Display subterranean facility."

The voice-activated system illuminated a three-dimensional map of the complex, enveloped in a hologram. Six rectangular objects were moving through the grid like hamsters in a habitat, some traveling up or down, others racing laterally. The seventh elevator remained stationary at the bottom of the hologram at Level-9.

"That's us," Lydia said, pointing to the car situated on the Maglev level. "As you can see, the complex has nine levels divided into twelve zones. These elevator cars can move horizontally as well as vertically—a necessity when dealing with the upper floors, which can run for miles in any direction. Our Cosmic Clearance allows us access to any compartment inside the facility; however it's always best to use Elevator-7, which is reserved just for us. Now, if you'll take a seat ..."

Jessica straddled the pole two rows down from Lydia and eased her weight onto the spring-loaded supporter.

The doors sealed.

She held on, her feet locating the chair's foot rest as the elevator launched vertically straight up its shaft. Reaching Level-5, the car slowed to a steady crawl before suddenly racing east, pulling a quick Gee that sent both women spinning around their support poles.

Jess held on, the butterflies in her stomach causing her to smile. A moment later, the car zagged to the south before settling at its destination and locking down, its doors opening to what looked like a hotel lobby.

Lydia led her to a "smart desk" which was overseen by a woman about Jessica's age, her blonde hair a shade darker.

"Dr. Gagnon, good evening. And this must be Dr. Marulli?"

Jessica gritted her teeth at the English accent. "You're not from Mickleover, are you?"

"Derby? Lord no, I'm from Kent."

Lydia smiled, knowing the source of Jessica's angst. "Dr. Marulli, this is Kirsty Brunt. Kirsty sees to the needs of all us Cosmic Clearance crazies."

"What I'm in need of is sleep."

"Then let's get you tucked in. We just need a retinal scan to generate your identification card."

Jessica jumped as a panel in the smart table top slid open by her elbow, releasing a small machine that resembled an electron microscope.

"Dr. Marulli, are you wearing contacts?"

"No."

"If you are, the machine will detect them."

"Then why bother to ask?"

"Because it's my job."

Jessica leaned over the machine and pressed both eyes to the rubber sockets, opening wide—the internal flash leaving purple floaters in her vision.

By the time she could see again, Kirsty had attached a black lanyard to her new I.D. badge. "Retinal access will get you anywhere you need to go, but it's best to wear the I.D. badge as well; sometimes the MPs get a little testy. We're on Level-5; you've been assigned Suite 512. I've already placed your belongings inside. Your cell phone won't work down here; all calls must go through our private Skype service available in your suite. You can place outgoing calls and receive text and voice messages through the system from an assigned number. All calls are monitored and on a seven-second delay, which takes some getting used to. If you're ready, I'll show you to your room."

"Go ... get some rest," Lydia ordered, returning to the awaiting elevator. "I'll find you when I need you."

Kirsty came out from behind the desk, leading Jessica down a concourse that was as wide as a three lane highway and seemed to run on forever. It was divided by a centrally-located elevated pedestrian walkway composed of a spongy red material sandwiched between two uni-directional Maglev tracks.

"The Maglev is only for hoverboards. Each side runs in one direction with the speeds varying from slow to fast from the center out."

They turned as an Asian man in a white lab coat shot past them on a three-foot-long object that resembled a small surfboard.

"Wow."

As they watched, he cut across the concourse, his speed reducing enough to allow him to flip the board out from under him. Crossing over the pedestrian walkway to the other side of the hall and the odd numbered suites, he entered a set of double doors labeled 505.

"Your work schedule has been programmed into the VC, along with a menu of personal selections. The gym on this level is located between Suite

146

530 and 532; the eatery is at 590. Most of my 'Cosmic Crazies' prefer room service, which is 24/7. To order, just summon your VC."

"What's a VC?"

"Sorry, your Virtual Concierge."

Jessica mumbled to herself, "… better not serve virtual food."

Kirsty led her down the catwalk servicing the even-numbered suites. As they stood before the door to Suite 512, a retinal scan locked on to Jessica's eyes, unbolting and opening the door and turning on the interior lights.

"Oh my …"

The apartment was enormous, the plush living room featuring a wrap-around taupe leather sofa and black easy chair. Part of the couch faced a twelve-foot-wide by fifteen-foot-high smart-glass wall that Jessica knew would function as a home theater, the other half looked upon a dazzling floor-to-ceiling night view of the French Riviera. The doors were open, leading out to a private balcony. A warm, balmy breeze flowed over the Mediterranean Sea to enter the dwelling, the humidity immediately neutralized by the air conditioning, the hypnotic sounds of the shoreline threatening to lull her into sleep while she was still on her feet—

—Jessica having to remind herself that none of it was real.

"This is incredible, and I love the sea—"

"—but what else is on the scenery menu … everyone asks the same question the first time they gaze upon that view." Kirsty pointed out an iPad held within a plastic sleeve anchored to the wall by the door. "There's a complete list of balcony settings on this device, along with your schedule, a built-in GPS that will get you where you need to go, and menus from each of our eateries and restaurants. But let's find out what the VC thinks you might enjoy."

Turning to the wall of smart glass she said, "Concierge, select Dr. Marulli's favorite scene."

Instantly the Mediterranean scene morphed into a dramatic second-story view of California's Pacific Coast, the ocean crashing violently against the rocks below, the humid warmth replaced by a northwestern chill. A fireplace ignited, the holographic flames taking the edge off the cold.

"Perfect. And it's so real."

"It also serves a purpose. No matter what scene you select, each reflects the time of day within our complex, helping to maintain our body clocks and with it, our mental health, which can be challenged when one lives underground for weeks or months at a time. Come on, I'll show you the kitchen and bedroom, then I'll let you get some rest."

The kitchen and dining area flowed to the right, the cabinets and chairs made of oak, the appliances camouflaged in the same wood. Jessica had never seen anything like the dark granite used on the countertops and matching table, the material seemingly alive with liquid splashes of color that changed as she altered her sightline. Forcing herself to look away, she followed Kirsty down a short hall to the master bedroom.

"Nice …"

The king-size bed faced another smart wall and the same fifteen-foot-high, floor-to-ceiling view of the Pacific Coast. Gusts of wind rattled the sliding glass doors, which were closed, the flames of the virtual fireplace adjusting its heat accordingly.

Jessica joined Kirsty by the walk-in closet where someone had already unpacked her belongings.

"As you can see, I had your closet stocked with uniforms, workout clothes, silk pajamas, undergarments, shoes, sneakers … everything you could possibly need. The personal items are yours to take with you when you leave, the uniforms stay with us."

"Thank you."

She followed the Englishwoman into the master bath. Decorated in Italian marble, the rectangular space was divided by its centerpiece—an enormous Jacuzzi tub. Behind the marble wall that contained its built-in waterfall was a step-down drain which handled his-and-her showers. A water closet lent privacy to a toilet and bidet; a small linen closet held a variety of linens and towels.

Overwhelmed by her accommodations, Jessica struggled to triage her immediate needs.

"I know you're exhausted, sleep as long as you want; your orientation doesn't begin until Monday morning at ten."

"Sorry, I can't remember … what day is it?"

"It's Friday evening. By the way, all holographic landscapes face west so that you won't be disturbed by the rising sun. I suggest you order in, shower, and then sleep in; you've got the entire weekend to be pampered. Remember, whatever you want, simply say 'Concierge' and it will be taken care of."

"Concierge … got it."

Jessica walked Kirsty to the front door, said good night, and bolted the lock.

A cold gust of salty air rushed into the apartment. Jessica closed the French doors, surprised to hear running water coming from the bathroom.

She entered to find the tub filling with hot water and scented bath oil beads.

"The bath oils were my idea."

She jumped, her heart racing at the Hispanic male's voice. "Who said that?"

"I did. I'm Raul, your Virtual Concierge."

She looked around, discovering—to her relief—the stranger speaking to her from the other side of the sink mirror.

Athletic and tan … she guessed he was about twenty-five, his wavy dark hair highlighting deep-blue eyes.

Nicely done …

"What did you say your name was?"

"Raul."

"Well, you scared the shit out of me, Raul. Are you going to be popping in and out of mirrors whenever you feel like it?"

"Only when you summon me."

"I didn't summon you."

"You were debating whether to bathe first or eat."

"You can read my thoughts? How …? Oh wait, the retinal scan … that's impressive. But I can't have a strange man popping in on me, even if he is a computer-generated creation, and especially when I'm in the bathroom."

"Perhaps you'd be more comfortable with someone from your childhood?"

Raul morphed into a stout gray-haired Swedish woman in her sixties.

"Ingrid? Oh my God, oh my God … I haven't seen you since I was seven years old. This is freaky, this is really freaky."

"But comforting, *ja*?"

"God, you sound exactly like her ... of course you do, you're pulling my memory of her straight out of the recesses of my brain."

"Your blood sugar is low; you need to eat. I ordered you something special. How does lobster thermidor topped with lump crabmeat and a velvety sauce sound, served on garlic whipped potatoes. And for dessert ... a decadent chocolate crème brûlée with a hint of Grand Marnier."

"That sounds ... incredible."

"Would you like to dine on the terrace?"

"It's too cold."

"Not in Tahiti."

She was about to respond when the doorbell rang.

"Ah, there's dinner. Go ... I'll meet you in the living room."

Jessica hurried out of the master bedroom, feeling as if she were in a dream.

An eight-by-ten inch video panel by the front door revealed the room service attendant waiting on the catwalk, his name and identity number— BENEDICT GUZZO, Q-766-22-1103—flashing in green.

Jessica opened the door, her stomach rumbling.

"Good evening, Dr. Marulli."

"Benedict."

"I understand you'll be eating on the main balcony, is that correct?"

"Yeah ... sure. God, that smells good."

"I'll only be a minute."

Feeling lightheaded, she stepped aside and watched as he pushed the dinner cart to the balcony—all the while her childhood nanny observing him from the living room smart glass, a cross look on the Swedish woman's age-weathered face.

Oblivious, the waiter methodically opened one side of the French doors and then the other. Gone was the pounding Pacific, in its place—a calm lagoon shared by several private cottages on piers, their balconies lit by torches. Jessica recalled Adam showing her travel photos of Bora Bora, each guest house set on its own private dock over the water.

She closed her eyes, listening to the computer-generated waves lapping beneath the balcony. A warm, soothing breeze entered the apartment, mixing with the intoxicating aromas of her main course which still remained concealed beneath its metal serving container.

What the hell is taking him so long?

She watched as the waiter carefully laid out a white tablecloth over the heavy outdoor table. He meticulously arranged a place setting, filled her water glass and left the pitcher, then struggled to light the dinner candle.

It was Ingrid who finally snapped, her bellow bringing with it a tide of memories. "My girl hasn't eaten in over a day and you stand there, fumbling with a candle? Why does she need a candle? Whoever heard of a romantic interlude for one … idiot!"

The red-faced attendant pocketed his lighter and returned to the cart, quickly carrying the hot dinner plate, salad, and dessert outside, not bothering to remove the covers.

Feeling embarrassed, Jessica attempted to apologize for her computer-generated nanny's outburst. "I'm sorry. Ingrid means well, but she's always had a short fuse when it comes to my well-being."

The waiter shot her a "what-the-fuck" look before pushing the empty cart toward the front door.

Ingrid would have none of it. "Guzzo—leave the cart by the door and take the attitude with you … *rövhål!*"

The man stopped in his tracks, staring hard at Jessica. "What did you call me?"

"Me? No, it was—"

"It was me, lard ass," Ingrid cried out, "and I called you an asshole! Since my English is sometimes not so good, I will spell it out for you. A-s-s …"

Benedict Guzzo exited the apartment, slamming the door.

"Ingrid, that was very rude of you. It's only my first day and already someone dislikes me."

"He was jealous; I could see it in his eyes. Just like those girls in middle school. Go and eat; I will put on some music that will soothe you."

Jessica stepped out on to the balcony, attacking her meal. Within minutes she had devoured the main course, using chunks of warm garlic bread to mop up the remains of lump crabmeat and sauce. She was about to start in on the chocolate crème brûlée when she realized why the waiter had taken an attitude with her.

There is no Ingrid. Everything she says is an extension of my thoughts.

She looked back at the living room smart glass. The image of her nanny was nodding at her.

"Virtual concierge, remove Ingrid!"

The dark smart glass went blank.

"No more images of people unless I verbally command it. Acknowledge command by shooting three fireworks over the lagoon."

A lone rose-red flame arced into the dark heavens, igniting into a pink, green, and blue blast of color over the water.

Nice.

"Leave the Tahiti setting; it might be nice to wake up to. Oh, and have Raul finish drawing me a hot bath ... with the oil beads."

She smiled. "Dress him in something ... revealing."

17

Charlottesville, Virginia
9:26 p.m.

"**WELCOME TO OUR MEDITATION CIRCLE** … does everyone have their circle buddy?"

Adam sat shivering in a folding chair, seeking warmth from an old wool sweater and a tattered baseball cap he had borrowed from Dr. Greer. They were situated in a six-acre clearing surrounded by woods, a good two hundred yards from the house. Wrapping his legs in a wool blanket, the Under Secretary of Defense now realized what the other twenty-two paying guests already knew—that there was a big difference in dressing for the weather and dressing for *prolonged exposure* to the weather.

Emily Greer had attempted to warn him. "I realize it's August, but it gets very cold out there. If you're going to join the group then we'll need to dress you in something warmer. Let me see if I can find you an old pair of Steven's long johns and—"

"—That won't be necessary. I Googled tonight's local forecast; it'll be a balmy 62-degrees Fahrenheit. I doubt we'll see any UFOs with all this fog, but weather-wise I'll be fine."

"The skies will clear around ten when the temperatures drop. Unless the group goes on break, you'll be stuck out there, and Steven gets very perturbed when his meditation circle is broken. At least bring a blanket."

Adam glanced up at the cloud-choked heavens. As predicted, he could feel the temperature dropping, a few patches of stars slowly starting to appear. They hadn't even begun yet and his teeth were already chattering.

Asshole. You should have listened to Greer and stayed inside to watch the damn baseball game instead of insisting on tagging along on this snipe hunt.

"Mr. Shariak, I'm your circle buddy. You okay?"

Adam glanced to his right where a woman in her mid-thirties—her name tag identifying her as Leslie Ann Mahurin from Park Hills, Missouri—was adjusting the volume on a machine emitting a rapid de-do-de-do-de-do sound.

"Missouri ... the 'Show Me' state. What exactly is that thing?"

She smiled. "This is a laser detector. I'm running a battery test. If it starts making that sound once we begin, it means an ET craft may be vectoring in."

"Vectoring in on what exactly?"

"The group's consciousness. Dr. Greer will explain."

The guests had begun arriving around six-fifteen, the CE-5 orientation meeting set to begin at eight. Plastic tags were worn on lanyards around their necks, identifying each person and their city and country of origin. The farthest trek belonged to a brother and sister team who had traveled from New Zealand. A married French couple in their thirties hailed from Paris, an older woman and her younger female companion had flown in from Munich, Germany, and he managed a short conversation with a heavyset Briton bundled in an orange parka. The others were from the States. A third of the guests had been on at least one CE-5 expedition before, Greer matching up each veteran with a pair of excited "newbies."

Adam stuck out like a sore thumb.

Greer had warned him. "These people were vetted before their applications were accepted; those who made it put in a lot of time and effort to get here. They were given instructions and a manual to study which included a waiver that allows me to dismiss them for any action or attitude that does not fit in with CE-5 protocol."

"What kind of attitude?"

"Anything one might describe as self-serving. We're here to welcome our ET ambassadors, Mr. Shariak, not to exploit them. If they sense the latter, they won't join us."

"How often do these ETs actually show up?"

"Every CE-5 expedition is different. Ultimately, the outcome is determined by the consciousness of the group. If I sense your presence to be a disturbance, I'll ask you to leave ... and not just the circle, but my home."

A cold wind whipped across the field, howling through the surrounding woods.

Adam looked up as their leader took center stage, the surrounding darkness pierced by sporadic blips of blue and green lights coming from an assortment of electronic devices held by guests within the circle.

"Good evening. A few basic rules before we begin. There's no smoking and please refrain from eating or drinking when we go into our meditation sessions. We'll take a bathroom break in a few hours, but if you have to go there are plenty of trees nearby. If you must go, please do your best not to disturb other people in the circle.

"We're positioned in a circle so the group has eyes on every direction. If you see something, you need to alert the group by calling out its location using a direction and degree of elevation. The horizon is zero degrees, straight up in the sky is ninety, so halfway in between would be forty-five degrees. As for directions, the house is to the east, the woods to my left, therefore, are west ... then north and south. We also have northeast, northwest, southeast and southwest. It's okay to lay your head back and watch the sky, but we have a no snoring rule ... if someone falls asleep and starts snoring their neighbors must wake them."

Removing a laser pointer from his jacket pocket, he turned it on, directing its powerful emerald-green light at a patch of star-filled sky overhead. "As you can see this laser is quite powerful, with a range that extends some 200 miles into space. I'm always careful not to use it whenever planes are around. It's not just a pointer; it is also one of our tools of communication. I remember the first night we used it. We were in the foothills of New Mexico when I flashed the laser at what I assumed was a satellite. The object flashed back at us before dematerializing into a cigar-shaped craft. It remained visible almost ten seconds before vanishing."

Using his laser, Greer traced a circle around two stars. "You can't quite see the entire constellation because of these clouds, but these two stars are part of the Big Dipper and they always point to Polaris, the North Star. Using our navigation points, we'd describe Polaris as what ... about thirty degrees northeast. Everyone understand?

"The bright object peeking out behind this cloud is Jupiter. Over here we have a formation of stars known as the Winter Triangle. The lower star is Sirius, the upper—Procyon, and the star pointing at three o'clock is Betelgeuse, part of the Orion constellation ..."

Adam closed his eyes, feeling himself nod off.

Leslie Ann shook him awake. "You were snoring."

"Sorry."

"I know you're all hoping for a vessel to dematerialize out of the sky like the one I just described, but there are many other ways for us to experience a close encounter with an ET. Back in the early 1990s, I came up with the idea of using radio transmitters like this one—Leslie Ann can you hold that up? When we used the transmitter to broadcast CSETI tones into the atmosphere, within minutes an omni-directional, non-local anomalous tone came back to us. This clearly demonstrates not only the ET's expression of intelligence, but their desire to communicate with us."

Adam rolled his eyes. *Or maybe your next door neighbor was using his ham radio ...*

"This next device is a magnetometer—a magnetic field sensor. We use it to detect an ET vessel as it phase-shifts from the higher dimensions of thought energy into our own physical world.

"This object here is a thunderbolt detector. We've discovered that a certain race of ETs—a very evolved, physically-imposing species who are extremely protective of what we are doing—will often let us know they're here by sending a distinct signal through this particular sensor. This isn't unusual by the way; many extraterrestrials, as well as souls in the spiritual world, often use electronics as a means of communicating across other realms.

"Now, as far as what to look for, an incoming ET craft can appear like a meteor, only they are moving more slowly, or a second meteor may follow the same path within seconds. Besides having no tail, an ET craft may streak directly down from the apex of the sky and go into the ground with no explosion or disturbance. A CSETI team witnessed a bright teal object do this in Joshua Tree National Park in November 1996.

"Some UFOs resemble stars. They might blink off and on randomly, sometimes moving slightly between the blinks. We once observed a whole squadron of craft in Sedona that blinked off and on for ten minutes in one area of the sky. When a laser was pointed at one of the objects it glinted off the craft.

"It's also important I mention orbs. They vary in size and can be craft or drones. They are often a uniform amber or gold, although they can appear in various colors. Orbs often will remain stationary for a period of time, though they do move about as well. These are not to be confused with flares which are often dropped by the military to confuse observers after a genuine sighting has occurred. A flare will float downwards at different rates and give off smoke.

"Orbs can also be huge. In 1998, observers in England saw a very large orange globe rise above the horizon, then dip back below, then rise again before it suddenly disappeared. This object was observed on two separate nights in two different locations. The second night, after it rose above the horizon for the second time, it 'dissolved' as it disappeared. Within thirty seconds, several British military jets and helicopters appeared in the area, one chopper dropping a flare in the vicinity where the object had been seen.

"There is also a phenomenon you need to be aware of known as a distorted sky. This happens when an ET craft hovering just beyond the crossing point of light causes a distortion in the star field, leaving a shimmering effect even though no object can be seen. If this occurs, and it has on numerous occasions, assume there may be ETs on the ground nearby or among the observing group. During such an event, members of the group may sense a change in atmospheric pressure which can be felt in the observer's ears, a sudden stillness or quietness, and the hair on your head, arms, or legs may stand on end. Don't be startled if the radar goes off.

"Interactions between ETs and individuals in a CE-5 group range from sensing a presence, to a loving personal acknowledgment, to full telepathic conversations. The sense of love is almost always present, no matter the level of the interaction, and the expression can be truly wonderful and unforgettable. The conversations are typically non-verbal. Field observers have reported shimmering-light ETs that have stood in front of them or sat on their feet for a prolonged time.

"Touch is another way an ET might engage with you. While we are meditating you may feel a gentle contact, as if something is touching you, only when you open your eyes nothing is there.

"Most important—remember our mission. We are here to ask our ET ambassadors and guests to appear to us in a form that is most safe to them. Sometimes an extraterrestrial may choose not to fully materialize, giving off sort of a sparkling light. When an ET does spin-shifts across the crossing point of light and dematerializes in our physical world, they become visible not only to us but to the military—a condition potentially dangerous to the extraterrestrial. If this happens, it's routine for us to be buzzed by Air Force jetfighters. So again when we go into our group meditation, each of us is asking the ET to appear using the method which they feel is safest both for them ... and for us."

Dr. Greer left the center of the gathering to take his seat within the circle.

"Let us begin. CE-5 is a close encounter of the fifth kind, the fifth kind defined as humans initiating contact with ETs. We do this through meditation and a technique called remote viewing. For those of you new to remote viewing, I'm going to walk you through it. As for the meditation, I'm going to give you a simple mantra. We use the mantra to keep our thoughts from straying. I'll repeat the mantra a few times; then you can join in with me."

Greer repeated it several times, the first syllable an upper tone, the second a full tone lower, with the last a half note in-between.

"Let's try it together."

Adam closed his eyes, feeling ridiculous as he chanted the mantra.

The group continued until Dr. Greer instructed them to repeat the chant only to themselves.

For several minutes it was quiet, save for the sound of the wind rustling through the surrounding forests and the occasional electronic chirp from a sensor.

In due time Dr. Greer began, speaking in a calm, melodic voice. "Now, as we become aware that we are all created by one light … one consciousness; that this cosmic mind allows each one of us to be awake and living together in peace … that we are all drops from the same ocean, the same pure being who is watching and standing with us.

"And now, desiring only to share our presence with that of another consciousness, we allow our minds to leave our bodies. Looking down, we hover over ourselves, registering the unified oneness of our meditation circle. Floating higher, we rise above the dark contours of the Blue Ridge Mountains, the traffic headlights distinguishing the highways as they curve around the Virginia landscape. We can see the lights of Washington, D.C., quickly fading as we soar above the eastern seaboard of the United States until we are high over the Atlantic. We're entering space now, gazing down upon the curvature of our planet as we feel the infinite love of Gaia—Mother Earth—and we vow to lift the burdens humanity has placed upon her.

"And now as we move off into space we see extraterrestrial vessels orbiting the far side of the moon and massive structures erected on the lunar surface. Leaving Earth-space, we race past Mars and head for Jupiter, registering the presence of a large extraterrestrial mother ship in orbit around the massive planet. Continuing beyond Saturn, we quickly leave our own solar system to travel light years past other stars until we find ourselves gazing at the Milky Way, a spiral galaxy composed of 100 billion stars, each system possessing its own planets, many of them inhabited.

"Circling our galaxy, we invite any ETs whose path we cross to join us. We vector them to us by focusing our thoughts on our spiral galaxy and the arm of Orion. From there we head back to our star system and the nine planets revolving around our sun. We lead our ET friends to our blue world, the third planet from the sun, escorting them to the eastern seaboard of North America and back to the dark contours of the Blue Ridge Mountains, beckoning them to join our community in this clearing, inviting them into our circle. We ask them to manifest in any form they feel is safe … in electronics, in sound, in physicality.

"Now I will remain silent while each of you repeats the remote viewing journey we just completed together, vectoring other civilizations to us, allowing your mind to connect with any interstellar vessels that cross your path."

Adam attempted the mental exercise, making it as far out as the moon before he drifted off into sleep …

The woman from Wisconsin shook him awake.

"… anyone else have anything they'd like to share? Yes, Andrew?"

The heavyset Brit rose to his feet, bundled in his orange parka. "Moving off into space, I thought I sensed the color yellow flowing in a counter-clockwise direction."

Adam coughed, attempting to suppress a chuckle.

Dr. Greer was not amused. "Colors, sensations, scents—anything can remind us of something we may have remote viewed without even realizing it. What's important, Mr. Shariak, is that you first believe something is possible in order to perceive it. If you had not first believed in aero-dynamics, you could never have flown a helicopter. There is a saying, 'as ye have faith, so shall your powers and blessings be.' This is faith, not in the religious sense, but in an affirmative confidence that something can be, and to that extent, it will be. Knowing this helps people get out of their own way.

"Anyone else?"

It was almost three in the morning by the time Adam found himself back in the Greer's guest room. Chilled to the bone, he thought about taking a hot shower until he sat on the queen-sized bed. Succumbing to gravity and fatigue, he managed to kick off his shoes and turn off the desk lamp before his head hit the pillow.

Moonlight violated the open slats of the Venetian blinds, casting a luminous pattern on the opposite wall. Too tired to move, Adam stared at the wall and the pattern of reflected lunar light, his mind drifting even as he realized …

There's someone looking through the window at me.

He could not see the face peering in through the gaps in the Venetian blinds, only the long shadow of its enormous head, and the bulbous compound eyes and antennae. Instinctively he knew the extraterrestrial was a species of insect—first because the praying mantis was five feet tall; second because it had two legs and two arms, with sharp spikes protruding from the forearms.

What was really bizarre was Adam's response. He simply continued to lie in bed, watching the being that was watching him. He had no doubt the Mantis-Man was intelligent and, like his own species, a product of evolution. The difference was simply the source material; humans having sprouted from primates, his visitor's race from insects.

He waved at the ET.

The ET waved back.

Comforted by the being's response, Adam rolled over and fell asleep.

"… huh?"

He opened his eyes to see Emily Greer hovering over him in her bathrobe.

"Come quickly, Steven needs you."

Rolling out of bed, Adam methodically placed his bare right flesh foot next to the mechanical version of his left. *Stand … and left … right … left—*

Leaving the bedroom, he headed for the stairs, fighting the urge to hop down on his right leg to save time.

What the hell …

Amber waves of sunlight were streaming through the open front door and windows, the light so bright he could not see the front entryway.

Steven Greer was standing outside in his bathrobe and gray sweatpants, looking up at the source of light.

Adam, come out here and join me.

The Under Secretary of Defense rubbed his eyes, attempting to wake up. Greer's words had echoed in his mind, and yet the man's mouth had never opened.

Yes, I can hear your thoughts and I know you can hear mine. Now come outside please and let them see you.

Them? Vaguely recalling something about insects, Adam strode awkwardly out onto the front porch, grabbed Steven's arm … and looked up.

"Whoa shit."

The extraterrestrial vessel was enormous, its chevron-shaped undercarriage, hovering fifty feet above the roof of the Greers' farmhouse, easily two hundred feet across. Three amber lights were aligned in the shape of an equilateral triangle, and everything within its borders appeared to shimmer.

Stay calm. They want to meet you.

As they moved away from the farmhouse, Adam registered a strange sensation—the air now still, the temperature noticeably warmer.

What's happening?

Removing the laser pointer from his robe pocket, Dr. Greer aimed it down the driveway and pressed the power switch.

The green beam of light traveled seventy feet before dispersing into a prism of color.

My God … Greer, are we inside the vessel?

Yes, only it's not completely phased in. I want you to meet a friend. Adam Shariak, this is Kindness.

As Adam watched, a luminous light appeared before him, materializing into the form of a woman. Her head was round and hairless, her eyes—almond-shaped, her features that of another species, yet still quite feminine. Only the lack of flaps around her ear holes identified her as something not quite human. She wore a one-piece outfit composed of a reflective silver cloth, and both the material and her pale skin seemed to shimmer.

She smiled at Adam, emanating an energy which exuded compassion.

Kindness was introduced to us through the spirit of my assistant, Shari, shortly after she died in 1998. Kindness is an ambassador to many species. While she still exists in the physical world, she shares a God-consciousness that allows her to function as an avatar in the spiritual realm. There are twenty-seven emissaries aboard this vessel, and many more that remain in orbit outside the crossing point of light.

Why are they here … oh!

For a brief, powerful moment Adam Shariak's consciousness suddenly bloomed, allowing him to observe the Earth from the vantage of a higher dimension—and what he absorbed was as enlightening as it was frightening.

Suckling energy from the star about which it orbited, the blue world functioned as a living, breathing complex synergistic system designed to incubate, birth, and sustain life. Its heartbeat was the rock-steady spin which perpetually circulated its life-giving fluids; its lungs were the Amazon rainforest; its kidneys the oceans. Ice at the poles and heat at the equator regulated its thermostat; magma regenerated its skin.

For the last three-and-a-half billion years, the Earth had served as an incubator for life, its ever-changing atmosphere, seas, and land evolving to serve the complexities of its species.

And now one of its offspring had given it cancer.

The malignancy was everywhere. The Amazon rain forest, once lush, dense, and green was decimated and dying, its breathing capacity operating at the equivalent of half a lung. This exacerbated conditions in the atmosphere, which appeared thick with carbon dioxide and other greenhouse gases.

Observing the planet, Adam could sense the effects of global warming through the attributes of his host. He could *feel* the deep rumbling of Antarctica's polar ice as it melted, fragmented, and collapsed; he could *taste* the acidification of the oceans … the seas poisoned with mercury, the marine life dying—the cancer spreading throughout the world's food chains.

The aftermath was a sobering, gut-punching lesson delivered by Mother Nature as terrifying images of humanity's obituary raced across his mind's eye.

Tens of thousands of acres of crops—America's breadbasket—shriveled beneath a dense smoke-gray sky, the drought delivered by changing weather patterns—photosynthesis disrupted by man's refusal to abandon fossil fuels.

The images accelerated into the very near future, mass starvation leading to riots, cities burning to the ground, the dying feeding off the dead, disease rampant …

As he bore witness to his species' demise, the terrifying scenes gradually disappeared behind a blizzard of snow which steadily blanketed Earth's continents.

Adam knew what had happened, he had felt the toxins blanketing the atmosphere, baking the planet and melting the polar ice.

Greenland's ice was melting—it had been for many years, releasing a steady tsunami of fresh water that was seeping into the North Atlantic Current—a warm water conveyor belt which circulated heat across North America and Europe.

It was saline that mobilized the current, and now Greenland's melting ice had finally and irreversibly shut it down—

—summoning an Ice Age and the extinction of man.

Adam opened his eyes as the extraterrestrial vessel silently shot straight up into the star-filled heavens and disappeared.

PART 3

"In a brazen challenge to international efforts to limit global warming, this is an all-out assault on the protections we need to avert climate catastrophe."

—Rhea Suh, Natural Resources Defense Council, on President Donald Trump signing an executive order that aims to reverse many of the climate policies introduced by President Obama

March 28, 2017

"According to some estimates, we cannot track $2.3 trillion in transactions."

—Secretary of Defense Donald Rumsfeld

September 10, 2001

"The Pentagon cannot account for 25% of what it spends."

—Pentagon Audit

EVALUATION REPORT—WINTER SEMESTER

Michael Andrew Sutterfield
SS #711-19-0878
GVP Unit: PA-762-32443
AGE: 13 years, 3 months
GRADE: 7
SEX: Male

ACADEMICS:
Student continues to make acceptable progress in mathematics, language arts, and history while demonstrating exceptional work in his elective classes in quantum physics.

SOCIAL SKILLS:
Moderate levels of disdain were demonstrated toward a BLACK (male) GVP instructor. Unacceptable levels of intolerance were demonstrated toward a MEXICAN (male) GVP instructor.

NEURO-BEHAVIOR PREDICTORS:
A flat line in neuro-synaptic activity was detected during Phase-IV (follow-up) of the Risch-Avery protocol, confirming potential sociopathic tendencies. Series S-7 through S-12 will be added to the curriculum and student retested in 12 weeks.

FURTHER RECOMMENDATIONS:
Mandatory private consultation with the subject's Parents.

North Philadelphia, Pennsylvania
January 8, 2033

Edward and Tina Sutterfield followed the academic aide into the school administration office's empty waiting room.

"If you'll have a seat, Dr. Mallouh will be right with you."

Edward Sutterfield dropped his 233-pound frame into one of the vacant chairs. "A ten-hour shift, and now you have me scheduled for a school conference? What the hell's wrong with you, Tina?"

She leaned in, mumbling under her breath. "Don't start with me, Ed. The person who called me last week said we both needed to be here."

"What's the point in enrolling our kid in virtual school if we can't have a virtual meeting to discuss whatever the problem is?"

"No one said there was a problem."

"Oh, please. You think we'd be here if there wasn't a problem?"

The door opened, revealing a Middle Eastern man in his early thirties. He was dressed in a white collared shirt and tan slacks, his black mustache and short-cropped beard matching his jacket and bowtie.

Edward glanced at his wife, his expression a tapestry of prejudice.

The brown-skinned academic flashed a smile. "Mr. and Mrs. Sutterfield? Sorry to have kept you waiting. Dr. Mohammad Mallouh, District-8 counselor. Won't you come in?"

The couple entered the counselor's office and sat.

Dr. Mallouh closed the door behind them and took his place behind his desk. "I'll get straight to the point: Michael has been diagnosed with Antisocial Personality Disorder."

Tina covered her eyes.

Her husband seemed more annoyed than shocked. "So he doesn't have many friends … that's a disorder now?"

"Ed—"

"Mr. Sutterfield, this is a bit more serious than not having friends. Your son has been diagnosed as a sociopath, a dangerous condition found in about three percent of the general population."

"Sociopath … is that like a psychopath?"

"The conditions are very similar."

"And you think you're qualified to render this kind of decision about my kid, *Mohammad*? I think maybe we should get a second opinion."

"This is not my diagnosis, Mr. Sutterfield. The GV pod's results have been checked and double-checked."

"What a hunk of crap. The porn pods decide who's crazy now, do they?"

"Actually, that was the reason they were originally designed. With the advent of zero-point-energy, the World Union required a non-intrusive means of identifying ASD subjects in order to prevent them from gaining access to zero-point weapons."

"I don't understand. The machine targets them?"

"No, Mrs. Sutterfield. It identifies them. It's the dark side of introducing an energy source as potent as zero-point-energy. There are always those individuals who would attempt to exploit it to power a weapon. The Global Village was devised as a means of tracking that particular segment of the population."

"Christ, you make it sound like the kid's a child molester."

Tina Sutterfield teared up. "I knew there was something wrong when we found those dead stray cats. Then this last time with the turtle—"

Edward took his wife's hand. "Our son is a loner, but he's not a terrorist."

"Can't you just prescribe a pill or something?"

"I'm afraid there are no magic pills. Mrs. Sutterfield. The biological seeds of sociopathic behavior are present in the person's brain at birth."

"What does that mean exactly?"

"It means, sir, that your son is missing the innate ability to care about others."

Edward felt his blood pressure rising. "So what's the solution? Do we lock him up and toss away the key?"

"Of course not. And for the record, punishment is an ineffective tool—at least when it comes to rehabilitation. A sociopath is unable to learn from their mistakes simply because they have no fear or remorse ... no conscience."

"And that's a crime?"

Dr. Mallouh closed his file. "We were just children at the time, but in the decade that preceded the disclosure of zero-point-energy, there was a tremendous gap between the top earners and the rest of the population. One of the reasons for this was the unusually high number of sociopaths who were hired as CEOs of major multibillion dollar companies. Their sheer ruthlessness and lack of anything resembling a conscience enabled them to abuse their work force and the environment in order to drive stock prices higher, all the while rewarding themselves with obscene amounts of money. It wasn't just CEOs; sociopaths had risen to power in Russia, North Korea, Hungary, and throughout the Middle East, South America and Africa.

The 'Rise of the Sociopath' culminated in 2017 when the Trump Administration essentially eliminated all federal laws safeguarding what was left of the environment. With the brakes off, the result was a runaway Greenhouse Effect. Polar ice melted, causing fresh water to infiltrate the North Atlantic current. Without getting too technical, ocean salinity is what moves this warm water highway and keeps our planet from moving into an Ice Age. Just as frightening, our crops began dying when dense smog clouds choked off the sun's rays, disrupting photosynthesis. In the critical four to five years it took to bring atmospheric scrubbers powered by zero-point-energy generators online, we very nearly annihilated life on this planet.

"In retrospect, we had allowed greed and fanatical religious beliefs to silence the scientific community. Elections were determined by money, not by the qualifications of the candidates running for office. The two political parties had produced so much gridlock and anger that nothing could be done. It was only after the masses revolted in the wake of near planet-wide starvation that the rules were changed. One of the new checks and balances that was put in place was to safeguard society against the rise of the sociopath in politics, the military, and the new sciences brought forth from *The Disclosure Event*. This includes Quantum Physics and CE-5 training—the very activities Michael has shown to have both an exceptional interest in and aptitude for."

Fresh tears flowed down Tina Soderfield's cheeks. "Don't ban him from that or we'll lose him. Please Dr. Mallouh—"

"We're not going to ban him. We're going to attempt to use these interests as a reward for Michael taking a positive interest in his own therapy. While he may not have the internal mechanism that allows him to feel, he needs to know that unless he respects the feelings of others—especially those who are different than him—then extraterrestrial contact will be forbidden … and not just by us, but by the Interstellars themselves."

18

Subterranean Complex—Midwest USA
Saturday

JESSICA AWOKE TO THE soothing crash and sizzle of waves dying outside her bedroom window. Rolling over, she glanced at the clock on the night stand.

Twelve forty-eight in the afternoon? No wonder my stomach's growling.

Rolling out of bed, she entered the bathroom and showered, then ordered a decadent omelet before dressing in one of the many workout outfits provided by the efficient Kirsty Brunt.

Forty minutes later she exited her suite, stuffed from lunch. Her intention was to walk to the gym to digest her meal—until she saw the concourse. While the center track was occupied with joggers, it was the Maglev lanes that grabbed her attention as people shot past her on hoverboards like they were snowboarding on air.

"Oh, I gotta try that!"

Returning to her apartment, she located a hoverboard in the hall closet, the smooth fiberglass top supporting adjustable foot straps, the denser underside composed of a hard gray porous material, similar to the surface of the Maglev track.

Jessica exited to the catwalk outside her dwelling and sat down at an empty bench, attempting to pick up a few pointers by observing the hoverboarders. She quickly separated the pedestrians using the Maglev as a means of getting from Point A to Point B from the "subterranean surfers." The latter occupied the faster outside lanes, cutting S-patterns in a torque-like maneuver which seemed to increase their speed, each change in direction generating a *zzzzzttt* of protest from the electromagnetic waves being repelled beneath their boards.

Fearing the embarrassment of taking a hard fall, she waited until the concourse was less crowded before she ventured on foot across the fifty-foot-wide expanse to the more forgiving jogging surface located at the center of the track. Checking both directions again to make sure no one was watching, she tucked her I.D. badge inside her workout top before bending over to place her hoverboard to the hard bare gray surface.

One moment she was registering an invisible cushion of resistance—the next she was being dragged across the cold Maglev surface, her right hand caught in one of the foot straps. Twisting sideways, she flung herself free, only to witness the cursed device shooting down the concourse without her.

Bruised, skinned, bleeding and embarrassed, Jessica stepped onto the center track and started jogging, hoping no one had noticed.

The cushioned surface was easy on her joints, but her knees were scraped and sore, forcing her to walk.

"Move to the side!"

She turned to see a quartet of male joggers bearing down on, a powerfully-built heavyset Caucasian man in his early fifties adamantly signaling her to move aside.

Unsure what to do, she jumped onto the Maglev track, nearly getting sideswiped by a woman on a hoverboard.

"Idiot!"

The herd thundered by, their annoyed leader calling out, "walk left, jog right!"

Jessica contemplated turning back when she saw the teen waving at her.

He was tall and lanky, with shoulder-length brown hair and bright blue eyes—she guessed his age to be sixteen. He was cutting figure-eights across the Maglev track, Jessica's hoverboard tucked under his right arm.

"Lose something?"

"I've never seen that board before in my life."

He smirked. "Want me to show you how to ride it?"

"No. Maybe. Will it hurt?"

"Only if you're dumb enough to try to mount it with the power on."

"There's a power switch?"

He tugged the leash attached to his board and right ankle, powering off the device.

"Now see, that makes sense. But my board doesn't have—"

Flipping Jessica's board back-end up, he unzipped a small plastic storage pouch and unraveled the leash.

"So that's where they hid it."

"I'm Logan ... Logan Remy LaCombe. You're new, aren't you?"

"Jessica Marulli. I arrived late last night. Aren't you a little young to be living down here?"

"My mom's a genetics engineer, my father works security. I've been here two years; they home school us kids by computer."

"Where's here?"

"Shit if I know. I spend most of my free time surfing the RC ... the Residential Concourse. Don't feel bad about wiping out; the same thing happened to Kari her first time on the Mag."

"Who's Kari?"

"Kariane Phillips. She's sort of my girlfriend. Her old man is one of the religious big shots and he's like, 'my daughter is not a box of candy; there will be no free samples.' And I'm like, 'Dude, I'm fifteen ... do you really expect me to marry her without tasting the goods?' So you know what he did? He moved his family to an apartment on Level-4, just so I can't see her."

"Well, that sucks."

"So, you wanna learn to ride or what?"

"Just don't hurt me. My first day of work is Monday and I'm already bruised. Is this the best way to get around? My meeting place seems pretty far, and those weird elevators gave me a headache."

"The Maglev is definitely more fun, but not the way the old farts use the board, you have to surf the fast currents ... the deeper waves."

Logan handed Jessica her board. "Rule #1: Always make sure the power light is off *before* you place the board on the Maglev. Next, slip whichever foot you prefer to steer the board with into the rear sleeve."

Jessica placed her right foot inside the rear stirrup, the left in front.

Logan leaned over and adjusted the straps. "You want these snug, but not so tight that you can't slip out of them." He placed the cuff around her right ankle and handed her the slack. "Hold the leash with your left hand. When you're ready just give it a tug."

She pulled on the cord, registering the *click* as the board powered up and levitated off the electromagnetic track, slowly propelling forward on an unseen cushion of energy.

Logan positioned his feet on his own board, yanked his power cord and quickly caught up with her. "See? Easy, right? Okay, you're in what we call 'the shallows,' the kiddie pool. To actually surf the Mag you have to go out into the deep."

Jessica watched as Logan aimed his hoverboard to the outer section of the track.

Veering to the right she followed in his path, feeling the EM field beneath her board intensify. Imitating the teen, she cut S-patterns back and forth across unseen waves of energy, her lower torso registering patterns within the EM field.

Quickly picking up speed, the two riders soared past the gym and continued on, the ride exhilarating and yet hard work, Jessica's flexed quadriceps and glutes taking a pounding as she dug into the Maglev equivalent of a river's rapids.

After several minutes her face hurt from smiling.

As they ventured farther down the concourse, she noticed the suites had become two-story row homes, the "neighborhood" seeming more middle-class. Logan pointed to the second floor balcony of Unit 545-B. "That's where I live."

Jessica offered a thumbs-up.

They continued along the Maglev track for another mile before the concourse dead-ended at an eatery and small shopping plaza. A domed ceiling loomed three stories overhead, projecting a blue sky that appeared anything but artificial.

She signaled him to pull over and the two riders powered down.

"Quitting?"

"I'm old. This is harder on the quads than cross-country skiing. Besides, I've never been down here; let's check out the shops."

"It's just a mall. Every residential level has one, The eatery has a small grocery store; the shops are kind of lame. But the movie theater's cool. Level-4 is even better, it has private—"

His expression changed, as if he had said too much.

Jessica brushed it aside. "Are you hungry?"

"I'm good. Anyway, I'm saving my credits for tomorrow. It's Dim-Sum Sunday. Three to six p.m. Definitely worth checking out."

"I'll keep it in mind, but today I'm buying."

"Oh? Okay, maybe a quick snack."

Carrying their boards, they entered the eatery—an open-seating café adjacent to three restaurants and a small market. Jessica estimated there were forty people in the complex but saw no staff. "Logan, how many people live down here?"

The teen had loaded a cheeseburger, soda, and two bottled waters onto his tray. "Couple hundred maybe, but that's just Level-5."

"What about the other levels?"

"Dunno. I've never been on another level. Only Cosmic Clearance can do that."

She smiled. "Come on, now. I know you and Kariane have been checking out those private boxes in the Level-4 theater. A quick peek at your father's security schematics and, you probably downloaded at least two secret access routes up to Level-4."

Logan offered a mischievous grin, holding up three fingers.

"Good for you." Jessica added an apple to the tray and then took over for Logan, sliding it beneath a scanner to tally the bill.

The machine spoke: "Your total is $7.28. Please swipe your identification and have a nice day."

Reaching for the lanyard hanging around her neck, she removed the I.D. badge from inside her shirt and glanced back at Logan. "Anything else you'd like before I swipe? Dessert?"

The teenager had gone pale, his jaw slack, his blue eyes staring at the I.D. card in her hand. "You're Cosmic Clearance?"

"Yes. So what?"

"I was lying. I've never been on Level-4, I swear."

"Okay. Logan, calm down—you're hyperventilating."

He wiped tears from his eyes. "I gotta be somewhere, I just remembered."

He jogged back to the Maglev track, stepped on his board and took off, accelerating down the concourse.

19

Charlottesville, Virginia
Saturday

ADAM LAY AWAKE IN BED, staring at the sun-drenched window. Ten hours before, he had been convinced a species from another world had been observing him from the other side of the glass.

Seven hours of sleep later, and he wasn't sure if it had really happened or if it was just a dream.

The scent of brunch and a freshly-brewed pot of coffee drove him from his bed. Guiding his pant leg over his prosthetic he dressed, used the bathroom, and made his way down the stairs.

He found Emily Greer in the kitchen, transferring a pan of hash browns into a serving dish.

She greeted him with a smile. "Good afternoon. How did you sleep?"

"Surprisingly well considering a spaceship from another world practically landed on your house.

Emily smiled. "Just another night at the Greers."

"Are you saying that this kind of thing happens often?"

"Not often, but it happens. However, you definitely received the VIP treatment. I made hash browns and scrambled eggs, and we have fresh bagels and cream cheese, unless you'd prefer toast. Go on and help yourself; I have to run into town before this afternoon's training session. Steven pushed it back until four p.m."

"Where is Steven?"

"Where else? In his study."

Adam fixed himself a plate of food, poured a cup of coffee, and crossed the hall.

He found Dr. Greer at his desk, reading through a file. He looked up as Adam entered. "Sleep well?"

"All things considered. What are you doing?"

"Reviewing the personnel files of this week's CE-5 group. I suspect at least one of our guests is not quite who they claim to be."

"CIA?"

"Or MAJI. The ETs knew, they always do. I think that's why they waited until the group left before revealing themselves to you."

"You knew they were coming, didn't you?"

"I always ask them to make an appearance; I never know if they'll actually show. As I said last night, every CE-5 session is different. But I did ask them to do something that would eliminate your doubts. And that was impressive."

"Ya think?" Adam sat on one of the folding chairs. "How do you communicate with another species and ask them to pop in for a visit? Do you have an ET hotline or something?"

"Thought-energy and consciousness is my hotline and it's theirs; it's how they communicate with one another across millions of light years. I meditate before each session. Last night I communicated to them that you were on a mission to help us, and if they felt you were worthy, then I suggested they do something to remove your doubts. Years ago, I did the same thing when I was in Phoenix preparing for an important briefing. Google 'Phoenix Lights' when you have a chance. That event was bigger; last night was far more personal. I'm sure you thought I was a bit of a kook."

Adam smiled. "It's the subject matter. When I tell my brother about what happened last night, he may dissociate himself from me."

"You need to understand—the ridicule attached with seeing UFOs … it was all intended. Back in 1953, the CIA actually hired Disney Studios to create cartoons about little green men so that the subject would never be taken seriously—de-fanging the whole issue into silliness. It will take a lot of courage to pursue this, not just in terms of one's own personal safety, but also your reputation. You're going to be ridiculed and laughed out of meetings; you're going to be ostracized. Everything terrible you can imagine has been said about me, and so what? I mean, you just expect it … but most people in the public eye don't want to go through it.

"I wrote a paper about this called, *When Disclosure Serves Secrecy*. It's on our website, SiriusDisclosure.com—I suggest you read it. The paper describes the dangers of doing what we've done and how the process of disclosure is being hijacked by charlatans who masquerade as disclosure supporters. It's an old CIA trick they've used time and time again to diffuse the threat of the public learning the truth about a subject from the inside. In my case, they attached nonsense to the body of evidence I compiled; things exacerbating the fear factor and the silliness—the whole *evil aliens are coming to eat us for lunch*. The CIA has gone to extraordinary lengths to perpetrate alien abductions in order to add fuel to the craziness associated with UFOs, keeping legitimate scientists from getting involved."

"But you got involved. You weren't afraid."

"I had a sighting when I was a boy, plus I had a near-death experience which somewhat inoculated me. Still, my goal was never to brief presidents and CIA directors, and I certainly didn't expect to have to deal with threats on my life, let alone see harm come to people I cared deeply about. I was working full-time as an emergency and trauma doctor in a North Carolina ER and I loved my work. Using meditation to establish peaceful contact between humans and these visiting Interstellars … I stumbled upon that when I was much younger. My only intention was to show our visitors that there is far more to the human race than the military establishment that was shooting them down. So I founded the Center for the Study of Extraterrestrial Intelligence—a grass roots movement that bypassed governments in order to make peaceful contact with these civilizations as citizen diplomats, much like *Physicians for Social Responsibility* were citizen diplomats to the Soviet Union during the darkest days of the Cold War.

"Our first really successful CE-5 experience happened with a group of about fifty people on a beach near Pensacola, Florida. Two of our participants were Air Force pilots, one was a colonel. That night we vectored in four ET craft and they materialized and were filmed—it was actually quite close but the night cameras back then weren't very good. The story ended up on the front page of the Pensacola paper and I suddenly found myself flying way above the radar of some very serious national security guys.

"In March of 1992, about a month after the close encounter in Pensacola, I was invited to attend a conference in Atlanta. Being naive, I thought it was just a UFO convention. Once I arrived I realized half the people there were part of MJ-12."

"Like who?"

"The former Head of Army Intelligence, the NSA, DIA—a lot of Intel spooks. And they were very confrontational, asking me, *What the hell do you think you're doing?* I said, *Well, you can read about it, I don't have any secrets."* I told them I was developing protocols and a team to make contact with these civilizations outside governmental channels because the government was broken. I was told it was none of my business and not to do it. My response was, *Try stopping me.'* We kind of had a *mano a mano* in a hotel room until three in the morning."

"What changed? How did you go from group meditations to briefing presidents?"

"A senior official at the CIA flew a trusted emissary down on a private jet to visit me in North Carolina. This man's family founded the California Institute of Technology, one of the most prestigious universities in America. He said, *Dr. Greer, do what you were planning on doing and don't give up. Someone's got to do this because it's out of control; moreover someone's going to have to spearhead a contact protocol—right now, the system is completely dysfunctional.'* I told him that I was an emergency room doctor and I was just doing this ad hoc between ER shifts and raising four children. All the time I'm thinking, 'why is this guy asking *me* to do something? Why don't they just do it themselves?' That was my initiation into this weird 'down the rabbit hole' world of secret projects.

"A few months later William Jefferson Clinton was elected President of the United States. Almost immediately I was approached by people who were friends of his who said, *This is something that the president is very interested in.'* Webster Hubble, who was third in command at the Justice Department prior to being convicted of some other problems, told me Clinton wanted

181

to know three things when he took office: Who really killed Marilyn Monroe, who killed Jack Kennedy, and what is all this UFO stuff? Apparently they made inquiries into the subject and were not happy with the answers they were getting, meaning they knew they were being lied to. At about that time, some military people who were in favor of disclosure approached me. These people had had UFO experiences, either on battle-ships or at strategic air command facilities where nuclear weapons were being kept, and they offered to assist me.

"One of these men was a naval commander ... very connected up in the Pentagon. When he showed up at my front door, my first thought was that he was a spy. Turns out he was a stand-up guy who did everything he could to set up a number of the deep background briefings that I did at the Pentagon. We decided to have a meeting to discuss how to put together a team that would brief the right folks in government and encourage them to end the secrecy. You have to understand, this was back in 1992-93, when I actually thought we had a functional constitutional government. Since then I've learned it's all window dressing, that there's a parallel governmental process that operates completely independent of the people we elect.

"Anyway, we had this meeting and it was decided that we should contact certain key people in the U.S. government to—in military speak—de-conflict the CSETI contact teams from Air Force and other military operations so that they didn't interfere with us and we didn't interfere with them. That was the whole purpose of the meeting, to make sure we weren't caught in the middle ... to prevent an accidental shooting. It seemed that whenever and wherever we were doing our CE-5, we'd have a run-in with military jets, helicopters, and all kinds of stuff coming into our contact sites ... and we still do to this day. All I wanted was to keep my people safe.

"My military advisor met with Admiral Cramer, the Head of Intelligence for the Joint Chiefs of Staff. After speaking with him he decided we needed to have a meeting with the Intel people at Wright-Patterson, the air force base where the Roswell remains were sent. This was in September of 1993. While that meeting was being set up, two more influential individuals came calling. The first one was Leah Ghali, the wife of Boutros Boutros-Ghali, the U.N. Secretary General. The second was Laurance Rockefeller.

"Laurance was the philosopher king of the family. David Rockefeller was the money guy with Chase Manhattan, and his nephew, Jay Rockefeller was Chairman of the Senate Intelligence Committee. If you recall from my talk, Nelson Rockefeller was the one who had set up the Rockefeller Commission of 1956 which completely reorganized the Department of Defense and the CIA, and led to the establishment of MJ-12—he was the group's first leader. It was also Nelson Rockefeller who made it so no U.S. president could contain, control, or penetrate MAJI or their unacknowledged UFO projects."

"You must have gotten some blowback—associating with a Rockefeller."

"I did, but I knew Laurance was different; I think he wanted to 'cleanse the family karma.' He knew what we were doing was really working—he had been sending his people to our CE-5 protocols where ET craft would appear and then disappear. Laurance invited me out to his ranch—the J.Y. Ranch in Wyoming which is where the Clintons vacationed. I was asked to go there in September of 1993 to share information about our CE-5 initiative.

"It was an eclectic crowd. Billionaire Robert Bigelow of Bigelow Aerospace was there, along with people of various backgrounds from the UFO sub-culture. Some were supportive regarding our work; some despised what we were doing. I found out later that the unfriendlies were working for the intelligence community.

"At some juncture over the weekend I was asked what else I was working on. I said, *We've initiated a project to brief senior government officials in the Clinton Administration and the Pentagon and members of Congress so that we can terminate secrecy on this issue and get the government to change policy because we understand that the incoming president is favorable toward that idea.*'

"Well, you could have heard a pin drop. Laurance Rockefeller asked about my plans and I told him I was going straight to Wright-Patterson Air Force Base after this meeting to brief the colonel over this Foreign Technology Division of the Air Force, and then, in a couple of months, I'd be briefing President Clinton's CIA director.

"Laurance wanted to be involved, but only from behind-the-scenes. He offered to host the president and first lady at his ranch so that I could show them the best available UFO photos and evidence.

"Meanwhile, the U.N. Secretary General's wife attended a series of events known as salons. A salon was a meeting in a private home attended by dignitaries. The well-to-do host would invite an interesting guest, someone like yours truly, who would inform these rich and powerful people about what was going on, which is exactly what I did. Mrs. Boutros-Ghali was so taken by the subject that she wanted to arrange a meeting at the U.N. so I could brief a lot of the diplomats and friends of hers who were supportive of ending secrecy and making peaceful interplanetary contact. Again, our objective was to provide accurate information to the president, his advisors, and the key people in Congress. We even gave them the perfect story to cover their asses as to why this information had been kept so long from the masses—that world leaders were simply waiting until the Cold War was over, not wanting to throw into the mix the fact that Earth was being visited by interstellar civilizations, and that our scientists had, in fact, reverse-engineered many of their technologies.

"In the fall of 1993, I was invited to speak at Colorado State University. The event was hosted by astronaut Brian O'Leary and Maury Albertson, one of the co-founders of the Peace Corps. Before roughly 800 people I laid out the entire manifesto which justified disclosure and how we should do it. At the end of that talk I noticed a bald man standing at the back of the room, waiting to speak with me. He said, *'Dr. Greer, my name is Petersen, and I think I can help you with this. I know some folks in Washington who want to know about this, but they're not getting any good answers.'* I assumed it was some low level staffer for some junior congressman, only he surprised me by telling me it was James Woolsey, the director of Central Intelligence. The two men were good friends and he said Woolsey wanted to be briefed.

"The meeting was eventually set for December 13, 1993. The cover story was a dinner party in Arlington at John Petersen's home. The CIA director and his wife, Dr. Sue Woolsey, who was the COO of the National Academy of Sciences, would attend along with Emily and myself. So we got a nanny for the kids, flew up to Washington, and had this meeting. I began by showing the director a portfolio of images, photographs, and documents.

After about ten minutes Woolsey stopped me. He said he knew UFOs were real, turns out he and his wife had a sighting in New Hampshire when they were younger. What he wanted to know was why no one would discuss it with him or President Clinton.

"My initial thought was that I was being set up. Three hours later I was convinced he knew nothing about these projects; that both he and the president were being completely deceived by those who had compartmented intelligence within the CIA. That was the moment I realized that we were living in a country that had undergone a quiet *coup d'état* decades earlier—a story that would never be covered by either *The New York Times* or *The Washington Post* because it would be the biggest scandal ever."

"What did you do?"

"I had come to the Woolsey meeting with a white paper which described what needed to be done by the president and his people in order to end the secrecy. I gave it to the CIA director as he was leaving. Woolsey looked at me and he said, *'How can we disclose something which we have no access to?'*

"Well, that was a very chilling question. If we were to push on this, it would unveil the biggest constitutional crisis in the history of the United States. No president wants to admit that they're out of the loop on important things. They tend to think in terms of activities being either classified, secret, or top-secret, never realizing within these classifications there are compartments. The compartments that are Unacknowledged Special Access Projects are only known to those individuals inside the compartment, and that includes the President of the United States.

"I'll give you an example of how even a high-ranking official is kept in the dark about a department he's in charge of. On September 10, 2001—the day before 9/11, Donald Rumsfeld announced that $2.3 trillion was unaccounted for in the Department of Defense budget, based on a recent audit ordered by one of your predecessors, the Under Secretary of Defense. Think about that a moment. The war in Iraq cost American taxpayers a trillion dollars, and Secretary of Defense Rumsfeld is saying there is more than twice that amount—not missing, but unaccounted for.

"I know an auditor who audits my uncle's old company, Northrop-Grumman. Just like Lockheed-Martin, they do a lot of top-secret work on certain kinds of aircraft dealing with anti-gravity propulsion. If it's an unacknowledged compartment with billions of dollars in it, the auditor will be told, *'You don't have a need to know what's going on with this,'* and it's just rubber-stamped as audited. The auditors have no idea where that money is or where it's going. It goes in the front door and leaves out the window, and no one knows where it ends up.

"My military advisor was involved in one USAP. He and a few others were taken into a SCIF—a Secure Communication Intelligence Facility—completely underground. Everyone's weapons were taken, their cell phones, watches … anything electronic. A security enforcement officer for that particular USAP escorted them below. The guy took a bullet out of his gun's chamber and said, *'If you tell anyone about anything going on in this project, there is a bullet with your name on it and it will find you … somewhere … somehow.'* This is not a movie. This is actually how that world works … the world I've been dealing with since 1993. That is serious stuff. Of all the projects that are unacknowledged … black bag operations of all kinds … special operations of all kinds … the blackest and most unacknowledged are the ones dealing with UFOs and extraterrestrial intelligence.

"Listening to this military advisor's story, I was ready to quit. I mean, here I am, an ER doctor used to dealing with shootings and stabbings … car wrecks and burns … and this bag of crap gets handed off to me and I'm expected to run with it?

"In early February of 1994, a friend of the president came to our home for dinner; I was told that he was a big fundraiser for Bill Clinton. We're sitting at the table eating dinner when he turns to me in front of my wife and kids and says, *'The president and his team are really very supportive of what you're recommending in this white paper, but they're concerned that if he does this, he'll end up like Jack Kennedy.'*

"I start laughing … I think he's joking. He stopped me and says, *'No, they're not kidding.'* We went into my library to talk in private where he tells me the president and his people were convinced that if he were to push on the UFO issue, he would be subject to TWEP—Termination With Extreme Prejudice. I'm hearing this, thinking—okay, then what am I supposed to do? It's not like I've got a Secret Service detail. He said, *'No … they want you to do this … go ahead and try to bring this stuff together.'* In other words, President Clinton is afraid he'll be assassinated if he attempts to bring disclosure to the UFO-ET subject, but I'm expendable. And guess what that makes you, my friend?"

"Damn …"

"Laurance Rockefeller gave me the same line … that it was too dangerous for him, that the money side of his family—the oil people—were already angry at him for pursuing this. He'd support our efforts and he'd arrange for me to meet the Clintons at his ranch—a get-together that finally happened in 1994 … my first presidential briefing."

"So what did you do—you know, when you found out your place on the totem pole?"

"Once I realized the president would never sign an Executive Order, I decided to approach potential allies in both houses of Congress and eye-witnesses in the military and government, believing there was safety in numbers—not just for them but for myself. Between the years 1995 and 1998 we identified dozens of potential witnesses with top-secret clearances who could be subpoenaed and would swear under oath about UFOs and the secrecy behind it. In 1997, we held a meeting at the Westin Hotel in Georgetown for several dozen of these people, along with a few members of Congress … a very private, closed event. Congressman Dan Burton, who was Chairman of the House Government Reform and Oversight Committee showed up; he was interested because one of his closest friends had had a UFO encounter in Indiana some years earlier and told him all about it. Burton was a mover and a shaker; he wanted everything we had on the subject. A short time later someone got to him and he backed off."

"Steven, how were you able to convince your eyewitnesses to violate their national security oaths in order to come forward and testify?"

"My military people provided the solution. They advised me to draft a UNOD letter."

"UNOD?"

"Unless Otherwise Directed. The letter basically stated that these USAPs exist and are being run illegally and have been unconstitutional since the 1950s; that the president and other key figures have been lied to, as have the oversight committees of the Congress. It also mentioned how similar illegal programs exist in the United Kingdom and other countries where I had briefings. Therefore, it was our assessment that the National Security Act and secrecy laws that are attached to oaths of secrecy were null and void, and that any man or woman who has knowledge of any document, material, or evidence attached to the UFO and extraterrestrial issue can disclose this information publicly without penalty of law. *Unless otherwise directed*, we intended to proceed with disclosing this UFO testimony and all related documents.

"To cover ourselves legally, we sent the UNOD letter to the president, the head of the Justice Department, the Pentagon, the CIA, FBI, NSA—basically the entire alphabet soup of the Intel agencies and we sent it return receipt requested to prove it was received. Danny Sheehan, the constitutional attorney who did the Silkwood Case and represented *The New York Times* in the Pentagon Papers, helped me—pro-bono—on this."

"I get it. If the programs are illegal, then the oath is invalid."

"It's basic constitutional law. The letter essentially exonerates every man and woman in the private and public sector, Intel or the military who ever worked on these projects from any legal penalties related to disclosing information. We used the document to protect every eyewitness and whistleblower that came forward to testify in 2001 for the *Disclosure Project*."

"You have to wonder why Eric Snowden didn't do this."

"Snowden's mistake was that he disclosed things that were legal—projects that were being overseen by the president and the Senate Select Committee on Intelligence. Even though those programs are Big Brother-esque, he should have limited his disclosure to operations that were unacknowledged and illegal. If he had done that, he would not be in legal trouble. He just didn't know. He was young, and the journalists and people who were working with him didn't understand the system that well. As a whistleblower it's okay to disclose the illegal programs, not the legal ones, no matter how outrageous they are. Of course, there are far more potential witnesses who will never come forward because of the threat to their families. This is the type of criminal behavior you'd associate with organized crime, which is exactly what it is … organized crime. I've had private conversations with several Apollo astronauts who told me that, when they returned from the moon they were briefed by members of the intelligence community who warned them that, if they ever went public about what they witnessed, their loved ones would be killed."

"Witnessed … on the moon? You mean extraterrestrials?"

"With the Interstellar community, it's all about consciousness. We tend to associate NASA with science, but the Apollo program was always an extension of the military industrial complex. When JFK set his challenge to put an American on the moon, the United States and the Soviet Union were at the height of the Cold War."

"You didn't answer my question. Are there ETs on the moon?"

"Their structures are located on the dark side. We have several *Disclosure* witnesses who have seen top-secret photos of these structures, so NASA knew they were there before the Apollo landing. When Neil Armstrong and Buzz Aldrin stepped out of the lunar module, the crater they had landed in was surrounded by Interstellar craft. NASA officials had prepared a fake audio transmission and video footage of astronauts planting an American flag, just in case of that very scenario. You can tell where they cut in because, in one shot, the fake flag caught a gust of wind and moved."

Adam shook his head. "Is everything about the space program a lie?"

"Which space program? There are two. One is NASA, otherwise known as the biggest white collar welfare program around. Do you have any idea how much American taxpayer monies have been wasted on antiquated rockets like the space shuttle?"

"What was wrong with the space shuttle?"

"For starters, like all rocket-propelled objects, these controlled bombs were inherently dangerous—the equivalent of riding a Roman candle into space. There were six shuttles; two of them blew up, along with their crews. The second and more important space program has existed for the last forty years, and we've had reversed-engineered anti-gravitic craft, built by humans. NASA's using a horse and buggy while Lockheed keeps the Maserati locked up in the garage."

Steven glanced at the antique clock on his wall. "We don't have much time; the group will begin arriving in about an hour. I'd like you gone before then. That way I can explain the CE-5 wasn't for you and I asked you to leave."

"One last thing: Before Emily woke me last night I had a weird dream … I dreamt an insect-man was watching me from the bedroom window. At least I thought it was a dream, now I'm not so sure."

"Interesting … There is an intelligent species of ETs that evolved from insects; they've become very protective of what we're doing. Did it have the head of a praying mantis but the arms and legs of a biped?"

"Then it was real? I wasn't sure … I was so tired."

"Maybe it came to you in a lucid dream."

"I don't know. But if you told me an insect creature would be staring at me from the bedroom window, I'm guessing my reaction would have been to freak out. And yet I never felt threatened, in fact, I felt perfectly at peace."

"We tend to fear things we don't understand. What you call an insect creature is simply another intelligent life form that evolved from a different exit point in the animal kingdom. I'm sure they were checking you out, evaluating you to determine whether you were worthy of the close encounter that followed."

"And the climate change message? Have you ever experienced that before?"

"We don't need our Interstellar friends to tell us our planet is in trouble. That's why we're trying so hard to get our hands on a zero-point-energy application and fund its development before we slide beyond the point of no return. Failing that, either a cataclysmic event or an existential emergency will arise."

"What kind of existential emergency?"

"The cabal has handcuffed human civilization to fossil fuels for nearly eighty years. As a result, little to nothing has changed—except for the number of people on the planet using the same resources … and that is a reality which is absolutely unsustainable.

"When the air becomes even more unbreathable and the lower class goes extinct, the masses will rise up and revolt to overthrow the center of power, which was always just an illusion anyway. When that happens, MAJI will unleash a False Flag event that will make 9/11 look like a church picnic."

"What kind of False Flag event?"

"A fake alien invasion using ARVs—Alien Reproduction Vehicles—and scalar weapons. It's their own apocalyptic version of *Independence Day*, and they've been preparing for it since the 1970s."

"That's insane? Why would they do this?"

"Because, Mr. Under Secretary, these warmongers would rather torch the Earth and murder billions of innocent people in a contrived interplanetary war than lose control. The gang-banksters and military industrialists running MAJI have united with the religious right to bring us their own version of the End of Days, and the algorithms to mass destruction are already in play."

20

Subterranean Complex—Midwest USA
Monday, 6:27 a.m.

THE MEETING ROOM WAS SHAPED like a horseshoe, its rows of elevated seating wrapped halfway around the speaker's dais, a large projection screen mounted behind the stage.

The guest speaker stood at the lectern, preparing to address a dozen cameras located throughout the near-empty chamber. The event coordinator was seated in the front row wearing a headset connected to an iPad. On screen were thirty-four numbered squares, all but two of them now lit.

A moment later the last two Council members logged on, causing the coordinator to signal to the scientist at the dais to begin.

"Good morning ... or evening, whatever the case. My name is Dr. Jessica Marulli, and as the new director of *Project Zeus*, I've been asked to provide a status report on the twenty satellites we hope to put into orbit before the end of the year. As far as the Defense Department is concerned, the *Zeus* array is simply part of the next generation *Space Fence*, a ground-based sensor system that had been responsible for tracking the more than 500,000 objects in orbit around Earth, most of which is classified as space junk—all of which is potentially quite dangerous to the International Space Station and our other satellites. While the old *Space Fence* array could track objects as small as a basketball up to 24,000 kilometers away, the *Zeus* satellites will provide the Space Surveillance Network with an entirely different set of tracking sensors.

"The *Zeus* array is, in essence, an ITS or Interstellar Tracking System. It has been designed to track objects as they pass from higher dimensions into our third dimensional physical universe. By deploying these twenty ITS satellites around the Earth, we'll be able to lock onto and track any extra-terrestrial vehicle passing through the crossing point of light anywhere between our sun and just inside of the asteroid belt which lies between the orbits of Mars and Jupiter.

"To handle the enormous energy loads required to power the satellite's ITS unit, as well as its onboard EM shield, our team turned to the same source of energy used to power the interstellar vehicles we'll be targeting: zero-point-energy."

Jessica held out her hand, allowing a hologram of a doughnut-shaped object to appear to rest in her palm.

"We initially used a first-generation rotary ZPE prototype which was based on a design by Professor John Searl at Cambridge. All human-invented ZPE devices are classified as first-generation units; the more advanced devices having been reverse-engineered from the interstellar craft downed over the last seventy years. Even though this unit is relatively small, the generator can still produce enough energy to power the Empire State Building for the next thousand years. Let me show you how it works."

She pretended to toss the hologram, which expanded across the stage until it was the size of a pick-up truck.

"A little stage craft, but at least now we can see how these amazing generators work. First, some quick basics: Energy is everywhere. The challenge is to convert it to power, defined as voltage multiplied by current to equal wattage. What Professor Searl designed is a closed circuit perpetual generator which produces a quantum vacuum flux field using zero-point-energy. It is powered by the electrons which perpetually surround us, producing clean and unlimited electricity."

Using her iPad controls, Jessica removed the top of the hologram, allowing her remote video audience to see inside the zero-point-energy generator.

"Looking down inside the doughnut, we can see it contains three circular ring plates, one inside the next. Suspended within these ring plates are rollers, each the size of a 9 volt battery. These rollers, along with their ring plates, possess a magnetic north and south pole. As a result, the rollers float above the magnetic field without actually touching the ring plate. The process of rapidly circulating these rollers around the ring plates in order to generate electricity begins when one powers up the unit's positively-charged neodymium core."

The inner rim of the doughnut hole glowed neon-blue, causing neon-red particles to suddenly appear out of thin air and race into the center of the device.

"As you can see, the red negatively-charged electrons, which exist all around us, immediately rush into the device like male dogs going after a pack of bitches in heat. They mate together to form boson pairs, color-coded in purple here. The boson pairs compress and then exit through the central core to the first outer ring where they cause the twelve rollers to accelerate to speeds averaging 250 miles an hour. From there they pass through a magnetic layer which both excites and pulls them through the second ring where they cause these rollers to revolve at a velocity exceeding 600 miles an hour. Finally, the electrons exit to the copper emitter layer where they join trillions of other boson pairs in ring three, spinning these rollers at over 1,500 miles an hour. A switch directs the generated electricity through standard coils, completing the electrical circuit. Unlike conventional generators which heat up after prolonged use, the zero-point unit remains cool no matter how long it runs. There's no fuel needed, no toxins released—the unit is powered solely by the electrons entering the unit and the internal tensions of the atoms. It is, literally, a source of endless clean energy."

Jessica shut off the hologram. "Powered by these zero-point-energy units, our team produced three different operational designs for the ITS, two of which scored above the minimum 92 percentile rating on the Oracle Computer Simulation. Unfortunately, during zero-gravity tests inside the CHIL—Lockheed's Collaborative Human Immersive Laboratory—the system reported targeting deviation errors exceeding three one-thousandths of a degree. That may not sound like much, but when you're scanning an area from the Earth to Mars and beyond—that's a major league whiff.

"The good news is that I was able to isolate the cause of the problem.

Turns out the moving parts of the zero-point-energy unit were causing the satellite to wobble just a tick. While it was barely perceptible in our dimension, in an area of space we refer to as the crossing point of light, it was creating quite a noticeable hiccup. Allow me to explain.

"To track a fast-moving object in space requires a laser. A laser is essentially an amplified beam of light. The light you see in this auditorium has a wave component which travels at 186,000 miles per second—a figure more commonly known as the speed of light.

"The crossing point of light is the boundary that separates our third dimensional space from the higher dimensions. We can't actually track an interstellar space craft moving through these higher dimensions, but we can lock on to the disturbance created when the ET vessel crosses over. To track this disturbance requires us to use a scalar wave.

"A scalar is a longitudinal wave that travels way beyond the speed of light and in multiple dimensions. The geeks working at Nellis Air Force Base back in 1947 discovered this when they used a scalar wave to track three interstellar craft as they passed through the crossing point of light—in other words, as they stepped down from a higher dimension into our physical dimension. The scalar wave caused two of the interstellar craft to collide. One crashed northwest of Roswell, New Mexico; the other about a hundred miles west of the first. We were able to salvage a treasure-trove of the ETs' technology.

"Getting back to the Interstellar Tracking System, I swapped out a first-generation zero-point-energy generator with one of the more advanced ZPE units reverse-engineered from the ET craft. These devices use nano-crystals as opposed to rotating gyros, thus eliminating the wobble. The results from my CHIL lab were perfect. Once we replace all twenty first-gen ZPE units with the nano-crystal generators, the satellites should be ready to launch. Are there any questions?"

Lydia Gagnon signaled from the vacant first row. "Dr. Marulli, we have multiple requests for you to expand upon how interstellar craft travel through space."

"First let me state that a rocket is a very inefficient method of propulsion; you're essentially pushing a craft through space. Interstellar craft travel by phasing in and out of higher dimensions where time and space do not exist.

"Think of these higher dimensions as an intergalactic short cut, linking any two points. To enter these higher dimensions requires an electromagnetic propulsion system which draws energy from the zero-point field. The process creates an anti-gravitic effect, or what we refer to as a bubble in space-time. Traveling inside the bubble allows a craft to access the higher dimensions. When it's accessed in the physical dimension, a craft can travel 20,000 miles an hour and then suddenly execute a 90 degree turn with no deceleration effect. All of this falls under what Einstein referred to as 'spooky magic.' It's what makes interstellar travel possible."

The event coordinator waved once more from the front row. "Dr. Marulli, several Council members would like to know why we haven't used zero-point technology to send our own ARVs on missions across the galaxy."

"Do we have the means to accomplish this? The answer is yes ... in fact we've had that ability since 1956. As to *why* we haven't gone ... it seems our Interstellar visitors have quarantined us."

From her vantage behind the lectern, Jessica could see Lydia's iPad screen light up like a Christmas tree.

"Dr. Marulli—"

"They want to know why humans have been quarantined."

"Correct."

Jessica Marulli stared back at Lydia Gagnon. The event coordinator had warned her on the elevator ride over this morning that this line of questioning would probably come up—that it was a litmus test for all new Cosmic Clearance members—the MAJI equivalent of asking a Supreme Court nominee their feelings about abortion.

"Dr. Gagnon, I don't think any member of *Zeus* is qualified to speak for an Interstellar. However, since it was the testing of the atomic bomb during World War II, and the hydrogen bomb a short time later, that appeared to summon our galactic visitors in droves, I think we can safely make a few assumptions.

"First, by our own definition, Interstellars are Type-3 civilizations, the highest rank a species can achieve on the evolutionary scale. By contrast, humans are the definition of a Type-Zero civilization—the lowest rung on the ladder. Violent and self-centered, we have yet to advance beyond the planet-polluting era of fossil fuels, while we continue to teeter between advancing as a species and initiating our own self-destruction. If you question that evaluation, pick up a newspaper. On any given day we're either bombing or shooting or stabbing one another. To be fair, the Interstellar communities that have shown interest in humanity have been around a lot longer than we have—maybe ten thousand years, maybe a million ... who knows? At some time during their own history, they no doubt dealt with their own equivalent of hatred, prejudice, and violence. *Homo sapiens* also had to evolve from the violent end of the gene pool, our primate brains are wired for conflict. Lest we forget, we did acquire the ETs' technology by force, shooting down their vehicles. Whether that gives them the right to quarantine the entire human race is a matter of opinion ... a quarantine, let me remind you, that includes our own moon. The Interstellar community made it quite clear during the last Apollo missions that they will not tolerate any more lunar landings or flyovers of the far side where their bases are located."

"One last question ... one of our senior Council members is asking about these CE-5 encounters where civilians—acting as self-appointed ambassadors for humanity—have been initiating contact with Interstellar species. Up until now, the efforts of our Air Force to discourage this unauthorized contact has been rendered ineffective by the speed of these ET craft and their ability to move into transdimensional space. The question, Dr. Marulli, is how effective will a fully-functioning *Zeus* satellite array be in discouraging these CE-5 encounters?"

Jessica flashed a grin. "You've heard the expression, 'like shooting fish in a barrel?' After *Zeus* vaporizes the first UFO foolish enough to cross into third dimensional space, I sincerely doubt our Interstellar guests will be responding to Dr. Greer and his followers."

21

The Pentagon
Washington, D.C.
Monday 8:27 a.m.

THE PENTAGON IS A CITY UNTO ITSELF—6.6 million square feet of office space supporting 23,000 people, all contained in a five-sided, five-story (with two basements) facility, its 17.5 miles of corridors laid out in ten wedges so that any two points can be reached on foot in ten minutes or less. The building is divided into five concentric rings, from A-Ring out to E-Ring, with the two basement levels extending out to G-Ring. There are ten entrances, a central courtyard, thirty fast-food restaurants, a gym, and a concourse in close proximity to the Metro-bus and Metrorail stations.

Senior officers have their choice of locations, most of whom have the opportunity select E-Ring which has the only offices with windows. The wedge housing the Secretary of Defense and his five under secretaries was considered prime real estate; its office windows facing the Potomac River.

Adam Shariak's office was located on the third floor, two floors directly below that of his boss, the Secretary of Defense. Seated behind his desk, he reread the document he had just revised for the sixth time in the last two hours. Satisfied with the last edit, he glanced at his watch.

Meeting's in forty-five minutes Are you going through with this or not?

Steven Greer had answered every question Adam Shariak had, save one—why had William Jefferson Clinton selected him to bring out zero-point-energy? He was neither a politician nor a military insider, held a low security clearance, and knew just enough about the private defense sector to be annoying.

The obvious answer was his brother. As head of the Appropriations Committee, Senator Randy Hall was the perfect person to lead an investigation into whether a compartmentalized entity within the DoD was secretly spending $80 billion a year on illegal Unacknowledged Special Access Projects.

As Dr. Greer had said, "Expose the USAPs and you'd expose the cabal ... and with it—the black-shelved energy programs."

"Okay, but how do I convince my brother that these programs even exist? I need something to show him—a project name ... something?"

Dr. Greer had unlocked a tall steel file cabinet, removing a manila folder from a file and made a black and white copy. "In 1997, Admiral Tom Wilson, the Head of Intelligence for the Joint Chiefs of Staff, asked me to hold a briefing at the Pentagon. Before we met, I had my military advisor send the admiral this top-secret document."

He'd handed it to Adam. "As you can see, it originated out of Nellis Air Force Base—the place the public mistakenly calls Area 51. The document was actually a security alert—some UFO spotters had managed to penetrate the perimeter of Nellis and the administrators were forced to shut down test flights of their EMG's—their electromagnetic, gravitic anti-gravity vessels. What makes the document so valuable is that it came from the National Reconnaissance Office. The NRO is the super-secret spy satellite operations part of the Air Force. As you can see, the document lists a number of compartmented operations by their code names."

"By compartmented operations, you mean—"

"USAPs."

Adam had stared at the list. "Red Flag, Dark East, Dark South, Black Jack Team, Black Jack Control..."

"All originating out of Edwards Air Force Base. There were also teams at Nellis and Apertec, as well as other sites. All the important USAP stuff is handled by defense contractors—Lockheed-Martin, EG&G, E-Systems, Raytheon, Northrop-Grumman, Booz Allen Hamilton ... Edward Snowden worked for Booz Allen Hamilton; they contract for the National Security Agency. The corporate world is where most of the

USAPs get centered; from there they interface with other USAPs within military and intelligence. Attempt to approach them from the government side, and a project gatekeeper will tell you it doesn't exist. Approach from the corporate side and it's privatized... a corporate secret, like Microsoft's code. In this way it's hermetically sealed from all inquiries—clever yes, but very illegal. Of course, the mafia is always very clever, and this is the biggest mafia in the world."

Adam turned to the second page, scanning the names of the defense contractors. *"Holy shit ... Kemp Aerospace?"*

Greer nodded. *"Maybe that's why Clinton's people chose you as their Trojan Horse; they wanted someone on the inside who could testify that these USAPs are real."*

"I need a pen."

Adam had read through the list of projects again, circling any code names he recognized. *"I count six projects that Kemp Aerospace was subcontracted to work on while I was managing director, another three that were grandfathered in by my predecessor, Brian Coker."*

"Are any of them zero-point-energy projects?"

"I have no idea. My clearance wasn't high enough to sit in on any of these meetings."

"But you knew the defense contractors involved and their budgets. You could provide that information to your brother ... unless of course he already knows it."

"What's that supposed to mean?"

"Adam, it's possible your brother is a gatekeeper. The covert government always keeps a few operatives in key positions to maintain the secrecy and deny the truth. Former Congressman George Brown of California was a member of the Science and Technology Committee, but he was also on MJ-12's payroll. Same with Porter Goss, the former CIA Director and Chairman of the House Intelligence Committee. When asked about ETs or Roswell, or any of these USAPs, a gatekeeper assures the person inquiring that he's checked it out thoroughly and nothing exists. Congressmen never question a gatekeeper, and you only need a few of them overseeing key points of control in these institutions to maintain secrecy."

"My brother isn't a gatekeeper for the cabal."

"There's only one way to be sure. Give him the list. If he tells you he checked into it and it's not true, then he's either on the payroll and he's lying or he's afraid of going up against Big Oil."

"You don't know my brother."

"You're right. But I know Dennis Kucinich. The congressman knew all about UFOs, hell, he'd seen them with his own eyes. Yet he refused to touch the subject—too afraid of the ridicule he'd be forced to endure—and he chaired the House Oversight Subcommittee on Information Technology. James Woolsey ... the guy was once a huge ally, now he's a gatekeeper."

Adam contemplated this. "Okay. I'll meet with Randy about this on Monday—"

"No. You can't take this information directly to your brother; you have to follow proper protocol."

Adam nodded. "The new Secretary of Defense."

It had not taken long before General James "Mad Dog" Mattis had butted heads with President Trump and his "personal advisors." The Defense Secretary's first "come to Jesus" talk took place on his tenth day in office when Trump began issuing Executive Orders without consulting the departments of government that would be affected by these decrees ... especially the military.

A few days later, Trump's chief strategist, Stephen Bannon, was predicting war with China and the general knew his days as Secretary of Defense were numbered.

Jordan T. Denny, the newly confirmed Secretary of Defense, stared at the document in his hand, his body trembling as he read.

August 7, 2017

TO: The Honorable Jordan T. Denny, Secretary of Defense
FR: Adam Shariak, Under Secretary of Defense–Comptroller

Mr. Secretary of Defense:
In preparation for an extensive audit of the Department of Defense, Fiscal Years 2000 through 2016, I pulled the contracts and sub-contracts awarded to Kemp Aerospace during the period I served as managing director (August 2013 thru February 2017), as well as those projects grandfathered in by my predecessor, Dr. Brian Coker

(December 1999 thru March 2011). The point of this exercise was to cross-check the Pentagon's numbers against Kemp Aerospace's account receivables, in order to verify the reliability of the DoD's reporting system.

To my surprise, I could find no DoD records pertaining to the funding of nine (9) projects subcontracted to Kemp Aerospace through larger defense contractors during the sixteen years in question. In referencing Kemp's receivables, I was able to identify the name(s) of the lead defense contractor(s) involved, and the amounts received by Kemp Aerospace. Based on these figures, I have estimated the aggregate value of these projects, all of which were clearly funded by the Department of Defense—despite the fact that no records pertaining to any of these transactions "officially" exists, either in the public record or inside the Pentagon. While I do not know the specific nature of these projects, I do know the individuals to subpoena to obtain this information.

Project Name	Amount Subcontracted to Kemp Aerospace	Estimated Project Budget
Royal Ops	$14.4 million	$75 million
Cosmic ops	$1.2 billion	$18 billion
Maj ops	$1.7 billion	$6 billion
Maji ops	$1.2 billion	$7.5 billion
Pahute Mesa MOC	$680,000	$5 million
Sally Corridor MOC	$1.5 billion	$5.5 million
Groom Lake MOC	$3.8 billion	$18 billion
Dreamland MOC	$2 billion	$12 billion
Ground Star MOC	$27.5 million	$150 million

Private Corporate Entities involved:

BDM	MITRE Corp.
Bechtel Corporation	Northrop Grumman
Booz-Allen and Hamilton Inc.	Phillips Labs
The Boeing Company	Raytheon
EG&G	SAIC—Science Applications

E-Systems
Lockheed Martin
McDonnell Douglas Corp.

International Inc.
TRW
Village Supercomputing
Wackenhut Corporation

Military Bases Receiving Kemp Aerospace Goods and Services

Edwards Air Force Base and Related Facilities:

Government Facilities:
Edwards Air Force Base
Haystack Butte
China Lake
Table Mountain Observatory—
     NASA
Blackjack Control

Aerospace Facilities:
Northrop "Anthill"—Tejon Ranch
McDonnell Douglas—Llano Plant
Lockheed-Martin—Helendale Plant
Phillips Labs—North Edwards
     Facility

The Nellis Complex:
Area 51/S4, Pahute Mesa
Area 19, Groom Lake.

New Mexico Facilities:
Los Alamos National Laboratories
Kirtland Air Force Base
Sandia National Laboratories—SNL
Defense Nuclear Agency
Phillips Labs

Manzano Mountain Weapons
     Storage Facility and Under-
     ground Complex
Coyote Canyon Test Site
     (N. end of Manzano)
White Sands Complex

Arizona Facilities:
Fort Huachuca, underground storage facility, NSA and Army
     Intelligence complex near Fort Huachuca underground

Others:
Cheyenne Mountain Colorado Deep
     Space Network
Lawrence Livermore Labs
Pine Gap underground facility in

Utah underground complex
     southwest of Salt Lake City;
     accessible only by air.
Dugway Proving Grounds out-

| Australia Majestic; U.S. and Australian | side Provo, Utah; classified airspace |
| Redstone Arsenal underground complex; Alabama | |

Conclusions:
Based on Kemp Aerospace's share of Defense Appropriations during the years in question, I have estimated that $80 billion to upwards of $100 billion of taxpayer monies are being channeled <u>annually</u> into these USAPs (Unacknowledged Special Access Projects). Because they are being funded without the knowledge, consent, or oversight of the U.S. government, they have been operating illegally and unconstitutionally, and are in direct violation of the RICO Act.

Recommendations:
As Under Secretary of Defense–Comptroller, I am moving forward with an immediate investigation into these matters. I am also recommending inquiries into these Unacknowledged Special Access Projects, as well as the facilities, agencies and entities listed above, by Senator Randy Hall, Chairman of the Senate Appropriations Committee.

Thank you for your assistance in this important matter.

Adam Shariak
Adam Shariak
Under Secretary of Defense–Comptroller

Jordan Denny reread the document twice and then massaged his eyes, as if not believing his Under Secretary was starting his week like this. After a few moments, he returned to the list of project names. "Mr. Under Secretary, which defense contractor subcontracted services to Kemp Aerospace in regard to this first project, cited here as 'Royal Ops?'"

"Sir, I believe that was SAIC."

Jordan Denny reached across his desk for his phone, hitting the intercom. "Angela, get me Barry Zuckerman over at SAIC."

"Yes, sir."

He scanned down to the next name on the list. "What about 'Cosmic Ops?'"

"That was Lockheed. You'll want to speak to Edward Canup, Jr.; he's stationed out at Edwards Air Force Base."

The intercom beeped. "Sir, I have Barry Zuckerman on line one."

"Thank you, Angela." He pressed the blinking key. "Barry, Jordan Denny. I'm with Under Secretary Adam Shariak and you're on speaker."

"Gentlemen. To what do I owe this pleasure?"

"Project Royal Ops—read me in on it, please."

A moment of silence ... followed by: "I'm sorry, Jordan. I can't do that."

Jordan Denny snatched up the receiver. "Barry, in case you forgot, I'm the goddam Secretary of Defense. Now read me in on Project Royal Ops."

Adam watched as his boss's face flushed red.

"What do you mean I don't have a need to know? If I'm asking you about ... hello? Hello?"

Adam winced as the Secretary slammed the receiver on the hook.

"Can you believe the son of a bitch hung up on me?" He pressed the intercom button again. "Angela, get me Edward ... sorry?"

"Canup."

"Canup. Edward Canup. He's at Lockheed?"

Adam nodded.

"He's at Lockheed, Angela. Thank you."

The Defense Secretary closed his eyes and took a few deep breaths. "Meditation ... my wife swears by it. Ever give it a try?"

"This weekend as a matter of fact."

"Did it calm you down?"

The intercom beeped, cutting off Adam's reply. "Sir, I have Edward Canup on line two."

"Mr. Canup, this is Jordan T. Denny, the Secretary of Defense. I want you to read me in on Project Cosmic Ops."

"I'm sorry, Mr. Secretary. I'm not familiar with Cosmic Ops."

"In that case, Mr. Canup, say hello to Adam Shariak. Before he was sworn in as my Comptroller, Mr. Shariak was Project Manager at Kemp Aerospace, a company you subcontracted and paid $1.2 billion to complete work on this unfamiliar Cosmic Ops."

"With all due respect, Mr. Secretary, Adam Shariak never had the clearance to discuss Cosmic Ops, and you do not have a need to know. Have a blessed day."

Jordan Denny's eyes widened in disbelief as he was hung up on yet again.

The intercom buzzed through. "Mr. Secretary, you have an important call on the Blue Line."

The Secretary of Defense picked up the receiver. "Denny here ... Yes sir. Stand by, General." Looking up, he signaled to Adam to wait outside the office.

The Under Secretary exited to the waiting room, feeling like a scolded child.

Angela Hatzileris stared at him from behind her desk. "I've served three administrations, and in all that time, I've never heard a general sound so upset. What is going on?"

"I don't know. Maybe a UFO landed on the White House lawn."

The administrative assistant chuckled, then covered her mouth as the door opened and Jordan Denny waved Adam back inside.

The Secretary of Defense looked pale. "Apparently, we poked the bear. In no uncertain terms, I've been told to cease these inquiries."

"Told by who?"

"Doesn't matter. Mr. Shariak, at this particular time, I am satisfied that the proper due diligence regarding the existence and nature of these projects was carried out or they would not have been funded. Therefore, in response to your report—"

"UFOs and extraterrestrial intelligence."

"Excuse me?"

"You wanted to know the nature of the USAPs. They involve the reverse-engineering of advanced technologies taken from interstellar craft that have been shot down over the last seventy years."

"Christ … are you out of your fucking mind?"

"Let me do my job and I'll expose this thing."

"Your job? What the hell do you think the president is going to say if I tell him my new Under Secretary wants to investigate a bunch of black budget projects dealing with aliens? Where do you think this investigation of yours is going to lead? How will you prove your case? Anyone you or your Senator brother subpoena from the defense sector is going to hide under the shield of 'exclusivity and trade secrets,' and no one in Congress will dare challenge that. This whole thing is a cluster-fuck and I want no part in it."

"No problem. When I announce that I just discovered the DoD has been secretly funding $80 billion to $100 billion or more worth of unacknowledged and unapproved special access projects every year—secret projects that neither the president nor Congress have any inkling of, I'll be sure to mention that you wanted no part in the investigation."

Adam headed for the door.

"Wait just a minute, goddam it! You want to investigate the matter—fine. But for now it stays an internal investigation inside your office. Funds are missing; we want them found and accounted for—period. I don't want to hear anything about aliens or UFOs or freakin' Bigfoot, am I clear?"

"Yes, sir. Thank you." Adam exited the Defense Secretary's office, his mind racing.

Jordan Denny remained seated behind his desk, gazing at the framed photos of his wife, three children, and two grandchildren arranged on the far corner of his desk.

Screw it. You tried to warn him … he didn't listen. Just keep him isolated so there's no blowback.

22

Subterranean Complex—Midwest USA
Monday Evening

IT WAS 5:41 P.M. WHEN JESSICA MARULLI summoned Elevator-7 to her location on Level-3, the uppermost floor in the subterranean habitat. After an intense first day, all she could think about was dinner, a hot bath, and bed.

Don't forget you scheduled a call with Adam …

Today had been the first time she had thought about her fiancé since she had boarded the Boeing 767 back in Baltimore.

Barely a week … was that even possible? Her schedule had been so non-stop and utterly disorienting, it seemed like she hadn't seen Adam in a month.

Today was the first time she had really missed him.

Her early morning lecture had been followed by a "meet and greet" with her staff in Lab-3C, the work place assigned to *Project Zeus*. Waiting for her outside the only entrance into the facility was a blue-eyed, brown-haired woman in a white lab coat.

Dr. Sarah Mayhew-Reece appeared to be in her early forties, though Jessica knew from reading her assistant's personnel file that she was fifty-eight and had earned her doctorate from M.I.T. while her new boss was still in diapers. At five-foot-one, the petite southerner seemed more of a doting mother than a rocket scientist, but by mid-morning Jess found herself more than a little intimidated by the sharp-witted, always probing 'thinkaholic' her colleagues teasingly referred to as "Ladybug."

"Dr. Marulli, so good to finally meet you. As you can see from my identification, I'm Sarah Mayhew-Reece, *Zeus's* assistant director. Ya'll can call me Sarah or Dr. May if you'd like … my last name gets a bit tedious. You'll find the staff prefers Ladybug—that's sort of a pet name my husband, Alton, blessed me with. Unfortunately, a co-worker heard him call me Ladybug on a personal Skype message two years ago; since then it's followed me around like an unwanted shadow."

"Sarah it is. Call me Jessica."

"You know, I think it best we keep it as Dr. Marulli. I find informality and beauty with one as young as ya'll to be a recipe for insubordination." She whispered, "Some of these men haven't been with a woman of the flesh for quite some time."

"Oh-kay … Did you happen to catch my lecture this morning?"

"I did, and I made some notes. We can go over them after you meet our tech team." Sarah swiped her identification card and pressed her brow against the rubber mold of the retinal scan, causing the bolt of the pneumatic steel door to open with a hiss of air.

Jessica followed her into an anteroom, a warning sign posted above a second pneumatic door.

Bio-Hazard Level 2 Containment
Nothing is permitted to leave the lab
without proper documents.

Sarah pressed a button and the interior door opened, the air pressure blasting them in the face before easing.

A howling wind accompanied the two women as they made their way single-file through a tight empty corridor. Up ahead was a golden-yellow glow coming from the end of the passage which was sealed behind a Plexiglas barrier.

Sarah waved her right hand at the motion detector, causing it to part.

"Welcome to the Hive."

Lab-3C was contained inside a four-story-high dome; its curved interior walls composed of three-foot-in-diameter honeycomb-shaped panels which radiated a faint golden light. Jessica recognized the material—an advanced polymer designed to block out electromagnetic waves.

More of an assembly area than a lab, the facility spanned the length of two football fields, the open space divided into twenty work stations. Each location encircled an 8,000 pound *Zeus* satellite, the monoliths lined up like giant dominoes.

Every fourth work station was separated from the next by an eight-foot-high, twenty-foot-long divider. From her vantage, Jessica could not see what these barriers were concealing.

Sarah frowned. "Look at them. They're like twenty lost children, waiting for their mama to send them off into space. C'mon, I'll introduce you to their keepers."

Jessica followed her assistant to the partition situated between work stations four and five. On the other side of the divider was a combination supply depot and break area. Hanging from numbered hooks were tool belts, uniforms and an assortment of bulky orange vests that resembled life-jackets. There was a kitchenette, and a lounge area which consisted of several sofas and recliners, and eight nap pods—all but two of them vacant. Four port-o-potties were paired off by gender, the combination toilet and enema designed to evacuate and "refresh" the bowels.

Project Zeus's station leaders were dressed in white jumpsuits, the extra padding around their knees and elbows stained dark from wear.

Lois "Lolly" Stern was the first to make an impression on Jessica. Strapped in one of the orange vests, the teal-eyed, forty-eight-year-old engineer was floating upside-down three feet off the ground, her long brown hair hanging below her face like a mop.

Jessica stared at the device strapped across her chest. "An anti-gravitics device? That's impressive. How high—"

"—three hundred meters; excuse me, Dr. Marulli." Sarah rushed over to the inverted woman whose face was flushed purple, the veins in her forehead popping out like tree roots. "Lolly, roll into a horizontal position at once before you pop an artery!"

"Dr. May? Did I fall asleep again?"

Sarah grabbed her by the ankles and dragged her into an upright position. Then she turned a harsh parental gaze upon the two men watching the spectacle from their leather recliners. "Mr. Mull … Mr. Mahurin, I thought I asked the two of you to keep an eye on her."

Chris Mull was in his late forties, his brown hair worn long and tied in a tight ponytail despite a receding forehead. The upper torso of his orange jumpsuit was tied by the sleeves around his waist, exposing his gray Dallas Cowboy's tee-shirt. "We were watching her, Ladybug. And in the course of watching her, we decided to kill time by wagering on when she'd pass out. I said nine minutes; Lukas went with fourteen."

"And if she dies from an aneurism?"

"Then all bets are off."

"No worries, Ladybug. Lolly has good veins." Lukas Mahurin held a carrot in his mouth like a cigar, his attention focused on the guinea pig feeding from the other end. "Isn't that right, Mr. Nibbles?"

"Ugh … do you see what I have to put up with, Dr. Marulli? Lolly, we agreed to a maximum of five minutes per session. Ignore my rules again and I'll ban you from all gravitronic devices."

"No you won't."

Jessica turned to the voice of dissension.

Jeffrey Emmette was in the kitchenette, working on his own assembly line, this one consisting of six deli subs. "Lolly has a herniated disc and frequent inversion is the only thing that takes the pressure off the nerves in her lumbar spine. Cut her off and we'll have to listen to her whine all day."

The self-appointed "Sandwich King" ran his eyes over Jessica. "What're you having, boss lady? I've got Italian, turkey-off-the-bone, and two pounds of fresh roast beef that's nice and bloody. We have another six hours before it starts to go bad."

"Thank you … maybe later. It's only nine-twenty in the morning."

"Around here we eat when we can; you never know when Ladybug is going to call for an all-nighter." Using a large carving knife, Jeffrey sliced a turkey sub in half, slid it onto a paper plate, then walked over to one of the sealed sleep pods and banged on top of the oval device with the palm of his

211

free hand. "Wake-up, R.B. Eats!"

The pod opened, revealing Rachel Barry, a long-necked, frizzy-haired Caucasian woman in her late thirties. "Did you put mayo on it?"

"Did you ask for mayo?"

"In fact I specifically said no mayo."

"Then there's no mayo on it."

Rachel accepted the sandwich and took a bite. "Asshole."

Jeffrey Emmette grinned. "Turkey's a little dry. With dry turkey you gotta add mayo. Ain't that right, new boss lady? So what's your poison?"

"Italian with oil and vinegar; hold the mayo and onions."

"You must have grown up in the northeast ... praise God. Not like the assistant boss lady, who kills every sandwich I make her with yellow mustard."

Ignoring him, Sarah scanned the break area, doing a mental head count. Grimacing, she approached a man soldering scraps of copper at a work table, his Marist College sweatshirt stained in grease. "Ian, where's Peter and Andrew?"

Ian Concannon never looked up from the ET figurine he was piecing together. "Pete's trying to fix the leaking A/C duct. I lost track of Andrew. Maybe it's tea time?"

"Grabowski's on the shitter," Lukas said, the guinea pig now feeding off carrot shards covering his groin. "Or should I say, the 'port-o-loo.'"

Lois Stern stretched her back, her complexion having returned to normal. "Did you know in Russia they call it a *unitas* ... as in, 'You Need Ass.' True story."

A tall athletic man with a slight paunch emerged from the men's port-o-potty, slamming the plastic door shut. "That's not a story, Lolly, it's more of an anecdote. A story is what our dear Ladybug will be spinning when I ask her—again—why maintenance still hasn't drained the sludge out of the men's shitter. What's the point of 'refreshing one's colon' if one has to smell it afterward? It's been two bloody weeks."

"I was told—again—that all maintenance services will revert to their normal schedules in the fall. Until then, and I quote, 'your ten zoo keepers can make do,' no pun intended."

Andrew Grabowski snorted a reply. "Next turd I vacuum out of my intestines will be in the woman's shitter; see how you like it then."

"Enough. This is Dr. Marulli—"

"The new head zookeeper, we know, Ladybug." Ian looked up from soldering. "Hey, boss lady, how long have you been a member of the Flat Earth Society?"

"I'm sorry?"

Jeffrey Emmette handed her a paper plate holding the two halves of an Italian sub. "What my esteemed colleague is referring to is this morning's speech. It was a bit … antiquated."

"It was bullshit."

Jessica looked up as a powerfully-built man with piercing hazel eyes and a neatly trimmed mustache floated down from the ceiling, a heavy tool belt hanging below his anti-gravitics vest.

"Peter Niedzinski, this is our new—"

"Ops Director, I know. Will you be offing yourself like your predecessor?"

Jessica felt the blood rush from her face. "Scott Hopper committed suicide?"

"Suicide's the 'official' report," Chris Mull said, hopping off the recliner. "Everyone who saw the body knows he was TWEP-ed."

"What's TWEP-ed again?" Lolly asked as she moved into a downward-facing-dog yoga pose.

"Terminated With Extreme Prejudice," Chris Mull answered. "You can bet the farm it was the bikers."

"You're wrong," Peter said. "Scott was poisoned. Poison is CIA."

"Yeah, well I spoke to his wife. After they poisoned him they yanked out one of his back molars. The dental calling card is strictly *Devil's Disiples*."

"Stop you guys; you're freaking Dr. Marulli out." Rachel wiped mayo from the corner of her mouth. "Besides, it could have been an overdose. I mean—you know, Scott. He had issues."

"What sort of issues?" Jessica asked.

"He had a conscience," Chris Mull replied. "Morality and MAJI go together like mayo on an Italian sub."

213

Sarah shook her head. "This is entirely improper. The walls have ears—"

"Not today they don't," Peter winked. "The Hive's security system is wired into the EMP shield. By removing one of the panels to access the A/C duct, I may have accidentally severed the circuit. Until I replace the panel we can speak freely."

"Then I'll start," said Ian, holding up his copper extraterrestrial. "Interstellars, new Boss Lady. Are you for 'em or against them?"

"Extraterrestrials? I can't really say. I mean … I know they're out there; I've just never crossed paths with one."

"But you helped create a satellite array designed to fry them as they cross into our dimension. Surely you must have something against them?"

"Sorry … Ian, is it? Ian, I think you have the wrong impression about *Zeus*. It wasn't designed to be a weapons platform; it simply tracks physical objects moving out of the higher dimensions—"

"—using a scalar wave-based targeting device, which can not only lock on to and track them, but with a bit more juice, it can also vaporize them … poof!" Ian crushed the copper ET in his fist, handing it to Jessica.

"Easy Ian," Rachel said. "Maybe she didn't know?"

"I didn't."

Lukas held his guinea pig up to his ear. "Hmm … Mr. Nibbles says you're a brilliant engineer but a bad liar. Any post-graduate physics major knows the only difference between a scalar tracking device and a scalar weapon is the strength of the wave. And … you … just … lobbied … Council … for … more … power," he said, pretending his pet was speaking

Chris Mull nodded. "The 'Rodent Whisperer' speaks the truth. You and the douche bags at Lockheed conjured up that whole wobble story in order to justify equipping each SAT with a nano-crystal zero-point-energy generator. With a device that powerful, you could take down that big mothership parked out by Saturn."

"Jupiter." Lois Stern groaned, coming up from her yoga pose. "Anyway, I seriously doubt the Interstellars will allow anything that powerful in orbit."

Ian retorted, "They won't know, Lolly, until *Zeus* starts picking them off like a game of *Asteroids*. MAJI is setting us up for a war mankind is clearly instigating and can't possibly win. This whole thing is insane."

"Then quit!" Jessica snapped, silencing Ian, as well as several cross-conversations. "I'm serious, if you don't want to be here—resign. That goes for any one of you. If MAJI's politics don't suit you, then come and speak to me in private and I'll transfer you to a job designing widgets."

She gazed around the break area, all eyes now locked on her. "As I said before, having never met any of these purported species, I have no reason to like or hate them, and the last thing I want is to start a war. But I'm an engineer and a physicist and I was hired to do a job. As far as jacking up the juice on the *Zeus* SATS ... yes, Lockheed's engineers made it clear that change was necessary. Does that mean I'm happy about placing a scalar device, powered by an advanced ZPE device, aboard these satellites? Hell, no. But no one asked me my opinion when I signed up for this gig and they're not asking for it now. As for initiating a war, the Air Force has been using scalar waves to shoot down these interstellar craft since 1947. Maybe the array's threat alone will be enough to convince our out-of-town guests to shut down their bases on the far side of our moon and go annoy some other Type-Zero civilization.

"But it's not our job to question Council's motives. My mother was a scientist working on a USAP back when the entity was still calling itself MJ-12. She taught me long ago never to discuss politics with anyone on the inside or outside because there's always another perspective you can't see from your limited scope in history. What if the American team working on the atomic bomb back in 1943 had taken the time to debate the ethics of killing tens of thousands of innocent Japanese men, women, and children? If they had, the delay might have allowed Hitler's scientists to finish their bomb first and we'd all be speaking German. As scientists, it's our job to provide our military with options; after that, all we can do is pray the powers that be know what the hell they are doing."

Her fists clenched, Jessica waited for what she anticipated would be an in-her-face rebuttal.

Instead, her staff shocked her by applauding.

Ian Concannon was among the loudest. "None of us want a war with the Interstellars, Doc. To be honest, the whole thing freaks us out. But it's like you said, each of us was recruited to do a job; now we just want to get it over with and go home to our families."

Jeffrey nodded. "Your predecessor was a good guy, but he took his work home with him, if you know what I mean."

She didn't, until Sarah clarified the statement.

"In dealing with UFOs and ETs, the wonderment of working with cutting-edge science comes with a harsh price. Constantly having to lie about what we do to our loved ones can cause emotional stress. The suicide rate among subterranean techs working on interstellar-related USAPs is over thirty-five percent."

Jessica turned to Sarah, "How do we requisition twenty of the advanced zero-point-energy devices?"

"That's Ian's department."

"I'm on it. Ladybug. Has Jessica seen the chariots?"

"Not yet. Why don't you get Dr. Marulli a vest and show her."

"The chariots?" Jessica turned to the engineer who was sorting through a selection of anti-gravitics vests and helmets hanging from hooks along the partition.

"Trust me, you'll enjoy this." Estimating her size, he held out a small vest for Jessica to slip her arms through. "Have you ever worn one of these?"

"I didn't know they existed until fifteen minutes ago."

He snapped the three horizontal straps in place, pulling them snugly across her chest. "The Hive's large enough, but as you'll see in a moment, this entire Atlas launch facility spans miles, making these vests invaluable. Ah, who am I kidding; we love using them. Inside the back of the vest is a ZPE unit. When you want to go weightless turn this gauge here," he pointed to the small knob by her left shoulder. "That will cause a high-voltage charge to strike the zero-point-energy field, creating an anti-gravity bubble around you and up you'll go."

"How do I steer?"

"That's a little bizarre. Put this helmet on, then think the direction you want to go, and you'll go in that direction."

"You're kidding?"

"That's how the Interstellars do it."

Her heart pounding with adrenaline, Jessica secured the helmet's chin strap in place and then turned the gauge by her left shoulder to the ON position.

A vibration rose from the bottom of her feet and up through her spinal cord, the sensation tickling her nose as she shed the gravitational forces of Earth and rose off the floor, giggling.

"Oh wow … I could definitely get used to this."

Securing his own vest and helmet in place, Ian joined her, the two engineers thirty feet above the group, Jessica banking from side to side to get used to sensation of being weightless.

"I love this! I feel like a bee in a hive."

He held out his hand and she took it, allowing him to tow her to the west end of the lab. Picking up speed, they soared over the satellite stations, quickly approaching the curved wall of a dead end.

When it appeared that he had no intention of slowing down, Jessica tried to jerk her hand free. "Let go! What are you doing?"

Seconds from impact, a section of the honeycomb-shaped panels parted like an expanding ripple on a pond and they flew through the dark opening.

"Oh my …"

The tunnel was immense, its ceiling easily thirty stories.

Perched upright on mobile launch pads were twenty Atlas-V rockets, each unmanned craft towering 191 feet tall. The rockets and their vehicles ran the length of the subterranean facility, which disappeared in the distance.

"Impressive." She realized Ian was still holding her hand. "You can let go now, Dr. Concannon. And I don't appreciate you scaring me like you did. Next time tell me the walls are sensor-activated."

"Sorry."

"Anything else you think I should know?"

"I'm single."

"I meant about this facility. I'm guessing the ceiling sections beneath each launch pad are retractable?"

"Yes."

"And where are they retractable to?"

"The surface."

"I meant the base location. Where the hell are we?"

"I don't know. The consensus among the group is somewhere in the Mid-West."

She continued on, flying over one Atlas rocket after the next, each launch station deserted, a series of blinking red lights framing the darkness ahead.

Ian caught up to her before she flew through the lit passage, grabbing the crook of her arm as she soared over the last vehicle. "Jessica, wait—" They spun in circles, each refusing to ease up.

"Let me go!"

"You can't go beyond the red lights!"

She stopped struggling. "Why not?"

"We're not authorized."

"I am."

"Not in an anti-gravitics vest. See those red warning lights? Fly past that boundary while you're inside a zero-point-energy bubble and you'll be hit by an electromagnetic pulse. Before you know what happened, you'll strike the concrete like a bug on a windshield."

Jessica squinted, staring ahead into the pitch. "What's out there?"

"I don't know, and I'm not supposed to know."

She hovered another thirty seconds, her eyes unable to pierce the darkness beyond the blinking red square of lights. "What happens if we land and try to walk past that boundary?"

"I'm not sure what they'll do to you, but a bunch of nasty Delta Force commandoes armed with M-16s will have me lying spread-eagled on the ground, and it won't be a pretty sight. Can we go back now?"

Jessica held on to her seat's support pole as Elevator-7 zigged then zagged horizontally before plunging two stories to Level-5. As the doors thankfully opened and her anxiety eased, she recalled the fear in Ian Concannon's voice as they had hovered in the darkness over the last Atlas rocket.

From that juncture on, the engineer had referred to her only as **Dr. Marulli**.

What was he so scared of? We weren't going to fly beyond those lights—

She waved to Kirsty Brunt as she headed for the catwalk leading to her suite.

Maybe he was afraid we'd see something we weren't supposed to see?

"Hey!"

Jessica glanced to her left as Logan LaCombe shot past her on his hoverboard. "Hey, you. I thought you were afraid to speak to me?"

He circled back. "I'm not afraid."

"Are you sure? After all, I am Cosmic Clearance."

The teen smiled nervously. "I'm sure. I mean … it's not like I did something wrong."

"Well, I almost did something wrong. Are you familiar with Level-3?"

"No. But my Dad sometimes works there. "What'd you almost do?"

"I almost flew through a restricted area wearing an anti-gravitics vest. A coupla more seconds and I would have gone *splat*."

"Geez. What part of Level-3 were you at?"

"The launch site."

"Cool. Did you see any ARVs?"

"What's an ARV?"

The teen's complexion paled. "I don't know. You're the one with Cosmic Clearance … what is it?"

"Logan—"

"Gotta go, Dad wanted me to pick up stuff at the mall for dinner. Laters …"

"Logan, wait … I'm just messing with you. I know what it is—"

She watched as he cut an S-pattern across the fastest section of the Maglev track, disappearing down the transit corridor.

Curiouser and curiouser …

23

Virginia Beach, Virginia

THE FOUR-BEDROOM TWO-STORY brick house with the candy-apple-red shutters was located on Broad Bay Island. It was not a huge property by any means, but the community was gated and every owner had their own private dock.

Adam arrived at his brother's home just after six o'clock. He was greeted at the door by his sister-in-law, Melinda.

"Hi, stranger."

"Ah, come on … I was here for Christmas." He leaned in for a kiss and entered the foyer. "Something smells good."

"It's called leftovers. Randy told me you were coming for dinner about an hour ago."

"My fault; last minute change of plans." He followed her to the family room where his niece and nephew were engaged in a video game.

"Jordan, Sean … look who's here."

"Hey, Uncle Adam."

"Hey."

Neither teen looked up.

Adam smiled. "Adolescence, my favorite years. Where's Randy?"

"Where else?"

The boat was a 37-foot Post Sport Fisherman which legally held up to twelve passengers, though Adam recalled his brother squeezing twice that

220

many on board at the Super Bowl-LI party. The captain was out on deck with a hose, cleaning out his fish holds.

"Permission to come aboard?"

"Permission granted."

Adam swung his right leg over the port rail, followed by his prosthesis, careful not to slip on the wet deck. "They biting?"

"Caught some Rockfish early this morning. Why don't you grab us a few beers; I'll finish up and join you inside."

Adam entered the salon, heading forward past the L-shaped dinette to the galley. Reaching inside the refrigerator, he removed two cans of Budweiser—

—only to be yanked backwards by the collar of his windbreaker and pinned against the stove top, his metallic left foot fighting for balance.

"Easy, slick … that's a new jacket."

"Do I look like I give a fuck? A few months in office and you're calling for an internal investigation of the Pentagon? Who do you think you are? Joe McCarthy?"

Adam pushed his older sibling back. "I found evidence of improprieties and presented it to my boss. Is that a problem?"

"When I get called out of a meeting on Capitol Hill to be told my younger brother's accusing two of our biggest defense contractors of criminal activity—yeah, that's a problem."

"So is informing the Secretary of Defense that he doesn't have a need-to-know about a defense-funded project when he makes an inquiry."

"Just because a project is compartmentalized doesn't make it illegal, Adam."

"If the president, congress, and the Secretary of Defense have no clue they exist while billions of dollars are flowing through them to God-knows-where, I'd say they were illegal. And don't tell me my fucking job! I need you to step up and do yours."

"Okay, Mr. Under Secretary … present your case."

Reaching into the interior jacket pocket of his windbreaker, Adam removed the folded copy of his report and handed it to his brother.

"Royal Ops … Cosmic Ops … Maj Ops? How would you even know

what these projects are? Most of the stuff you handled at Kemp was way above your shitty little douche-bag clearance."

"There still has to be a paper trail if funds are coming out of the U.S. Treasury."

"Not if they're being funded by the CIA."

Adam felt his face flush. "Is that conjecture or fact, Senator?"

"Let's just say I recognize a few acronyms."

"Like MAJI?"

"Who told you about MAJI? Steven Greer?"

"You spying on me, Randy?"

"Just doin' my job as big brother."

"Boy, if that's not a Freudian slip." Adam pushed past him and flopped onto the wrap-around couch. "Are you a gatekeeper?"

"Fuck you and your conspiracy theories. I don't have time for this bullshit."

"Eighty to a hundred billion taxpayer dollars a year in Unacknowledged Special Access Projects? As Head of the Senate Appropriations Committee, I think you'd better make the time."

"Is that a threat, Adam?"

"I don't threaten family. But I'm also not going to shit in my pants like the Defense Secretary did this morning. That copy of my investigation you have in your hand—it's addressed to Senator Hall, not Secretary Denny. Consider my report officially submitted."

Randy glanced at the first page. "Son of a bitch ..."

"So what happens now?"

"Now? Now you get the fuck off my boat."

His heart pounding, Adam left the unopened beer on the coffee table and exited the salon to the stern. Climbing over the rail, he limped across the pier, following it around the two-story red brick house to his car.

Randy Hall watched the 2011 silver Jeep Grand Cherokee drive off before dialing a memorized number on his cell phone.

"It's me. I'd say we have a problem."

Adam arrived at the five-story apartment building at 9:47 p.m. Parking in his reserved spot in the private lot, he turned off the engine, grabbed the still-hot pizza box, and exited the car. He hobbled to the front entrance and keyed in, never noticing the black Ford Mustang that had been following him over the past eight hours as the driver parked across the street.

Apartment 208 was a one-bedroom dwelling on the second floor, the view from its living room balcony overlooking the parking lot and the dumpster poised beneath the building's garbage chute. While the view and its associated trash collection sound effects were less than desirable, Adam had signed the two-year lease because he liked the fake hardwood floors, affordable rent, and the building's location, which was within walking distance of a 24-hour gym and the Metrorail's Greenbelt Station. Having all but moved in with Jessica, it was rare that he ever used the apartment or the gym. He was only here tonight because the Skype call with his fiancée was scheduled for 10:00 p.m. EST and he didn't want to miss it.

A musty scent greeted him as he opened the door and turned on the lights. The living room was just large enough to hold a couch, coffee table, and a recliner. Chocolate-brown drapes had been left drawn to cover the balcony's sliding glass doors. To his left was a small kitchen, to his right a short hall which led to a bathroom and his bedroom.

Piled behind the sofa were cardboard boxes filled with his personal office belongings and two prosthetic devices he had been working on before he had resigned from Kemp Aerospace.

Tossing the pizza box onto the coffee table, he hurriedly relieved his bladder and washed his hands and face, the cool water reviving him a bit. He looked as tired as he felt, but he missed Jessica, and the call was important.

Duane Saylor, Steven Greer's attorney, had explained it when the two had met in his Maryland office earlier that afternoon.

"A Dead-Man's Trigger only works if the people who are a threat to kill you know it exists, and are convinced the information that will be released upon your death is far

worse than anything you can deliver alive. When is the press conference scheduled?"

"Wednesday afternoon at 5:15. That way, I can go live on the evening news."

"And the call with your fiancée?"

"Tonight at ten."

"Then we'd better get busy, you have a lot of documents to sign."

"Hey, babe! Oh my God, it seems—"

Adam waited several seconds for the frozen image of Jessica Marulli to re-animate.

"—so long since I've seen you."

"I know. Jess, this is a bad connection … the image is freezing up."

"It's security … there's a seven second delay. So don't say anything about our sex life."

The image froze on her mid-laugh.

"Jess, I need to speak to you about something important."

For the next several minutes, Adam spun a tale about how his meetings with defense contractors had motivated him to perform an audit by cross-checking the last decade's worth of projects subcontracted to Kemp Aerospace.

"Jess, nine of our projects could not be accounted for by the Pentagon. Based on what we were paid just for our share of the work, we're talking about tens of billions of dollars worth of contracts. When the Secretary of Defense asked two of the defense contractors to brief him, they refused, and the blowback was enough to soil Jordan Denny's underwear."

"Adam … what are you planning to do?"

"Denny's letting me run with the ball."

"You're opening an investigation?"

"The president wants accountability. Kemp's share of these projects is nothing. We're probably looking at $100 billion a year secretly being channeled into these Unacknowledged Special Access Projects."

"If these are CIA—"

"They're not. It's something much bigger … something unbelievable.

Jess, if anything should happen to me … I made arrangements for the evidence to be released to the public."

"Adam, what did you just say? I couldn't hear—"

The image of Jessica froze mid-sentence.

Adam waited, only this time the transmission didn't clear.

"Jess, can you hear me? Jessica?"

The screen went black before returning to the Skype logo.

Okay, Shariak. You've tossed enough shit for one day; let's see how long it takes for it to hit the fan.

24

Subterranean Complex—Midwest USA

THE TWENTY NANO-CRYSTAL zero-point-energy generators, and their four armed escorts from Delta Force, arrived at Lab-3C at 1:35 p.m., each device secured within the padded foam confines of an aluminum case. Sarah Mayhew-Reece wasted no time in dividing her technicians into pairs, assigning Chris Mull to work with Jessica at Station-3.

Swapping out the man-made zero-point-energy units for one of the far more powerful nano-crystal devices required removing a section of each satellite's electromagnetic shield in order to access the circuit board.

Wielding his power ratchet as if the tool were an extension of his hand, Chris Mull had the internal workings exposed before Jessica had donned her orange jumpsuit.

"That was fast."

"Your predecessor taught me well."

"I take it you and Dr. Hopper were close?"

"We grew close because of our politics." Using a flathead screwdriver, Mull pried open a plastic control panel, exposing two columns of buttons. Pressing the third one down caused a horizontal drawer to slide out like the tray of a DVD player.

Inside the unit, connected to a series of red and green couplings, was the hockey-puck-size zero-point-energy device.

"As Dr. May likes to say; the walls have eyes and ears. Be careful what you say."

"Fuck Ladybug, and fuck MAJI. See this watch? It blocks any sound or video within ten meters with white noise. If I have something to say, I'm going to say it." Disconnecting the rotary generator, he held it up for inspection. "See this miniature power plant? It wasn't designed by an advanced race of extraterrestrials; it was conceived and invented by human scientists, many of whom who were murdered. Do you know what their crime was? They were attempting to make the world a better place to live. What right does an oil executive or the CEO of a bank have to keep this technology from the rest of us? Who died and appointed them masters of the universe?"

"I'm not going to debate the issue with you, Mr. Mull."

"Then debate it with your fiancé. He's investigating these unauthorized programs. From what I'm told, he intends to bring zero-point-energy to the rest of the world. And we're going to help him."

"Who told you that? And who is *we*?"

"I can't tell you the *who* until you help me with the *how*."

He opened the aluminum case, revealing a platter-shaped, nano-crystal generator packed in form-fitting foam, its circumference twice the diameter of the unit it was replacing. A smaller doughnut-shaped cut-out lay vacant beside it, intended to hold the manmade ZPE unit it was replacing.

Glancing around to make sure none of the other members of their team were watching, Chris Mull quickly reached inside a compartment of his jumpsuit and removed a rotary-style zero-point energy device, pushing it firmly inside the accommodating vacant foam hole.

"Where did you get that?"

"It's not real, it's only the outer casing, but it'll fool security." Popping the real rotary generator from the satellite's power pack, he slipped it inside the hidden compartment of his jumpsuit.

"Mull, put it back—now."

"There's a firm in India that can mass-produce these units if we can get a working model to them—Scott made all the arrangements weeks before he was terminated. We can't have the unit on us when we leave the lab—security performs an external and internal body scan as we exit the Hive—but I can get it out through the kitchen."

"You're wasting your breath; I'm not doing this."

"Tonight will be a late night. Tomorrow you'll order dinner in. I suggest the lobster thermidor topped with lump crabmeat and a velvety sauce, served on garlic whipped potatoes. Oh yeah ... and for dessert—a decadent chocolate crème brûlée with a hint of Grand Marnier."

Jessica's lower jaw dropped. "Oh my God ... you hacked into my suite's private server."

"All room service meals are covered by fancy aluminum covers. The one that will be keeping your lobster thermidor warm will be composed of a lead alloy that will appear solid to the security sensors; in reality, it has a false bottom that pops open to hold the rotary ZPE—just like the one you used to smuggle this empty ZPE shell to me your first night in this facility. Who gave it to you is anyone's guess ... Lydia Gagnon? Kirsty Brunt—"

"Bastard ... you set me up!"

"Shh. Wish I could take the credit, but that belongs to someone far higher up on the totem pole. Now pay attention, because your life and your fiancé's life depends on it. Tomorrow night you'll order the same lobster meal. The waiter will bring you the hot plate top which will contain the real ZPE unit. At precisely 2:33 a.m you'll summon Elevator-7 and take it down to Level-23. Only Cosmic Clearance personnel know the lower floors below Level-9 even exist. Exiting the elevator, you'll proceed to the first checkpoint. The Delta Force commando on duty is named Josh LaCombe ... I believe you know his son."

"Logan?" Jessica felt queasy.

"Give Captain LaCombe the package; he'll get it to our people on the outside. You'll have exactly seven minutes to complete the transaction before the security cameras aboard Elevator-7 and on Level-23 cease their video loop."

"I'm not doing this, Mr. Mull! Now put the real unit back."

"Too late for that, Dr. Marulli, you're already involved and implicated. Turn me in, and I'll squeal like a pig to my MAJI interrogators, confessing that I'm working for you and your accomplice—Under Secretary of Defense, Adam Shariak."

Pentagon Press Briefing Room
Washington, D.C.

"The Pentagon has a long history of mismanaging funds. The last reported gaff happened in Fiscal Year 1999 when the Department of Defense somehow 'misplaced' $2.3 trillion. When Former Secretary of Defense, Donald Rumsfeld, went public with this information on September 10, 2001, he blamed the problem on an inability of DoD computers to communicate. Others have called the situation systemic in that the CIA and other intelligence agencies have been operating for decades in a vacuum of secrecy without any Congressional oversight."

Gripping the edge of the podium, Adam shifted his weight in an attempt to relieve the sciatic nerve pain in his left buttocks.

"The need to maintain secrecy does not give these agencies the right to conduct operations without the knowledge and consent of the President of the United States, nor does it allow them to write blank checks to their partners and associates in the military industrial complex. And yet that is exactly what has been happening. These secret programs, known as Unacknowledged Special Access Projects, or USAPs, have been siphoning approximately $80 billion to $100 billion from the U.S. Treasury every year, generating billions of dollars in unreported revenue for defense contractors. These criminal activities must be stopped and the participants prosecuted to the fullest extent of the law.

"The challenge is in piercing the gauntlet of lies, greed, and corruption that permeates an industry where retiring military officials routinely enter the private sector as high-salaried lobbyists, and well-connected defense contractors leave the private sector to accept top government military posts. I am an example of that very process. While serving as the managing director at Kemp Aerospace, I accepted billions of dollars worth of subcontracts for defense projects—the specifics of which remained hidden from me for, what I was told were, security reasons.

"What could not be kept from me were the names of these projects, their budgets, and the supervising defense contractors involved. Armed with this information, I was able to cross-check these projects against the allocations of dollars funded by the Pentagon. To my surprise and disgust, I discovered the existence of nine USAPs—projects that were clearly funded by the Department of Defense, despite the fact that no records pertaining to any of these transactions officially exists, either in the public record or inside the Pentagon. While I may not know the nature of these projects, I do know the individuals to subpoena in order to obtain that information.

"These nine projects represent the tip of a massive iceberg of corruption. What is even more troubling is the existence of a shadow quasi-government that has operated under a variety of names over the last six decades, hidden under a transnational umbrella organization composed of rogue elements of the military industrial complex, Wall Street, private banks, and monopolies within the energy sector. This transnational entity not only controls these projects, but clearly possesses their own agenda—an agenda intended to keep them in power by preventing advanced energy technologies from being shared with the rest of the world.

"This, then, is the dirty underside of the iceberg that must be exposed, prosecuted, and permanently shut down. With the support of the Trump Administration, the Comptroller's office intends on doing just that.

"I do not expect this process to be an easy one. For those individuals working under these umbrella organizations, who have suffered under the pressure of secrecy for so long, I offer complete amnesty and financial incentives if you come forward now and provide information and evidence against these criminals. Once my office issues subpoenas, the financial incentives of this whistleblower program shall be rescinded.

"For those of you out there seething in the shadows, let me assure you— I have come into possession of a list of names and the nature of their crimes against humanity. Should something happen to me or any of my loved ones, the incriminating evidence I have compiled shall be released to the public, and you and yours shall follow us to the grave."

Having finished reading from his prepared statement, Adam looked up at a sea of raised hands and shout-outs from the attending members of the media.

"I'm sorry. I know you have questions but that's all I can say at this time."

Collecting his notes, Adam exited to his right and down a short flight of steps to a small conference room where Secretary of Defense, Jordan Denny, was watching the end of the press conference on a wall-mounted flat screen television, the event broadcast on a two minute delay. Rolled up in his hand was the list of names of those defense contractors Adam wanted to subpoena.

He turned as the Under Secretary entered. "*A shadow government has been in existence for the last sixty years* ... are you insane, Shariak? Where the hell are you getting this information from? You sound like a conspiracy nut."

"How would you have explained it?"

"I wouldn't have even brought it up! Two days ago you came to me wanting to investigate misappropriated funds; now you just announced to the world that there's some transnational umbrella organization out there, made up of the military, Big Oil, and God-knows-who else. How are you going to prove that? By subpoenaing the CEOs of the biggest defense contracting firms in the world? Are you expecting them to confess to being involved in some New World Order? The Illuminati maybe?"

"Who threatened you the other day?"

"No one threatened me, Shariak. But your actions and accusations have sure threatened the defense contractors that keep America safe. And I'm not going to allow you to go on a witch hunt."

"There's billions of dollars that cannot be accounted for, Mr. Secretary. Unless you can figure out a better way to shut that deluge of funds off, stay out of the way and let me do my job."

Snatching the list out of Jordan Denny's hand, Shariak left the conference room and strode awkwardly down the hall to an emergency exit. Yanking open the metal fire door, he exited the basement floor, limping and dragging himself up two flights of concrete stairs.

He was exhausted by the time he exited the stairwell, emerging on the ground floor of the Pentagon.

A sign indicated he was in C-Ring, Corridor-7.

Patting his pants pockets, Shariak located his iPhone. Stealing a quick glance at the screen, his fingers spun through his contact list as he maneuvered his way through the rush hour crowd, his eyes searching faces for lingering stares.

"Hello?"

"It's Shariak. Where are you?"

"Where are *you*?"

"C-Ring, Corridor-7."

"North exit—got it. I'll meet you outside in four minutes."

Following the crowd, he headed in the direction of D-Ring.

He was hobbling badly by the time he entered E-Ring. Two minutes later he found himself outside of the north exit beneath threatening gray skies, the change in atmospheric pressure causing the leaves on the surrounding trees to invert.

Up ahead, a black Mustang screeched to a halt by the curb, former Tech Sergeant Eugene Evans waving at him from the open passenger window.

Yanking open the door, Adam climbed in, wheezing from the effort.

"You okay, Captain?"

"I need ... to speak ... to Greer."

The bodyguard removed his iPhone from its charger on the console, scrolled through his contacts, and handed the device to Shariak.

"Greer?"

"Well, Mr. Under Secretary, you certainly rattled a lot of tiger cages for one day. How do you feel?"

"Like I'm about to be eaten. How will they come after me?"

"First they'll offer you money—more money than you can spend in a lifetime. Assuming you turn that down, they'll try to break you ... tarnish your image, accuse you of molesting puppies—anything to prevent you from forcing these defense contractors to testify. Not that they will anyway. They'll simply plead the fifth."

"It's not their answers that are important, Steven. It's all about starting the conversation by posing questions about UFOs and ETs and zero-point-energy systems on C-SPAN and across the mainstream media. The more they plead the fifth, the more the public will become convinced they're really hiding something."

"Don't be so sure, Shariak. It only takes one well-positioned gatekeeper to derail the entire train."

25

Oval Office, White House
Washington, D.C.

PRESIDENT DONALD JOHN TRUMP paced like a caged tiger in the Oval Office behind the sitting area as he unleashed his pent-up rage at the members of his National Security Council.

"Since when does some goddam Under Secretary take it upon himself to call a press conference? There's only one star of this show, and that's me. What the hell does an Under Secretary even do? Can someone explain that to me? Domenik?"

Domenik Davis, the president's latest addition to his National Security Council, felt everyone's eyes upon her. "The Under Secretary serves under the Secretary of Defense. As comptroller, Shariak has oversight responsibilities for all military programs. While he may have blindsided Secretary Denny with some of the things he was suggesting in his press conference, he was essentially doing his job."

"Domenik ... sweetheart—forget Denny, Shariak blindsided *me*!" He glanced at his watch. "Where the hell is Jordan Denny? Teresa, I specifically asked you to make sure the Secretary of Defense was in this meeting."

Teresa Ann Hurtienne—one of the president's three personal assistants— nodded, hoping the affirmation would blunt the anticipated negative response. "Sir, Secretary Denny apologizes; apparently he had an urgent personal matter to attend to and—"

"Fuck him! I'm the goddam president! He'd better be in the goddam hospital dying of fucking cancer to miss this meeting."

233

Trump turned to Kellyanne Conway. "Adam Shariak ... Kellyanne, who is this guy? Did he work in the campaign?"

"No, sir." The president's counselor searched her notes on her iPhone. "He was a General Mattis appointment ... an Apache helicopter pilot who served in Iraq ... a Purple Heart recipient. Says here he was a war hero."

"What'd he do?"

"Apparently, he lost his leg in Iraq when his chopper was shot down."

"I don't get that. In my book, a war hero is someone who kills the enemy or dives on a loose grenade to save his fellow soldiers. Someone who gets shot down isn't a war hero, he's a lousy pilot."

He turned to the Chairman of the Joint Chiefs. "General, according to Shariak, there are military operations being conducted without my knowledge."

"Not military operations, per se," General Wade Snuggerud stated. "He referred to them as USAPs. That stands for Unacknowledged Special Access Projects."

"Do I know about them?"

"No, sir. These are most likely black budget programs run by the CIA and other Intel agencies."

"Still, $100 billion is a lot of money."

"Yes sir, it is. And the last president who tried to pull in the CIA's reins got the back of his skull blown off in Dallas. In my opinion, Shariak has opened a can of worms. He has no idea the size of the shit storm he'll be summoning if he starts issuing subpoenas to our defense contractors."

The president turned to Stephen Bannon, his former campaign manager and most trusted advisor. "Stevo, what do you think?"

"Shariak's expendable. At the same time, the public supports his investigation."

"You're not telling me anything."

"Mr. President, what's important here is that none of this happened on your watch."

"Exactly. This is another Obama-Hillary mess."

"There's your talking point," said Bannon.

"Good. Make sure Spicer has that. In fact, I think I'll put that in a tweet." The president removed his iPhone from his jacket pocket. "That's why you're here, Stephen. You get what's important."

Los Alamos, New Mexico

The knuckles on Colonel Alexander Johnston's fists were white as he gripped the padded steering wheel of his Chevy Suburban and waited for the wrought-iron gate to open. Growling through clenched teeth, he nudged the slowly parting fence with the truck's front bumper before accelerating up the winding driveway to his estate home.

"Yvonne?" The colonel entered the house, stalking past the grand marble-columned entrance and down the hallway leading to his private study.

"Yvonne!"

"I'm in your office."

He pushed open the solid oak door to find his wife at his desk, busy at his computer.

"You heard?"

"I caught it on CNN." The gaunt, dark-haired practicing Satanist kept her eyes on the computer screen while her husband continued his rant.

"They never listen. I told them twenty years ago we needed to kill Greer!"

"Greer? Who said anything about Greer? Shariak's the problem."

"He's only the problem because we allowed Steven fucking Greer to brief him. Well, I'm through listening to General Cubit and the rest of those bleeding hearts on Council. This time I'll handle things *my way*."

"Alexander, no one's going to buy Shariak's suicide or a diagnosis of stage four cancer hours after announcing his first investigation as Under Secretary."

"Then we'll wait a few weeks. Make it look like an accident."

"Shariak's a wounded war vet. Killing him, no matter how it's staged, will only add credibility to the information that will be released upon his death."

"What information? Shariak only knows what Greer has been spewing on YouTube over the last sixteen years."

"Yes darling, but in the wake of his press conference, Shariak's death could elevate information relegated as fringe into the mainstream. I found a better way to deal with this … come and see."

The colonel walked around to her side of the desk to peer at the array of monitors. "Shariak's war story? How does that help us?"

"When he was captured and tortured, Captain Shariak was aided by a young Iraqi girl in her teens. *'My captor was quite clear; if I died, she died.'*"

"So?"

"Can you gain access to Shariak's statements that were taken right after his rescue? I need the girl's name."

"What for?"

Yvonne Dwyer-Johnston smiled. "Darling, the first step in killing a war hero is to tarnish his medals."

26

Subterranean Complex—Midwest USA

TUESDAY HAD BEEN A NIGHTMARE.

Chris Mull had gone on non-stop for nearly an hour, briefing her one moment about where to hide the zero-point-energy device once it was delivered to her suite (we equipped your Maglev hoverboard with a wider-than-usual compartment to stow your leash), and bragging to her the next about the strength of their movement (surely you must have wondered how someone with your fiancé's credentials could have been appointed Under Secretary of Defense), until Jessica's overwrought nerves had finally reached their breaking point. The moment she had finished running diagnostic tests on the satellite's power pack she had fled their station to find her assistant, like a distraught second grader being teased by the classroom bully.

"Sarah, I can't take it anymore, the man is turning my stomach."

"Mull? What's he doing?"

"He just won't shut up about Scott Hopper and his damn conspiracy theories."

"Mr. Mull can cross the line at times, but he's one of my best techs."

"Then you deal with him, I've had my fill."

"That wasn't the plan. The objective of having me set up a rotation was to give you an opportunity to evaluate each member of our team before they leave on break. In fairness to Mr. Mull, can you at least wait until after lunch? Otherwise I'd have to—"

"No, *Ladybug*. I've had all I can handle from Mr. Mull—switch me now!"

Sarah's expression had chastised Jessica even more than her words.

237

"Really, Dr. Marulli? Did ya'll really want to lower yourself to that? You won't last very long down here with such thin skin."

"Excuse me, Dr. Marulli?"

They had turned to find Chris Mull walking toward them, a power drill in his hand.

"I finished testing the scalar wave converter like you asked; everything's working fine. But I'll need your help repositioning the outer casing."

"Chris, Dr. Marulli and I are going over a few things. Ian's finishing our exchange; when he's through, I'll ask him to join ya'll at Station-2."

Mull raised his eyebrows in innocence. "Dr. Marulli, did I do something wrong?"

"Did you not just hear Dr. Mayhew-Reece? Wait for Dr. Concannon at your station."

The tech feigned confusion, then appeared hurt. "Ma'am, if I said something inappropriate, I sincerely apologize."

Not so sure I won't turn you in, are you—you smug little shit. And what's with the drill? Is that supposed to scare me?

Turning on his heel, Chris Mull walked away slowly, casually pressing the trigger on the power drill every few strides, as if sending a message.

The conversion of the twenty *Zeus* satellite generators from zero-point-energy rotary units to the far more advanced (and lethal) nano-crystal power plants had been completed by late Wednesday afternoon. Over the next two weeks, each satellite would undergo a battery of environmental simulation tests to make sure the equipment would perform in the frigid confines of space. Barring anything unforeseen, *Project Zeus* would then be greenlit for launch, its payload crew sent home.

Home was where Jessica wanted to be. She had barely slept; her every waking thought consumed by the implications of Chris Mull's actions and threats. Their paths had not crossed again Tuesday, but he had given her one last push when the work day ended Wednesday afternoon.

"Nice to get off early after yesterday's all-nighter, huh Dr. Marulli? If you're ordering in dinner tonight, you should try the lobster thermidor topped with the lump crabmeat. I had it last night; I'm telling you it's to die for."

"Actually, Mr. Mull, I hadn't decided what I'll be doing for dinner. I might even catch a movie and eat in the mall."

She had walked away, only to hear, "How's your fiancé? I hear he's holding a press conference in about ten minutes. Any idea what that's about?"

Rushing back to her suite, she had caught the last few minutes of Adam's speech on C-SPAN.

"These nine projects represent the tip of a massive iceberg of corruption. What is even more troubling than the nature of these projects is the existence of a shadow quasi-government that has operated under a variety of names over the last six decades, hidden under a transnational umbrella organization composed of rogue elements of the military industrial complex, Wall Street, private banks, and monopolies within the energy sector. This transnational entity not only controls these projects, but clearly possesses their own agenda—an agenda intended to keep them in power by preventing advanced energy technologies from being shared with the rest of the world ... "

"Jesus, Adam, what are you doing?"

"Good evening, Jessica."

Startled, Jessica turned to find the two-dimensional projection of her stout gray-haired Swedish nanny addressing her from the other side of the living room mirror.

"Ingrid, what are you doing here; I didn't summon you."

"Your low blood sugar summoned me, you need to eat. I ordered you something special. How does lobster thermidor topped with lump crabmeat and a velvety sauce sound, served on garlic whipped potatoes. And for dessert ... a decadent chocolate crème brûlée with a hint of Grand Marnier."

"That sounds incredibly disgusting. Cancel the order; I'm going for a workout."

She stripped as she headed for her bedroom closet, the determined computer program following her from mirror to mirror. "Child, you cannot work out on an empty stomach."

"Then I'll have a piece of fruit; eating a rich dinner before exercising will make me puke." Down to her bra and panties, she grabbed a workout outfit as Ingrid suddenly morphed into Raul.

"I am sorry to disturb you, *Senorita*, but the waiter is at the door."

"What's Spanish for—go fuck yourself?"

"Vete a la mierda."

Ignoring the sexy male concierge, Jessica quickly pulled on a one-piece bodysuit, then located her sneakers and slipped them on as the doorbell rang. Retrieving the hoverboard from the hall closet, she opened the door to her suite to confront the waiter.

"I didn't order dinner, Mr. Guzzo. Take it back."

Pulling the door shut behind her, she jogged to the Maglev track, dropped the board on the grooved surface, positioned her feet inside the straps and gave the leash a hard tug.

The device hummed to life, propelling her above the electromagnetic concourse. Bending deep into each zig and zag, Jessica increased her speed until she was flying down the avenue at more than 25 miles per hour.

The neighborhood changed quickly—too quickly—as she found herself soaring by the 500 block of the townhomes, passing her destination—Unit 545-B.

Her first instinct was to execute a U-turn.

Jessica opened her eyes to throbbing pain coming from the left side of her skull. She was lying on a worn beige sofa in an unfamiliar room, cold droplets of condensation dripping down her left cheek to pool at the nape of her neck.

"Dad, she's awake."

Repositioning the ice bag, she saw the teen with the bright blue eyes and shoulder-length brown hair. A man she assumed was Logan's father joined the fifteen-year-old, his brown eyes matching his short-cropped hair, his black jumpsuit the uniform of a security officer.

"Captain Josh LaCombe. My son is a terrific Maglev rider but apparently he's a lousy teacher. Lesson number one: Know your turning radius and its limitations. The poles along the track are uni-directional, matching the bottom of your board. Like forces repel and propel, opposites attract. If you alter the orientation of the poles beyond ninety degrees—"

"I know, I know. It's like hitting a brick wall."

Logan shook his head. "I was trailing maybe sixty feet behind you when your board suddenly stopped and you slammed head-first into the track. It was sick. To be honest, I thought you were dead."

"Not yet, but the day's not over." Jessica winced as she attempted to sit up. "Logan, I need to speak to your father in private. Would you give us a minute please?"

Logan's complexion paled as his father gave him a hard stare. "Dad, I swear—"

"Go wake your mom; she needs to get ready for work."

He hesitated.

"Go on."

The teen left the room.

"Relax, captain. I'm here as a friend. Is this room secure?"

"Ma'am?"

"Is there somewhere we can talk?"

"If you mean without Big Brother eavesdropping, I activated white noise dampeners before Logan and I brought you inside."

He turned as an attractive brunette wearing a pink satin bathrobe entered the room. "Jessica Marulli, this is my wife, Dr. Joyce LaCombe."

"Call me Joyce. Logan told us he made a new friend. I hope he hasn't done anything to disrupt your work."

"Not at all. However, I need to ask you both a few questions. Do either one of you know a man named Chris Mull? He's an engineer in Lab-3C."

"No. Josh?"

"Never heard of him."

"Well Captain, he sure acts like he knows you. Apparently, he was close to my predecessor, Scott Hopper and—"

His wife slammed her palm against the bar top. "Happy now? I warned you not to bring her up here."

"She was hurt."

"She probably wiped out on purpose."

"Whoa ... easy guys. Maybe I should leave."

"You'll leave when we say you can leave." In one motion the Delta Force officer reached over to the dining room table and collected his taser, powering up the device.

Jessica's heart raced, her head pounding from the increased blood flow. "Are you threatening me, Captain?"

"I need to know what you value more—my son's life or that Cosmic Clearance badge dangling from your neck?"

Jessica sat up painfully, tossing the ice bag onto the coffee table. "I think the world of your son, which is why I was en route to your home before I did a head-dive onto the Mag. Mull is setting me up to help him steal a zero-point-energy generator ... he demanded I bring it to Captain Josh LaCombe on Level-23, tonight."

The couple looked at one another, unsure what to think.

"Look, I'm just an engineer. The politics of the job ... I try not to think about it. But I don't trust this guy. He may be telling me the truth, or he may be setting us all up for a firing squad. What I do know is that my life and your family's lives depend upon us trusting one another, and that means giving me straight answers to the questions I came here to ask you."

Josh LaCombe glanced at his wife, who nodded.

"Captain, how well did you know Scott Hopper?"

"I'm the one who knew Scott," said Joyce. "We were recruited from the same Ivy League school and were promoted to Cosmic Clearance together. And yes, we believed—as a majority of the members of MAJI now believe—that zero-point-energy and the other advanced technologies reverse-engineered within these facilities belong to the masses."

"If the majority feels that way then what's the problem? Bring the damn thing out."

"This isn't a democracy, Marulli," Captain LaCombe replied. "There are three rings of Council operating in North America—figure seventy-two members, give or take. Worldwide, you're looking at about three hundred individuals who set policy. Thirty to forty percent of those members are hard line conservatives. Included among them are two dozen seriously maladjusted individuals armed with psychotronic weapons. The sociopaths are the ones who keep the silent majority silent."

Joyce opened a liquor cabinet and poured herself a drink. "MJ-12 used to be a science-dominated entity. Once the military industrial complex took over in the late 1950s, they began recruiting primarily from the Council on Foreign Relations, the Trilateral Commission, and the Bilderberg Group. This ensured MAJI would be controlled by a three-headed monster made up of the banks, the military, and Big Oil. Council's agenda is now entirely driven by money. Money buys weapons, weapons keep the oil flowing, oil generates money."

Joyce drained half her glass, then topped it off again before returning the vodka to its cabinet. "I did some checking … Your fiancé is investigating the $100 billion a year that gets lost in the Defense Department's USAPs. He's right when he says that's the tip of the iceberg. MAJI's annual budget is easily over a trillion dollars."

Jessica reached for the ice pack, pressing it again to her throbbing head. "A trillion dollars every year? What do they spend it on?"

"Half that money is spent on maintaining these subterranean complexes, another thirty percent is payroll. What's amazing is the effectiveness of compartmentalizing everything; the majority of the recipients have no idea who they're working for. Then there's the religious fanatics, the hired killers, the media, and of course, the politicians. MAJI's tentacles are everywhere; they're in the West Wing, on Capitol Hill, inside the Pentagon, the intelligence services, private industry … British Parliament. It's metastatic cancer, and as Eisenhower feared, it's grown completely out of control."

"Where do even they get that kind of money?"

"If I told you that, it would make you physically ill."

"I'm already physically ill; tell me."

The captain nodded. "They sell everything … from cocaine and heroin … to women and children. They support rebel forces and sell them guns. They support dictators and terrorists in order to steal their nation's resources. Most of all, they profit off of endless warfare that has been going on non-stop for forty-plus years. Saddam, Gaddafi, Osama bin Laden … now ISIS. It was our intelligence agencies who recruited and armed those lunatics."

"Nine-eleven?"

"Please. Do you really believe nineteen Saudi hijackers who could barely operate a crop duster managed to take out their targets while outmaneuvering the most powerful air force in history? Dick Cheney's been a high-ranking member of MAJI since before you were born; he was running war game exercises the morning of 9/11 that placed fake hijacked blips on the FAA's screens, using them to divert the F-16 interceptors."

Joyce drained her glass. "Iraq was all about oil, but not in the way you think. MAJI didn't want the crude; they just wanted to control the flow in order to set the market. Afghanistan, of course is about heroin, a product controlled by the CIA and delivered by MAJI." She glanced at her husband. "If you knew how they were delivering it …"

"Of course," the captain said, cutting her off, "none of that compares to the next war they've been planning for more than thirty years."

"Okay … enough," Joyce snapped. "We have a major problem with this Chris Mull character. Where's the zero-point device now?"

"I don't know." Jessica said, feeling queasy. "He managed to sneak it out of the Hive using the food services. When I order room service tonight the unit will be concealed within one of the serving dishes. I'm then supposed to wait until 2:30 in the morning and bring it to you."

"It's a set-up," the captain stated. "Once you leave your apartment with the zero-point unit they'll have you on video. That removes Mull from the equation and implicates you. From that moment on, you're Mull's pawn. He'll be able to do whatever he wants with you. Trust me when I say this … there are some pretty sick individuals working down here."

Feeling the bile rising in her esophagus, Jessica pushed past Joyce LaCombe and hurried down a short hall. Quickly locating the bathroom, she dropped to her knees before the toilet and wretched.

27

Greenbelt, Maryland

IT WAS AFTER TEN P.M. BY the time Adam and his new personal bodyguard, Hershel Eugene Evans, arrived at the Greenbelt apartment. It took the former Air Force Tech Sergeant twenty minutes to tap into the building's security system cameras, allowing him to observe the parking lot, entrance, stairwells and elevators on his laptop computer.

The two men were in the middle of gorging on take-out Chinese food when the intercom buzzed, indicating a guest was waiting outside the building entrance.

Adam checked the small security screen by the front door; Eugene his laptop. "Captain, you know this guy?"

"Yeah. It's my old boss."

Dr. Michael Kemp looked tired. At 10:52 at night, this was hardly a social call.

Adam tossed an old army blanket over the Kemp Aerospace cardboard boxes stacked behind his sofa before opening the door. "Michael, what are you doing here?"

"Cut the bullshit and let me in." The CEO of Kemp Aerospace Industries pushed his way inside, pausing when he spotted the armed man seated at the kitchen table. "Who's this?"

"An old military buddy. Eugene Evans, Dr. Michael Kemp."

"Adam, is there someplace we can talk in private?"

"Balcony or the bedroom; take your pick."

"It's starting to rain."

Eugene grabbed his plate. "Talk here, I can eat in the bedroom."

Kemp waited until the bodyguard had closed the bedroom door. "What the hell are you doing to me? I set up a division of my company to develop the prosthetic device you're wearing; I paid you well. Is this how you repay me—by accusing Kemp Aerospace of subcontracting illegal projects? By threatening the defense contractors who feed us their scraps?"

"Michael—"

"You stabbed me in the back, Adam. And for what? Because you found a few bookkeeping discrepancies? Why didn't you come to me first? I would have explained those black op projects were funded by the CIA. I know you're new to the job, but the Central Intelligence Agency is not required to open their books to the goddam Under Secretary of Defense–Comptroller."

"Do you think I just fell off the back of a turnip truck, Michael? *Pahute Mesa* is not a CIA project. Neither are the *Groom Lake* nor *Dreamland* MOCs. Those names correspond to something entirely different and you know it. And just because billions in funding were wired out of a CIA account doesn't it make it acceptable or legal."

"So that's it then? You're going to shut me down?"

"No. I was planning on granting you immunity to testify as part of the whistleblower program."

"Screw your damn whistleblower program. Do you think Lockheed or SAIC or any of the majors will touch us after you subpoena them? You'll make Kemp Aerospace radioactive. You'll get nothing out of them, and you'll get nothing out of me."

"If that's the case then why are you here?"

"I'm here as an emissary. The powers that be are willing to give you a sneak peek behind the curtain in exchange for your cooperation. They've asked me to invite you to a special meeting scheduled for next Tuesday evening at 7 p.m. at the Wrigley Mansion in Phoenix, Arizona. I suggest you hear them out."

"Tell them I accept, on one condition: I want Jessica at the meeting."

Subterranean Complex—Midwest USA

"Dr. Marulli, we're outside your suite. I need you to open your eyes for the retinal scan. Dr. Marulli?" The nurse leaned over the wheelchair and gently squeezed Jessica's shoulders until she opened her eyes—

—the retinal scan positioned above the entrance to Suite 512 immediately locking on to her eyes, causing the door to unbolt and swing open. The interior lights bloomed brighter as the nurse pushed the lethargic woman inside her quarters.

"What happened?"

"You had an accident on the Maglev track; you have a second degree concussion."

"Why am I so sleepy."

The I.V. we gave you at the clinic contains a sedative to help you rest. Do you want to lie down on the sofa or in bed?"

"Help me to the recliner. What time is it?"

"Nine-fifteen … at night."

"No wonder I'm so hungry."

"Concierge, report."

Ingrid appeared in the living room mirror. "My goodness, Jessica. What happened to you?"

"She had a little accident on the Maglev. Order her some dinner and see to it she rests. If she needs any further medical care, summon me at once." The nurse held her I.D. badge up to the smart mirror and then left.

The Swedish woman tut-tutted. "I warned you that your blood sugar was low … when will you ever listen?"

"Just order me some food."

"I already did."

The front door opened and a waiter entered, pushing a cart. "Will you be dining on the terrace tonight, or should I just set you up in front of the recliner?"

"Right here is fine, Mr. Guzzo. What did the concierge order?"

"Your favorite—the lobster thermidor with the crabmeat and garlic whipped potatoes, and the chocolate crème brûlée for dessert."

Jessica picked at her dinner, barely able to keep her eyes open. She yearned to sleep, but first there was work to do.

Having dismissed the computer-generated concierge, she unscrewed the inside of the metal container that had covered her main course and removed the zero-point-energy device. She located her hoverboard in the canvas pouch of the wheelchair and popped open the compartment that held the leash. Sliding the device inside, she closed the lid, leaving the hoverboard on the recliner.

Lying on the couch, Jessica summoned Raul. "Wake me at two a.m. please." She was asleep the moment she closed her eyes.

Jessica's body jerked awake as the doorbell rang. "Raul ... who is it?"

"Logan LaCombe."

"What time is it?"

"Ten-fifteen p.m."

"Let him in."

The door unbolted and opened, allowing Logan to enter. "Jess?"

"Over here."

The teen laid his hoverboard on the recliner next to Jessica's board and knelt by her side. "How do you feel?"

"My head still hurts, but I'm okay. Thanks for getting me to the clinic. They gave me a sedative ... let me sleep, okay?"

She closed her eyes and drifted off.

Logan waited another moment then grabbed one of the hoverboards and left.

Jessica's eyes flashed open as the doorbell rang again. "Raul?"

"It's Logan LaCombe. He says he accidentally took the wrong hover-board."

"Pain in the ass kid. Let him in."

The front door opened and the teenager entered. "Sorry. Guess I grabbed your board by accident. It's set to your fingerprints or I would have ridden it home." He grabbed his board, left hers on the recliner, and was gone.

Jessica rolled over, but this time sleep evaded her. Sitting up, she reached over to the room service tray and collected the dessert plate and a fork, consuming the chocolate crème brûlée in three bites. Shuffling in her stocking feet to the bedroom, she entered the master bath and showered, washing the dried blood from her scalp.

When she crawled naked into bed it was 11:47 p.m. ...

"Jessica? You asked me to wake you. It is oh-two-hundred hours ... two in the morning."

"Thank you, Raul. Now go fuck yourself, please."

"I'm sorry. How do I—"

"Consult the concierge manual."

Forcing herself out of bed, Jessica selected a black unitard and matching sweatpants and sneakers from her closet and dressed. Her head was still sore to the touch, her legs a bit wobbly, but she was dealing with a small window of opportunity. Checking the time, she realized she was ahead of schedule.

Don't want to get to the elevator too early ...

She entered the bathroom and feigned using the toilet, wondering if she was peeing into a urine detector. *They probably know everything that's going on inside my body ...*

She brushed her teeth and checked the time.

2:18 ...

Exiting the bedroom, Jessica retrieved her white lab coat from the closet and put it on; verifying the small device Captain LaCombe had given her hours earlier was in the side pocket. She was nearly out the door when she remembered the hoverboard. She located it on the recliner and left her suite.

The thoroughfare was empty, the lighting dimmed to simulate the lateness of the hour. Crossing the Maglev track to the southbound lane, she placed the hoverboard on the track ... and hesitated.

If you're questioned, how will you justify using the hoverboard with a concussion? Force of habit? Or you could just say you forgot ... although it's obvious to anyone watching that you're thinking about it now.

Retrieving the board, she tucked it under her arm and walked back to the cushioned jogging track, calculating how long it would take her by foot to reach the elevators. *Don't go too fast, you don't want it to appear like you're on a schedule.*

She reached the Level-5 lobby at 2:29. Elevator-7's doors opened as she approached, beckoning her in.

Scanning the internal panel, she noted there were no levels listed below the Maglev Train Station on Level-9.

"Lab 3-C. Half speed please, I'm nursing a concussion."

Sorry, Mr. Mull, there's been a change of plans.

Jessica entered the Hive at 2:35 a.m. She hurried across the assembly area to Sarah's private office, her head pounding with each painful stride. Locating the security panel outside the door, she noted the current time on the built-in digital clock as it advanced to 2:38.

Reaching into the pocket of her lab coat, she removed the matchbox-sized device Captain LaCombe had given her and pressed its magnetic side against the wall directly below the keypad, moving it around until she felt it adhere to the circuits embedded inside the wall.

She watched in amazement as the digital clock on the security panel rotated backwards to 2:31 a.m., the electronic dead bolt clicking open.

You've only got seven minutes ... move!

Opening the unlocked door, she entered Sarah's office.

The twenty aluminum carrying cases were piled in four stacks of five on the floor by her assistant's desk. She quickly located the metal attaché labeled Station-3 and removed the fake zero-point-energy unit given to her by Chris Mull. Selecting the Station-16 attaché from the last stack, she swapped out the two devices, placing the working ZPE generator into the Station-3 container, the fake device inside case sixteen.

She had explained her plan to Logan's parents after the captain had showed her how to use the scrambler to "loop time" on the Hive's internal security system.

"I'll order dinner and place the ZPE unit inside my hoverboard as Mull instructed. Send Logan down to check on me around ten o'clock. Have him 'accidentally' take my board when he leaves. As he walks out to the Maglev track, he needs to remove and pocket the zero-point-energy generator, using the board to conceal what he's doing from the security cameras. When he gets out to the track the board won't power up. Realizing his mistake, Logan will return to my apartment, swap boards, and leave. Instruct him where to hide the unit. If he gets caught with it—"

"We'll handle it. What about you?"

"At 2:30 in the morning I'll enter Elevator-7 with my hoverboard as instructed, only instead of delivering the device to you at Level-23 I'll go up to the Hive. After I deactivate the lab's security system, I'll swap Mull's fake device for one of the real ones we removed from the satellites. If Mull is setting me up, the ZPE unit in attaché three will be real, eliminating any evidence against me—and you'll have a real zero-point-energy generator."

Jessica returned the two attaché cases to their proper stacks and exited Sarah's office. The security scrambler was at 2:36, forcing her to wait another two minutes before she could power off the device. The moment the scrambler's digital clock advanced to 2:38, she deactivated the unit, watching as the time jumped ahead seven minutes, resetting the Hive's internal security to 2:45—

—as a heavy baritone rumbling suddenly rattled her eardrums.

Her heart raced—*could her actions have triggered an alert? Was the Hive being sealed?*

Then she realized the source of the disturbance—the subterranean complex's roof was retracting!

Were they preparing to launch an Atlas rocket? If only there was only a way to sneak a quick peek without having to open a section of the Hive?

Then she remembered the leaking air conditioner duct.

Crossing the lab to the nearest satellite work station, she removed an anti-gravitics vest and helmet from the supply wall, contemplating her next move carefully.

I could say I was in the Hive catching up on some work when the ceiling started shaking and panels started falling. So I flew up to take a look, afraid the entire A/C duct might collapse on one of the satellites ... Bring a roll of duct tape with you to secure the damaged panels.

She located a tool belt which held a roll of silver duct tape as the rumbling abruptly ceased. Slipping off her lab coat, she placed the tool belt around her waist and then slid her arms inside the anti-gravitics vest. Tightening the straps, she secured the helmet's chin strap and powered up the antigravity unit—searching the ceiling for the gap.

There ...

She had barely focused her eyes on the water-stained spot when she felt herself levitate off the concrete deck, the vest accelerating her toward her intended target.

She slowed to hover beneath the six-foot-in-diameter hole, catching her breath. The octagonal ceiling panels surrounding the gap were moist, giving her the confidence she needed to proceed. Prying loose the most damaged of the neighboring panels, she allowed them to fall to the ground in sections before levitating inside the twelve-foot-wide gap.

She found her way easily around the labyrinth of ducts and cables to a thin cobalt-colored tin foil sheathing she knew separated the Hive from the tunnel. Searching her tool belt, Jessica removed a large screwdriver and used it to slice open a three-foot slit in the foil ceiling, making a mental note to duct tape the hole closed when she was done.

Ignoring the sudden urge to pee, she pushed herself head-first through the opening.

From her vantage atop the Hive, she had a clear view of the massive launch tunnel. Ahead were the vertical gantries supporting the twenty Atlas-

V rockets. At the far end of the site, it appeared as if a section of the subterranean roof had indeed retracted, the gap outlined by a rectangle of green lights and a sliver of starry night sky.

For several long minutes nothing happened. And then, just as she was about to abandon her perch and return to the Hive, the UFO appeared.

The ship was disc-shaped—about a hundred feet in diameter, with a coned top. Around the edge of the disc were dazzling multi-colored lights—red, blue, green, and yellow. While the disc was spinning counterclockwise, the lights were circling in both directions—fusing and blending into one another in seemingly random patterns, the intensity and quality not of this world.

And yet by its presence within the subterranean structure, Jessica knew the vessel had to be man-made ... an Alien Reproduction Vehicle.

She watched, incredulous, as the ARV set down.

I'm too far away to see. I need to be—

Before she could curtail her internal thoughts Jessica shot out of the top of the Hive like a bullet, soaring past the first six gantries before her mind could shout the telepathic command to stop.

She hovered in the semi-darkness, thirty-three-feet above the nose of an Atlas-V rocket, the only sound coming from her heaving chest.

Despite her sprint, the ARV was still a good distance ahead.

If you're going to do this, you'll need an explanation as to why you're buzzing around the Atlas launch site.

"I was working in the lab when the ceiling started to rumble and panels started falling from the ceiling ... hell, I thought it was an earthquake. My Cosmic Clearance gives me access to everything, so I left the lab to check it out ... is there a problem, marine?"

Satisfied with her story, she flew another quarter mile before spotting the outline of red warning lights which separated the Atlas rockets launch sites from the rest of the tunnel. Ian Concannon had warned her about the boundary being armed with an electromagnetic pulse that would disable her anti-gravitics and she had no interest in crashing twice in one evening.

Jessica landed feet-first in the shadows of the second-to-last gantry. Removing her tool belt and anti-gravity gear, she stowed everything behind a four-foot-thick concrete pillar before speed walking the rest of the way—keeping to the tunnel's darker periphery.

Detecting movement, she hid behind a vertical steel buttress.

A hatch was opening beneath the saucer section of the ARV, summoning four men in black uniforms from an interior complex out of her line of sight. They were pushing what looked like an extremely large laundry cart. Positioning it as close as they could to the hatch, the men formed a receiving line.

Another man wearing headgear and a black jumpsuit leaned out of the craft—Jessica took him to be the pilot. He quickly became engaged in a heated argument with one of the four worker bees as the ARV's co-pilot began tossing cinderblock-size parcels wrapped in dark plastic out of the craft to the first loader in line.

"We're light twenty kilos, and before you start in on your shit, this is the third time in the last two months the fucking FAC had Kfir Fighter Jets waiting for us as we entered Colombian air space. Plus there were another dozen of whatever they call their UH-60 Blackhawks—"

"—*Arpia*," said the co-pilot as he tossed another plastic-wrapped cinderblock out of the ARV.

"Right, *Arpia*. How do you expect us to set down in a fucking jungle patrolled by armed *Arpia* helicopters?"

"We went over this. You pull a bunch of Mach-30 zig-zags across their radar screens and they won't know where you'll set down."

FAC … he's talking about the Fuerza Aerea Colombiana … the Colombian Air Force. Jesus, they're using goddam Alien Reproduction Vehicles to smuggle cocaine into the states!

"You! Hands where I can see them … nice and slow."

She turned, confronted by a brilliant white light, its 500 Lumens occupying her entire field of vision.

"My name is Dr. Jessica Marulli …" she held up her I.D. "As you can see, I'm Cosmic Clearance. Now get that goddam light out of my eyes before I have you demoted to parking lot attendant."

She never saw the taser nor felt the sting of its two needle-like prongs as they struck her in the chest and left thigh. By then her mind was already surfing a blinding, deafening 60,000 volt wave of pain which slammed her into unconsciousness.

28

Wrigley Mansion
Phoenix, Arizona

THE WHITE STUCCO DWELLING was set high on a knoll over-looking the Arizona Biltmore Hotel and the city of Phoenix, its orange Spanish roof tile matching the sunset-drenched backdrop of desert mountainside which rose behind the property. Built during the Great Depression by gum magnate and Chicago Cubs owner William Wrigley Jr., the 16,000-square-foot mansion had changed hands several times before eventually being restored as a historic landmark. A popular tourist destination, with an on-site restaurant open to the public, the mansion nevertheless remained a private club that served as a favorite meeting venue for one very well-to-do client.

Former Tech Sergeant Eugene Evans drove the Cadillac limousine up the winding path to the valet station, the vehicle's tinted rear windows too dark to see the passenger riding in back. The usually open iron gate guarding the main entrance was closed, a posted sign explaining the circumstances:

PRIVATE PARTY TONIGHT
By Invitation Only

A man dressed in a black suit and sunglasses rapped on the tinted driver's side window with his knuckles, his ear piece intended to give away his presence as security.

Eugene Evans rolled down his window. "Under Secretary Adam

Shariak."

"This is as far as you go, pal. We'll escort Mr. Shariak inside; you can park down below in the Biltmore's lot."

A second "valet" opened the rear driver's side door. "Good evening, Mr. Under Secretary. If you'll come with me …"

Adam exited the limo, his escort leading him on a long walk to the front of the mansion. He was perspiring by the time they reached the main entrance which was accessible from two parallel flights of steps which framed a decorative mini-garden.

Adam followed the security guard up the staircase on the right, noticing the telltale bulge of the handgun pressing against the back of the man's jacket. "So, I guess everyone on staff must be excited about the Cubs' ninth inning rally last night to beat the Dodgers. Think they'll make it back to the World Series?"

"This is Diamondback territory; no one here gives a damn about the Cubs. The main entrance is through that portal, they're waiting for you inside." He smirked. "Try to blend in."

Thanks, douche bag. Try not to blow your ass off with your 9mm.

Adam made his way to the double doors set inside the alcove entrance, the roof of which served as the bottom of a Juliet balcony. Entering the mansion, he was greeted by a cold blast from an air conditioning vent. Before him was a grand staircase and a dazzling chandelier hanging from a high dome ceiling. As he took in the guests, he quickly realized that everyone was dressed for a black-tie affair … except him.

Michael, you bastard … you could have told me.

A cluster of women in evening gowns and men in custom-fitted tuxedos toasted him from across the room. Adam bowed in his navy-blue blazer and tan slacks and entered the main foyer.

Pretending to be interested in the mansion's history, he stared at a series of framed black and white photos—using the reflection to track the two Caucasian males in dark suits approaching him from across the room.

"Mr. Shariak, if you'll come with us, your party is waiting for you upstairs."

He followed them back out of the foyer and up the winding steps of the grand staircase, his sciatic nerve on full meltdown by the time he reached the second floor. They proceeded down a narrow hallway to a closed door, distinguished from the others by a plaque indicating that Elvis Presley had once slept there.

"She's waiting for you inside."

Adam entered, anxious to see his fiancée. The bedroom was empty, but he could see Jessica standing outside on the balcony, her back to him, her shapely figure filling out the topaz evening dress.

Juice …

He caught a whiff of her favorite perfume as he stepped outside and wrapped his arms around the blonde's narrow waist from behind. He nuzzled her neck—his groin responding as her hand reached between his legs to playfully squeeze his crotch as she turned to face him—

—revealing herself to be another woman.

Adam backed away, his pulse racing. "Who the hell are you?"

"Kelly Kishel, counter-intelligence. I was sent by the Air Force Office of Special Investigations to brief you."

"Were you also sent here to grope me?"

"Let the record show, Mr. Under Secretary, that you initiated the physical contact. I was just rolling with the punches."

"Where's Jessica?"

"Dr. Marulli apologizes, but she could not afford to leave her work at this time. She said you would understand."

"Get her on the phone; let me speak with her."

"I'm not authorized to do that. However, I can ask someone to arrange a call the moment your meeting concludes."

"My terms of this meeting were simple, Agent Kishel. The fact that the Air Force just happened to select you—a blonde look-alike wearing Jessica's perfume, sure reeks of a CIA set-up to me."

He glanced over her shoulder at the flower pot hanging from the ceiling—the lens of a miniature video camera reflecting the sunset. "I am so out of here—"

She reached out and grabbed the crook of his arm as he turned to leave. "Wait. I've been authorized to offer you a small sum to call off your investigation ... $75 million to be exact. That figure represents the amount of money you'd be saving the American taxpayer for cancelling these hearings."

"What about the $100 billion in taxpayer monies spent annually on these so-called Unacknowledged Special Access Projects? How do you propose we save them that chunk of change?"

She forced a smile. "You have no idea what you're dealing with, do you?"

"Let me take a guess ... UFOs, ETs, and the advanced technologies uncovered by these illegal USAPs for the commercial gain of a group of defense contractors whose CEOs will be receiving subpoenas from my office—that sound about right to you?"

She was about to reply when she received a communiqué over her earpiece. "They want to meet you."

"Forget it."

"It's important you do this ... for Jessica's sake." Without waiting for a reply she led him out of the bedroom and down the hall to a set of double doors guarded by the two security bookends. Turning to face him, Agent Kishel brushed lint from his lapel with one hand, slipping a folded business card into his jacket pocket with the other. "These are nasty people. Don't try to be a hero, *hero* ... or things will turn out bad."

Opening the door, she motioned for him to enter.

The chamber had been originally designed as a game room. Mixed in with the antique Cubs' baseball paraphernalia, dart boards, two pool tables and three green-felt octagonal card tables, was a large flat screen television and six smaller monitors which occupied one entire wall. The high ceiling was buttressed in a dark-stained oak which matched the bar; the remaining three walls were covered in expensive oil paintings of plump nude women which dated back to the sixteenth century. The rest of the furnishings were ornate, the arched windows curtained in cherry-red drapes, the scent of cigar smoke and age embedded in the heavy fabric.

The caterer had set up eight rectangular aluminum serving dishes which held hot entrees on two long folding tables. A third table displayed the remains of what had been an assortment of desserts.

Seated around a white linen-covered dining table were a dozen Council members representing the inner circle of the group formerly known as Majestic-12. All were Caucasian and male; the youngest was in his mid-forties, the oldest pushing eighty-five. Half had served in either the Armed Forces or the intelligence community; a few had crossed into politics. Of the six businessmen, two were American, one was English. The Scandinavian owned a private bank; the Australian was an engineer; the Russian an industrialist with ties to the KGB. Though they hailed from different backgrounds and countries, they were all billionaires who preferred to operate their empires from the shadows.

Four of the men were hardliners who were convinced that the only sensible solution to the planet's diminishing resources was to eliminate the middle class while systematically reducing the world's population.

The youngest member of the group—an American CEO—looked up at Adam Shariak with a Cheshire-cat smile. "Under Secretary Shariak ... so nice of you to join us. You must be hungry; make yourself a plate."

"I'm good, thank you."

"You seem a bit uptight. How about a drink ... or perhaps a lady of the evening? Our clients downstairs are enjoying the local talent but I've got a few Asian delights stashed in one of the upstairs bedrooms for our VIPs."

"I think I'll pass, but it's nice to see you're in such good spirits, Mr. Laskowski. I look forward to questioning you before Congress."

"And I look forward to pleading the fifth."

A few of the men laughed.

The Russian stomped out his cigar. "There is reason we wished to meet you. We have heard you are man of strong character, *da?*"

"You'd have to define character to me, Comrade."

"For me this means family-first."

Adam felt a sweat bead trickle down his armpit. "Whose family?"

"Yours, of course," said the lanky white-haired Englishman. "There's your step-brother, Senator Hall, and of course ... your fiancée. She's lobbied hard for us to bring you in."

They're lying ...

"Oh, and just to clarify ... the $75 million Agent Kishel mentioned on the balcony is merely a fee for ending your witch hunt. The starting salary is $36 million a year, plus perks—one of which is that you would be able to work with Dr. Marulli."

"So that's a $75 million signing bonus and $3 million a month for selling my soul. Just one quick question before I exercise my strong character and tell you to go fuck yourselves—what exactly is it that you people do?"

"We provide … balance," the tan, fit-looking Scandinavian replied. "Think of us as a western-leaning think tank possessing extraordinary influence. When the world slips off-kilter, we have the means to right the ship."

"Provided the ship runs on diesel fuel … yes?"

The younger American stood and applauded. "Bravo. In one short sentence you've managed to demonstrate your complete ignorance of world affairs. Gentlemen, I give you our new Under Secretary of Peace and Love. I'm sure we'll all sleep better with Mr. Shariak installed as our newest non-voting member of Council."

"Actually Mr. Laskowski, it's *Captain* Shariak. And while you and your rich pals have apparently been manipulating dictators and armies like pieces on a chessboard, grunts like me have witnessed first-hand the death and destruction your narcissistic decisions have wrought upon the masses."

"Save that lecture for the obstructionists occupying Capitol Hill. And for the record, our interests do serve the masses."

"If that's true, gentlemen, then prove it to me right now, and I'll reconsider your offer."

"How can we prove it," the Australian asked.

"Climate change is destroying Mother Earth like a metastatic cancer. Take a vote right now on phasing out fossil fuels over the next three years by introducing zero-point-energy into the public domain. Leave a legacy that saves our planet … do the right thing, and I'll do whatever I can to support you."

A heavy silence fell over the chamber. The six men in favor of Adam's proposal quickly identified themselves by leaning back in their chairs and offering supportive glances while the three individuals who opposed his request—the Russian, the older American businessman, and the Brit seemed clearly perturbed by the Under Secretary's audacity even to ask.

And yet the other three men appeared unsure. The Aussie was clearly mulling it over, his hazel eyes intensely focused on the table top, while the gray-haired former National Security Advisor seated directly across the table from him was embattled in his own internal struggle.

And then there was Laskowski. The youngest member of the billionaires' boys club seemed like a deer caught in headlights—the headlights being the hawkish gray eyes of the older American staring down at him from the opposite end of the table.

He was frail and pale and in his eighties, his receding hairline covered in liver spots. Stooped over from scoliosis, the old man's aura nevertheless weighed heavily in the chamber like a black hole, his presence clearly affecting Laskowski, who circled the dessert table, helping himself to a slice of chocolate cake as he attempted to regain his composure. "Upending the free markets would cause chaos, Mr. Shariak, and chaos is not in the best interests of the masses."

"Did the personal computer cause chaos? Did the iPhone? Zero-point-energy could be phased in like any other new technology and the free markets would respond in a positive way."

"One day, perhaps. Not today."

"Not today?" Adam glanced around the room. "How many todays do you think we have left? Surely some of you have children and grand-children? Don't they deserve a planet where the air can actually be breathed? Step up to the plate, gentlemen … do the right thing. Or is it more important to allow your oil oligarch pals downstairs to suck every last drop of oil out of the ground? For God's sake, how many billions of dollars do you people need?"

The Aussie looked up … he was about to speak—

—when the old man slammed both palms on the table. "How dare you insult the Eternal Father and His Son—our Lord and Savior—by speaking of money! It is only through the atonement of Christ than mankind shall be saved and not by employing an energy device invented by the devil. This man—this heathen—is not a member of Council; nor should he ever be. He has not accepted Jesus Christ into his heart; he does not believe in the restoration of the ten tribes or that Zion, the New Jerusalem shall be erected on American soil. When the minions of Satan are vanquished from the skies, then Christ shall reign. Then and only then shall Mother Earth be renewed and mankind shall bask in all His glory."

The man stood, his face a mask of hatred as he pointed a calloused index finger at the Under Secretary of Defense. "Leave our sanctuary ... now!"

Adam glanced around the table, tallying the averted expressions. Exiting through the double doors, he pushed his way past the two security goons and Agent Kishel as he retrieved his iPhone from his jacket pocket. Gripping the rail of the grand staircase with his right hand, he speed-dialed with his left, the heel of the shoe of his prosthetic leg nearly twisting off as he hurriedly descended the narrow steps.

"Meet me out front in thirty seconds; I'm done here."

29

Subterranean Complex—Midwest USA

JESSICA SAT UP IN THE HOSPITAL BED as the attendant wheeled in her lunch, replacing the cart which still held her breakfast. Lifting the plastic cover, he saw that she hadn't eaten a thing.

"Ms. Marulli, if you don't eat then how do you expect Dr. Spencer to discharge you?"

"I've been here six days which is five too many. Today starts Day 1 of a hunger strike."

"That won't be necessary."

She looked up as the Canadian-born physician entered her room, accompanied by his wife, a registered nurse.

Like most of the medical staff serving MAJI's subterranean complexes, Dr. Ken Spencer had begun his career in the military. He had met his wife, Robbin, during the first Gulf War, the couple returning to Alberta where they opened a private medical clinic. But once a year they reported to the complex outside Edwards Air Force Base where they were whisked by Maglev train to one of the secret subterranean complexes—the six week rotation tripling both of their annual salaries.

"Good afternoon, Jessica. And how are we feeling today?"

"My head feels better, my left forearm's slightly sore from where that asshole tasered me last week. Other than that, I'm fine."

The physician inspected the quarter-size welt along her biceps where he had been ordered to implant the tracking device. "Give it another day; I'm sure it'll feel better by then. The good news is that you passed your concussion protocol."

"Does that mean I'm free to leave?"

"Just give Nurse Robbin a few minutes to remove your I.V."

Lydia Gagnon watched her friend's daughter from behind the one-way glass, her skin crawling from the presence of the sociopath who had just entered the viewing area.

Colonel Alexander Johnston's crystal-blue eyes glittered beneath the fluorescent light, the soft pink flesh covering his bony cheeks yielding to the silver-white whiskers of a five o'clock shadow. The man known as Dr. Death smelled of baby powder and formaldehyde, the scent coming from his hands and the frayed sleeves of his black turtleneck sweater.

General Thomas Cubit gagged at the stench. "Christ, Colonel—this is a medical facility, not a morgue. There's a new invention … maybe you heard of it—it's called soap."

"Why are you here?"

"Dr. Marulli serves under my command. I will not allow you to subject her to your psychotronic mind control."

"She's a security risk."

"She is not a risk," Lydia shot back. "Mr. Mull tested her and she refused to comply, returning the ZPE device to the lab."

"Mr. Mull isn't convinced and neither am I. Her activity in the Hive the night she witnessed the ARV is very suspicious."

"That's only because the two of you are paranoid schizophrenics," General Cubit said. "I'm releasing her, and I'm taking her off probation, allowing her full access to the facility."

Alexander Johnston turned to him, speaking through clenched yellow teeth. "You're making a mistake."

"And you're outvoted," Lydia said.

With a grunt that sounded like a wounded animal's growl, Colonel Johnston turned for the door, kicking a wastepaper basket on his way out.

Lydia ran her sweaty palms across her lab coat. "I despise that man.

What do you think he had the doc inject into her arm?"

I don't know, but the more active she is, the quicker it will pass."

"What happened with Shariak?"

Cubit smiled. "They tried to bribe him and he turned it around. If the old man hadn't tossed him out there would have been a sea-change in the inner ring."

"That's why Dr. Death's on the war path."

"Yes, and you can bet the hardliners won't go quietly into the night."

Capitol Hill, Washington, D.C.

Senator Randy Hall, Chairman of the Senate Appropriations Committee, sat back in his desk chair and re-read the list of names his brother had prepared for the first week of hearings.

"Adam, who the hell are these people? I don't see a defense contractor's name among them."

"I'm saving the CEOs for week two. Week one are scientists and members of the Armed Forces who can attest to the existence of the Unacknowledged Special Access Projects we're investigating."

"If they haven't received money from the treasury, then their testimony is irrelevant. I told you I wasn't going to allow you to waste the Appropriations Committee's time."

"First, this is a joint hearing and I'm riding shotgun. Second, every defense contractor we call upon to answer questions about these illegal black ops projects is either going to deny they exist or plead the fifth. By calling these witnesses first and establishing that these USAPs exist, taking the fifth will seem more of an admission of guilt instead of an action to protect a top-secret weapons system."

"I assume these people have high security clearances ... how are you going to get them to violate their national security oaths in order to come forward and testify?"

"You prepare the subpoenas and let me worry about that."

PART 4

"We'll know our disinformation is complete when everything the American public believes is false."

—former CIA Director William Casey

"The business of the journalist is to destroy the truth; to lie outright; to pervert; to vilify; to fawn at the feet of mammon, and to sell his country and his race for his daily bread. You know it, and I know it, and what folly is this toasting an independent press? We are the tools and vassals of rich men behind the scenes. We are the jumping jacks, they pull the strings, and we dance. Our talents, our possibilities and our lives are all the property of other men. We are intellectual prostitutes."

—John Swinton, former managing editor,
The New York Times **&** *New York Sun*

"The CIA owns everyone of any significance in the major media."

—former CIA Director William Colby

North Philadelphia, Pennsylvania
March 2, 2033

The three-foot-high by four-foot-long double-paned barrier of glass stood upright on the table top. Wedged inside the half-inch spacing separating the two glass panels was an ant colony, the insect habitat composed of an edible neon-blue gel.

Michael Sutterfield's eyes followed the intricate pattern of tunnels channeling the perpetual activity of the nest. "They're like a well-trained army."

Dr. Mohammad Mallouh acknowledged the comment from the other side of the table. "They certainly function as a collective consciousness."

"And not a sociopath among them, huh Dr. M? No ants committing impulsive acts … every ant doing their job. Because if an ant were to go off the rails, the others would probably have to kill it."

"Ants are not people, Michael."

"You're right. The colony wouldn't exclude one of its own kind unless the ant first did something wrong. But me—I'm banned from CE-5 training because of something I could 'potentially' do against the Interstellars?"

"It's not fair, but after what happened years ago with the sociopaths in MAJI and the climate change deniers, the world is taking no chances."

"Didn't President Trump ban those victims of wars from entering the country because he believed Muslims were terrorists?"

"The Syrian refugees … yes."

"Do you know a lot of Muslim terrorists?"

"I don't, no. Your point is well taken, however—"

"I got an email yesterday from an Army recruiter. I thought maybe it was just something they send out around your thirteenth birthday, but I did some checking. Turns out military recruiters target sociopaths. Turns out a lack of conscience is a good trait to have when your government asks you to murder thousands of enemy soldiers and innocent civilians."

"Your points are well taken."

"But you still won't let me participate in CE-5?"

"It's not up to me. I'm sorry."

Michael stared at the ant farm, his pulse a steady 63 beats per minute. "I was wrong, Dr. M. There is one sociopath among the colony—it's the queen. She's the reason they stay in line."

Lifting the ant farm in both hands, the teen smashed it upon the table, his right fist emerging from the blizzard of blue goop with a shard of glass which sliced through the air, opening Dr. Mohammad Mallouh's throat.

There was no spurt of blood, no aftermath. The lights in the Global Village Pod simply flashed on, atomizing the hologram so that only the teen remained, his sensory suit popping loose as he rose from the bucket seat.

Climbing out of the pod, Michael Sutterfield left the basement to join his parents at the dinner table.

His mother smiled. "You're just in time. How was school?"

"Good. Dr. Mallouh said to say hello."

30

Dirksen Senate Office Building, Room 108
Capitol Hill, Washington, D.C.

ADAM GAZED AROUND THE wood-paneled chamber as the eight Democrats and twelve Republican senators made their way to their high-backed leather chairs positioned around the half-moon-shaped dais. The chamber was filled to capacity, the audience squeezed into tightly-packed rows, Dr. Steven Greer among them. More important was the presence of the two C-SPAN cameras, one aimed at the members of the committee; the other at the witness table where the Under Secretary now sat with the individuals scheduled to give testimony during the morning session.

Senator Randy Hall took his place at the center of the dais. It had taken a lot of persuasion and the calling in of several terms worth of favors for the chairman to put together a quorum of committee members in what many in the Beltway were publicly touting as a "Department of Defense witch hunt." It was one thing to talk about "plugging the Treasury's leaky dam," but no elected official wanted to be placed in a position to have to punish a defense contractor … not if they had any hope of being reelected.

Senator Hall turned on his microphone. "Good morning. "As it appears we have the minimum number of senators present to declare a quorum, I will ask everyone to take their seats so that we can begin. For the record let me state that this Hearing of the Appropriations Committee was requested by Adam Shariak, the Under Secretary of Defense–Comptroller as part of an internal investigation regarding the potential existence and funding of unaccounted for programs, collectively defined as Unacknowledged Special

Access Projects. These USAPs are considered illegal if they lack approval by either the President of the United States or Congress.

"Because of existing family ties between the Under Secretary and myself, I am now going to recuse myself and turn the chair over to my esteemed colleague from Michigan, Senator Karen Sampson."

The six-term Republican accepted Randy Hall's handshake and gavel before situating herself in his chair. "Thank you, Mr. Chairman. Under Secretary Shariak, before we call on your first witness to testify, perhaps you would explain to the committee what relevance Mr. Sheehan brings to this investigation."

"Yes, Madam Chair. Because the witnesses we'll be calling on to testify today and throughout the week were issued top security clearances and have taken a national security oath, it's imperative that both they and the members of this committee understand that their testimony regarding illegal activities conducted by individuals or entities operating both within and outside the United States government in no way conflicts with that sworn oath. Mr. Sheehan's experience in these matters qualifies him to address this issue and provide a necessary comfort level so that we may proceed."

"Very well. If the witness will state his name and occupation for the record."

The hulking man in his early seventies, with the mop of curly white hair, adjusted his microphone as he leaned in to address the members of the committee. "My name is Daniel Sheehan. I am an attorney, admitted to the bar of New York and Washington D.C. I have practiced civil law for almost forty years since graduating from Harvard Law School in 1970. Some of my more high profile cases as a constitutional trial lawyer include serving as one of the five defense attorneys assigned by the Cahill Gordon firm representing *The New York Times* in the Pentagon Papers case. I was one of the three trial lawyers in F. Lee Bailey's firm assigned to represent James McCord in the Watergate burglary defense, and it was our office that persuaded Mr. McCord to write the letter to Judge John Sirrica which helped trace the chain of command of the Watergate burglars back to the White House. I was also chief counsel in the Karen Silkwood case against the Kerr McGee nuclear facility in Oklahoma, as well as the civil case against the illegal

Steve Alten

enterprises of Richard Secord and Albert Hakim, the gentlemen who were working with Lt. Colonel Oliver North.

"Prior to today's hearing, I met with the Under Secretary and spoke with each eyewitness in regard to their involvement with these USAPs. Madame Chair, having done a great deal of analysis of the constitution, I am completely confident that the funding of these black ops projects is a violation of the Neutrality Act. The Neutrality Act is a federal statute under Title 18 of the United States code that prohibits private citizens from engaging in any type of war-like activities against any other non-United States entity without authorization from Congress. The Oath these eyewitnesses took, known as the *Oath Upon Inadvertent Exposure To Classified Security Data Or Information*, does not pertain to illegal activities which violate the Constitution and, therefore, the oath cannot be enforced."

"Does the Committee have any questions for Mr. Sheehan? No? Then Mr. Sheehan you are excused. Under Secretary Shariak, you may call your next witness."

A green-eyed, slightly balding Caucasian man in his early sixties took the microphone.

"Please state your name and occupation for the record."

"My name is Jonathan Graham Wade and I make a living designing furniture. Prior to that, I spent thirty-seven years with the United States Air Force as a counter-intelligence officer in the Office of Special Investigations. My first assignment to what the Under Secretary refers to as a USAP occurred in the summer of 1979 when I was transferred to the Nevada Test site, which is now the Nevada Security Site. There are actually two different locations out there. There's the test site—known as the DET-3 Test Center—and then there's Groom Lake, better known as Area 51. I was with a detachment of test personnel from Edwards Air Force base assigned to the Groom Lake Complex. Because my primary responsibility was to conduct counter-intelligence operations at the base, I was briefed or read in on an Unacknowledged Special Access Project."

"Can you tell us what that project involved, Mr. Wade."

"Yes, ma'am. The project involved the United States government's investigation of UFOs and the Air Force's involvement with extra-

272

terrestrials."

The chamber erupted with the buzz generated from a hundred side conversations.

Adam looked over his shoulder to steal a quick glance at Steven Greer. Instead of appearing pleased, the UFO expert had a grim look on his face.

The repetitive rapping of Senator Sampson's gavel eventually quieted the crowd. "Another outburst like that and I'll be forced to clear the chamber." She stared down at the witness from her perch. "Really, Mr. Wade? This committee is investigating the potential existence of illicit defense funding and you want to turn this into a circus?"

"Senator, I was asked to testify about these Unacknowledged Special Access Projects. The reason they're 'Unacknowledged' is because the individuals running them don't want the public, your committee, the President of the United States, or even their own employees to know about them, and the biggest, most secret USAPs all deal with UFOs and ETs. Many of you may not be able to handle that fact, but if you want to dismiss the truth by labeling it a circus or conspiracy theory, or those of us who came here today to testify as nut-jobs, then you ought to consider two things: First, every one of us was entrusted with duties requiring security clearances far above top-secret; second, dismissing anyone who comes forward to discuss this topic as being crazy is exactly what the intelligence agencies and the people in charge want you to do. I know that because hiding the truth in plain sight by attacking an eyewitness's credibility is exactly what I used to get paid a lot of money to do."

Catcalls of "let him testify" and "we want the truth" filled the chamber.

Senator Sampson held up her hand for quiet. "Alright, Mr. Wade, you have our full attention … please continue."

"As I was saying … while I was stationed at the Groom Lake Complex, I conducted investigations into the UFO phenomenon, with my primary mission focused on UFO sightings and any threats imposed by these extraterrestrials on Air Force or Air Force-related properties."

"And have you actually seen a UFO?"

"Yes, senator. I saw them when I was stationed at McGuire Air Force Base in Montana—they were always buzzing the bases where the nuclear weapons are kept. I also saw footage of an aerial demonstration at Nellis where they would accelerate to incredible speeds, stop on a dime, and execute a ninety-degree turn.

"But tens of thousands of civilians have seen them as well. Back in 1997, the ETs gave us an incredible show over Phoenix that was witnessed by tens of thousands of people and, of course, was immediately dismissed by the authorities."

"Mr. Wade, it's hard to believe so many people have had these … encounters, and yet there's never anything in the news or on TV."

"Senator, maybe you still believe in Santa Claus and the Easter Bunny, because if you actually think we have a free press, then you're fooling yourself. Thanks to Ronald Reagan and deregulation, a handful of CEOs now decide what the news is, and they take their marching orders from the CIA, who will fabricate or kill any story in order to protect their own agenda. As for members of the Armed Forces, any military personnel who speak about these encounters in public or to members of the media often find themselves transferred to some remote base far from home. Soldiers in the field who were first responders to a UFO crash have been intimidated, and in some cases beaten, by arriving members of our Blue Teams, where it is Standard Operating Procedure to physically threaten the soldier or even to kill him and his family should he ever go public with what he witnessed. I'm ashamed to say that I've seen one of these elite Delta Force guys crack open an American soldier's skull with the butt of his assault rifle simply because the sentry glanced at a photo of a downed UFO."

A brief exchange among the committee members was interrupted by Senator Tiffany Townsend from Florida. "Mr. Wade, you stated that your job was to assess any threats imposed by these extraterrestrials on our Air Force facilities. Are these aliens a threat?"

"Senator, that's a concern which dates back to late June of 1947, the first time our radar systems knocked two of these ET craft out of the sky."

"Are you talking about Roswell, Mr. Wade?"

"Yes, Madam Chair, only the craft didn't actually go down at Roswell. The first crash site involving two of the three ships was located southwest of Corona, New Mexico. It took the military two years before they found the second crash site, which was way out west of Magdalena. When they read us in on *Yankee Black*—that was the security code on this particular USAP—the first thing they did was show us a 16mm movie of the recovery. There were dead extraterrestrials at the Corona site, along with the one survivor. The bodies at the Magdalena site were too decomposed to salvage."

"Excuse me, Mr. Wade—did you just say the authorities managed to capture a living ET?"

"Yes, ma'am. They named it EBEN, short for Extraterrestrial Biological Entity. It was taken to Kirtland Air Force Base and then on to Los Alamos. We saw footage … they kept it alive for a few years. The other bodies were sent to Wright-Patterson field in Dayton, Ohio, and placed in a deep freeze."

"Can you describe this creature for us?"

"He was a Grey biped and male—all of the Greys were thought to be male. He was about four feet tall and hairless, with a large skull, big eyes, an indentation for a nose, and no visible ears. The Grey's hands were slender, with four fingers and no thumbs, and the fingers had suction devices on the tips. Their outfits were skin-tight and they wore an apparatus on their head with what appeared to be an ear piece for communicating with their craft, which were saucer-shaped. Not all of the craft are saucers; some were oval, others cigar-shaped. There are big ones that look like a kid's top. Different species … different craft."

"How many different species have visited Earth?"

"That's hard to say. One source told me nine; though I've heard as many as thirty-seven. Mind you, I've only seen photos of four different species. The most bizarre one looked like an insect, with big bug eyes, a large head, and a small body. They had two different hands on each arm and several joints in their legs."

Multiple discussions broke out, quelled by the Chair's gavel. "Senator Townsend asked you whether the ETs pose a threat. Do they, Mr. Wade?"

"Let me answer that first from the perspectives of the Eisenhower-Truman Administrations, then post-JFK. You have to remember that the majority of these encounters first began when the United States was testing the atomic bomb, culminating in the detonations in Hiroshima and Nagasaki. Those events definitely caught our visitors' attention, and throughout the late 1940s and 1950s there was a lot of UFO activity around our nuclear installations. Roswell had the 509th Bomb Wing—the only nuclear-capable strike force in the United States at that time, so it's no surprise they frequented New Mexico, which was also home to the lab in Los Alamos and other nuclear testing grounds. Kirtland Air Force Base had nukes, which again drew a lot of ET activity. Between the development of the hydrogen bomb and the Cold War with the Russians, our paranoia was running pretty deep, and now Eisenhower had these ETs to deal with. Were these reconnaissance flights? A prelude to an invasion? You can hardly blame the president for wanting to keep a tight lid on everything.

"A lot of the physicists who had been involved in the Manhattan Project were assigned to the ET problem, so secrecy was second nature to them. But there were no Intel groups back then, it was just the military and the scientists.

"Things changed during the Truman years. You had the establishment of the NSA, the CIA, and the eventual engagement of a group called MJ-12, which became the agency overseeing all things ET. That's when things evolved from assessing the threat to reverse-engineering the downed interstellar craft for our own use. That required secret bases and serious black budget defense funding and that's when Truman lost control. Once the Military Industrial Complex and MJ-12 took over, the president and Congress no longer had a need to know, and suddenly the money started pouring in.

"JFK knew about the ETs and these black budget projects and wanted to pull back the reins, beginning with the CIA. I realize that sounds like more conspiracy theory, but if you believe in the free press, then you probably believe in magic bullets and Lee Harvey Oswald too."

"I think we can do without the sarcasm, Mr. Wade. We're still waiting for you to answer Senator Townsend's question … are these extraterrestrials a threat?"

"Madam Chair, if these Interstellars wanted to destroy us, they could have done so at anytime. God knows we've certainly provoked them, taking out several dozen of their craft since 1947. In my opinion, the bigger threat to humanity are these USAPs. Trillions of dollars have been siphoned out of the U.S. Treasury to pay for these vast subterranean complexes located miles beneath our air force bases—the Under Secretary has a pretty accurate list. The people working down there are well paid, but everything is kept extremely compartmentalized. The most advanced projects are run by our biggest defense contractors: E-Systems, Lockheed, Northrop-Grumman, Johnson Systems, Sandia, Livermore, Los Alamos, Techtronics … GE. Motorola had a huge facility where they were trying to figure out how the ETs' communications worked."

"These reverse-engineering projects, Mr. Wade—what have they accomplished?"

"Well, you know about the F-117 Stealth Bomber and fiber-optic cable. What you don't know is that we solved anti-gravitics along with the energy problem more than fifty years ago. As Ben Rich, the late CEO of Lockheed-Skunkworks once said, 'we now have the ability to take ET home.'"

Once more the chamber erupted in conversation.

"Mr. Wade, are you saying we may one day see flying cars?"

"No. I'm saying we've had the technology for decades. Unfortunately, it's been black-shelved."

"Black-shelved? What does that mean exactly?"

"It means the powers that be have purposely kept it from the masses by denying patents, confiscating inventions, and then murdering the scientists who made the breakthroughs. That's the real crime you should be investigating."

Applause broke out, overwhelming the proceedings.

Senator Sampson waited for the chamber to quiet down. "Who's in charge of these programs, Mr. Wade?"

"Essentially, it's a secret faction operating independently and without the knowledge of the government. Some choose to label it a New World Order … call them what you will—they run it all, just like the Under Secretary spoke about … it's all true."

Adam was about to pose a question of his own when he noticed Steven Greer waving at him from two rows back.

"Madam Chair, could we have a ten minute recess … it's important."

"Very well. We'll reconvene at eleven o'clock."

A buzz filled the chamber as conversations broke out among the charged-up crowd. Adam patted Jonathan Wade on the back before joining Dr. Greer at the rail separating the witness area from the spectators.

"What's wrong?"

"Everything. C-SPAN's off the air; the bastards are jamming the signal just like they did sixteen years ago during the first hour of *The Disclosure Project*. Cell phones are out as well."

"Damn it! Okay, let me speak to Senator Sampson—"

"Forget her, she's useless."

"Then my brother—"

"He's long gone. Nothing said in these chambers will ever be covered by the media. Face it, Shariak, you've been set up and shut down, and don't expect to find any allies on that committee. You can bet the farm they're being issued specific instructions on what to say and how to proceed; just like the 9/11 commission was given back in 2002. I hate to say I told you so, but I've been down this road before. Washington is toxic with money and everyone is in on the take ... hey, where are you going?"

Adam homed in on the court stenographer, her badge identifying her as Adeline Russell.

"Excuse me, Adeline, there's been an emergency. I need you to email the transcript of this morning's testimonials to my iPhone right away."

"I can't. The Internet's down and no one can get a phone signal."

"Then print me out a hard copy."

"I still have to transcribe it. It's all in shorthand."

"How long will that take?"

"I don't know ... twenty minutes."

"But you can read what you wrote, correct?"

"You mean the shorthand? Of course."

"Then get your machine, you're coming with me."

"But the hearing—"

"Your assistant can take over; I need you with me ... *now* please." He waited impatiently while she unplugged her machine and rolled up the cord.

"Where are we going?"

"I'm holding an impromptu press conference on the steps of the Capitol

Building. When I say, I'll need you to read the Jonathan Wade testimony aloud to the media."

Pushing his way through the throng, he led her up the center aisle past security and out the rear doors of the chamber, his awkward gait helping to clear a path.

He found himself in the mezzanine where a crowd was assembling around a circle of reporters and their camera crews. "This is perfect. Come on." Grabbing hold of the crook of the stenographer's right arm, he worked his way closer until he could see the person the reporters were interviewing.

It was a Middle Eastern woman, dressed in a black one-piece Abaya—the coat-like garment topped with a matching scarf which concealed all but the bangs of her raven-colored hair. Though she was only in her early thirties, the dark eyes that scanned the crowd had witnessed several lifetimes of suffering.

Adam froze. He knew those eyes ... he had seen them in a thousand dreams.

He was about to call out when Eugene Evans intercepted him. "Captain, we need to get you out of—"

"There he is!"

Suddenly all eyes and camera lenses were focusing in on him, his bodyguard, and the stenographer, who was backing away as the crowd parted before them, bringing him face-to-face with his past.

"Nadia?"

The Iraqi woman's face contorted in horror. "Infidel warrior! Are you surprised to see me still alive after you murdered my father and left me for dead?"

Sweat beads broke out across Adam's face. "Nadia ... what are you talking about?"

"My father and I saved your cursed life after your death chopper crashed. We pulled you from the wreckage and carried you up three flights of stairs to our apartment in order to hide you from the *Fedayeen*. We risked our lives by helping you ... and how did you repay us? By scorching me with a pot of boiling oil before stabbing my father to death, murdering him as he slept ... leaving me screaming in agony as you made your escape ...

the American hero!"

Adam could hear the cameras click, the lights and flashes blinding his peripheral vision. "Nadia, nothing you just said is true. Why are telling these lies?"

"We shall see which one of us is lying." Tearing off her scarf, she exposed the back of her hairless skull and the lump of flesh from a butchered skin graft, the burn scars and welts continuing down her neck and back.

"Now the world will see who you really are, Captain Adam Shariak. Now the world will know the truth!"

31

Subterranean Complex—Midwest USA

A COOL MOUNTAIN BREEZE rustled the sheer curtains framing the bedroom balcony's open French doors, the "Nature Alarm Clock" rousing Jessica Marulli from a heavy sleep. She had set the hologram to a "Colorado lake scene," hoping a change in her routine might curb the recent bout of depression brought on by her extended stay in the infirmary. But even the tapestry of gold splaying over a Rocky Mountain horizon had little effect on her wounded psyche.

Five days of I.V. drips had left her feeling toxic. Every breath was accompanied by the scent of medication. The veins in her arms were bruised; her tongue tasted of metal. After being discharged, she had promised Lydia that she would exercise in order to burn off the drugs in her system, but having awakened with a dull headache, a workout was the last thing on her agenda.

What she really wanted to do was finish her job and leave.

She had arrived more than a month earlier harboring the excitement of a freshman going off to college. While the requisite thirty-six-hour security marathon had tarnished her promotion, she understood the necessity of the interrogation and the five-star accommodations had made up for any bad feelings. But those in charge seemed more interested in testing her loyalty than her actual work. She realized that her personal relationship with Adam and his recent announcements were obviously causing a few members of Council to feel ill at ease, but there were other red flags that were giving her serious doubts about her own career choices.

At a time when climate change was arguably the most serious challenge facing the planet, why was zero-point-energy still being kept from the masses? Equally disturbing—why were alien reproduction vehicles being used to traffic drugs?

Forcing herself out of bed, she used the bathroom and then dressed in her lab attire. No longer trusting room service, she searched her refrigerator for something edible but found nothing.

Locating her hoverboard, she left the apartment, bound for the eatery.

The thoroughfare was busy with the usual morning traffic as the community of techs, security personnel, laborers, and engineers headed off to work. Watching the scene, Jessica realized that none of the commuters were speaking to one another. Even neighbors emerging from their abodes at the same time rarely exchanged a greeting.

They've established an Orwellian culture of fear …

Walking out onto the Maglev track, she set down the hoverboard and positioned her feet before giving the power cord a tug. Her pulse quickened as the device rose beneath a cushion of magnetic waves, propelling her forward.

Jessica remained in the pedestrian lane closest to the center divider, her confidence shot since the last accident. She looked around for Logan LaCombe, but the teen was probably still asleep. She passed his parents' home without so much as a glance in case the authorities were watching her … which they probably were.

Hunger pangs sent her drifting into the faster peripheral lanes and she soon found herself approaching the mall.

Pulling on the power cord, she shut down the device and carried it to the eatery where a breakfast buffet was being served. Her stomach growled as she fixed herself a heaping plate of scrambled eggs, hash browns, and a bagel. Too impatient to wait in line to use the toaster, she poured a coffee and situated herself at the nearest empty table.

"Mind if I join you?"

She looked up, momentarily choking on a mouthful of eggs as Chris Mull occupied the chair across from her.

"Leave or I'll call security."

"I am security … counter-intelligence, to be exact. Every new Cosmic Clearance Council member is on probation until a C.I. officer checks them out."

"And did I pass?"

"If you didn't, we wouldn't be having this conversation."

"Is that what happened to my predecessor?"

"There's a reason these facilities were built … a reason for all this security. You and the other eggheads are working with technologies that can alter the path of human evolution. There are two reasons an insider turns traitor—money and morality. We counter the former with an over-generous salary. The latter, unfortunately, can only be resolved one way."

"You terminated Dr. Hopper?"

"With extreme prejudice; as we do with all traitors. Knowing the repercussions of any of these secrets reaching the masses, what would you do, Jessica?"

She pushed away her tray of food. "I'm not sure what sickens me more—when you refer to me and my colleagues as 'eggheads' or when you call me by my first name. Don't."

He smiled with his mouth, but the eyes were vacant. "Enjoy your breakfast."

She waited for him to leave the vicinity before she hurried off for the nearest women's room. Locating a vacant stall, she barely had time to aim before she lost her breakfast.

It was nearly noon when Jessica exited Elevator-7 onto the third floor. Tea and toast had soothed her upset stomach; a two-hour respite at the apartment settled her nerves.

She hustled through the anteroom and interior corridor, the air stream blasting her in the face as she headed for the Plexiglas barrier at the end of the wind tunnel and entered the Hive—

—startled by the level of activity taking place before her.

The far end of the four-story-high lab had been retracted, revealing the vast space launch complex containing the towering Atlas rockets and their gantries. Moving through the lab was a steady procession of *Zeus* satellites. Each of the twenty four-ton rectangular devices had been loaded onto anti-gravitic platforms which were floating six feet off the ground in a procession that ended at their assigned Atlas-V rocket—next stop … Earth orbit.

Jessica watched as Dr. Concannon escorted one of the satellites as it rose on its anti-gravity pedestal past the Atlas's engine and booster before it disappeared into the open payload fairing atop the rocket. Her eyes locked onto Sarah Mayhew-Reece as she flew into the Hive from the tunnel and landed next to her.

"We finished prepping the SATS while you were in the infirmary," she said, removing her anti-gavitics vest.

"I feel like I should be out there helping."

"The *Zeus* crew can handle it."

"I don't see Mr. Mull."

Ignoring Jessica's comment, Sarah pointed to the ceiling above their heads. "The air conditioner duct leaked again; must have happened the night you were brought to the infirmary. Ceiling panels fell … it was quite the mess. Rats must have chewed through the security system's electrical wires. They finished repairing everything a few days ago."

She's warning you that we're being watched.

Sarah turned to Jessica, scrutinizing her pallid complexion. "You look peaked my dear; are you hungry?"

"A little."

"Come with me; I have just what you need."

Sarah led her across the empty expanse to her office. The stacks of containers holding the zero-point-energy devices were gone and it appeared from the open cardboard boxes on the floor that her assistant was in the process of packing her personal belongings.

"Are you getting ready to leave?"

"My last day is Friday. I'm meeting my husband for a month-long vacation in Hawaii."

"Sarah, that's wonderful. When is my last day?"

"I don't know. I heard Council has meetings scheduled through mid-

October; I'm sure you'll be leaving soon after that."

"Two more weeks?"

"It's not so bad; I haven't seen my family since April. Do you like to cook?"

"Not really. Why?"

"Come with me … I'll show you the hobby that keeps me sane."

Sarah led her to a door sealed with a padlock. "I had to put a lock on the door when I caught my staff stealing from my private stash."

Jessica pondered what kind of secret life her assistant could be leading while Sarah removed a key hanging from a lanyard around her neck and opened the lock and door.

Inside was a modern kitchen, complete with a walk-in refrigerator, aluminum prep stations, ovens, and two floor-to-ceiling wine racks—no doubt Sarah's "stash."

"This is … wow. I wouldn't have expected such an elaborate kitchen in a lab."

"I've been working for the organization going on twenty years. It's in their best interest to keep me happy."

She walked over to a gas stovetop where a large cast iron pot was simmering on a low flame. "Like you, I never had time to cook. However, I quickly tired of eating Jeffrey's lunch meat sandwiches, and the room service entrees are too rich to eat every day … I must have gained ten pounds every time I had to report on assignment. Last year I decided I was going to learn how to cook—a virtual chef taught me how right in my apartment—and guess what … I love it."

Sarah removed the lid from the cast iron pot, releasing an aroma that filled the room.

"Mmm … what is that?"

"Chicken and dumplings … a new twist on my grandmother's recipe. There's drinks in the walk-in—help yourself. Grab me a sparkling water, would you my dear?"

Jessica pulled on the metal handle of the vault-like refrigerator and entered.

Stacked on the floor were open wood-slat containers holding fresh fruit, heads of lettuce, and an assortment of vegetables. Shelves held large bricks of different cheeses and milk, along with the remains of a carton of thirty-six brown eggs.

She found an open case of sparkling water on the floor and extracted two bottles.

Sarah had set their lunch on a small folding table covered by a vinyl red and white checkered cloth. Steam rose from the two heaping bowls of chicken and dumplings, the scent causing Jessica's mouth to water.

Before she could dip her spoon into the food, Sarah reached across the table and grasped her hands. "Would you like to say grace?"

"I'm a little out of practice. Would you mind?"

Sarah closed her eyes. "Dear Lord, we thank you for the food we're about to eat and pray you'll keep us safe from harm. Amen."

"Amen. That was simple."

"Spirituality is simple; religion complicates everything. As for grace, that's simply asking God for a blessing we haven't earned."

"I like that."

"Silly me … I forgot the sourdough bread. I made it from scratch last week and froze several loafs. It'll take about four minutes to defrost in the microwave; go on and start eating while I heat up a loaf."

Jessica waited until Sarah disappeared inside the walk-in refrigerator before dipping her tablespoon into the lumpy broth. "Oh my God, Sarah … this is amazing."

She looked up as her assistant placed an object inside the microwave—only it wasn't a loaf of bread. She set the timer for four minutes and pressed start, filling the room with static white noise.

Sarah returned to her seat, her expression now all business.

"The object I placed in the microwave is designed to scramble any security devices that could be eavesdropping on us, along with any psycho-tronic waves. As you've probably guessed by now, Mr. Mull was never a member of *Zeus*—he works in counter-intelligence. His boss is a sick bastard named Colonel Alexander Johnston, or as he prefers to be called—*Dr. Death*. Johnston fits the definition of a sociopath and recruits military personnel who also share this abnormality.

"A sociopath is wired differently than the rest of us, Jessica. A sociopath lacks the capacity to love. To these individuals, God is a black hole; morality a compass they were never equipped with at birth. While we may feel sorry for them, I can assure you they do not feel sorry for us. History has been poisoned by their rise through the business, political, and military ranks; millions have been tortured and murdered by their calculated cruelty. Pol Pot, Saddam and the sadistic members of his Republican Guard who now run ISIS ... Kim Jung Un, Vladimir Putin ... all sociopaths. Hitler was a madman, but it was psychopaths like Josef Mengele who ushered Satan into the Third Reich. Like moths to a flame, the sociopaths who ran European and American banks and corporations during World War II never hesitated to do business with the Nazis, and when the war was over, they offered them sanctuary.

"It is from this pool of soulless agents that MJ-12 recruited its most hardcore members during the fifties, sixties, seventies, eighties, and into the nineties. As the Cold War ended, things began to change. Today, most of the younger members of Council, as well as the scientists and military intelligence who work for the organization now calling itself MAJI, are moral individuals who realize that we have at our fingertips an endless clean energy source that can reverse climate change and end poverty, hunger, and disease ... that if we simply put aside our differences we can evolve as a species and travel across the galaxy."

"If the sociopaths are the minority, as you say, then what's the problem? Kick the bastards out ... or terminate them. I won't be shedding any tears."

"Hitler's generals had made similar plans. They tried, failed, and were executed. Any revolution in the ranks must account for Dr. Death, who has access to psychotronic devices that can drive you into madness. His version of the S.S.—the Sociopathic Security—remain loyal to him."

"Why are you telling me this?"

"I'm trying to protect *you*, Jessica. The air conditioning duct ... punching through the foil shield that surrounds the Hive—I had to cover your tracks. I found the anti-security device in your lab coat. I assumed you used it to access my office."

Jessica felt the blood drain from her face. "I didn't break in ... I was

287

thinking about it when the ceiling started falling … when the roof retracted—"

"Don't lie, Jessica. We both know you wanted to steal one of the rotary ZPE devices."

"Okay, I did break in, but not to steal one of the units … to return it. Mull was blackmailing me … he switched out the rotary ZPE from SAT-3 with a fake device, then had the real thing delivered to my room. Instead of handing it off to some mysterious contact, I broke into your office and returned it."

"Who gave you the looping device?"

"Why do you need to know?"

"I need to know in order to determine if I can trust you, Jessica."

"And I need to know if I can trust *you*, Sarah. If you respect that, then you won't ask who helped me."

"Let me see your forearms."

Jessica hesitated, then she held out her arms.

Sarah inspected each limb, tracing the veins along her assistant's biceps.

"What are you doing?"

"This area along your left arm … is it sore?"

"Yes."

"The physician who treated you implanted a nano-device inside your brachial artery. Dr. Death obviously doesn't trust you either."

"How do I get it out?"

"It will dissolve by itself in a few weeks before you leave; in less time if you exercise."

That's why Lydia wanted me to work out. She knew …

"Jessica, it's very important that you not leave the facility until after the device dissolves. If the colonel arranged this, then you can bet the farm he equipped it with a charge that functions sort of like an electrical dog collar and fence."

"I don't understand."

"If the dog passes outside the boundaries of the electrical fence it receives a shock. If you leave the electromagnetic shielding that surrounds this facility before that unit dissolves, a tiny charge will cause the device to explode inside your arm like a firecracker. The brachial artery is a major blood vessel; you'll bleed to death before anyone can help you."

32

Washington, D.C.

THE CURVY REDHEAD SEATED ACROSS from him in the beige business suit adjusted her reading glasses, revealing the wrist tattoo.

"Mr. Shariak, my name is Kim Mather and I'll be serving as lead counsel. The purpose of this meeting is to determine the best course of action in dealing with what has quickly become a P.R. nightmare for the president."

"Is that why he flew to Beijing three days early?"

"President Trump asked the Chinese to move up trade talks so an agreement could be in place prior to November's Climate Change Summit in Boston. I'm sure the change in schedule had nothing to do with you."

"Of course not."

Ignoring the comment, the redhead opened the sealed military file before her. "We've reviewed the Army's report detailing your Apache being shot down over the city of Karbala, as well as a statement from your co-pilot, Chief Warrant Officer Jared Betz."

"And you have my report?"

"We do. But I'd rather you tell us what happened … in your own words."

Adam gazed around at the oval conference table at the other eight attorneys—all men. He wondered whether Ms. Mather would have been included in the "boys' club" had his accuser been a male.

He directed his response to the woman. "The cockpit had collapsed around me. Jared attempted to move me but my left leg was badly injured, the femur had snapped on impact and the pain was pulling me in and out of consciousness. I vaguely remember him telling me that he was going for help. The next thing I know I was being removed from the wreckage by men wearing masks."

"Was the woman with them?"

"You mean Nadia? She was fourteen at the time ... hardly a woman. No. I didn't meet her until I came to inside the cellar."

The attorney checked her notes. "Ms. Kalaf claims that she and her father carried you up three flights of stairs to their apartment."

"I don't know who carried me or where they took me, but the place I was kept was quite small and definitely underground. They were using it as a weapons cache."

"What makes you so sure it was below ground?"

"Concrete floor ... concrete walls. No windows. Sound was completely muted; they never worried when either one of us screamed."

Kim Mather paused from jotting notes on her legal pad. "Tell us about Abu Anas al-Baghdadi."

"At the time all I knew was that he was a commander in Saddam's Republican Guard. Years later our military hired him to recruit members of the Shia Badr militia into the Wolf Brigade, the 2nd battalion of the interior ministry's special commandos. Essentially, the interior minister hired them to terrorize insurgents. They wore red berets and sunglasses and drove around in convoys of Toyota Landcruisers. They had a reputation for torturing Iraqi prisoners using electric drills. These are the same sick fucks who are now running ISIS."

"Tell us about the girl."

"She told me she had been kidnapped and made a sex slave. Nadia's mother had been a nurse; in Ali's mind that qualified her to keep me alive. My leg was in horrible shape ... my foot had swollen to twice its normal size and gangrene was setting in. Baghdadi spoke to me in English, claiming he was negotiating a prisoner exchange. What he never realized was that I understood enough Farsi to figure out that his plan was to get as much information from me as he could, then take me to a bridge located just south of Baghdad and publicly behead me.

"He quickly grew frustrated as all I ever did was babble incoherently. Some of this was exaggerated, but by the end of the first week I was in such bad shape that they no longer bothered shackling me.

"I was close to death the morning two guardsmen arrived carrying boxes of fliers. They warned Nadia not to touch them and ordered her to prepare me to travel. They'd said they'd be back in thirty minutes and left.

"The two of us were alone in the basement, but we could hear men walking on the first floor above us. I knew they were going to kill us; I just had to convince Nadia. I begged her to read one of the fliers. She translated the Arabic for me: 'This American soldier killed innocent Iraqis and raped the girl. He has been slaughtered in accordance with God's will.'

"When Nadia read that, she knew they were going to kill her, too. Unfortunately, there were no weapons left, but there was a small wooden table and four chairs set up in a corner for cards. With Nadia's help, I unscrewed one of the legs and then returned to my spot on the floor, covering my makeshift club with a blanket.

"When the two men returned, they found me unconscious and Nadia naked, in the process of getting dressed. She tried to fend them off, but they quickly had her bent over the table … never noticing the missing leg—until the table collapsed.

"Nadia and the guardsman who was sodomizing her went down in a heap. By then I was standing behind his partner, who was laughing hysterically. I took him out with one blow to the back of the skull. I had his gun in my hand before his partner could react. The girl took the table leg from me and beat him senseless."

"You said there were soldiers upstairs … how did you manage to escape? Could you even walk?"

"My leg couldn't bear any weight. I grabbed one of the guard's weapons and made my way up the ladder leading out of the cellar. Nadia walked out ahead of me to draw the soldiers' attention and I came out firing. We managed to make it outside to a main thoroughfare where she flagged down one of our Hummers. The rest is a blur."

"Was that the last time you saw Ms. Kalaf?"

"Yes. Until she showed up yesterday, I had no clue whether she was dead or alive. But I certainly didn't rape her or pour boiling oil over her scalp."

Kim Mather finished writing a note before turning to one of the firm's senior partners. "Sean?"

"Why do you think she showed up now, Mr. Under Secretary?"

"I think a fifth grader could answer that. This is a classic CIA counter-intelligence move designed to focus the public's attention on my credibility and away from the investigation and the testimony my witnesses were in the process of disclosing."

"And what was that, Mr. Shariak? What is the big secret?"

"You're kidding, right? It's not in your notes?"

The female attorney searched quickly through her folder ... shaking her head.

"UFOs ... extraterrestrials! These Unacknowledged Special Access Projects that have been secretly channeling trillions of dollars into covert programs which successfully reverse-engineered advanced alien technologies ... and yes, I know I sound like a complete and utter asshole, but it's all true. And the Intel organizations preventing public knowledge and access to these technologies—which include free, clean zero-point-energy generators—basically shut down the message, as they have done for the last seventy years."

Adam's gaze fell upon the redhead's wrist tattoo. "Courage ... Strength ... sorry, I can't see the last word—"

"Faith."

"Faith ... of course. Certainly words to live by, but words without action don't effect change. I never claimed to be a war hero, Ms. Mather, but I think you can see I'm no war criminal ... that Nadia has been coerced into doing this.

"The question now is whether the Trump Administration has the balls to see this thing through."

33

Subterranean Complex—Midwest USA

IT WAS LATE IN THE AFTERNOON by the time Jessica returned to her suite. She had spent two hours in the gym and the last twenty minutes buying groceries from the mini mart. After setting the perishables inside the refrigerator, she grabbed a bottle of water and flopped down on the recliner.

Her iPhone dinged with a text from Sarah. **"TURN ON CNN!"**

The live CNN report showed General Ronald Rahn, Head of the Defense Intelligence Agency, standing behind a podium before a room filled with reporters.

"… the president wants to make it perfectly clear that the Under Secretary has the White House's full support and confidence. However, due to the sensitive nature of these accusations, all parties felt it was best that Mr. Shariak step down until the issue can be properly investigated."

They fired Adam? What the hell happened? She glanced at the engagement ring on her finger. I need to call him—

"General, doesn't it seem a bit odd that this Iraqi woman would suddenly appear out of the blue on Shariak's first day of the DoD's hearing? How did she get here? Who sponsored her trip?"

"There's little doubt Ms. Kalaf timed her announcement to grab the media's attention. As for your other questions—"

"What about the Under Secretary's investigation? Will these secret projects be looked into now that Captain Shariak has been dismissed?"

"The Department of Defense will continue to cooperate fully with the

Senate Appropriation Committee's investigation. It's the Chairman's decision when the hearing will resume."

"General, at least two dozen eyewitnesses who were in the Dirksen Senate Chamber that morning have come forward claiming these unacknowledged projects deal with advanced technologies reverse-engineered from UFOs that crash-landed … beginning with the incident years ago in Roswell, New Mexico. Can you comment on that?"

"I wasn't in the hearing, but that sounds pretty crazy."

"Why were C-SPAN's cameras shut down?"

"They weren't shut down, there were technical difficulties."

"Is that what happened to everyone's cell phone service?"

"Will you be making the transcript available?"

"That's all people … thank you."

Jessica muted the television. Reaching for her laptop, she Googled her fiancé's name, quickly accessing the story:

Defense Secretary Accused of War Crimes.

She scanned the article, her pulse pounding in her neck. *Lousy bastards. Adam tried to challenge MAJI and they crushed him. You're a part of Council—you could have warned him. You could have …*

She had been glancing at the giant screen, the muted sound causing the closed caption to describe what her eyes were seeing.

"Oh my God …" Jessica turned up the volume.

"*… the neon blue spiral appearing in the night sky over Beijing was witnessed by more than a million people. At first it was thought to be a special effect intended to honor President Trump's arrival earlier in the day, however, a military expert we spoke to indicated it was more likely the testing of a space-based weapon, something officials in both the United States and China firmly deny.*"

Grabbing her hoverboard, Jessica fled the apartment and dashed across the thoroughfare to the side of the Maglev track heading toward the elevators. In less than three minutes she was aboard Elevator-7, the multi-directional car weaving its way to Level-3, Section-C.

Sarah was already pressing her face to the lab's retinal scan when Jessica arrived.

"You saw the blue spiral on the news?"

"Of course I saw it."

"You think they've begun deploying *Zeus?*"

"We need to find out."

The two female engineers made their way through the connecting corridor and into the Hive. Wasting no time, they donned anti-gravitic helmets and vests. Thirty seconds later they were soaring over the empty expanse of concrete, heading toward the wall separating the Hive from the launch facility.

Red warning lights flashed as they approached. The automated doors failed to open, forcing the two women to pull up and hover.

Sarah squeezed her eyes shut, focusing her thoughts on the barrier of octagonal panels before them.

"Sarah—"

"Shh! Let me focus."

"Listen! Do you hear that rumbling?" Moving closer to the wall, Jessica pressed both palms to the framework. "I think the roof is opening. Is there any way we can see what is happening?"

"I forgot ... the panels are tinted!" Sarah focused her thoughts on several octagonal panels, causing them to turn opaque, then transparent.

From out of the darkness, a patch of blue sky appeared in the distance, illuminating the far end of the dark cavity.

"You were right; they're getting ready to launch another satellite. Jessica, how many rockets can you see?"

Before she could get a count, the Hive's walls began vibrating as if struck by a giant tuning fork, the thunderous reverberation followed by a brilliant orange flame which unleashed a tsunami of white smoke and an avalanche of sound.

The two women hovered before the blinding, deafening blizzard, mesmerized. Through the smoke they saw a spark rise beneath one of the Atlas's boosters seconds before the rocket and its satellite payload rose majestically out of the subterranean complex and into the patch of blue on its journey to space.

Seconds later the scene appeared to replay in reverse as high-powered exhaust fans rapidly inhaled the smoke, returning the subterranean launch deck to its pre-flight visual.

The Eiffel Tower shimmered gold in the Parisian night sky, its presence dominating the rooftops visible from their balcony perch.

Sarah adjusted the quilt higher on her chest before pouring herself a second glass of wine. She left the bottle on the table between the two lounge chairs, glancing at Jessica. "Are you cold? I have plenty of extra blankets."

Jessica sipped her wine, hoping the alcohol would ease the edginess of her rattled nerves. "Why don't you just tell the computer to make it warmer?"

"This is the accurate temperature for Paris in autumn. This view ... it's the actual view from our flat. My husband and I plan on spending three weeks in Paris after our trip to Hawaii."

"They've launched two satellites, Sarah. What's the minimum number of SATS needed to engage the *Zeus* array?"

"Thirteen."

"Why didn't they tell us they were launching?"

"My dear, everything around here is strictly 'need to know.' We may be Cosmic Clearance, but we're just Indians, not chiefs." Sarah closed her eyes. "No more talk. We've talked all day and night and now I'm tired. You can have my bed if you want to stay over; I'm going to sleep out here with my wine and my view of Paris. Lovely Paris ..."

"It's not real, Sarah."

"Sweetie, as John Lennon once sang, *nothing is real*. Life is just one big video game ... when we're out of time God tallies the score and sees if we've done enough good things to earn our way back inside the pearly gates ... *strawberry fields forever*."

Jessica reached over and took the wine glass from Sarah's hand as the older woman passed out. "Good night, Ladybug."

"Level-23, please."

Jessica held on as the elevator plunged eighteen stories in under five seconds, an illuminated sign above the map of the complex flashing as the magnetic brakes took over:

Level-23
WARNING: RESTRICTED AREA

The doors opened and she stepped out to white polished marble floors which led into a small circular lobby, its two-story domed ceiling illuminated bright emerald-green. From this starting point there were three long white empty corridors; one directly ahead, the other two on either side. All three appeared to run on forever.

There was not a soul in sight.

"Direct me to Dr. Joyce LaCombe."

The corridor in front of her remained lit, the other two vanishing into darkness.

"Thank you." She walked forward, her third stride disappearing into a gelid barrier—

—her body emerging on a grass-covered knoll overlooking a winding stream. The sun, still high in a cobalt-blue sky, warmed her face—even as a chilled mountain breeze blew in from the distant snow-covered Rockies to compensate.

Jessica inhaled the fresh air, feeling invigorated. It was the scene she had awoken to this morning. Whatever it was—a hologram or a drug-induced dream—she couldn't fathom. Regardless, it was impressive.

Follow the brook downstream ...

Joyce LaCombe's voice cooed in her brain, and yet the words had not been spoken, they had appeared in her mind's eye as a whisper of wind.

She made her way down the knoll to a footpath bordering the three-foot drop-off that was the brook. As instructed, she followed it downstream, its trickling waters providing a soothing chorus of sound. Gradually the diminuendo over shallow beds of pebbles and stone deepened to a crescendo of moss-covered chasms of rock as the brook widened into a swiftly-moving river, its shorelines hedged in by a forest of pine.

She stayed with the footpath as it abandoned the waterway and cut through the trees, the sound of the river steadily deadening, the air cooling noticeably as the canopy of branches grew thick overhead.

Jessica stopped dead in her tracks, her eyes catching movement up ahead. "Hello? You can come out; I know you're there."

The being stepped out from behind the trunk of a tree ahead and to her right. Gray-skinned and three-and-a-half feet tall, it possessed a large, hairless bulb-shaped skull which accommodated two oval eyes, the immense sight organs completely black. The being's upper body seemed emaciated yet powerful, the cord-like tendons of its limbs making up for a lack of muscle mass. The long four-fingered hands were delicate but dexterous, ending in concave tips. From the neck down it was clothed in a sheer microfiber body suit, the fabric of which appeared to be blending in with everything it touched—the bark of the tree, the dirt path …

As she watched, the being leaned closer to the Pine tree and disappeared—

—only to step out from behind another tree trunk a second later, this one ten paces to her left.

"Well, that was a neat trick."

It disappeared again, this time reappearing six paces ahead of her and to her right. And then it was seemingly everywhere, randomly appearing and disappearing, popping in and out of existence so fast that Jessica was convinced there had to be at least a dozen of them.

Dr. Marulli has been secured. Cease mind-control and reveal yourself.

Jessica heard a click and then the sky and forest collapsed into a trillion droplets of water, evaporating as they struck the unseen floor.

In its place was the inside of an extraterrestrial space ship. Jessica found herself lying on her back on a metallic table, unable to move.

There were three Grey ETs visible. Two appeared to be operating the vessel from a central hub; the third was hovering over her lower abdomen and groin which had gone completely numb.

Her blood pressure dropped as a wave of anxiety rushed over her.

It's probing me!

Why did you launch the scalar weapon? Our treaty does not permit the placement of advanced weaponry in space.

Treaty? What treaty?

If another satellite is launched you will be removed from this planet.

Please ... I didn't know—

Zero-point-energy field generators are not permitted on your planet. If the quarantine is broken then both you and your mate will be abducted and removed from this planet ... and your pregnancy terminated.

"Ahhh! Ahhh! Ahhh!"

Jessica sat up and expelled a blood-curdling scream as the lights came on, revealing her bedroom suite and a hologram of the nurse who had treated her back in the clinic.

"Dr. Marulli, are you alright?"

Still shaking from the night terror, her tee-shirt soaked in a cold sweat, Jessica fled the bedroom—

—the hologram re-engaging in the bathroom mirror. "Dr. Marulli, should we send help? Please respond."

Dropping to her knees, Jessica bent over the toilet and puked.

34

Greenbelt, Maryland

IN THE END, IT HAD COME DOWN to Newton's Third Law of Motion—for every action there had been an equal and opposite reaction, only in his case it wasn't equal, he had fared far worse.

When Adam had attempted to use the power of his office, they had threatened his boss, the Secretary of Defense.

When he had publicly announced his investigation, they had bribed him.

When he had brought forth witnesses, they had shut down all media coverage.

When he had attempted to enlist the public's support as a war hero, they had tarnished his reputation; when he refused to back down they had taken his job.

And now, this afternoon, when he had called a press conference to present his side of the equation …

Using the TV remote control, Adam switched from station to station, his excitement waning, changing from frustration to outright anger.

MSNBC: "… the ousted Under Secretary of Defense claiming that eighty to one hundred billion dollars a year of taxpayer money is being spent on—are you ready for this—advanced technologies reversed-engineered from UFOs that crash-landed as far back as the late 1940s."

FOX NEWS: "… extraterrestrials. According to the former Under

301

Secretary, man-made flying saucers known as Alien Reproduction Vehicles, or ARVs, have been secretly reverse-engineered. Where are these man-made flying saucers, you ask?"

CNN: "... stored in secret subterranean military bases all over the country. When asked where these bases are, the former Under Secretary had this to say, "I don't know.""

"Huh? That's not what I said! I gave out the locations ... Edwards Air Force Base, Haystack Butte, China Lakes, Nellis, Los Alamos ... You bastards edited them out!"

He clicked back to MSNBC: "Chris, how will Shariak's appointment and sudden ouster affect the Trump Administration?"

"I'd say the blowback is more on Shariak's brother. Senator Randy Hall is up for reelection next year and—"

"Ugh!" Adam threw the remote as hard as he could at the flat screen TV, the impact cracking the surface.

Six months ago he'd had it all ... a good job, the love of an incredible woman who was the girl of his dreams. Now he was jobless and blacklisted ... rendered unemployable. Steven Greer had been right when he had said, "there are things worse than death." His enemies had succeeded in making him *persona non-grata* while setting him firmly on a path of self-destruction.

How long will Jessica stay with a man who can no longer support himself?

Could her family accept a son-in-law who the public believed had committed a war crime?

More important—where was Jessica? Was she safe?

The knock on his apartment door startled him. "Jess?"

He hobbled to the door, the smart-prosthetic sent off-kilter by his thoughts.

The DHL delivery man looked up from his scanner as the door opened. "Adam Shariak?"

"Yes?"

"I have a package for you ... just need you to sign here please."

Adam took the inkless pen and signed his name on the tiny screen.

The delivery man scanned the package's barcode and handed the small box to Adam. "Say, aren't you—"

"No!" He slammed the door as he eyed the label, his heart racing as he saw Jessica's name under SENDER. Expelling a grunt, he tore open the four-by-six inch cardboard container.

The iPhone rang the moment he removed it from its bubble wrap.

"Hello?"

"Do you recognize my voice?"

Female … definitely not Jessica. "Give me a clue."

"I gave you a reach-around in Phoenix."

The blonde from counter-intelligence … what was her name? He searched his wallet and found her card … Kelly Kishel.

"What do you want, Kelly?"

"Paybacks are a bitch; I thought you deserved one. I'm texting you an address. Memorize it and then dispose of this phone. I'll see you there in twenty-four hours. Come alone."

Los Alamos, New Mexico

The home office was windowless and sound-proof—a pentagon-shaped room with a two-story-high ceiling. Three of its five walls were covered by oak bookshelves, the upper levels of which were accessible by a matching built-in ladder on wheels. The wall directly before the horseshoe-shaped desk displayed a five-by-seven-foot flat screen television, along with six smaller monitors, the signals of which were fed in from two large satellite dishes situated in the backyard.

When asked about the enormous objects, Yvonne Johnston told the homeowners association that her husband was an avid sports fan.

Of course, the only sport Colonel Johnston ever engaged in was psychotronic warfare.

The black and white images rotating across three of the small monitors were originating from two different spy satellites and a drone. Only a few members of Council's governing body knew the colonel had tapped into the

NSA's network, but the rumors alone were enough to maintain a healthy dose of paranoia among the junior members of MAJI.

The cabal's tentacles reached throughout all branches of the intelligence services and the colonel never hesitated to eavesdrop on the private conversations and texts of those Council members whose "politics" were suspect. When former CIA director William Colby had asked a personal friend in the military to contact Steven Greer, the colonel's response had been swift—the TWEP order issued before the long-time member of MAJI could deliver a black-shelved ZPE generator and $50 million in start-up capital to mass produce the clean energy device. It was a professional hit involving two wet teams; the first one assigned to kidnap and kill Colby and safeguard his remains long enough to allow the victim's internal organs to decompose beyond the point of identifying a cause of death. The other team planted his sand-filled canoe along a Potomac River shoreline so it could be discovered the next morning. As with any TWEP on a public figure, there were unanswered questions—why would Colby choose to take his canoe out on the river so late at night; how had it taken the authorities nine days to locate the body so close to where the canoe had been found less than twelve hours after he had gone missing. In the end, the coroner had ruled death by drowning, the suspicious circumstances swept away as conspiracy theory.

The colonel's latest challenge was a bit more complicated.

Like Colby, Jessica Marulli's parents had powerful allies in Council and the evidence against their daughter was circumstantial at best. Moreover, the importance of *Project Zeus* could not be understated. If a technical problem arose, the engineer's expertise would be needed, therefore, she could not be sanctioned.

Dr. Death's solution: Psychotronic intervention.

A Level-3 abduction was ordered two days after the subject had been admitted to the infirmary. The time-released drug that had been injected into the subject's artery was a powerful hallucinogenic developed by the CIA as part of Project MK-Ultra. This enabled Colonel Johnston's psychotronic warfare team to implant a holographic scenario directly into Jessica Marulli's subconscious—in this case a staged alien abduction intended to put "the fear of extraterrestrials" into the scientist's psyche.

Similar "abductions" had been used over the years on family members of royalty, politicians, and billionaires in an attempt to sway their opinion about Earth's interstellar visitors. What had made Dr. Marulli's experience especially effective was the Grey alien's knowledge of her pregnancy—a secret she had yet to share with the fetus's father, but which had been discovered through the clinic's blood tests. The emotional and psychological trauma the *Zeus* director had experienced virtually guaranteed Dr. Marulli would not be a risk to MAJI after she left the complex.

Her fiancé, however, was proving to be quite the nuisance.

Colonel Johnston tapped his right index finger atop the armrest of his chair, his eyes glued to the large flat screen projecting a real-time black and white image of morning traffic moving along Interstate 495, the spy satellite locking on to the signal coming from Adam Shariak's iPhone.

Johnston knew Shariak was a passenger inside the Uber-registered vehicle heading to Dulles International Airport. The round trip airline ticket to Phoenix had been purchased the previous night at 21:23 hours using his VISA card, but there had been no prior calls in the last week referencing the flight or his ultimate destination.

The fact that Shariak had been to the Wrigley Mansion in the last thirty days was not lost on the colonel, but the face-to-face meeting had taken place at a scheduled MAJI event and there were no personnel of importance permanently stationed in the area.

There were also no direct flights to Phoenix. Shariak's American Airlines itinerary would take him by way of Minneapolis and then Chicago's O'Hare airport en route to Sky Harbor International. It would be almost twelve hours before he arrived at his destination—the now jobless former Under Secretary of Defense forced to ride all three sold-out flights in a middle seat in the back of coach the entire way.

The colonel smirked. *As soon as he arrives in Phoenix, we'll put him out of his misery.*

Dulles International Airport
Washington, D.C.

The United Airlines baggage check-in line inched forward. Adam waited until he was two passengers from being called before switching his iPhone to airplane mode. Unzipping his suitcase, he shoved the device deep inside the load of dirty laundry.

"Next."

Adam handed the female attendant his ticket.

"One way to Phoenix. Are you checking any bags?"

"Just this one." He lifted the suitcase, placing it on the scale."

"That will be thirty-five dollars."

She swiped his debit card and gave him his receipt and boarding pass. "Gate 27C. Have a good flight."

Subterranean Complex—Midwest USA

"... and so I think it is imperative that we launch the other satellites and complete the array as quickly as possible, before the Interstellars detect the advanced energy devices aboard the *Zeus* satellites and destroy them."

Jessica Marulli finished reading her report and looked up from her iPad. There were seventeen Council members in the chamber and six following along on Skype. Most were male and Caucasian, the exception being an Indian couple, herself, and Lydia Gagnon, who was seated at the oval table on her right.

General Cubit, being the most senior member in attendance, had been asked to chair the meeting, and he was clearly not pleased by his protégé's comments.

"Launching twenty satellites in a short time span ... how do we justify that kind of payload to POTUS, let alone the Russians and Chinese?"

"That's your problem, General. Mine is protecting *Zeus*. A minimum of thirteen satellites is required to be placed in orbit before the array can protect itself."

"Understood."

"Understood? General, the blue spiral that appeared over Beijing was clearly a scalar burst."

"What can I tell you, Dr. Marulli? Council obviously wanted to test the weapon."

"While the president was in China?"

Heads turned; all eyes now on Jessica.

"What are you inferring?"

"I'm not inferring anything. As I stated in my report, testing any *Zeus* satellite before the array has been established is not only dumb, it's dangerous. You need to tell Council that they can't play head games like they did with Obama. The difference between a scalar shot using a crystalline-based ZPE generator and the rotary unit powering that missile blast over Helsinki is the equivalent of a lighthouse beacon going up against a flashlight."

"Duly noted."

"It's also in direct violation of our contract with the ETs, isn't it General?"

Lydia reached out under the table, prodding Jessica's thigh with her thumb.

"To what contract are you referring, Dr. Marulli?"

Jessica's face turned red. "I don't know. It's probably just some Internet nonsense I read. Sorry ... I didn't get much sleep last night."

General Cubit stared at her for a long moment, debating where to take the discussion.

"You've had a rough few weeks, Jess. When are you scheduled to head home?"

"Not for another three weeks, sir."

"How 'bout we give you time off for good behavior. Dr. Gagnon, would you arrange a private jet for Dr. Marulli to take her back to D.C.—today if possible."

"I'll get right on it, sir."

Jessica's eyes welled with tears. "Thank you, General."

"Okay then, unless anyone else has any other conspiracy theories they'd like to discuss, I think we're done here."

The chamber emptied quickly, General Cubit pulling Lydia aside. "What the hell was that all about?"

"Dr. Death gave her a level-three mind-fucking last night."

"Oh, Christ ..."

"We can't let her out like this, Tom. Her expertise combined with Shariak's dismissal makes her a news-worthy loose cannon."

"Then we need to find a way to fix it, or Council will."

"How?"

"Take her to La-La Land."

35

O'Hare Airport
Chicago, Illinois

"THANK YOU AGAIN FOR FLYING UNITED. The local time in Chicago is 2:14 p.m."

The jumbo jet's engines powered off, the cabin lights illuminating, initiating a traffic jam in the aisle as a third of the two hundred and twenty-three passengers simultaneously attempted to retrieve their carry-on luggage from the overhead compartments in order to quickly exit from a plane whose doors had yet to even open.

Adam stood as well—not because he felt the need to hold his small gym bag stuffed with personal items, but because his irritated stump was in terrible pain. It had been several years since he had worn the bare steel prosthetic leg he had switched to this morning; having been wedged between two fairly large human beings over the last four hours had not helped.

In due course, the twenty-six rows ahead of him cleared and he lumbered off the plane. Upon reaching the concourse, he checked the departure board for his connecting flight to Phoenix. *Just under an hour layover, plus the four hour flight … figure five hours before your suitcase and iPhone arrive in baggage claim. They won't know if I got off in Minneapolis or Chicago, and by that time, I'll be out of the area … unless they've got eyes on the ground here?*

Adam looked around before heading for the nearest restroom. When he emerged he was wearing a gray sweatshirt, black sweatpants and sneakers, a Cubs baseball cap and sunglasses—the sports jacket, slacks, dress shoes and carry-on bag having been shoved into the trashcan in one of the handicapped stalls.

Tilting the brim of the cap down low, he followed the signs for baggage claim, trying his best to conceal any trace of a limp.

The white van advertising *Betz Electronics* followed the airport signs for arrivals. Entering Terminal 1, the driver spotted a familiar-looking tall man in a gray sweatshirt seated on a bench outside the United Airline's domestic baggage claim. Flashing his lights twice, he pulled over to the curbside pick-up.

Adam climbed in the front passenger seat, exchanging a quick embrace with his former Apache co-pilot. "You look good, J.B. How's the family?"

Jared Betz waited for a cop safeguarding a pedestrian crosswalk to wave him back into traffic. "Wife's good. Kids are good. You're the one I'm worried about. What's all this about, Captain?"

"Trust me, the less you know the better."

"You'll have to do better than that if you expect me to supply you with a loaded weapon."

Adam nodded. "The powers that be who brought in the girl from Iraq to make me look like a war criminal may be holding my fiancée against her will. This may be my only chance to get her out."

"By powers that be, are you referring to this secret government you've been talking about on the news networks?"

"You don't believe me?"

"I'm here, aren't I?" For a long moment Betz remained silent, focusing on staying in the correct lanes that led out of the airport complex and south onto Interstate 294. "Where's the meet?"

"Thirty-two miles outside of Detroit."

"What time?"

"Oh-two-hundred hours."

"I guess that explains why you wanted the night-vision glasses."

"Were you able to get a gun?"

"This is Chicago, Cap. Anyone who wants a gun can get a gun."

"And the tasers?"

"I picked up two King Cobras; each one packs about three million volts."

"Nice. What about the copper wire?"

"Everything you asked for is in back. I had my cousin drop off the rental car at a rest stop about ten miles from here."

"Thank you."

"Cap, that RPG strike over Karbala … it should have killed us. You saved my life."

"Consider the debt paid."

"It's a four-hour ride to Detroit; at least let me drive so you can get some rest. I can always rent another car for you once we get there."

"Appreciate the offer, Jared, but I can't let you do that. The element I'm dealing with … they don't mess around. If they knew you were helping me they would come after you and your family. But I'll definitely need your help rigging the tasers before I get on the road."

"What are you planning on doing with them?"

Adam smiled. "Let's just call it my version of shock and awe."

Subterranean Complex—Midwest USA

It took Jessica less than fifteen minutes to pack. Her heart was racing with adrenaline; she felt like a prisoner on death row who had just received a last-minute reprieve from the governor.

Not wanting to spend another night alone in her suite, she had hounded Lydia after the meeting. "I don't need a private jet. Just get me to Edwards Air Force Base, I can find my own way home from there."

Her supervisor had promised to do her best.

She jumped as her Hispanic holographic concierge materialized in the living room mirror. "Pardon, *Senorita*. There is an incoming message from Dr. Gagnon."

"Put it through."

Lydia's image replaced Raul's. "Bad news, Jess. I can't get you out of here until seven a.m."

"I told you, I don't need a private jet."

"And you're not getting one. The problem isn't flying you home; it's getting you to Edwards. Maglev trains don't make regular pick-ups like the D.C. Metro, they have to be scheduled in advance. Enjoy your last day; I'll come by your suite tomorrow morning at six-thirty."

The mirror went blank, Lydia's words hanging in the air.

Enjoy your last day ...

Her heart pounded as the doorbell rang twice, the security video displaying the image of her visitor in the mirror.

Logan?

"Let him in."

The door unbolted and the teen entered, carrying his hoverboard. "Wow, you're actually here. I haven't seen you literally in forever."

"I've been busy."

Logan spotted the luggage. "You going somewhere?"

"I'm heading home. I leave tomorrow morning."

"Damn." He slumped sideways into the recliner. "Were you even going to tell me?"

"In fact, I was just on my way to see you. Have you had dinner yet?"

"No, but I know a really cool place to eat ... let me take you."

"Okay. Do I need my hoverboard?"

"Of course."

Jessica located the board in the hall closet and followed Logan out onto the Maglev track, the teen crossing the center pedestrian walkway to the opposite lane.

"Where are we going?"

"Elevators." Stepping onto his board, he yanked on the power cord and idled, waiting for her to follow suit.

Jessica slipped her feet into the two straps and activated the electro-magnets beneath her board, chasing after Logan.

They rode straight to the fifth-floor lobby, their presence eliciting a friendly wave from Kirsty Brunt seated behind her work station. "I heard you'll be leaving us tomorrow. I'm so sorry to see you go."

"No, it's all good ... flying home ... can't wait." She waved, once more rolling the parting phrase in her mind until she mentally kneaded it into an unhealthy snack of paranoia.

The lanky teenager pressed the wall button to summon Elevator-3, the doors of which opened instantly. He stepped inside ... holding his palm against the door's rubber seal to prevent it from closing on Jessica, who entered ahead of him and took a seat—

—as Logan stepped off, offering her a quick wave before the doors sealed shut and the elevator plunged more than a mile down the vertical shaft.

Chicago, Illinois

Jared Betz had labored for two hours in the back of his electronics van to rig Adam's taser until the improvised weapon functioned to the former Apache pilot's liking. When they finally finished, the two war vets embraced and parted company.

Adam ate lunch at one of the rest stop's fast food restaurants. He used the bathroom before making his way to the rental car parked on the south side of the parking lot. The black 2015 Ford Taurus had been paid for earlier that morning using Jared's cousin's credit card.

It was 4:25 p.m. by the time Adam pulled onto Interstate 294 southbound, heading east toward Indiana.

He had lied about his destination in order to protect his friend. The address Kelly Kishel had texted to him the night before was located in southwest Michigan only two hours from the rest stop. Earlier that morning he had stopped for coffee at an Internet café, using one of the establishment's computers to take a Google Earth view of the property and memorize the directions.

Adam did not trust the blonde Air Force intelligence officer. She had already played head games with him once and knew all the right buttons to push. He estimated his chances of walking into a trap that would end in his own execution at over eighty percent, but according to Steven Greer, he was already a dead man anyway.

"First they'll destroy your reputation, then they'll render you an outcast before they finally issue the orders to Terminate With Extreme Prejudice. Before this happens you need to run. Leave everything behind but the cash in your bank account; be sure to toss your cell phone and destroy your credit cards. If you have no other choice but to use your car, swap out the license plate and remove any automated toll booth devices. Stay off the grid, Mr. Under Secretary. Any form of technology will lead them right to you."

Interstate 294 had become I-94 East by the time he had passed through Indiana and entered Michigan. Merging onto US-12, he found himself driving in a rural countryside where he backtracked north on State Route 60.

It was dusk by the time he entered the village of Cassopolis.

Situated close to Diamond Lake, one of the largest inland lakes in Michigan, Cassopolis was a typical rural Midwestern town with a population just over 2,000. Adam had eight hours until the rendezvous, and knew he needed to sleep. But before he found a safe haven to sack out, he needed to know what he was dealing with. After a few tries he managed to guess his way out of the center square of buildings and shops until he found himself on the right stretch of country road—the two-lane tarmac bordered on either side by cow pastures and surrounded with barbed-wire fencing.

Adam slowed as he approached the mailbox marking the private gravel driveway leading up to the gray-roofed, white stucco farmhouse. He knew the residence sat on ninety-three acres of farmland. A quarter mile north of the house rose a pair of silos and an immense three-story A-roofed barn which looked like it had been erected at the turn of the 19th century.

There were no lights on inside the dwelling nor were there any vehicles present—save for a rusted jalopy rotting in the weeds by a small garage adjacent to the house.

Adam continued driving, searching for potential places to leave his car when the time came. The only viable option appeared to be an old gas station located three miles down the road, a realty sign indicating the property was for sale.

Walking three miles in the new prosthetic leg was not an option.

It was 8:20 p.m. by the time he found his way back into town. He grabbed a grilled chicken sandwich from a fast food drive-thru and then went shopping for supplies at a nearby 24-hour Walmart, purchasing a navy wool blanket, a battery-powered alarm clock, several bottles of water and trail mix, two 1000-lumen tactical flashlights, a black backpack, bolt cutters, and a 5-speed bicycle which he stowed in the trunk. Backing his car into a peripheral spot away from the lighted entrance, he set the alarm clock to wake him at 11:30 p.m. and laid down in the backseat beneath the blanket, placing the loaded 9mm on the floor by his side.

36

Subterranean Complex—Midwest USA

JESSICA BARELY MANAGED A SCREAM before the elevator free-fall suddenly terminated in a cushioned one-G stop.

The doors opened, revealing Joyce LaCombe. Logan's mother wore a white lab coat and a terse smile. "We meet again. Please don't be upset with Logan, I instructed him to send you down here."

"Where is here?"

"A little slice of the future we call La-La Land."

"You didn't answer my question."

"We occupy levels twelve through twenty-three which are accessible only from the bottom up."

"Level-23?" The blood rushed from Jessica's face, her limbs trembling.

"Now don't freak out on me, Marulli. Come on out of there and I'll show you—"

"No. I've been down here. Take me back!"

"You've never been down here, Jess. The colonel blasted your brain with a psychotronic device which separated your consciousness from your body. He implanted an alien abduction scenario into your subconscious that was designed to make you fear ETs."

"No … this was real. This Grey … it knew things about me that I've never told a soul."

"Let me guess … you're pregnant."

Jessica's eyebrows raised. "How—"

"Please. You're highly emotional and you threw-up in my apartment.

I'm sure they ran blood tests on you after my husband stunned you with his taser."

"That was Captain LaCombe?"

"Delta Force runs security down here. When they detected you inside the launch area he intervened. He felt bad about tasing you, but he couldn't let you identify him." Joyce stepped inside the elevator. "You don't have to worry. Down here I'm Sheriff Glinda and the Wicked Colonel of the West isn't welcome."

Placing her arm around Jessica's shoulder, she led her off the elevator to a security station resembling a pedestrian version of a toll booth. An office enclosed in bullet-proof glass divided two walkways, the men's entry on the right, the women's on the left.

A female guard wearing a black jumpsuit addressed them from inside the women's area. "Swipe your identity cards and go on through one at a time."

Joyce nodded. "I'll be right behind you."

Jessica removed the lanyard from around her neck and slid the card's magnetic strip along the slot, causing the rotary bar lock before her to open. She walked through, waiting by a door designated "Women" by its stick figure.

Dr. LaCombe passed through security and pushed open the door.

Inside was a well-kept locker room. Bathrooms and showers were to one side, rows of lockers on the other. "Strip down and stow all your belongings in a locker. Then take the key and your I.D. badge and follow me into the showers."

Jessica selected a locker across from Joyce and removed everything but her I.D. lanyard. Placing the locker key's elastic band around her left wrist, she grabbed a clean towel from a stack and entered the showers.

Joyce cupped her hand beneath a soap dispenser, the motion detector activating the water pressure. "Lather up from head to toes. We have to pass through a bacteria detector; if you fail you'll have to repeat it until you get it right."

Jessica did as she was told. Rinsing the anti-bacteria body wash from her hair, she squeezed out the excess water from her blonde strands and then passed through the bacteria detector without a glitch. Joyce led her into a another locker room equipped with hair dryers and scales. Racks of scrubs and shoes were organized by size.

"Dry your hair, then swipe your card on one of the scales and weigh yourself. Once your birthday suit weight is logged in you can get dressed. Purple scrubs are for guests. You'll find clean bras and underwear in those drawers."

"Joyce, do you have to shower every time you enter wherever it is you're taking me?"

"Yes. It's for their protection, not ours."

Their protection? Jessica grabbed a gun-shaped dryer from a wall rack and quickly dried her hair, an uneasy feeling tightening in her gut.

"Stop worrying. I would never endanger you or your baby. By the way, does Adam know?"

"No. I haven't spoken to him in almost three weeks."

"Well, I'm sure he could use the good news."

Cassopolis, Michigan

Adam awoke five minutes before the battery-powered alarm clock went off. The car windows were steamy, his undershirt soaked in sweat. Unlocking the doors, he climbed out of the backseat and looked around.

It was a cool autumn night, the air muggy with humidity. The Walmart lot was empty save for three cars parked close to the entrance. Peeling off his tee-shirt, he tossed it in back and pulled on his gray sweatshirt. Then he climbed in front and started the car, the digital clock above the radio reading 11:32 p.m.

Adam drove through the center square of Cassopolis, only to follow the wrong road to a dead end. Retracing his route, he located the two lane highway that led to the closed gas station.

He parked the car and shut off the engine. Removing one of the powerful flashlights from the plastic Walmart bag, he got out to check the two bay doors and the office. Finding everything locked, he returned to his car and popped open the trunk, locating a tire jack.

Adam walked back to the gas station office. Making sure no one was around, he jammed the flat edge of the tire iron between the door and its frame and popped open the lock.

Entering the dark office, his light revealed bare shelves and a layer of dust that indicated no one had been there for quite a while. Using the tire iron to brush aside cobwebs, he entered the service area, making his way carefully to the last bay where he slid back the bolts on either side of the roll-up door before opening it.

Returning to the car, he organized his supplies. He consumed a bag of trail mix and a bottled water before placing the items Jared had acquired for him inside the backpack, along with the flashlight and bolt cutters. He checked the safety on the 9mm and climbed out of the car, tucking the gun into his waistband; the night vision glasses going around his neck. He removed the bicycle from the trunk and restarted the car, backing the Ford Taurus into the open bay. After rolling down the windows, he powered off the engine and left the keys inside the ashtray. He then sealed the garage door and exited through the office.

Adam surveyed the area using the night vision binoculars. The country-side appeared green in the glasses—the stars, glowing specks in the sky. Satisfied there was no one in sight, he secured the backpack over his shoulders and climbed onto the bike, sliding his left shoe in the peddle strap before pushing off with his right foot, following the deserted country road to the northwest.

He quickly realized his prosthetic was not going to cooperate and was forced to adapt a one-legged spin with his real leg. After a few minutes he found himself winded; after ten he stopped to gauge his bearings again with the night glasses.

He could see the farmhouse half a mile up ahead, a soft glow of light coming from one of the first floor windows.

That's close enough ...

He climbed off the bike and removed the bolt cutters from the backpack. Examining the barbed-wire fence, he selected the nearest wood post and snipped each of the three horizontal lengths of wire. After replacing the tool, he dragged the bike through the opening, laying it flat along the tall grass.

Using the night vision glasses, he headed for the farmhouse.

Orange flames danced around a log in the stone fireplace, the random crackling and popping in contrast to the rock-steady cadence of the ticking grandfather clock.

Air Force counter-intelligence agent Kelly Kishel huddled beneath the down comforter on the dining room floor. From her vantage she had a clear shot at the front door of the farmhouse, as well as most of the first floor windows. The back door, accessible through the kitchen, was her one vulnerable point. To gain entry her target would first have to enter the screened-in porch, its rusted springs alerting her to his presence. Once inside he would still have to pass through the kitchen and into the dining room, again entering her kill zone.

She had arrived at the property shortly after receiving confirmation that Adam Shariak had boarded United Flight 6324 out of Washington, D.C. The farm's caretakers—both retired field agents—had vacated the black ops location the day before and would not return for seventy-two hours. To their credit, the couple had actually become novice dairy farmers. The sixteen cows they cared for certainly lent to their cover, though the supplemental income was far from necessary with what MAJI was paying them.

The dark screen of Agent Kishel's laptop suddenly illuminated, revealing an aerial view of the property. Sensors had picked up a break in the security fence along the northwest access road, heat sensors locking on to the intruder as he circled the farmhouse to the north.

Kelly Kishel felt for the prescription bottle in her purse and popped her second 20mg Fluoxetine in the last two hours, chasing the megadose of serotonin with the remains of her coffee. She removed the Glock 27 from its holster and then released the safety, her eyes tracking her invited guest on her monitor as he made his way to the farmhouse.

Adam surveyed the two-story dwelling from behind the trunk of an oak tree. The driveway leading to the front door was gravel, the back door accessible only through a screened-in porch. He imagined the hinges and springs of the patio door would be rusted.

He checked the time … 12:36 a.m. He had purposely arrived early—not that it really mattered. The counter-intelligence agent was expecting him; the question was how many reinforcements were inside with her and how many more were on the way.

Kelly's eyes followed the blinking figure on screen, her medicated pulse rock-steady as her visitor crossed the gravel driveway.

The counter-intelligence agent drew a bead on a chest-high dining room window panel that looked out to the front stoop. *Atta boy … Coupla more feet and it's nighty-night.*

For several minutes Shariak remained ten to fifteen feet outside the front door. Then he appeared to have second thoughts; circling around to the southeast side of the house.

Sweat beads rolled down her neck as she heard the screen door's rusted springs squeal open. *No problem. From her vantage she could put a bullet in her quarry no matter which door he entered through.*

And then the window by the kitchen sink shattered, causing her to drop to her knees. Before she could discern what the hissing sound was, a second object punched through the dining room window and rolled beneath the table, the smoke trail quickly filling the room and burning her eyes.

Tear gas!

Barely able to see, she ducked beneath the blanket with the laptop, quickly determining Shariak was heading around to the back porch. Gun in hand, she ran stooped over to the front door and flung it open, desperate for fresh air.

The light ignited from somewhere directly ahead, blinding her. Squinting and curling into a ball, she aimed her gun at the 1000-lumen tactical flashlight, firing twice before she felt the barrel of the 9mm pressing against the back of her neck, the voice coming from behind the gas mask muffled in her ear. "Hand me the weapon very slowly."

She swore under her breath, angry at herself for falling for the diversion.

She held up the Glock—Shariak yanking it out of her hand. She heard him tuck it away before his hand slid up the back of her neck, his fingers entwining her blonde hair into a fist.

"Walk toward the light … move!"

Looking down, she moved ahead until she was at the source.

"On your knees."

"Sounds kinky, Shariak. Is that how Jessica prefers it?"

The CIA agent never registered the blow to the back of her skull, only the gravel as her face struck the driveway, her consciousness inhaled into the sparkling purple darkness.

Subterranean Complex—Midwest USA

Freshly showered and having weighed in and dressed in purple scrubs and tennis shoes, Jessica followed Joyce LaCombe out of the women's locker room and down a long, white-tiled corridor. Every twenty feet they passed below a translucent black-tinted half-sphere mounted in the ceiling, the objects no doubt containing security cameras.

"Joyce, why did you bring me here?"

"After what Dr. Death did to you, we felt it was important you know the truth."

"Who's *we?*"

"We are the silenced majority that needs to be heard."

"Maybe you could start by telling me where *we* are."

"We're in Dulce, New Mexico … or more accurately, we're beneath a mountain not far from Dulce, New Mexico. Construction on this underground base dates back to 1948 when access tunnels were expanded from out of the natural cavern system that runs through these sacred Indian grounds. The complex was originally disguised as a lumber camp; its initial source of power came from the Navajo Dam. Dulce is part military base, part genetics lab; it's also the largest underground hub in North America.

From here you have access to all of the other subterranean bases, including Los Alamos National Laboratories. Crazy story—when Bechtel's excavating machine was completing the tunnel from Dulce to Los Alamos, the vibrations in the bedrock caused a humming sound that drove the residents of Taos, New Mexico crazy. They called it the *Taos Hum*. Some New Agers actually thought it was Gaia speaking to them."

"How many subterranean bases are there?"

"Enough to warrant changing Bechtel's mascot to a mole. You know about the complex beneath Haystack Butte at Edwards; that's where most of the pulse beam and stealth research is carried out. A fifty-mile shuttle links the 'Butte' with the Tehachapi facility in Southern California. Heading east you have two of the more infamous underground complexes in Groom Lake, Nevada and Dugway Proving Grounds in the desert outside Provo, Utah. I heard there's a really deep complex located below Denver's International Airport, though I've never been there. Then there's Fort Huachuca near Tombstone, Arizona—which serves as Army Intelligence headquarters—and bases in Burley, Idaho and Oklahoma City.

"The wildest underground facility I've ever visited is located about eighteen kilometers from a town called Alice Springs in Australia's Northern Territory. The base is known as Pine Gap; to locals it simply appears to be a satellite ground station which is jointly operated by the Americans and Aussies. Anyway, they flew us in at night by helicopter. The ground station is surrounded by mountains, and suddenly, it looked like we were about to crash into one. I let out a scream ... as we flew *through* the mountain, which was actually a hologram that concealed a massive base built deep inside the mountain. Among other things, it's where they keep the largest triangular Alien Reproduction Vehicle ever made."

The T-shaped corridor dead-ended; branching off to their right and left in identical white-tiled hallways.

"And what do they keep here in Dulce ... besides my *Zeus* satellites and a bunch of empty corridors that lead nowhere?"

"I'm going to show you." Instead of turning right or left, Dr. LaCombe took Jessica by the elbow and walked her straight into the wall—

—the two female scientists stepping through the hologram into an immense hangar which resembled the flight deck of an air craft carrier, only ten times larger.

Instead of F-16s, the underground air strip held an armada of extra-terrestrial vehicles.

They were floating in holding pens, each about half an acre in size. Most were saucer-shaped discs like the ARV Jessica had witnessed entering the Level-3 launch complex. There were also cigar-shaped and diamond-shaped UFOs, and several ten-by-twenty-foot oval craft.

"These are all man-made?"

"Correct. You can tell by the seams. The real deal is seamless and they function almost as life forms."

A herd of colorful drones whipped by, each semi-transparent object the size of a basketball. Jessica was about to inquire what these objects were when she caught sight of an imposing dark triangular vessel hovering twenty feet above the deck, its mass easily occupying a square mile of the hangar.

"A mothership? Joyce, why did they build a mothership. For that matter, why build any of this if you're just going to keep it hidden under-ground?"

"All good questions that deserve answers. Come with me, I'm going to show you."

Crossing the immense deck, they headed for an alcove marked by six vertical plastic tubes, each five-foot-in-diameter device disappearing up through the ceiling.

Joyce ducked inside one of the tubes. "There are elevators, but this is closer and more efficient."

"Looks like something out of *Willie Wonka and the Chocolate Factory*. Remember, I'm pregnant."

"It's safe up to the second trimester. Climb in and grip the rail by your sides and that will prompt the computer to ask you to state your destina-tion."

"Good evening, Dr. LaCombe. Please state your destination."

"Genetics Complex."

Before Jessica could respond, Joyce shot straight up the vertical shaft and disappeared.

Cassopolis, Michigan

Repositioning the gas mask over his face, Adam carried the unconscious woman back inside the house and up the stairs to the second floor and the master bedroom. He laid the blonde on her back on the queen-size bed and opened the window before searching the closet.

Five minutes later he had secured her wrists and ankles to the four bed posts using an assortment of belts and ties. When he was finished, he glanced at the clock on the end table.

Almost one a.m. Better pick up the pace, Shariak.

He unzipped the front pocket of the backpack and removed a small medical kit. Inside were two syringes and a small vial of clear liquid. Unscrewing the cap, he punctured the foil top with the needle and drew 20cc's of the elixir into the syringe.

Then he rolled up the counter-intelligence agent's sleeves, examining the veins in her forearms …

Kelly Kishel's eyes rolled forward as she inhaled fumes from the ammonia-soaked paper towel Adam held beneath her nostrils. A second later her head snapped back against the bed board, the impact causing her to wince.

She attempted to wipe tears from her watering eyes, only to realize her limbs had been bound. "Kinky."

"Where is Jessica?"

She looked up at Adam, her voice inflection flirtatious. "What do I get if I tell you?"

"You get to live."

The agent smiled. "Am I supposed to be scared? We ran your psychological profile … I think we both know you're not going to hurt me. Unfortunately the people I work for don't share the same love for humanity. If I don't report back at the top of the hour you can say bye-bye to the future Mrs. Shariak."

She wrinkled her nose. "My face feels funny."

"That's probably the Scopolamine kicking in."

She squirmed in her bonds, attempting to view her left forearm. "You injected me with truth serum?"

"Actually, this stuff is better than sodium pentothal. With Scopolamine you won't remember any of this."

"It won't work, Adam."

"It will if you *want* to tell me, and I think you do. That *is* why you sent me that cell phone, isn't it?"

"Yes."

"So then, why am I here?"

She closed her eyes, attempting to focus through a barbiturate fog. "There's a movement among many of the members of MAJI to release zero-point-energy to the masses; the challenge is smuggling one of the devices out of these underground military bases. We finally managed to do this—with the help of your fiancé. The device should arrive sometime before dawn."

"And you wanted me to have it?"

"God, no. I've arranged a buyer … an Indian billionaire with strong government connections. If you've ever been to New Delhi, you'd understand his interest."

"Where is Jessica?"

"She's in one of the underground complexes."

"Which one?"

"Dulce. It's a shithole town in New Mexico. The facility is located beneath a mountain. There are access points that will take you through the natural canyons to security checkpoints. Of course, Delta Force isn't about to let *you* inside."

"Is she being held against her will?"

"I don't think so."

"If you're not giving me the device why did you ask me to meet you here?"

"You're the reason the pilot agreed to risk bringing the ZPE unit on this run; he thinks he's delivering it to you."

"Who is he?"

"I don't know, my boyfriend set the whole thing up."

"Why meet me out here?"

"The farm is a drop point."

"For what?"

"Drugs. The CIA moves a couple hundred billion dollars of coke and heroin into the States every year through MAJI depots like this one."

She paused to listen as a vehicle turned into the farm's driveway, its wheels grinding gravel. "They're early. Guess it's bye-bye time."

Adam peeked out between slats in the Venetian blinds as a black van rolled to a stop in front of the barn. Two men and a woman exited the vehicle, all three dressed in leather and jeans.

"Looks more like a motorcycle gang than *Men in Black*."

Kelly Kishel's jaw dropped. "Bikers? Are you sure?"

"I said they look like bikers … they're driving a van." Remembering the night vision binoculars, he fished them out from beneath his sweat shirt and zoomed in on one of the men as he opened the van's rear doors. With his back turned, Adam was able to make out an insignia on the big man's jacket.

"*Devil's Diciples*."

"The *Diciples*? Are you sure?"

"They spelled Disciples wrong, but yeah … I'm sure." As he watched, one of the bikers rolled back the interior carpet and unlocked a hidden panel … revealing a cache of weapons.

"Shit."

"Shariak, the *Diciples* are MAJI's hired assassins."

"No kidding."

"Shariak, listen to me! If the colonel sent the *Devil's Diciples* then he must have put out TWEP orders on both of us."

Ignoring her, he dumped the contents of his backpack on the floor. Searching through the pile, he located the tactical flashlight he had rigged to power on when Kelly had fled the farmhouse.

He froze as one of the gang members kicked open the front door.

"Shariak, untie me! You'll need my help."

Pulling the 9mm from his waistband, he aimed it at the blonde. "Quiet."

❖ ❖ ❖

Brent "Snowman" Snowden was a 280-pound bull of a man, his shaved head and thickly-muscled tattooed arms bulged out from the sleeveless black leather Harley-Davidson jacket. Stepping over the downed front door, he entered the farmhouse, his eyes immediately burning from the remnants of tear gas.

Rather than retreat, he simply positioned his white bandana over his nose and mouth so that the fabric's skull design aligned with the lower half of his face. Holding the Mossberg .12 gauge shotgun out in front of him with the heel of the gun's butt pressed to his right shoulder, he motioned to "Big Tommy" Thompson to enter.

The former Army Signal Support Systems Specialist fought to see the miniature screen of the electronics device in his hand, its direction finder pinpointing the location of the cell phone that had led them to the farm. He quickly found Kelly Kishel's iPhone on the dining room floor next to her laptop.

A creak in the floorboards overhead caused both bikers to look up.

Snowden took the lead, ascending the stairs two steps at a time. Reaching the landing, he crouched low and listened.

"Hello? Will somebody help me?"

Big Tommy recognized the woman's voice, having eavesdropped on her cell phone conversations on the ride over from Detroit. Signaling Snowman to wait, he held the .38 snub-nose revolver with the barrel up as he crept to the closed bedroom and kicked the solid wood door off its eighty-year-old hinges.

For a moment the biker just stood in the entrance, staring.

"Well? Is she in there?"

"Stay there … I got this." Big Tommy entered the master bedroom, his watering eyes drifting from the open window to the blonde agent. Spread-eagled on the bed, she was completely nude, her wrists bound to the bedposts with a pair of silk men's ties, the quilt concealing her legs from the knees down.

Kelly looked up at the biker. "Are you here to rescue me or eye-fuck me?"

"Where's Shariak?"

She nodded to the open window.

Big Tommy looked out in time to see a man in a gray sweatshirt lower himself out over the ledge of the A-framed second story roof by holding on to the rain gutter.

When he turned back, his biker pal was staring down his .12 gauge shotgun at the naked agent.

"Snowman, Shariak's on the roof, northeast side of the house. I got this, go help Sasha!"

The big man nodded and left.

Big Tommy circled the foot of the bed, his eyes transfixed on Kelly Kishel's body. "Now what am I gonna do with you?"

"What would you like to do with me?"

"I'm supposed to kill you."

"But if you do that, who will get all the money?"

Big Tommy's eyes looked up from her groin. "What money?"

"Drug money. That's why I'm here, I'm a courier."

"How much money we talkin'?"

"It's usually somewhere between five and seven million. My job is to report the amount and deliver the cash to a private bank in Detroit."

"Why do they want you dead?"

"Obviously they think I've been skimming off the top. I haven't been, but that doesn't matter anymore if they put out a TWEP on me. So let's make a deal ... I'll take you to the drop zone and you free me with my cut of the cash."

"Why should I trust you?"

"Why should I trust *you*? You've got the gun. I'm lying here, tied up and naked. Either way I'm screwed." She glanced down at her vagina. "We've got a few hours until the drop ... see anything you like?"

Sitting down next to her right leg, he placed his right hand and the gun flat on the mattress by her left leg and leaned over, burying his face in her groin.

Kelly moaned—

—her right hand releasing the loose necktie and snaking its way beneath the pillow ...

Sensing movement, Big Tommy looked up—his right eye staring into the barrel of the Glock.

"Nighty-night."

The shot blasted a Rorschach pattern of brains, blood, and skull fragments against the back wall of the bedroom and out the open door.

Kicking her legs free of the dead biker, Kelly hurriedly pulled on her pants, grabbed her shoes and sweater, and peeked out into the dark hallway. Hearing nothing, she slipped the sweater over her head and the shoes onto her feet and then entered the hall—

—managing two strides before a swarm of steel buckshot plastered parts of her neck and sweater to the age-yellowed wallpaper.

The counter-intelligence agent dropped to her knees, gagging on a stream of blood rising from the back of her throat. Still holding the gun, she aimed the Glock into the darkness, getting off three rounds before her body slumped over sideways.

Brent Snowden rose from his seated position at the top of the stairs. Pumping in another round, he placed the barrel of the .12 gauge shotgun inside the dead woman's open mouth and fired, splattering her remains across the upstairs hallway.

Adam was dangling twenty feet off the ground when he heard the first shot. Forcing himself to stay focused, he worked his way hand over hand along the length of rain gutter, his target—the thick limb of an oak tree. Feeling something solid beneath his right shoe, he released the gutter, managing to maintain his balance long enough to squat and then straddle the thick branch.

He was crouching on the ground when he heard two more shots—these from a shotgun.

Ducking by a pile of firewood, he retrieved the night vision glasses from around his neck and quickly looked around.

There were three bikers. From the sound of the fired shots Kelly had taken out one of them before the second had most likely killed her.

That left two *Devil's Diciples* ... and the pilot—whoever he was.

Adam had a full clip and a bullet in the chamber. The night glasses offered him a slight advantage, the woodpile served as temporary cover from anyone approaching him from directly ahead, but he remained vulnerable from behind where one of the bikers could use the northeast corner of the house for cover while blasting him with their shotgun.

The sound of the kitchen door being kicked open sent him hobbling on his prosthetic leg to the northwest corner of the dwelling, the gravel driveway, garage, and barn now visible up ahead.

Targeting the black van, he leaned out to see around the corner of the house—

Whomp!

Sasha Moulder straddled the unconscious man. Spitting on his back, the female biker raised the shotgun over Shariak's skull to strike him again when Brent Snowden grabbed her wrist.

"No, babe. We need him alive."

"MAJI wants him dead."

"I heard the girl telling Big Tommy this farm is a cash drop zone. Shariak may know the details. We'll waste him after we get the money."

Handing Sasha his weapon, the big man grabbed Adam Shariak by the arm and tossed him over his broad shoulders like a fireman.

"Snowman, where's Big Tommy?"

"Dead. But don't shed any tears; he went out with a smile on his face."

37

Subterranean Complex—Midwest USA

JESSICA DUCKED INSIDE the clear plastic tube and stepped on a round platform covered with quarter-size holes. She gripped the rails by her side, prompting the onboard computer.

"Good evening, Dr. Marulli. Please state your destination."

"Genetics Complex."

Jessica felt the rubber soles of her shoes being suctioned to the porous floor a split second before she was transformed into a human bullet, soaring straight up, then sideways so fast she lost all orientation—

Stop!

Somehow she was upright again. The suction eased, her legs wobbling beneath her as she stepped out of the tube to a transportation hub, the six vertical shafts now aligned across from four elevators.

Dr. LaCombe was waiting by an impressive polished steel vault door. "Are you all right?"

"From now on, let's take the stairs. Where are we? Fort Knox?"

"The vault contains a Faraday chamber which blocks out all electric and electromagnetic waves." She pressed her face to the rubber housing for a retinal scan.

Eight bolts situated around the steel vault simultaneously retracted, the huge door whisper-quiet as it swung open.

"There are white noise dampeners inside; we'll receive headsets before we enter. Make sure you keep yours on at all times."

Jessica followed Joyce inside the vault entrance, immediately registering

332

a faint buzzing sound in her ears. Ahead was a set of smoke-glass doors adjacent to another Plexiglas control booth, a male security guard seated inside. As they approached, a metal box similar to the ones found at a bank drive-thru ejected from inside the checkpoint.

Joyce reached in and removed two headsets wrapped in cellophane. She handed a pair to Jessica, who quickly secured the device over her ears.

The white noise disappeared, replaced by the guard's voice, which was crisp and clear. "Evening, doc."

"Good evening, Monroe. I assume you received security clearances for Dr. Marulli?"

"Yes, ma'am, she's all set. I alerted Dr. Lara that you just arrived."

"How much time do we have?"

"Prep started twenty minutes ago. At your request, the procedure was moved to TDS-2 so your friend could watch."

"Excellent. Tell him we're on our way."

Joyce headed for the glass doors which were already parting outward, releasing a stream of cool air. Once inside, she turned left down a corridor, Jessica hustling to keep up.

"Procedure?"

"A little something that falls under the description Weird Science and Frickin' Magic. Since we still have some time before the show begins I thought I'd show you a bit of history."

The wall on their right illuminated into a ten-by-twelve-foot section of smart glass. As Jessica watched, a slide show began, featuring black and white photos taken of the 1947 UFO crash site in Corona, New Mexico. These were augmented by 16mm footage showing the remains of the vessel, along with military personnel recovering the dead bodies and the extraterrestrial vessel's lone survivor.

The scene jumped to a series of graphic autopsy slides of the deceased ETs, which were narrated by the Army's Medical Examiner.

"… as you can see, the EBEN's brain possesses eleven different lobes as compared to the eight lobes of a human brain. The optic nerves are also larger and far more sophisticated than ours, and their eyes operate from different parts of the brain.

"In regard to the EBEN's internal parts, one organ appears to function as both a heart and set of lungs. Multiple stomachs are responsible for different digestive processes. There is also an organ designed to remove the moisture from whatever they eat, eliminating the need to consume a large amount of fluids. The reproductive organs are internalized; the vocal cords nonexistent. While communication between the surviving EBEN indicates female Greys do exist, the ETs aboard the crashed vehicles all appear to be male."

Joyce tapped her shoulder. "We need to cut this short; Dr. Lara is ready to begin."

The two women followed the corridor signs heading for TDS Suites 1-4. Glass doors parted with a *hiss* of air pressure and they entered what appeared to be a hospital wing, the corridor walls covered in green tile.

Joyce led Jessica up a narrow flight of steps to an observation galley. Below was a surgical suite that looked like it had been designed by a modern-day Dr. Frankenstein.

Half-a-dozen six-foot-tall, sickle-shaped transformers surrounded a rubber-insulated surgical table like an electronic ribcage. Strapped to the table was a balding Caucasian man in his mid-forties, sporting an unkempt brown beard and mustache and wearing a pale-blue dressing gown. He was unconscious; his right leg covered in rubber pads connected to electrodes which ran from the exposed flesh of his lower right limb to a circuit board situated outside the central dais.

Jessica could see that the man's left leg was gone, having been amputated above the knee. *Just like Adam ...*

The only other person in the suite was a dark-haired man dressed in black scrubs who was seated at a computer terminal.

Joyce switched channels on her headset to converse with him. "Dr. Juande Lara, say hello to Dr. Jessica Marulli. Dr. Lara is our resident specialist in TDS ... Transdimensional Surgery."

The Spaniard continued typing out commands on his keyboard, never bothering to look up. "Tell me, Marulli, are you familiar with TDS?"

"Never heard the term until you just mentioned it. From the looks of your lab, I assume it has something to do with the zero-point-energy field."

"Correct. Scientists have known for decades that animals use bioelectrical signals to regenerate body parts—this is how tadpoles regenerate their tails. Two components are required: a proton pump to remove hydrogen ions out of the cell surface, and sodium ions which flow across the cell membrane. This bioelectric state stimulates regeneration-specific genes to multiply, allowing nerves to develop in the direction of the new growth and new cells to replace the damaged ones—including those in the spinal cord, essentially reversing paralysis."

"That's amazing."

"No, Dr. Marulli, amazing is what happened after we used stem cells to crack the bioelectric code and applied the regeneration recipe in a zero-point-energy field."

Dr. Lara walked over to the man whose three limbs were grounded to the rubber-insulated surgical table. "Our patient this evening is Mr. David Griggs. Mr. Griggs worked for MAJI as a ... well, let's just call him a bounty hunter. Unbeknownst to Mr. Griggs was the fact that he had diabetes, which was left untreated for eighteen years, resulting in gangrene and the eventual amputation of his left leg.

"These six electrodes are powered by zero-point-energy. When I activate them, it will surround the patient in a transdimensional field similar to the bubble generated by the extraterrestrial vehicles. At that exact instant, the bioelectric code to regenerate Mr. Griggs' left leg will be juiced."

Returning to his console, Dr. Lara typed in a few commands on his keyboard, causing a neon-blue aura to surround the surgical table.

Jessica watched in amazement as the patient's left leg began growing from out of his stump, forming a new limb from the inside out within sixty seconds.

"Oh my God ..."

"You got the 'God' part right. The new limb is fully functional, the neurons channeling directly to Mr. Griggs' brain."

Joyce smiled. "Tell Dr. Marulli what else we can do."

"In a word ... everything. There's not a disease we haven't cured or an injury we can't heal within minutes of the application."

Jessica could barely contain her excitement. "This is incredible. Is this still in the trial phase? When will it be announced to the rest of the world?"

"It won't be announced," Dr. Lara said. "The cabal will keep it black-shelved forever, along with zero-point-energy."

Jessica felt numb. "But why?"

"I think you already know that answer. There's far more money to be made in treating the symptoms of a disease with prescription medicines that have to be reordered every month than by actually curing something. Eradicate a disease, and you've eliminated a trillion dollars from the economy. Big Pharma and the Bankocrats don't want cures—except for themselves, of course.

"As for the amputees and the paralyzed ... the diseased and the dying—MAJI could care less. This is all about money and controlling the masses—the less of them to deal with, the better."

Jessica's feeling of utter helplessness had quickly evolved into anger by the time Joyce had dragged her out of the debate and down the hall.

"I wasn't through!"

"You were preaching to the choir, Jess. Dr. Lara and his colleagues would love to bring these discoveries out, only they're scared. Physicians and biochemists who claim to have found holistic cancer remedies get shut down ... or worse."

Jessica adjusted the tension on her headset which was squeezing her temples and giving her a headache. "Watching that man's limb grow out of his stump ... all I could think of was Adam—"

She stopped walking, forcing Joyce to turn back. "What?"

"That's why you wanted me to see that procedure ... you even found a left leg amputee, just like Adam."

"That was a coincidence."

"Bullshit. You're lobbying me against Council. Admit it, Joyce."

"Okay, I admit it, only it's not what you think."

"What I *think* is that I've had enough. I'm going home."

Jessica spun around on her heels, causing her headphones to slide off her head. As she reached out to catch them, her brain was accosted by a symphony of clicks and whispers, screeches and grunts.

Disoriented, she lost her balance, her legs folding beneath her.

Joyce grabbed her as she fell, minimizing the impact. She quickly returned the headphones to Jessica's ears, tightening the tension. "You okay?"

"No. What the hell was that?"

"That is why I brought you here … to show you MAJI's real secret."

Joyce helped her to her feet then led her down the hall to another corridor guarded by two members of DELTA Force. She glanced at a sign posted above a set of double doors.

Genetics Lab
Dr. Joyce LaCombe: Director of Operations

Cassopolis, Michigan

The garage was situated between the farmhouse and the barn and was the newest structure on the property. An assortment of tools and farming equipment hung from the back wall. Open cardboard boxes held plastic containers of engine oil, a gasoline pump fed diesel fuel from and an underground storage tank housed beneath the concrete slab.

There were two vehicles parked inside. The silver Audi A4 had been leased under a phony name and provided to Kelly Kishel for her use. The candy-apple-red 2013 Case IH Steiger 550S 4x4 tractor belonged to the agents working undercover as farmers.

Adam Shariak opened his eyes to the scent of diesel fumes. He was arched backward over one of the tractor's enormous pair of rear tires, his arms outstretched painfully over his head, his wrists and ankles duct taped to the vehicle's undercarriage. The tape had been hastily secured around his left sock, indicating the biker hadn't noticed the artificial limb.

Barely able to turn his head, he looked to his left and saw the dark-haired female *Devil's Diciple* rummaging through a tool chest.

"Baby, do you want a molar or a front tooth?"

"Sasha, I'm on the phone." The big man with the shaved head and thickly-muscled tattooed arms gave the edge of his hunting knife several slow passes against the silicon carbide stone sharpener while he waited for the secured line to process the call.

"It's Snowman. The job is done but we'll need a clean-up crew."

"How many?"

"Two in the house, one in the garage."

"Understood."

Adam tested his bonds—the duct tape around his wrists was cutting off his circulation, but there was some play on his right ankle. As for the prosthetic, the sock was loose; he knew he could slip the bare metal hinged foot out of his shoe at anytime.

He looked up as the woman filled his vision, her human tooth necklace an ugly foreshadowing of what was about to happen. Gripping his lower jaw, the female biker jammed a pair of needle-nose pliers into his mouth. In a well-practiced motion, she forcibly yanked one of his upper right molars out of his gums.

Adam's groan was choked off by a wad of blood gushing down the back of his throat. Turning his head as far as he could, he spit, only his head was too far back and he ended up dribbling it across his chin and sweatshirt.

The big man approached, the blade of the hunting knife gleaming beneath the bare fluorescent lights anchored beneath the garage roof's crossbeams. "Sasha … she don't mess around. Me? I like to take my time. But I'll make you a deal. You tell me where the drop point is and I'll end things quick and easy with a bullet to the brain."

"Detroit … the drop-off is in Detroit."

"Where in Detroit?"

"A warehouse near the football stadium. I don't know the address, but I can take you there."

"He's lying," said Sasha, who was busy at a work table, fitting a drill with a narrow bit.

Brent Snowden leaned over Adam. "Are you lying?"

The former Apache pilot and prisoner of war spit again, this time managing to hit the biker in his face. "Maybe that ugly bitch is the one who's lying?"

The biker wiped his right cheek with his skeleton bandana. "Babe, bring that drill over here."

Sasha finished drilling a hole in Adam's pulled tooth, then walked over to the tractor and handed the tool to her boyfriend.

Adam's eyes went wide in terror. "No, no … please God, not in the knee!"

With a maniacal leer, the biker squeezed the trigger, his muscular right arm jamming the spinning drill bit straight into the fabric of Adam's left pant leg and down through the metal appendage—

—as Adam's thoughts commanded the robotic limb to hyperextend.

The sudden movement powered on both of the King Cobra tasers that Jared Betz had rigged to a briar patch of stripped copper wiring around the prosthetic leg, sending a combined six million volts of electricity through the metal and into the biker's body, instantly stopping his heart.

For a surreal moment the *Devil's Diciple's* two-hundred-and-eighty pound torso continued to convulse in place. And then the dead man toppled forward onto Adam's lower legs—

—the impact snapping the duct tape around his right ankle and freeing both legs!

Sasha laughed. "Snowman? Baby, get up."

It took her a moment to realize her motionless boyfriend was dead.

Adam flipped his legs up and over his head so that he was now facing the tire. He gnawed at the twisted mess of duct tape around his left wrist with his blood-drenched teeth like a deer caught in a bear trap.

The biker chick screamed at him, venom in her eyes. "Where the fuck do you think you're going?" Prying the hunting knife loose from her dead boyfriend's hand, she wheeled upon Adam—

—who had freed his left hand and was now brandishing a second 9mm that he had removed from a holster hidden inside the struts and springs of his artificial limb, the gun's barrel aimed at Sasha's right eye.

Without hesitation he pulled the trigger, the slug tearing through the woman's cornea and brain before exploding out the back of her skull.

He spit out a wad of blood. "That's for making me have to go to the dentist."

Adam quickly chewed through the tape around his right wrist that was still pinning him to the tractor. He slid down the back of the double tires as the last piece of silver tape gave way. Locating Snowden's knife, he cut loose the remains of his bonds.

He managed two steps—only to realize the damaged prosthetic was wobbling badly.

Fix it … then get out of here before the clean-up crew arrives.

Slicing off the pant leg, he inspected the damage to the hydraulic knee, which was bent beyond his ability to repair it.

Maybe Kishel left her keys in the car?

He attempted to limp over, only the prosthetic leg buckled. Searching the garage, he found a push broom. Inverting it, he tucked the broom's head under his left arm and used the stick like a crutch in order to make his way over to the silver Audi.

A quick inspection turned up nothing.

And then the garage window panes startled to rattle …

38

Cassopolis, Michigan

ADAM STOOD BY THE GARAGE WINDOW, staring at the roof of the three-story barn. The A-frame of the dilapidated structure had split open like a giant pair of praying hands, its weathered shingles and struts conceal- ing a pair of aluminum doors anchored on hydraulic rollers.

Exiting the garage, he hid behind the rusted jalopy and gazed up at a starry night sky and a bizarre amber-red light.

The disc-shaped UFO was fifty feet in diameter, with a band of multi- colored lights that circled randomly around its circumference. Descending rapidly, the ship stopped to momentarily hover above the barn's still open- ing gullet—revealing tell-tale seams along its hull in the process— confirming to Adam its identification as a man-made Alien Reproduction Vehicle.

The craft disappeared inside the barn, the A-frame roof closing to seal the vessel inside its secret port.

Leaning on the broom, Adam made his way across the gravel driveway to the barn door and pressed his ear to the heavy reinforced barrier to hear two men yelling inside—

—the argument ending with a shot of gunfire.

Adam hid behind the barn door as it swung open, releasing a Caucasian man in his forties, his brown hair receding in front but long in the back, ending in a tight ponytail. He was dressed in a black Delta Force jumpsuit, a Beretta handgun in his right hand, the pilot's helmet in his left.

"Drop the gun or I'll drop you where you stand."

The commando stopped; his back to Adam. "Sounds like a bad western.

How am I supposed to know if you're really armed?"

Adam fired a shot between the man's feet.

"I guess that settles the matter." He lowered his gun, allowing it to fall to the gravel-covered driveway by his right boot. "Your move, cowboy."

"Who did you shoot inside the barn?"

"The guy MAJI sent to kill you. You are Adam Shariak, yes?"

"And you are?"

"Chris Mull. I work with your fiancée. May I turn around just to confirm who you are?"

Without waiting for a reply the commando turned to face Adam. "Ah, it is you … fantastic. About a week ago we learned a TWEP order had been placed on you. Jessica begged me to save your sorry ass. I managed to change the duty roster in order to accompany the hit man. His name was Captain Joshua LaCombe. The body's inside the barn."

"What about the girl?"

"Girl? What girl?"

"Kelly Kishel. MAJI sent her to kill me."

"Never heard of her. Where is she?"

"Dead."

For a brief second the commando's eyes went vacant like a predator's, devoid of a soul. "You killed her?"

"No, the bikers handled that. But I thought you said this guy, LaCombe was sent to kill me?"

"Apparently MAJI brought in back-up."

"Where's the zero-point-energy device?"

"What zero-point-energy device is that?"

The bullet splintered the gravel between Chris Mull's feet.

"Take it easy, Shariak. I'm on your side."

"That remains to be seen. Now show me the device."

"No problem, it's inside the ARV." Mull walked back toward the barn, slipping the helmet on his head as he approached Adam. "Jessica told me you flew Apaches in Iraq. You'd love flying one of these ET ships. The helmet links your thought commands to the—"

"Stop."

"Stop ... start ... get the ZPE unit ... make up your mind."

"I said stop!" Adam fired again, causing the man to halt a few paces away. "The headpiece ... take it off and hand it to me."

"It won't work for you."

"As long as it doesn't work for you."

Chris Mull's smile cracked a second before he whipped the headpiece at Adam, the helmet knocking the broomstick out from under him.

Balancing on his only leg, Adam attempted to shoot his assailant, only Mull had circled behind him. As he turned, the MAJI agent launched a front thrust kick, catching him flush in the solar plexus and driving him backward through the open barn door.

Adam flopped on the hay-covered concrete slab like a fish out of water. He wheezed but could not draw a breath, the air driven from his lungs, the bundle of nerves below his ribcage momentarily paralyzed. He tried to raise the gun—

—only to have the Delta Force commando kick it out of his hand.

"You killed Kelly, didn't you?"

The instep of the man's boot struck him on the right side of his chest, bruising two ribs.

"You're in a world of hurt, my friend. After I take care of you I'm heading back to Dulce to deal with your fiancée. Me and Jessica ... we're going to have a lot of fun as I—"

Chris Mull leaned over to retrieve Adam's gun—and vaporized.

Adam looked up in disbelief. One moment he was there, the next ... *poof.* All that remained was a dispersing trail of humidity.

Unable to breathe, Adam rolled over onto his back, each wheezed breath managing to push a little more air into his starving lungs. Thoughts raced at him, demanding answers but breathing was his first priority, pain a close second.

Opening his eyes, he found himself staring at the underside of the man-made space craft. There was no landing gear; the vessel was simply floating ten feet above the barn's concrete floor.

And then he heard a voice.

"... to your right. Shariak, pick up the headpiece."

He glanced to his right and saw it lying six feet away.

Forcing himself onto his belly, he crawled to the device and placed it on his head, registering a *zzzzztt* of current in his brain.

"Shariak, can you hear me?"

"Yes. Where are you?"

"Far side of the barn ... by the bales of hay."

Adam diverted to a metal rake and used it to lean on as he circled the floating vessel.

He saw the trail of blood ... then he saw the man.

Captain Joshua LaCombe was leaning back against a bale of hay, his blood-soaked hands pressing weakly against an entrance wound in his abdomen and an exit wound in his left lung. He was pale and bleeding out very fast.

"How did you vaporize Mull?"

"Head-piece. ARVs are fully weaponized ... just don't use them in space. Listen carefully. Inside the lower level are three gravity amplifiers. Omicron configuration ..."

He ceased talking, the blood gurgling in his windpipe.

Adam reached for him, only the commander's telepathic voice interceded.

Shariak, focus! Omicron configuration flies sublight speed using one gravity amplifier. Delta configuration uses all three as a bow-wave to go transdimensional. I rigged the ZPE unit to eject from your console when you go Delta.

"You expect me to fly this thing?"

No choice. MAJI will terminate my wife and son, along with Jessica and your unborn kid. Get to Dulce and shut them down.

"But how am I—"

An ARV is like an Apache ... just think and it moves. Beware of Zeus SATS ... they're armed.

"Okay. Anything else?

Tell Joyce and my boy ...

Adam watched as Joshua LaCombe's eyes glazed over. "Captain?"

Did he say my unborn kid?

He looked up as the sound of motorcycles approached in the distance.

Leaning on the rake, Adam limped to the barn door and sealed it, then returned to the hovering disk. Looking up at the curved underside, he noticed a hexagon-shaped honeycombed configuration.

"*Think* the hatch open."

Open, please.

The honeycomb pattern pixilated, collapsing upon itself to become a hatch.

Okay, that was cool. Adam balanced on his right leg fourteen feet beneath the opening. *Now how am I supposed to climb up in there?*

A strange sensation made him smile, then he laughed out loud as his body became weightless and the ARV's anti-gravity bubble swept him up inside the ship.

Subterranean Complex—Midwest USA

The Genetics Lab occupied two levels and more than six square miles of the subterranean complex's lower floors. Promising to limit the tour to two locations, Joyce escorted Jessica to an ET repository—a dark chamber where the preserved remains of several dozen interstellar life forms were floating in clear vertical tubes of liquid.

"My God ... How many different Interstellar species have visited Earth?"

"The reports vary. I've heard anywhere from sixteen to thirty-five. My genetics team was assigned to work with the three most prevalent extra-terrestrial species. This first tube holds a rare specimen—a very human-like ET known as a Nordic. We believe they've been infiltrating society for quite some time."

The specimen was a female and startlingly human in appearance, save for a slightly narrower skull and cat-like irises.

"With a pair of contact lenses, it would be nearly impossible to distinguish them from us. What do they want?"

"We don't know. But neither the Nordics nor any of these other Interstellars have ever been hostile—even though we've repeatedly shot them down."

"What about the times they've shut down our nuclear ballistic missiles?"

"I don't consider that hostile. It's more like a parent taking away fire-crackers from a preschooler."

Joyce led Jessica to the next vertical container, the contrast between the Nordic and this creature startling. The six-foot biped possessed the head of a praying mantis and a pair of hand-like appendages on each upper limb.

"That is seriously ugly."

"Don't judge a species by its appearance. While we trace our beginnings to primates—one of the most violent life forms in the animal kingdom, this Interstellar species evolved from insects. They happen to be an extremely advanced and peaceful race that has taken a real liking to man."

The last two rows of vertical tubes contained the remains of the Grey species that Colonel Johnston had used to infiltrate Jessica's subconscious.

"These are Greys, of course. We believe they come from a planet in Zeta Reticuli, a binary star system about 39.5 light years away. There is increasing evidence that the Greys manipulated our genetic code as many as sixty times over the last several million years."

"Why would they alter our genetic code?"

"There are a lot of reasons. Most fall under the category, 'to accelerate our evolution as a species.' Earth is a wonderful habitat, Jess, but over most of its six billion year history it has experienced multiple epochs of glacia-tions, each of which nearly wiped out every life form in existence. The evolution of *Homo sapiens* happened only because Earth has been experienc-ing a temperate period between ice ages."

"And you think it's possible the Greys accelerated our simian develop-ment in order to give us the best chance to survive?"

Joyce nodded. "And now, because of fossil fuels, we're accelerating Global Warming. What the average American and the Climate Change deniers in Washington refuse to understand is that Global Warming causes ice ages. When Greenland's ice melts, all of that fresh water will inundate the North Atlantic Current, diluting its saline content. Salt water is what circulates the thermohaline, and the thermohaline is what keeps Europe and North America warm.

"Unless we drastically reverse carbon emissions, the thermocline *will* stop. And when it does, the Earth's temperature will plummet. Within

346

months, most of North America and Europe could be covered in snow and ice."

"Is that why you brought me here, Joyce? To smuggle a zero-point-energy unit off this base in order to stop Climate Change?"

"Yes and no. The zero-point-energy unit is being delivered to your fiancé as we speak, along with access to off-shore accounts totaling a hundred billion dollars."

"My God ..."

"Unfortunately, there's another threat that supersedes Global Warming. Come with me, and keep your headpiece on."

They left the repository and approached a set of sealed doors which opened as Dr. LaCombe approached. Jessica followed her inside to a balcony located several stories above a gymnasium-size mosh-pit.

Milling about below were hundreds of Grey extraterrestrials.

"Welcome to La-La Land."

The ETs appeared delirious, bumping into one another, walking into walls.

"What the hell, Joyce? Did you capture these beings?"

"God, no. They were biologically cloned; we call them PLFs ... Programmed Life Forms. We manufacture them here in Dulce and in the Pine Gap facility in Australia. Their neural complexes have been fitted with a microchip implant which scrambles their thoughts, forcing them to obey our commands. The lab is surrounded by a very powerful Faraday Chamber, otherwise the ETs would simply walk through the walls and disappear."

"Why are you cloning them?"

"We're cloning them for the same reason we're building hundreds of ARVs. MAJI has been preparing for a fake alien invasion for decades; only in this Orwellian nightmare we are both the *us* and the *them*. The fake ships and aliens ... it's all a false flag event staged to look like a real *Independence Day*."

"This is insane. Why would MAJI do this?"

"Mostly because they're power-hungry ... and endless war allows them to control the planet and regulate the human population. Then there is a religious faction of MAJI who believes Armageddon will lead to the Second

Coming. So you have the military sociopaths and the religious fanatics joining forces to launch their new campaign against terror which will unite what's left of the world against Satanic species from other worlds."

"No ... I don't believe it."

"Scott Hopper was assigned the task of programming the array's target list; he revealed it to me two days before they poisoned him. The West will get hit first of course ... London and Los Angeles, then Moscow and Beijing. Syria and ISIS will be incinerated, along with a billion innocent Muslims, and Iran will get theirs too. Jerusalem will be attacked but will manage to survive in order to appease the radical Christians rooting for the return of their savior. After that, America will stage a comeback as our *Zeus* Space Defense System, quote-unquote 'becomes operational.' Putin and Trump will play starring roles, their egos left to fight on Twitter as to which one of them actually saved the world.

"It should be one helluva show ... a lesson on how to reduce the human race by eighty percent, brought to you courtesy of the wackos running MAJI."

39

Cassopolis, Michigan

ADAM WATCHED IN AMAZEMENT as the hexagon-shaped hatch sealed beneath him.

He was weightless because he had wished it so, just as he knew he could instantly restore gravity within the tight confines of the ship with only a change of thought.

The lower level was as tight as an attic. Three large gravity amplifiers, each equipped with two-by-four-foot-long rudder-like objects that occupied most of the space.

He rose past ladder rungs leading up to the main deck. A circular console occupied the middle of the chamber, its three crew seats positioned at intervals around the controls.

Adam grabbed on to one of the seatbacks and pulled himself in, then thought away the zero-gravity setting … his body mass returning like a concrete suit.

"I need to get—" *I mean, I need to get to Dulce, New Mexico. Better open the barn roof first.*

Nothing happened.

The eleven *Devil's Diciples'* motorcycles rolled past the closed gas station, following the deserted two-lane highway to the northwest. Reaching the farm, they turned up the gravel drive and parked next to the van, shutting down their engines.

Aaron Edward Rahn, A.K.A. "Fast Eddie," ordered his crew to search the farmhouse and garage. Having taken over as warlord following his predecessor's conviction on RICO charges, Fast Eddie had moved the gang's business from meth to Murder, Inc. The "contracts" were provided by a former Vice Admiral who Rahn's father had served under, the victims considered enemies of the state who needed to "disappear." The bikers had proved to be fast, reliable, and extremely ruthless, their only shortcoming—an affinity for the killers to wear the teeth of their victims on a necklace.

This job was a bit different. Adam Shariak's body would be found in a hotel room. The woman hired to do the hit would get whacked herself, their naked corpses arranged in what was supposed to look like a lover's tiff.

"Eddie, there's two bodies in the farm house—the girl and Big Tommy. We found Snowman and Sasha in the garage ... both dead. There's no sign of Shariak."

They turned as two bikers waved at the warlord from the barn door, one holding up Adam's night glasses. "Over here!"

Adam tried rephrasing the thought command a dozen different ways. He searched the vessel for some kind of hydraulic controller. Desperate, he even tried all three pilot seats ... only nothing would raise the barn roof.

Mull said the headset wouldn't work for me ...

A warning light flashed as the forward panel went translucent. He could now see through the ship and the barn door into the night where one of the bikers was removing something large from the van's hidden compartment.

The weapon illuminated and enlarged on the screen.

"Christ ... that's an RPG."

Open barn roof! Prepare to activate Omicron configuration.

Still nothing.

Adam's eye tracked the biker as he stood before the barn door and hoisted the rocket-propelled grenade launcher upon his right shoulder.

Screw it. Activate Delta configuration!

Select destination.
I don't know ... how about Jupiter.

Adam opened his eyes ... which, in retrospect, indicated he had closed them. Strangely, he hadn't remembered closing them ... or leaving the barn, or for that matter, experiencing any hint of a passage of time. And yet here he was, looking out a 360-degree view of space dominated by the monstrous planet whose southern hemisphere loomed over him like the epitome of creation.

Adam stared at the goliath ... how could one not? The island of hydrogen, helium, and churning bands of sulfurous clouds was more than three hundred times the size of Earth, its volatile winds whipping three times faster than a Category-5 hurricane. And yet the behemoth was beautiful, its atmosphere colored in blues, browns, reds and whites; its ice rings sparkling like diamonds.

Gazing at him from the belly of the beast was the leviathan's crimson eye—the Great Red Spot—large enough to engulf two Earths. And then there were Jupiter's moons; four immense gravity-affecting toddlers and sixty-plus smaller tykes, all of which appeared to be trolling above the planet's exotic seas like tiny orbs ... each a world unto itself.

As he watched, a dark speck came into view, rotating counterclockwise with the planet. Too oddly shaped to be a moon, Adam realized it was following a geosynchronous orbit and would pass directly between his craft and the planet.

And now he could see it ... an immense triangular Interstellar mothership that dwarfed his tiny vessel in the same manner Jupiter dwarfed Earth.

Filled with wonderment, he reached out telepathically with a greeting. *I am Adam.*

Greetings, Adam. You are the first to venture this far.

I come in peace.

There are no boundaries in peace. Safe travels, friend Adam.

In that moment, in the emptiness of space, he was at one with the universe and the universe was at one with him ... his soul a spark of the single creation that had given birth to the Big Bang and every atom in the physical universe.

Adam was overcome by such a feeling of brotherhood and unconditional love that he wept.

Having strapped in, he had not realized the cabin was experiencing zero gravity until the object ejected from the main console. He reached out for it as it floated by—the device an island of energy, a buoy to a future denied to humans by those who had sought only to erect boundaries.

Engage Delta configuration ...
Take me back to Earth.

40

Dulce Subterranean Base
Dulce, New Mexico

DR. JOYCE LACOMBE topped her cup of coffee off with a second shot of whiskey. "Do you know who I admire?"

Jessica passed on the offering. "Who do you admire, Joyce?"

"The blissfully ignorant."

"You mean the ones who define technology as an iPhone-7, but believe it's impossible to run a car off of anything but gasoline?"

"Exactly. I'd love to just wake up one morning and have a blissfully ignorant life with a husband who drove a truck, or a son who could play sports instead of reside in a bunker four months out of the year."

"Know what I think? I think you're jealous of the ignorant, but I don't think you admire them … that's what I think."

Joyce took another swig of her drink. "You know me that well, do you?"

"I know *me* that well. I wouldn't want to *not* know the truth … the truth is beautiful. It's the lies that are ugly."

"And have you decided on whether you'll be helping us to spread the truth?"

"Tell me what I have to do."

Joyce leaned in to whisper, even though she had rigged her private office with white noise dampeners. "Getting hold of a zero-point unit was never on our radar, you sort of walked that option home. Far more important than a working device are its schematics. We've been able to copy the plans for three different zero-point-energy generators onto several USB flash drives. The challenge is getting them out of this facility—not an easy task given the ultra-high security present in these lower levels."

"But you came up with an option?"

"Not an option but a real solution. The option is whether you are willing to accept a small amount of temporary discomfort in order to make the world a safer, better place for your unborn child."

Dr. Lara ushered the two women into Transdimensional Surgical Suite-4. "Everything is set. The entire procedure should take less than four minutes."

"Well, I've got about eight minutes worth of questions," Jessica replied quickly. "Just so I understand this, you want to amputate one of my fingers and grow back a replacement finger with the flash drive grown under my skin?"

"Correct. The flash drive will be placed beneath the tendon and bone where any skilled surgeon will be able to slide it out."

"Without removing my new finger?"

"Correct. Again Dr. Marulli, there should be no lasting effects other than a small scar."

"Which finger?"

"That is a legitimate question; let us take a look."

Reaching into his lab coat pocket, Dr. Lara removed a small flat flash drive sealed in white rubber latex. Holding up the object to each finger, the TDS surgeon measured the width.

"You said you were right-handed?"

"Yes."

"Then I would say the best results should come by replacing the fourth digit of your left hand."

"Hello? That's where I'm wearing my engagement ring."

"That's an engagement ring?"

"Yeah, wise ass. Maybe I should castrate you and we can smuggle the flash drive out in your new ball sack."

"Take it easy," Joyce said. "Dr. Lara, use the ring finger on the right hand ... it's only a twenty-four hour inconvenience ... she'll manage."

Jessica eased herself onto the rubber table top and laid back, looking up at the underside of half a dozen six-foot-tall sickle-shaped transformers.

Dr. Lara prepared a syringe. "I'm going to give you a few injections for the pain, then administer a local anesthetic. Dr. LaCombe, if you'd start the I.V."

She winced at the cold spray preceding the two numbing injections, her heart beating rapidly as Joyce inserted an I.V. tube into a vein in her left forearm.

She glanced at the face of a large wall clock as the antibiotic drip entered her bloodstream.

It's 04:17. Only two hours and forty-three minutes before I get ... to ... go ... home ...

Joyce watched as Dr. Lara engaged the transdimensional bubble around Jessica's right hand. "The vortex will prevent any bleeding when I remove the finger ... like ... so—"

Joyce found herself turning away as he clipped off the digit.

"Are you squeamish, Dr. LaCombe? You should have seen what our teams went through when we were amputating the limbs off street people. The remains we left buried in the desert still give me nightmares."

Using a probe, he positioned the flash drive beneath the flexor tendon connecting Jessica's right hand to the fourth finger's lower joint. "As you can see, I'm going a little lower so she'll still maintain a bit of flexion in the—"

The detonation shook the Dulce complex, rattling the fluorescent lights mounted in the ceiling.

Dr. Lara looked up, his focus momentarily broken. "What was that?"

"I don't know. It felt like an earthquake."

A second tremor shook the subterranean facility; the disturbance followed a moment later by a deafening siren and whirling yellow lights.

Joyce felt the blood rush from her face.

"What the hell is going on?"

"That siren is a warning. Strategic Command is about to go into a full alert."

"What would—"

"I have no idea," she yelled, ripping off her surgical gown, "but you need to finish up without me. If we go into a full alert, anyone not wearing a Zebra badge or higher will have exactly sixty seconds to vacate the facility before they are shot and killed … and that includes my son!"

General Thomas J. Cubit climbed out of a transport tube, his hair and clothes disheveled from having been "vacuum-flushed" twenty-two stories out of his suite. "Christ, I hate these damn things … speak to me, gentlemen."

"Sir, one of our ARV's is hovering above Dulce Mountain firing low level scalar bursts at us."

"Who's piloting the craft?"

"According to the duty roster, Captain Joshua LaCombe is the pilot—"

The lights blinked off and on as another scalar shot penetrated the complex's electromagnetic shielding.

"—only the ship's computer isn't getting a DNA match. The co-pilot is listed as Captain Jeffrey Allen … only I can't even get a corroborative history on him."

"Somebody get me a goddam headset and connect me by thought-wave."

"General, three visiting Council members are demanding to know why Strategic Command hasn't gone on full alert."

"There are civilians with young children living here; I'm not about to give an order that leads to marines shooting kids."

"Sir, *Zeus-2* will be in firing range in seven minutes."

"General, we have a pit crew loading an interceptor drone onto an elevator platform. ETA for launch … under sixty seconds."

A tech arrived with a headset, offering it to General Cubit who snatched it from him and powered the device on.

This is General Thomas Cubit. Would the pilot or pilots of the ARV firing upon our facility please identify themselves.

Just me, General Cubit. Small world.

Shariak? My God ... you actually made it through the rabbit's hole.

"General, ARV-2 is on the platform. ETA for launch is twenty seconds."

Adam, listen to me—I'm on your side ... we were the ones who selected you. There's an ARV interceptor drone ready to launch. You need to hit us with a Level-Six EMP ... quickly!

The powerful electromagnetic pulse passed through the subterranean complex at near light speed, shutting down the electrical grid, reducing the Dulce facility to emergency power.

Good. That should shut down power to the lifts and buy us a few minutes. Shariak, how did you acquire the ARV?

Someone put out a TWEP on me. One of the would-be assassins was a counter-intelligence agent at OSI. Her boyfriend arrived aboard the ARV ... apparently they had plans to sell a ZPE unit. The boyfriend shot the pilot ... the pilot vaporized the boyfriend.

Do you know their names?

The pilot was LaCombe. The OSI agent was Kelly Kishel; her boyfriend ... Chris Mull.

Colonel Johnston ... you bastard—

"General, are you able to communicate with the pilot?"

"Yes. This was an unannounced test of the EMP Shield. Stand down warning."

Shariak, I know who issued the TWEP order and I'll handle it. Get the hell out of here before the Air Force arrives or a Zeus satellite vaporizes you.

What about Jess?

She's safe ... she'll be heading back to D.C. today.

Why me, General?

MAJI's silent majority is making a move against the ruling fringe element. The movement selected twelve potential access points to release zero-point-energy. Each access point was assigned an escort.

And I was yours?

No. Jessica was mine. You were Barbara Jean's.

Jess's mom?

Never mind that now. Implanted in the fourth finger of your fiance's right hand is a flash drive with schematics for three different ZPE generators. Get it to Greer; he'll know what to do with it.

What about the ARV?

Crash it or ditch it. Zeus was designed to target and destroy any vessel crossing over into our physical dimension. There are already three of them in orbit … one is moving into firing range as we speak!

The forward view screen suddenly zoomed into space, focusing upon a rectangular object …

Recognizing the killer satellite, Adam quickly engaged the ARV's Delta configuration, slipping the ship into transdimensional space.

41

JESSICA GAZED OUT OF THE FIRST-CLASS passenger window at the autumn sky. Dusk bled over the darkening city in crimson and purple, the lights of Dulles International Airport beckoning to the east.

Her mind drifted back three thousand air miles and fifteen hours ago … She had found herself stumbling down a dimly lit corridor illuminated by yellow emergency lights while strangers in lab coats raced by. Her mouth was dry, her right hand felt strange, and someone had taped a gauze pad to her left forearm.

Twenty minutes later the power had returned, along with the memory of being prepped for surgery.

A security guard escorted her back to the women's lockers. Stripping down, she was weighed and searched by a female attendant, then sent through the showers to the other side. Locating her locker, she dressed, and at 6:37 a.m., rode the elevator up to the Maglev train station on Level-9, her packed bags already there along with eight other techs, all of whom seemed excited to be going home.

Sarah had packed her a breakfast sandwich and a container of freshly-squeezed orange juice. Lydia had refused to allow her to leave Dulce until she was given medical clearance. They had held the train up forty minutes before Dr. Spencer confirmed her bloodstream was clear of any foreign objects.

Finally she had boarded the train, receiving nasty looks from the other passengers. Selecting an empty row in back, she took the window seat, reclined her chair and dozed off …

"Excuse me? Are these two seats taken?"

The train had stopped at Los Alamos to pick up a single passenger—a raven haired woman, bearing the gaunt, pale complexion of someone who had spent far too many months working indoors.

"I'm sorry ... what?"

"I asked if these seats were taken."

The train suddenly accelerated, causing the woman to lose her balance. She fell forward across Jessica's lap, her right hand grabbing hold of Jessica's bare left arm to keep from tumbling head-over-heels.

"I'm so sorry."

Jessica wiped the woman's sweat from her biceps. "It's okay."

The Maglev train arrived at the subterranean complex beneath Edwards Air Force Base at 8:13 a.m. Fifteen minutes later Jessica found herself standing beneath an actual cloudless blue sky, breathing the fresh desert air.

She could have taken a private jet bound for Pittsburgh and Washington, but turned the offer down. Instead she accepted a van ride to LAX and booked a ticket on the next direct flight to D.C., wanting nothing more to do with MAJI.

She called Adam at the airport, but only got his message machine. "Hey babe, it's me. I'm coming home tonight, arriving in Dulles at 6:15 p.m. on Delta. I can't wait to see you and hold you ... and just love on you. I missed you so much."

Jessica's heart raced as the wheels touched down, her left forearm sore where the woman had dug in with her nails. She rubbed it, conscious of the stiffness coming from her fourth finger.

Maybe Adam knows an ER doctor who can take this thing out tonight.

Adam stood at the security checkpoint which separated ticketed passengers from guests.

Twenty thousand air miles and fifteen hours ago he had found himself knocking on the Greer's back door, the ARV hovering ten feet off the ground in the clearing behind him.

"Morning, doc. I'll swap you a pair of crutches for an ARV and a zero-point-energy device."

Adam shared his tale over a four a.m. breakfast. Thirty minutes later they had made plans with the man who had spent the last thirty years communicating with extraterrestrials receiving an in-flight tutorial on how to operate the man-made UFO.

They embraced outside the closed gas station in Cassopolis, Michigan. Adam watched the ARV shoot straight up into the graying sky, leaving him alone on the deserted country road.

Remembering the bikers, he rolled up the garage door and climbed in the rental car. Locating the keys in the ash tray where he had left them, he started the vehicle and sped away.

Returning to Chicago was all about establishing alibis. Adam had flown into O'Hare International a day earlier; therefore, he needed to depart from O'Hare.

He had received Jessica's voice mail when he had landed in D.C. at 3:25 p.m. He just had time to return to his apartment, shower, and strap on his regular prosthetic leg before Gene Evans arrived to drive him back out to Dulles.

The petite blonde with the athletic figure broke into a wide smile as she dashed up the inclined corridor and past the velvet ropes, leaping into her fiancé's arms. Wrapping her lower limbs around his waist, she locked in their kiss until Adam's legs began to buckle.

"I'm pregnant."

"Wow, that was some kiss."

"I'm serious. We're going to have a baby!"

He hugged her. "That's the best news I've had in a long time."

"Asshole!"

Adam and Jessica turned to find a middle aged woman glaring at them.

"If I were you, missy, I'd leave this scumbag before he abuses you, too."

They watched the woman walk away while others stared and pointed.

Adam shook his head. "I guess we have a lot to talk about."

"And even more we can't. Doesn't matter. I've decided to take a year off from work."

"A year, huh? You do realize I'm unemployed."

She slid her arm around his waist as they walked together toward the escalator leading down to baggage claim. "I'm sure we'll manage to get by."

Ten minutes later they had Jessica's luggage and were waiting for Evans to circle around with the car. The bodyguard pulled the black Mustang over to the curb by the passenger pick-up zone and popped open the trunk. He loaded Jessica's bags while the couple squeezed into the tight back seat.

"Adam, wouldn't you rather stretch out in front?"

"No, I like it back here with you."

The bodyguard climbed in the driver's side, rummaging through a gym bag he had retrieved from the passenger seat.

"Jess, this is Gene Evans. We served together in Iraq."

"Nice to meet you, Gene."

The bodyguard spun around, a big smile on his face—

—a Beretta in his hand.

He managed to fire two rounds before Adam grabbed hold of the barrel. Using both hands, he twisted the gun toward his assailant—the third shot striking Evans in the right temple, killing him instantly.

"Jess?"

"I'm okay … I'm okay."

He turned, relieved to find one slug had hit the seat between them, the other burying itself in the quadriceps of his prosthetic left leg.

Jessica smiled nervously, her hands shaking from the adrenaline rush. "Not much of a shot for a bodyguard, was he?"

Tears of relief poured out of Adam's eyes. "I guess not."

The white van rolled up next to the Mustang's driver's side door. A hand reached out of the open passenger window ... holding a palm-size controller.

The explosion splattered blood across the back windshield, blinding Adam. He spit the warm liquid out of his mouth as he screamed Jessica's name, desperately wiping at his eyes to locate what remained of his beautiful fiancée.

42

Annapolis, Maryland

THE IMAGE COULD HAVE INSPIRED a Norman Rockwell painting; the leaves golden and red and purple with fall, the church white, the sky cobalt-blue. Autumn in America—a pastel of life ... invaded by grief.

Men in black suits, women in black dresses, veils and purses. Black limousines occupied the church parking lot, the news vans relegated to film behind a barrier patrolled by police officers in black uniforms.

The explosive that had blown off Jessica Marulli's left arm had caused her to bleed to death in under thirty seconds, making the mortician's work especially difficult. The casket had been ordered closed, the viewing chamber limited to the immediate family and close friends.

Captain Al Marulli refused to wear his dress uniform. His wife, Barbara Jean, had to be heavily medicated before she could be led inside the limo. For forty minutes the parents of the deceased attempted to be gracious hosts—the polished-wood casket situated at the front of the room carrying its own gravitational weight.

Adam sat in the second row next to his brother, Randy, and his sister-in-law. Dr. Steven Greer was seated behind him.

No one spoke. Everything that had to be said had already been said. There were no more tears to be cried, all that remained was to channel the anger.

In due course the reverend entered the chamber to announce that it was time to begin the ceremony. Senator Hall and his wife joined the procession

364

line of guests exiting to the chapel.

Last in line, Captain Marulli led his wife past their daughter's fiancé. Barbara Jean paused to brush her hand along the top of Adam's head. Then she looked at Dr. Greer, who remained seated behind him.

"Be respectful ... be quick."

The two men waited until the chamber emptied. Adam quickly locked the doors, turning his back on Dr. Greer who opened the casket. Removing a thin carrying case from his jacket pocket, the former ER physician took out a scalpel and tweezers and set to work on the deceased woman's right ring finger.

In less than a minute he had the flash drive in a small zip-lock bag and the casket was closed.

Adam waited until Greer patted him on the back before opening the door to allow the pallbearers to wheel his fiancée's remains into the chapel.

Dulce, New Mexico

General Thomas J. Cubit stood in the assembly hall, addressing the members of Council who were watching him on video by invitation only.

"The zero-point-energy unit was stolen by counter-intelligence agent Chris Mull, one of Colonel Johnston's top men. Mull and his lover, OSI agent Kelly Kishel, intended to sell the device. Against the recommendation of the majority of Council, Colonel Johnston took it upon himself to issue a TWEP order on Adam Shariak in order to cover up Mr. Mull's tracks.

"In order to steal the ZPE unit, Mull acquired a fake device and attempted to blackmail Dr. Marulli into assisting him with the crime. Mull's plan was to implicate the director of our *Zeus* program, along with our best ARV pilot, Captain Josh LaCombe. It was the ARV that would provide Mull with a means of removing the zero-point-energy unit from Dulce.

"Things went sour for Mr. Mull when he arrived at the MAJI drop-site in Cassopolis, Michigan by ARV, only to discover Colonel Johnston had double-crossed him by issuing a TWEP order on both him and his girlfriend, Agent Kishel.

"Why would the colonel issue a TWEP on Mr. Mull and his girlfriend?

Because Dr. Sarah Mayhew-Reece, the assistant director at *Zeus*, had learned that Dr. Marulli had replaced Mull's fake ZPE unit with the real device in order to prevent the crime. She reported Jessica's actions to Dr. Joyce LaCombe, Captain LaCombe's wife, and the head of our genetics department.

"Our clean-up crew arrived at the Michigan drop point to find the bodies of Agent Kishel, who had been killed by members of the *Devil's Diciples*, and Captain LaCombe, who was shot and killed by Mr. Mull. There were also three dead bikers, one terminated by Agent Kishel, the other two by Mr. Mull.

"In a fit of rage, Mr. Mull then returned to Dulce aboard the ARV, intent on enacting revenge on Colonel Johnston. I attempted to talk him down while we readied our interceptor drones. He fired a disruptor burst and fled when one of the *Zeus* satellites moved into firing range."

A Council member from the United Kingdom addressed him via audio hook-up. "Where is the ARV now, general?"

"It was last tracked over India."

"Who gave the TWEP order on Dr. Marulli?"

"Again, that was *Dr. Death*. Shariak's driver was hired to take out Shariak; the biological explosive had been adhered to Dr. Marulli's skin during the ride to Edwards Air Force Base by Colonel Johnson's co-conspirator, his wife, Yvonne.

"Gentlemen and ladies, the aftermath of these crimes is devastating to MAJI. Dr. Jessica Marulli was not only the brains behind *Project Zeus* and an invaluable young mind, but her parents both served MAJI loyally for a combined seventy-plus years.

"Dr. Marulli's murder firmly splits MAJI into two camps. There's the old guard; a radically conservative minority that has controlled MAJI's agenda through a campaign of fear, orchestrated by Colonel Johnston and his MK-Ultra psychotronic threat. Then there is a progressive majority who feels it is time we disclosed our technological advances to the rest of humanity in an attempt to prevent an environmental cataclysm and thwart a radical false flag event that, if launched, will slaughter billions.

"Gentlemen and ladies, it is time for MAJI to crawl out of the shadows and into the light. Either we make bold changes immediately and stop this insanity, or there will be nothing left of humanity to salvage."

Annapolis, Maryland

The procession of black limousines continued rolling through the gated entrance of *Wardour on the Severn*. Relegated to the main house, the mourners fed on deli platters and attempted to comfort their hosts.

Captain Marulli and his wife remained with their guests until 5:00 p.m. when they excused themselves to adjourn to their private carriage home set along the waters of the Chesapeake River.

Entering the cottage, they made their way down the spiral stairwell into the wine cellar, where the other twenty-two members of their war Council had already assembled. They had arrived from all over the world to mourn the loss of their colleagues' daughter and to initiate an event that would send ripples around the world.

Each man and woman held a silver goblet filled with Chateau Mouton-Rothschild 1945. Captain Marulli had paid $310,000 for a double magnum of the wine ten years earlier, intending on opening it on a special occasion. Regarded as one of the greatest red wines of the previous century, the 1945 vintage was purposely chosen, for its date marked the year two atomic bombs had been detonated over Hiroshima and Nagasaki—an event which had sent its own ripples across the galaxy.

Al Marulli raised his goblet, his companions following suit. "To all the innocent lives stolen … and to our precious child, Jessica, whose courage led to the birth of this new day."

"To Jessica …"

Seated before her laptop, Lydia Gagnon pressed *enter* on her keyboard. The command initiated the download of the three zero-point-energy generator schematics to alternative energy websites around the world, along with information on how they could withdraw start-up capital from the $100 billion donated under the name J.M. ENERGY, LLC.

"Barbara Jean, where's Dr. Greer?"

"Upstairs in one of the guest rooms, meditating. I was told the message has been sent."

"Lydia, contact the admiral."

U.S. Naval Station
Norfolk, Virginia

Admiral Mark Hintzman, Commander-in-Chief of U.S. Fleet Forces, stood out on the balcony of Conference Room-A, watching the real-time images of the moon displayed on the theater's main screen.

Expecting the call, he answered his iPhone on the first ring.

"Stand-by, Lydia. We're getting some activity ... there!"

Three bright sparks ignited from the moon's dark side—three salvos streaking toward targets in orbit around the Earth.

Within seconds, the scalar strikes destroyed the three *Zeus* satellites, atomizing each four-ton object into tiny particles.

"You're good to go, Lydia. The road has been paved."

"The admiral says we're good to go."

Al Marulli nodded to his wife, who ascended the spiral stairwell. Exiting the cottage, she found Adam at one of the docks overlooking the Chesapeake. With him, sharing a bench as they watched the river, was a dark-haired woman and her fifteen-year-old son.

Adam turned as his fiancée's mother joined them. "Barbara Jean Marulli, this is Dr. Joyce LaCombe and her son, Logan. It was Captain LaCombe who saved my life."

"I'm so sorry for your loss."

"Yours, too." Joyce motioned to the teen. "Logan taught Jessica how to use a hoverboard."

"She was really good."

"Well Logan, thanks to your dad and my little girl, maybe the rest of the world will finally get to experience anti-gravitics." Barbara Jean turned to Adam. "The road is paved. Are you ready?"

Adam nodded.

Reaching beneath the bench, he pulled out a brown paper bag and removed the ARV helmet. Placing it on, he stared at the serene surface waters until they began to percolate—

—displacing the 50-foot-in-diameter, fifteen-ton vessel which rose from the river, having just reentered the physical dimension.

Barbara Jean gave Adam a hug and then pinched his earlobe, giving him a stern look. "Finish this."

"Just give me the ball, coach."

Adam commanded the hatch to open. Then he allowed himself to be inhaled by the zero-gravity vortex.

A moment later the vessel was gone.

Dulce, New Mexico

"Strategic Command is on full alert! All personnel are ordered to evacuate through the canyon exits. Marine and Delta Force security are ordered to stand down. I repeat, Strategic Command is on full alert. All personnel are ordered to evacuate through the canyon exits—"

The ARV hovered a thousand feet above Dulce mountain. Inside the craft, Adam took a moment to survey the damaged complex now appearing on his main viewing screen. The scalar blast had vented the subterranean launch site to the surface, along with the seventeen remaining Atlas-V rockets, each vehicle harboring a *Zeus* satellite.

The second scalar wave sent them tumbling over sideways and igniting.

Wasting no time, Adam engaged the Delta configuration, slipping the vessel beyond the crossing point of light and back into transdimensional space—

—directing it through twenty stories of solid concrete and steel until the craft reemerged in a massive underground runway filled with man-made extraterrestrial vehicles.

Destroy all of them.

Colonel Alexander Johnston was livid beyond reason. General Cubit had lied about Chris Mull and now he had the evidence to prove it, his psychotronic equipment confirming it was Shariak, and not Johnston's counter-intelligence officer, who had been operating the ARV.

It was obvious that Cubit was staging a coup, but the colonel knew he could beat it back into submission by alerting key leaders in Europe and Australia. All he had to do was get from Dulce to the Dugway Proving Grounds—a seven minute Maglev train ride. Then he'd enact his revenge.

I think I'll begin by ripping Cubit's soul from his body ...

Bypassing the elevators, the colonel descended the stairwell to Level-9. Texting his assistant, Scott Muse, he ordered a private Maglev car sent immediately to Dulce.

The colonel emerged from the stairwell, winded but in good spirits. The platform looked deserted—

—and then he saw the bodies.

They were hanging from nooses tied to the lampposts—each man having been a member of the cabal for more than forty years. Johnston paused to gaze up at the nearest corpse, the thanatologist in him observing the angle of the cord cutting into the dead men's Adam's apples, making strangulation the cause of death opposed to the more traditional and expert snapping of the victim's neck.

He exhibited no reaction as his blue-gray eyes fell upon the face of the last body.

Yvonne ...

Seated on a bench beneath the dangling corpse of the colonel's wife was General Cubit. "We had thought about burning her at the stake, but everything was so last minute. Pretty sick ... using your wife to rub combustion crème on Jessica's arm. You two made some pair. No worries, Dr. Death, I'm sure she'll be waiting for you when you arrive in hell."

Six Delta Force commandos stepped out of the shadows. Aiming their

M-16s, they let loose a lead rope which severed Colonel Alexander Johnston's twisting torso in half.

The ARV shot straight up through the atmosphere into space, then executed a ninety degree turn to the east.

Having removed the threat of *Zeus* on the Interstellars, and having impeded the chances of an alien false flag event, there was one last thing for Adam Shariak to do.

Nationals Park
Washington, D.C.

"Bob Costas here. If you're just joining us, Game One of the National League Playoffs between the Cubs and the Nationals has been a real pitcher's duel, with neither team able to advance a runner past second.

"And now, as advertised, joining us for tonight's seventh inning stretch to lead the crowd in a special rendition of '*Take Me Out to the Ball Game*' will be Lady Gaga."

The singer/songwriter made her way to home plate wearing a National's jersey, the partisan crowd rising to give her a standing ovation.

"Hey, D.C.! I'm gonna need some help here, so I want everybody to sing along. Are you ready? Here we go …

"*Take me out to the ball game … take me out with the crowd—*"

Suzanne Tomas was looking up when she saw the object drop straight out of the sky to hover five hundred feet above second base. "That is so cool. Is that going to be in all of Gaga's shows?"

"*Buy me some peanuts and Cracker Jack … I don't care if I never get back—*"

Arie Forma videotaped the object as it circled around the inside of the stadium, the hair on his arms standing on end as it passed overhead. "That's not a real UFO, Ellie!"

"No kidding," his older sister shot back as she refocused her iPhone on the immense saucer-shaped craft.

"Let me root, root, root for the Na-tion-als … if they don't win it's a shame—"

Lady Gaga waved at the ARV as it hovered ten feet above the pitcher's mound.

"For it's one… two … three strikes, you're out at the old ball game."

"Bob, that's one helluva special effect."

"Looks like a hatch is opening … maybe there's little green men inside."

Adam dropped out of the ARV onto the pitcher's mound, dazzled by the bright lights and sparkling flashes. Three cameramen followed him as he hobbled to home plate, unsure if the moment was really happening or if this was just a lucid dream.

Was that Lady Gaga coming out to greet him with a microphone?

"Hi! What's your name, and where can I buy one of these?"

"My name? My name is Adam Shariak—"

The crowd quieted as his face appeared on the ballpark's massive video screen.

"Up until last week, I was the Under Secretary of Defense. The anti-gravitics machine you see before you is man-made … it can travel across our galaxy in mere minutes. It was built in secrecy by the covert government I was investigating. Trillions of your tax dollars have been spent on these Unacknowledged Special Access Projects over the years. Much of this incredible technology originated from friendly extraterrestrials whose craft the military have been shooting down and reverse-engineering since 1947."

Adam paused as the crowd reacted.

"That's right …UFOs are real and the species visiting us are friendly. This Alien Reproduction Vehicle, or ARV, is powered by zero-point-energy … a clean, abundant and free energy source that would have eliminated hunger, poverty, disease, and fossil fuels fifty years ago, only the bastards acting illegally as its self-appointed gatekeepers refused to allow the technology to be shared by the rest of the world."

A cascade of boos erupted.

Adam raised his hand for quiet. "All that changes tonight. As we speak, the schematics for three zero-point-energy generators are being emailed to some of the most advanced green energy companies in the world, along with the means to apply for $100 billion in grant monies."

Cheers erupted from the crowd—so loud that Adam couldn't think.

"The price …" he signaled again for quiet, "the price for this gift is very high. Many people—many scientists—were murdered to keep zero-point-energy a secret … including Dr. Jessica Marulli, my fiancée"—he choked out the words "—and our unborn child."

A hush fell over the crowd as the string of recent news stories fell into place.

And that was it … Adam had nothing more to say … nothing more to do. Surrounded by forty thousand people, he felt completely alone, his life spent. He had no desire to re-enter the ARV … he just wanted to crawl in a hole somewhere and die.

It was at the moment that the mothership which had appeared at the Greer's home dropped from out of transdimensional space to hover over the stadium … the triangular-shaped vessel so immense it blotted out the night sky.

The video screen powered off.

The stadium lights shut down.

And then, in the midst of this uncharted moment in human history, a message of light appeared on the scoreboard:

There is no future in war and hatred.
There are no boundaries in peace.774

PART 5

"In the councils of Government, we must guard against the acquisition of unwarranted influence, whether sought or unsought, by the Military Industrial Complex. The potential for the disastrous rise of misplaced power exists, and will persist. We must never let the weight of this combination endanger our liberties or democratic processes. We should take nothing for granted. Only an alert and knowledgeable citizenry can compel the proper meshing of the huge industrial and military machinery of defense with our peaceful methods and goals so that security and liberty may prosper together."

—President Eisenhower

January 1961

374

"There exists a shadowy Government with its own Air Force, its own Navy, its own fundraising mechanism, and the ability to pursue its own ideas of the national interest, free from all checks and balances, and free from the law itself."

—Senator Daniel K. Inouye

August 11, 2007

"Every great change is preceded by chaos."

—Deepak Chopra

EPILOGUE

Ocean City, New Jersey
April 23, 2033

THE UNLIT FIVE-MILE STRETCH of public beach had been zoned from nine p.m. through three a.m. as a CE-5 area. Groups of twenty or more could reserve a designated locale on the city's webpage, while individuals seeking to join a larger circle could sign up.

Michael Sutterfield's seventh grade class was on their third night of a six-day field trip. The first two sessions had been uneventful and the teen was beginning to fear that his "condition" was blocking communication with the Interstellars.

Dr. Mallouh had attempted to reassure him that his presence had no bearing on the lack of extraterrestrial activity.

"Over the last decade we've learned that Earth is a complex self-regulating system which seeks a physical and chemical environment optimal for advanced life forms to evolve. Many processes necessary for the conditions of life—from microorganisms to the salinity of the planet's oceans—adapt as they interact with each other, in essence moving life along the path it was intended to follow.

"Like all of us, Michael, you are one of these organisms; the question is whether you can adapt to function within a system that has finally self-regulated to continue humanity's intended evolution."

"Which is what?"

"Unity."

"I'm a sociopath, Dr. Mallouh; you diagnosed me so yourself. I'm incapable of fitting in."

"Not true. Being aware of the limitations imposed by a condition can sometimes be enough to prevent one from stepping off that slippery slope. Besides, unity is not dependent on loving your fellow man; just as important is accepting their right to exist. Life, liberty, and the pursuit of happiness are not just words, they're a birth right. For seventy years a segment of our population remained convinced that the only way they could maintain their way of life was to deny it to the rest of us. These selfish acts nearly led to our own extinction because they ran counter to our very nature—our nature being the essence of the Creator, which is to share."

"What made you change your mind about allowing me to participate in the CE-5 field trip?"

"We're hoping your desire to communicate with the Interstellars exceeds your lack of restraint. Remember, every living organism possesses a spark of the Creator which unifies and connects all of us to every living organism in existence."

Connection? Who was Mallouh kidding?

Seated in a circle beneath the stars with his classmates, Michael Sutterfield knew he was different ... knew he didn't belong.

He waited for the group meditation to begin, then he left the circle.

The radar and electro-magnetometer sounded simultaneously. A moment later an amber-orange light appeared over the water, the object as large as the moon.

"Boys and girls, we have a major event. Everyone please stay seated."

"What is it, Dr. Mallouh?"

"It's a large ETV ... an Extraterrestrial Vehicle. They emerged from the sky but they're hovering just above the water about two miles out."

Steve Alten

"Look ... there's another one!"

A second identical object appeared next to the first, the ETVs poised on the horizon like a fiery pair of eyes.

"I'm looking through the night scope, they are definitely not flares."

"Connect to them with your consciousness and welcome them. Open your heart chakra and send them the beauty of humanity. Thank them for coming."

Dr. Mallouh looked for Michael, only to realize the teen was missing from the group. Using his night vision glasses, he searched the beach, locating a lone figure standing by a dune.

Leaving the group, the principal headed for the rise.

"Michael? Are you okay, son?"

"They're so ... beautiful."

"They are, aren't they? Dr. Greer says it's a color you never forget."

"I saw it before they appeared ... the color. It was in my head ... I can't explain it."

"You've obviously made a connection."

They watched together as the first object faded into transdimensional space, followed a moment later by the second.

"Come on, we should rejoin the group."

"If it's okay, I'd like to stay here a moment."

"Of course. I'll be with the group if you need me."

"Dr. Mallouh?"

"Yes. Michael?"

"Thank you."

The guidance counselor smiled, tears in his eyes. "You're very welcome."

THE END

Undisclosed

To learn more about the hidden history behind UFOs, ETs, and
Unacknowledged Special Access Projects, read:

UNACKNOWLEDGED:
An Exposé of the World's
Greatest Secret

by

Steven M. Greer, M.D.

Edited by Steve Alten

In Memory

Jessica Marulli

March 29, 1976–February 16, 2016

THE BIGGEST LIE IN HISTORY IS ABOUT TO BE SHATTERED.

UNACKNOWLEDGED

By STEVEN M. GREER M.D.

70 years of lies uncovered about UFOs, ETs, and the advanced technologies reverse-engineered from downed insterstellar craft dating back to Roswell.

Features documents and exclusive testimonials from eyewitnesses in the military, intelligence agencies, NASA, and defense contractors— some published for the first time since after their passing.

ON SALE
APRIL 25, 2017

THE MUST-READ COMPANION BOOK TO
UNDISCLOSED

A & M Publishing
ISBN: 978-1-943957-04-0 $25.95